THE DUNGEONEERS
and the
TREASURE OF ROAN

Joel McKay

Publisher:

Birchwood Press
British Columbia

Library and Archives Canada Cataloguing in Publication
McKay, Joel, 1984- author

ISBN 978-1-7782312-5-4 (perfect bound)
ISBN 978-1-7782312-6-1 (eBook)

Editor: Amnet Systems
Book cover & interior design by – Deena Rae; E-BookBuilders, adaptation for ebook

File version: 202503008 .019

OTHER WORKS BY JOEL McKAY

Novella

Wolf at the Door (Birchwood Press, 2022)

Collection

It Came From the Trees and Other Violent Aberrations (Birchwood Press, 2024)

Short Stories

"Number Hunnerd" (*Water: Selkies, Sirens and Sea Monsters*, Tyche Books, 2021)

"Hands" (*Blood in the Soil, Terror on the Wind*, Brigids Gate Press, 2022)

"Don't Rock the Boat" (*Water: Elemental Cycle Book Three*, Eerie River Publishing, 2023)

"The Ministry of Labour Transition" (*Bewildering Stories*, 2023)

"Tales of the Crypto" (*Locust Candy*, 2023)

"Shambling Gary" (*Tales of Sley House 2023*, Sley House Publishing, 2023)

"The Lighthouse Keeper" (*That Witch Whispers*, Black Cat Books, 2024)

Contents

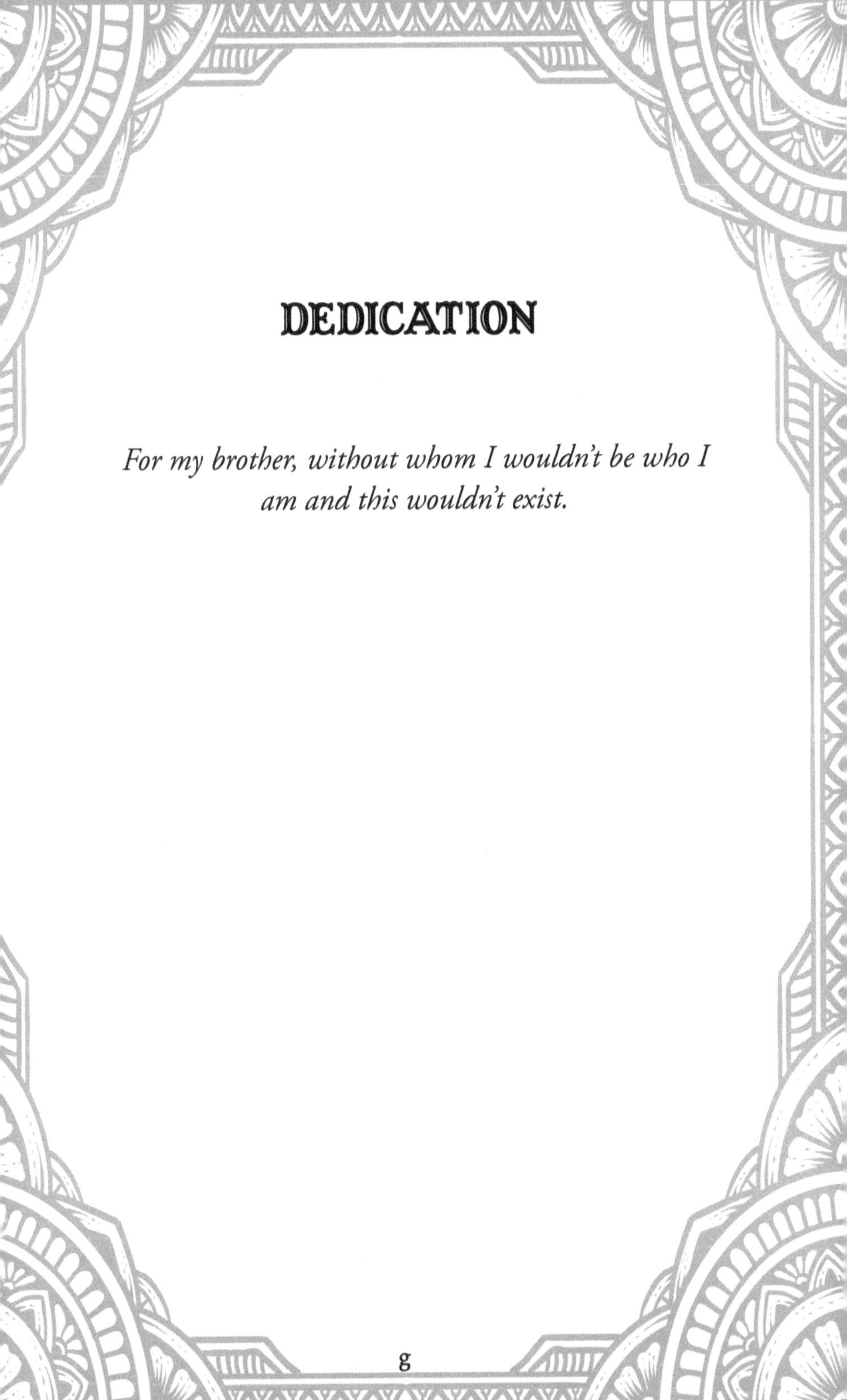

DEDICATION

For my brother, without whom I wouldn't be who I am and this wouldn't exist.

THE DUNGEONEERS AND THE TREASURE OF ROAN

Two thieves. One legendary treasure. Zero trust.

When washed-up burglar Wincott stumbles into the cursed city of Roan with a horde of pissed-off goblins on his tail, the last person he expects to save his hide is his estranged son—Sish Torren, a liar, scoundrel, and aspiring solo act in the crime world. But with a deadly mystery buried beneath the mountain and mercenaries, monsters, and myth-chasers closing in, the only way out... is through.

Now, this dysfunctional father-son duo must team up (again) to survive ancient traps, backstabbing allies, and their own baggage if they want to get their hands on the legendary Treasure of Roan—assuming it doesn't get its hands on them first.

A darkly funny, fast-paced fantasy adventure packed with grit, grudges, and unexpected heart, The Dungeoneers and the Treasure of Roan is what happens when the wrong people go looking for the right reasons—and find everything they didn't bargain for.

THE DUNGEONEERS
and the
TREASURE OF ROAN

Chapter One

NO ONE LIKES GOBLINS ANYWAY

WINCOTT WAS TIRED OF RUNNING. It didn't help that the snow was waist-high. He had short legs to begin with. His large gut didn't encourage swiftness or agility either. And then there was the murderous band of goblins that trailed him through the forest, their rusty blades at the ready. Yet those weren't the worst part of his predicament. The worst part was the crusty midwinter snow that crunched over the top of his boot cuffs, slid down his ankles, and pooled coldly beneath the soles of his feet. Wincott hated having cold feet.

"Hell," he growled.

Snow flung left and right as his stubby legs churned through the winter muck. The goblins had been chasing him for half a day. That surprised him; normally, they gave up after a mile or two. Goblins were, after all, notoriously lazy. Except for these ones. These ones were persistent, and he was tired of their tenacity. He hadn't made matters easier for himself by stealing a purse of coins from their den and slitting two of their throats in the process.

But he was a thief, and that's what thieves do, and on occasion, the ancient and exalted profession of thieving warranted murder. Besides, it wasn't as if he was killing real people; they were only goblins. And no one liked goblins anyway.

As he fled through the wintry forest, he wondered if it was time to retire. He had been thieving for nearly fifty years, far longer than most in his profession. And truthfully, he was a lot slower, fatter, and clumsier than he ever had been. Many years had passed since he'd been at the peak of his professional abilities.

Gone were the days of weeklong raids, palace capers, and high-handed hijinks.

The friends of his youth were dead, and what few thieves remained were no friends of his, and so he thieved alone. And when you throw a slower, fatter, clumsier, older thief with no friends into a den of goblins, he is bound to make a few mistakes.

In this instance, the mistake had been a cast-iron frying pan placed precariously atop a pile of rubble next to a smoldering fire. Wincott clumsily knocked it over as he'd taken the coin purse. Sure enough, the closest two goblins were on their feet in seconds. His knife hand, still quick despite his thick fingers, was just as fast. But their squeals of pain woke the rest of the band, and the chase was on.

It was enough to make a veteran thief think twice about his future. But not for long. Truth is, a man doesn't live half so long as Wincott without learning a thing or two about his strengths and weaknesses. Wincott loved stealing things. After all these years, it still gave him a rush to abscond with someone or something else's property.

And so, halfway across a snow-encrusted valley with ten frozen toes, Wincott decided he would continue stealing things as long as he could. If the goblins didn't get him first.

THE RIBBON WAS FROZEN SOLID, or so it looked anyway. The trouble with large rivers, even in the coldest months of the winter, is that parts can be frozen solid while other parts only *look* solid. Wincott had an eye for ice, a skill gained after a lifetime spent in the north, where time was measured in winters, not years.

The ice is thickest where the current is slowest. He stopped at the riverbank and tried to picture in his mind this section of the Ribbon when it ran free of ice during those few months each year that passed for summer in the north. Where did it move slowest?

He tugged thoughtfully on the stub of wiry gray hair that jutted from his round chin. He didn't venture this far into the valley often. The loot was scarce, and the risks high, especially during the colder months when a twisted ankle could leave a man stranded. Unfortunately, a man must make a living, and the valley—cold and isolated as it was—was better than starving on the streets. Besides, he was no longer welcome on the streets anyway—the Company had seen to that.

He stepped gingerly onto the ice. He decided on a route across the river, hoping he was correct. He was halfway across when he heard the goblins. A rush of jabbering voices clambered out of the frozen stillness of the forest behind them. The goblins looked black against the powdery white snow that blanketed the riverbank and weighed down the heavy branches of cedar and spruce trees.

The murderous creatures did not hesitate when they saw the rotund burglar making his way across the ice-bound river. Half a dozen of them leaped onto the ice without a second thought. Wincott moved more quickly, picking his way among the cakes of ice that had jammed against the far side of the river.

Whump. The ice moved. Wincott's stomach leaped into his throat. He stopped. The snow was too thick where he stood to know for sure if the crack was beneath his feet or elsewhere on the river. Balancing between two blocks of ice that jutted from the surface, he glanced precariously over his shoulder to see three goblins crash through the whiteness in an icy splash. More jabbering.

"Shit," he grumbled.

Wincott scrambled across the ice onto the far side of the river as a rusty spear whizzed past his head and pierced a snowbank ahead. The forest was no less forgiving on the east side of the valley, the trees and brush so thick he had to keep his hands at eye level to make a trail through the branches. Another glance over his shoulder revealed two dozen goblins making their way across the river. Several plummeted through a weak spot in the ice. Wincott vanished into the trees.

DUSK PLUNGED THE VALLEY INTO an eerie gloaming by the time Wincott reached the line of mountains that guarded the eastern edge of the valley. It was still only midafternoon, but winter days were short, and the temperature was already dropping. The old thief felt ice crystals in his beard, and his feet were numb. He needed to find shelter soon, or he wouldn't survive the night, goblins or not. He hadn't heard or seen the bloodthirsty creatures for at least an hour, but his gut told him they were still in pursuit.

He gauged the mountains and saw an opportunity: the abandoned city of Roan. It was not a place he would happily venture into, but given his circumstances, he felt it was his only option.

The ruins scarred the mountainside above him. The smiths and miners of old had carved Roan from the mountain, their tools leaving only right angles and hard edges that were not the least inviting to visitors. Now, centuries abandoned, its great rectangular entranceway stared across the valley like a gaping black maw, toothless and waiting to swallow whatever passed beneath its shadow.

It was said that even the dragon Myyrhmyth did not tread near the city, fearing whatever lay hidden in its depths. Of course, no one knew what was in its depths. Probably nothing but cobwebs and old junk, Wincott mused, but certainly, it looked like the type of place that would be home to more than a few things you didn't want to mess around with. Maybe that was the point, he thought, and the city was full of normal people going about their daily lives, content with the fact that their best defense from intruders was a scary-looking entranceway. But he doubted it. Roan had a one-way reputation: Things that went inside didn't come out. Yet with numb feet and a band of goblins on his heels, Roan suddenly didn't seem so fearsome.

Wincott started up the mountainside, but the grade was so steep he was forced to scramble on his hands and knees. Halfway toward Roan's gaping mouth, he slipped on ice and could feel the loose scree give way beneath his feet. Rocks tumbled down around him, shattering the valley's quiet winter solitude. He paused to listen. Nothing from the forest, but he thought he felt a great vibration in the ground beneath his hands.

The serrated peaks of the Knifepoint Mountains towered above him, their facades sulking forebodingly beneath a dusk-darkened light. Not for the first time he worried about an avalanche. And then he heard it, a low nattering at first that soon became a chorus of raucous gibberish that echoed out of the forest to the mountainside where he crept upward. The goblins. He looked back, but amid the evening gloom, he could not discern them from the trees.

Cold and out of breath, Wincott cursed and continued upward, trudging forward one hand and knee at a time. His only hope was to get inside the city's black gate, find a place to hide, and pray its fearsome reputation kept the creatures at bay.

As he neared the entrance to Roan, he was taken aback by the sheer immensity of the forgotten city. Stone steps, cracked and broken like the ancient bones of the mountain laid bare, formed a tongue-like path that led into the city's cavernous entranceway. All around him, great pillars of stone jutted from the ground, many of them broken.

Still, the goblin's voices urged him onward. He pushed on, climbing the cracked stone road until the air thinned and the white-clad valley below dropped away. At this altitude, the Ribbon lived up to its name and was little more than a line of ice twisting through the frozen forest far below.

At the city's threshold, he stopped and listened again. Wincott was not normally a fearful man, but Roan's visage caused the hair on his neck to stand on end. He hesitated. His stomach churned with apprehension. Was there another option? He scanned the horizon in each direction but found none. The snow crunched loudly beneath his feet. Below, he could hear footsteps scrambling up the loose shale toward him.

"Hell," he cursed again.

He turned and stepped into Roan but not before a heavy branch swung out of the dark and struck his head. Wincott crumpled to the ground. The world went dark.

TWO THIEVES WALK INTO A DUNGEON

SISH TORREN HAD NO ILLUSIONS about who he was. He knew he was a scumbag. A thief. A liar. And probably a bunch of other things as well. Knowing that, he didn't feel the least bit guilty about the fat thief who lay crumpled at his feet.

Almost three years had passed since the last time he had laid eyes on his dad, Wincott. The years, though few, had not been kind to the old man. The light from Sish's small campfire played off Wincott's face, revealing a lifetime hard lived: a bulbous, misshapen nose, pockmarks, a jagged scar down one cheek, thinning gray hair, and a fistful of wiry beard that sprouted from his chin like the thin roots of a clump of grass. He looked more like a brawler than the cunning thief he had once been, but things change, and men grow old.

What was he doing out here?

A shriek from outside the cave drew Sish's attention. He drew his short sword and crept out from the deep stone hollow where he'd made his camp. The gaping entranceway to the city was dark and empty. He moved stealthily along its outer edge until he neared the entranceway, where a winter moon bathed the mountainside in a pale glow.

Sish could see small, black shapes milling about at the far end of the stairs outside the city's great gate. Goblins. *Fool thief has brought them here.* He watched them for a while longer and gathered they were too fearful to enter the city at night, though once daybreak came, he wasn't sure their fear would be so palpable. He needed to move quickly if he was going to gain entry to the city and take what he wanted from Roan.

He snuck back to his makeshift camp to find Wincott sitting up and warming his naked toes next to the fire. The old thief looked at him calmly.

"Oh," he said, "it's you."

Sish froze, somewhat taken aback by his dad's calm demeanor.

"What does that mean?" he asked.

"Exactly what I said," Wincott shot back. "Oh, so it's you who smacked me across the forehead and dragged me into the cave."

Sish waved his short sword at the old thief. The blade glimmered in the firelight.

"Aren't you at all afraid I might gut you with this?"

Wincott shrugged. "Not really. If you meant to kill me, I wouldn't have woken up." He wiggled his toes next to the fire and let out a satisfied sigh. "Besides, after the day I've had, I wouldn't be opposed to dying now anyway. At least my feet are warm, though I'm afraid I've lost feeling entirely in both my pinky toes. And I've got a hell of a headache."

The old man rubbed his hand thickly across his forehead and frowned at Sish.

"I should kill you," Sish said matter-of-factly.

"Go ahead," Wincott replied, staring evenly at the younger man.

Sish pursed his lips and thought about it. To what end? He sheathed the sword.

Wincott nodded toward the city gate. "They still out there?"

Sish sat across from him and nodded. "Yes, though I think it's unlikely they'll venture beyond the entranceway while it's dark."

"Cowards," Wincott spat.

"But they will come for us in the morning."

"I guess that short sword you're waving about might finally come in handy then," the older man said, his voice full of ridicule. He paused and caught his son's gaze across the fire. "How long has it been?"

Silence descended on their small camp, the fire between them flickering silently.

"Not nearly long enough," Sish answered.

"Ha, no doubt there," Wincott said with a nod.

The old thief positioned his boots and woolen socks in front of the fire to dry them out. Sish watched as Wincott patted down the pockets of his heavy canvas jacket and vest beneath, revealing several seemingly random tools and implements he piled neatly on the ground next to him: knives, flint, steel, loose coins, a flask, a lockpick, and a pry bar, among them.

He stopped the ritualistic inventory and stared bitterly at Sish. The other man only smiled.

"The coin purse, where is it?" Wincott demanded.

Sish patted a small backpack next to him and folded his arms confidently across his chest. "Call it payment." *For being a shitty dad,* he thought though didn't say.

"For what?"

"Providing you with a warm, safe camp for the night."

"I could've done that myself," Wincott retorted.

Sish shrugged. "Well, here we are, regardless, sitting next to *my* fire. You know, I took a closer look at that coin purse. The markings on it led me to believe it came from the vault beneath the old garrison at Fort Shatterstill."

"What's it to you?" Wincott asked.

"Well, I find it interesting that a fat, old thief such as yourself would travel such a long way through snow and ice for a single coin purse. Seems a bit much, doesn't it?"

Sish twisted his lips in a sneer, waiting to see whether he could bait his dad into an argument that would allow him to make use of the short sword in his hand. He'd gotten pretty good at drawing the old man's ire over the years, though he was three years out of practice. It wouldn't sadden him to end their relationship here and now. Wincott ignored him and began putting his tools away.

"Equally strange that a smart-mouthed brigand such as yourself would find himself alone in an abandoned city in the mountains," Wincott shot back.

"Brigand? Am I not worthy of the title of *thief?*"

The old man stretched his hands over the fire and wriggled his fingers delicately. He said, "Brigand only because you rarely have the gonads to travel alone, which, I might add, is why *I* find it stranger still that you're here in Roan. But also because your particular brand of thievery is more akin to ambushing and robbing unsuspecting targets. You have no finesse."

"Finesse! Well, I've been called many things but not that," Sish said. He sheathed the sword and went on, "Fact is, times have changed, and a man must change with them. A lockpick and short legs don't generate nearly the same plunder they once did, old man. A thief must have a variety of skills in this day and age and an ability to perform them in tandem."

Wincott folded his arms and snorted, "Multitasking is the shortest route to mediocrity. Finesse and focus, those are the two most important skills of a good thief. You're just a robber."

It was Sish's turn to laugh. "Oh, now I'm a robber? Please do educate me, master thief. Unlike you, I have no romantic illusions about this business. We both steal things for a living; we just have different ways of going about it. You're happy to settle for a goblin's coin purse while I'm"—Sish gestured to the massive stone walls around them— "more adept at pursuing worthwhile causes."

"It wasn't just a purse I was after!" Wincott spat.

Bingo. So, the old man was up to something else at Shatterstill. Sish leaned over the fire and smiled gleefully at Wincott. "I knew it. So, there's more booty left in Shatterstill than we thought?"

Wincott grunted and changed the subject. "Tell me what a robber wants in a city long abandoned? There's nothing here but shadows and monsters."

Sish considered telling him. There was a time, a few years ago but not so many years ago, when they had been, well, thicker than thieves. Back then, Wincott had been a halfway decent mentor, as much as a lying, cheating, thieving, fat, old criminal can be anyway. It had lasted too long for Sish's taste, but that was the nature of growing up with someone. You don't get to choose; you only hope you can survive it. The last time Sish had seen Wincott, the scar on the older man's face was still red with blood, the younger man having carved it in a fit of rage.

"Only a great fool would reveal his intent," Sish said finally.

"Bullshit," Wincott said. "You're here for the Treasure of Roan."

Sish stirred the coals in the fire and said nothing.

Wincott shrugged again. "No matter. I've been around long enough to know there are only ghosts and goblins left in this valley."

Sish smiled. "Good. Then you'll have no qualms about departing our little camp as soon as your boots have dried. You can take the goblins with you."

Wincott sat forward and raised a finger. "Ahh, and therein lies the problem, doesn't it? I'm not so stupid as to go back out there until those goblins are good and gone. And it doesn't look like they're leaving any time soon. In fact, as you say, they'll likely come in here to skewer us both once the sun's up."

"Your point?"

Wincott tugged on his beard and smiled. "Did I ever teach you the third-most important skill for a good thief?"

Sish rolled his eyes. The only thing he liked less than working with his dad was listening to his junkyard wisdom and half-cooked speeches. He was about ready to draw his sword and finish the job he'd started three years before when a rare moment of compassion struck him, and he let go of the weapon. He exhaled slowly and offered a glib smile.

"Do tell," he said curtly.

"Luck." The old thief smiled. "Finesse, focus, and luck. The three skills. As *luck* would have it, I managed to escape from Shatterstill and find my way here. And as *luck* would have it, you were already here. Now, those goblins outside are either going to tail me back across the valley when I escape, and they will eventually catch up with me and kill me, or they're going to come in here and kill us both. Let's face it, neither of us are great fighters. On balance, if I had to pick, I'd prefer they killed us both than just me. Call it old-fashioned selfishness, but I'm not inclined to play martyr and draw that band of goblins away from the city so that you can go about doing whatever it is you intend to do here."

"What are you suggesting then?" Sish asked, his eyes narrowing.

"We either leave together, or I become a full partner in whatever fruitless treasure-hunting scheme you're currently pursuing," Wincott said. Then, almost as an afterthought, he added, "Or you could kill me now and carry on. But that doesn't deal with the goblins, and besides, you couldn't do it before, and I don't think you have the guts to do it now, that pitiful sword of yours notwithstanding."

Sish thought about it for a while before answering. The fire between them flickered weakly. Wincott reached toward the pile of loose branches next to them and tossed a few on the fire to burn. The crackling of the wood echoed off the walls around them. As the fire grew brighter, it illuminated the dark stone bulwark of Roan's inner-city gate, revealing a gargantuan room with a ceiling that arced several hundred feet over the top of their heads. The mineralization in the mountain's bones sparkled in the firelight, reminding the young thief why he was in the city in the first place.

He didn't relish the thought of working alongside his dad again, but he also wasn't a cold-blooded murderer. Worst-case scenario, the old man would tag along for a while, and eventually, he'd do something dumb, and they'd go their own way. Or maybe something awful from the depths of Roan would eat him. Very tragic, but such is life.

"Okay, you're in. But only a 15 percent cut of the return," Sish said, not intending to honor it whatsoever. *Back pay for being a shitty dad*, he chuckled in his head.

"Twenty-five," Wincott retorted.

"Twenty," Sish replied. "But you're all in—that means taking on whatever comes our way together. You can't just slip away in the dark and expect me to handle it."

"How about *20 percent* of whatever comes our way?" Wincott said with a wink.

Sish sighed, and they shook on it over the fire.

"I have to say, it's strange the goblins pursued you this far," he said. "Normally, they give up after a mile or two. What did you do?"

Wincott grinned. "Killed two of them. One, I think, was important. Maybe a chieftain."

"Well, I wouldn't feel guilty about that," Sish said.

"I don't."

"No one likes goblins anyway," they said in unison.

Chapter Three

A SLIP AND SLIDE INTO ROAN

WINCOTT DREAMED OF A COLD river. A mother's screams for her child echoed in his ears. The water was dark blue, cold. There was fire overhead, as if from a battle nearby, burning houses, and smoking ruins. The sound of heavily armed soldiers thumping across the muddy ground not far away. A child struggled in the water, his tiny, desperate arm reaching out for his mother. Wincott dived in. The cold tightened around his chest like a vise, forcing the air from his lungs, needling his skin wherever it was exposed. He gasped for breath and inhaled a mouthful of cold water. The child drifted away into the darkness. *This is it*, he thought, *we're not coming out.*

He awoke gasping for breath. The cave was silent save the steady crackle of Sish's small campfire. He was warm, not freezing. There was no river, child, or battle, only the long dark shadows cast by the firelight that danced along the rock face at the gates of Roan.

Sish stood a dozen feet away, studying a circular hollow in a rock face, his back to Wincott. The cave was tall and flat there, as if sculpted by ancient tools, but there was no indication as to why.

"Quiet," he said, not turning away from his study, "the goblins are camped just outside."

Wincott stifled a cough and sat up. A rough wool blanket was laid over his legs. It wasn't his. He looked at the young thief. "I must've dozed off."

"Must've," Sish said.

"What're you doing?"

Sish ran his fingers over the circular depression in the rock face. "Looking for a way in. I had hoped to find it before you woke."

And disappeared to leave me for the goblins to hack up, Wincott mused. The old thief pulled on his wool socks and boots, both of which had finally dried. He could feel his toes again, too. Well, most of them anyway.

He leaned back, propped up on his elbows, and stretched out his legs, feet crossed. He watched Sish struggle with the narrow impression in the rock for a few minutes. The young man paced back and forth, his fingers drumming thoughtfully on his chin. Wincott noticed he had a weak chin. *Too much overbite,* he thought. *Women don't like weak chins.* He reflexively rubbed his fingers over his own chin and tugged on his beard. *Mine's just fine,* he thought with a smile.

"You won't get in that way," he observed.

Sish stopped and glared at him. He pointed to the depression in the wall. It was slightly larger than a man's hand and looked like it had been carved to serve a specific purpose.

"This is clearly intended to be here," Sish said. "I just need to find where the door is."

Wincott laughed. "There isn't one."

Sish glared at him. "We're at the city's main entrance. Of course, there's a door here."

Wincott got to his feet and walked over to where Sish was standing. "There was, once. Look at the stone—it's been sealed off. This isn't a door; it's a barricade."

Far above them was a narrow crevice in the stone that ran along the ceiling of the cavern, parallel to the wall. It looked like a wide, rectangular black hole. A place that a giant slab of stone might've dropped down from.

"That opening is where this barricade came from," Wincott explained, slapping his hand against the wall. "The depression was probably a pin used to hold it in place in the cavern ceiling. I'm sure if you looked, you'd spot a few more."

The old thief grabbed one of the branches from the fire and used it as a torch to light the cavern wall. The firelight pushed back the cavern shadow to reveal a handful of similar pinhole impressions punched into the stone a dozen feet above their heads.

He guessed the wall in front of them was a defensive mechanism the city's inhabitants had created in the event of invasion. It had likely been dropped when the city was attacked, though he'd never heard of an invasion of the city, at least not in his lifetime. Legend had it Roan was abandoned.

"There must be another way in then," Sish said.

Wincott shook his head. "Likely not from here. These types of barricades were designed to keep people out—this entrance is sealed. We'll have to find another way in."

Sish's shoulders slumped. Wincott could tell the younger man was more than disappointed that it wasn't going to be as easy as he thought to enter the city. The old thief wondered what was suddenly so inviting about the legendary Treasure of Roan that the boy had hiked, alone so far into the valley. Wincott had traipsed through the woods of the valley his entire life, and not once had he conjured a good enough reason to venture into Roan, certainly not alone.

"We need to find a way in," Sish said, a note of desperation in his voice.

"How badly do you need to get in, boy?"

Sish ran his front teeth over his lower lip and inhaled deeply. He didn't say a word. Wincott didn't need him to. He knew Sish well. The boy's mannerisms were a dead giveaway—the young thief was in deep trouble, and the goblins were the least of his worries.

"I can get us in," Wincott said.

Sish looked at him with hope.

"For a price," the old man said, grinning, his crooked teeth glinting beneath the torchlight.

Sish threw his head back and sighed. "Fine, how much?"

"Fifty percent," Wincott replied.

Sish swore. "Thirty."

"Forty."

"Done."

Wincott smiled. "And whoever said there was no honor among thieves?"

"You do, frequently, and there isn't," Sish shot back. "Okay, old man, how do we get in?"

Wincott pointed at a small collection of stones next to the campfire and flicked his fingers, beckoning Sish to hand him one. Wincott stood closer to them, but he liked having the upper hand to the extent he could order the boy around. Sish sighed impatiently and tossed him a stone. Wincott turned and walked back toward the entrance to the cave. Just before he passed beneath the stone archway that led out to the valley, he looked up and hurled the rock as high as he could. It disappeared into the dark. Sish expected to hear it smack off the side of the wall, but instead, it landed and skipped along a ledge hidden in shadow.

"Where did it go?" Sish said, rushing forward.

Wincott took the torch and heaved it in the same direction. The flaming stick spun up through the darkness and landed on a small, roughly square alcove twenty feet above their heads behind the archway, leading out from the city.

"A ventilation shaft," Wincott said. "I worked in a mine some years ago. Every underground mine has ventilation, otherwise, the workers will suffocate. I noticed that one when I regained consciousness."

"And you waited until now to tell me?"

"Got me an extra 20 percent, didn't it?"

Sish ignored the comment. "Fine. So how do we get up there? The sun'll be up shortly and your friends outside not far behind it."

Wincott wandered over to the wall directly below the ventilation shaft. He pressed both hands to the rock, feeling around like a magician performing some sort of trick, paused briefly, and assessed the rock. He found it within seconds—a gap in the rock not visible to the naked eye, but behind it lay a tall, narrow alcove. He slipped behind it and heard Sish question where he'd gone. The old thief stuck out his hand so Sish could mark where he was and urged him to join.

Ahead of Wincott, a fold in the wall not easy to spot revealed a series of rough ledges that had been crudely cut into the stone and led up toward the ventilation shaft. To the naked eye, they looked natural, camouflaged by their surroundings to conceal the path upward. Wincott was impressed by the cleverness of the city's designers. The route up to the ventilation shaft was hidden in plain sight.

"It's a ladder," he said, pointing up.

"You first," Sish said, looking somewhat concerned about the climb.

A clatter and voices from beyond the cavern reminded the two thieves the goblins weren't far away. A dull gray predawn light filtered tentatively into the cavern. The creatures had stirred earlier than anticipated.

Sish elbowed Wincott out of the way and was halfway up the stone ladder before he slipped and sent a series of small stones and rock dust cascading onto Wincott's head. Same old Sish.

Despite their time together, it pained Wincott to admit the boy was not a natural thief. Nor was he particularly courageous, though he'd surprised Wincott a time or two. For a long while, he blamed himself, believing he was just a bad teacher. In fact, he was certain he was a bad teacher, but he had hoped the boy would pick up at least a few of his lessons, but no, Sish was naturally clumsy, favored strength over precision, and lacked the patience needed for a night burgle or a long job. That said, the boy had no shortage of gumption and pride. He was a self-starter with a natural charm and easy good looks that had brought jobs their way, and he could throw his weight behind a weapon or a punch when it counted.

And he had one other gift. Sish Torren was an exceptional liar. Better even than Wincott. The old thief had seen the boy spin a few yarns and talk his way out of more than a few troublesome situations. Wincott wished he could claim responsibility for it, but lying was not his strong suit, and the last thing a man wants to do is lie about being a good liar when he is not—the truth will come out.

As his stubby, sausage-like fingers dug into the sandpaper-like wall, the cold stone cutting into the flesh on the underside of his fingers, he admitted to himself the boy was probably playing him. Wincott was sure he had no intention of honoring their bargain and would look for the first opportunity to leave him behind or worse. He smiled bitterly at that, a strange pride swelling in him. The boy's lack of trust would keep him alive.

Sish's left foot slipped at the top of the ladder, swinging backward to nearly strike Wincott on the forehead. The foot missed, and the old man received only a fine dusting of rocky grit in his mouth and eyes. He swore and spat it out. Sish didn't apologize.

At the top, after he'd wiped the dirt from his face, Wincott had a sudden urge to kick Sish and send him reeling to the ground for the goblins to feast on. He didn't mind hitting his kid but watching him get eaten alive was taking things a bit far. Besides, he was genuinely curious to see where the boy led them—maybe there was treasure still to be had in Roan.

He stood on a flat, square ledge that overlooked the cavern. He could see the small camp they had made on the ground below, and to his right, beneath a finely carved archway, the path out of the city to the icy valley below. He had forgotten to snuff out the fire before they ascended the ladder and wondered if it might lead the goblins to their trail.

The younger man pointed to the fire. "Should we climb back down and put it out?"

Wincott peered over the edge, careful not to get too close. He hated heights. It always felt like some invisible force was pulling him down. Consequently, he'd avoided jobs over the years that had any element of verticality. And if they did, he'd sent Sish or someone else for that part. Some might call that cowardice, he mused, but Wincott just thought it was good leadership—people should play to their strengths. Heights were not his.

He shrugged. "You could if you wanted. I'm not going back down. Doubt they'll find their way up here either way. Your call."

Just then, a dark shape ambled into the cavern below the archway. A goblin. The dark-skinned creature was only about four feet tall and walked on legs that seemed to extend horizontally from its pelvis before hinging on knobby knees and extending to the ground. The creature moved with a rocking motion that reminded Sish of someone trying to walk in a squatting position. In its left hand was a torch, and in its right, a rusty meat cleaver. The goblin wore a loose chainmail vest and leather leggings that, to Wincott's eye, appeared to have some value. He wondered who had died so the goblin could have them.

The meat cleaver was clearly a kitchen tool and had likely been lifted, or taken violently, from some hapless camp cook who had the misfortune of being part of a fur trading party in the valley. The appearance of the meat cleaver, wielded by a lone goblin, told Wincott two important things:

One, Meat Cleaver had either drawn the short straw among his compatriots and been compelled to venture into the ruined city alone, or he was a leader. But no other goblins seemed to follow. They were losing their nerve, the old thief thought. Whatever remained in

Roan, the goblins were wary of it. And two, Meat Cleaver and his band were not well-armed or organized.

He watched the gangly creature pad around the campfire searching for the thief they'd chased from Shatterstill. Meat Cleaver looked like a lost puppy, and for the briefest moment, Wincott felt sorry for him. Then he remembered what he was looking at, and he considered chucking a rock at the creature's head for good measure. Suddenly, it turned and looked up, as if sensing his presence. Wincott slipped back into the shadow, clamping a hand over Sish's mouth as he bumped into the younger thief. The goblin sniffed the air, a surprisingly loud, raspy sound. It hissed.

Turning to Sish, he gestured for them to slip into a square corridor that disappeared down the length of the wall where they stood. A warm, almost tropical air billowed forth, pushing away the damp winter coolness of the cavern below. Wincott wondered apprehensively what would make the air so warm, quickly deciding that whatever it was, it probably wasn't good. He motioned for Sish to take the lead.

THE VENTILATION SHAFT WAS NARROW, barely wide enough for the old thief's squat but broad shoulders. It was roughly square in shape and crudely chiseled from the bones of the mountain. Here and there, edges of granite scraped against their shoulders and arms as they stepped carefully along its path. After a few hundred feet, when the weak light from the cavern behind had faded to pitch-black, Wincott knelt and struck his flint and tinder to light a short torch he had tied to his belt.

Sish turned away a moment, clearly blinded by the eruption of orange light. Wincott shone the torch forward, revealing a long, straight tunnel that stretched into the darkness beyond the light's reach.

They made their way along the tunnel in silence, Wincott worried their voices would echo into the cavern, alerting the goblins to their whereabouts. More than once he felt a light gust of warm wind against his face, a strange feeling in a land where winter so rarely loosened its grip. It smelled of minerals and damp. It was good news to Wincott because it suggested the shaft's connecting point to the city deeper in the mountain hadn't collapsed in the years since it was abandoned. The journey to Roan had not been an easy one for him.

He wondered again about the boy and his journey to the city. Had his son really come all this way in search of a treasure that was little more than legend? By himself? He was certainly capable, but there were other things afoot that made Wincott feel a larger game was at play. Sish knew more than he was letting on, of that he was certain, and he intended to find out what it was. But something else gnawed at him too, a thought that felt just out of reach but felt … dangerous almost. It had been too easy to convince the boy to let him come along, but he wasn't sure why. He tried to push it out of his mind, but it wouldn't dislodge.

The last time they'd run into each other, Sish had sliced Wincott's face open and promised to do worse. The wound had scarred the old thief in more ways than one. He traced a finger along it, thinking back and recalling the vicious look in his son's eyes. One thing he knew about Sish was that when the boy decided something, he did it. Wincott doubted Sish had made peace with that anger. He thumbed a short knife hidden in his vest as he walked behind the younger man. Best be ready for anything, he thought.

The tunnel widened ahead where water gushed from a crack in the wall. Beyond that, the floor was checkered with square holes that ran in a line as far as the light from the torch extended. The air reminded Wincott of being next to a lake on a hot summer's day— humid and thick.

He handed the torch to Sish and knelt next to the spouting water for a drink. It splashed over his face and beard, cold and fresh. A large pool had formed below the natural spout, where the water trickled across the checkered floor and splattered its contents into the mountain's black throat. Wincott held his hand above one of the holes and felt the rush of warm air.

"It comes from below," he said.

Wincott drew back his hand and saw it was slick with beads of moisture. He had no idea what was below, but he guessed there was a lot of water. He studied the checkered floor ahead of them. Each hole was narrow enough to jump over, and there was enough stone floor between each to stand and make ready to jump to the next one.

There was only rock above them, suggesting the only way forward was to leap across the holes. He grabbed the torch from Sish and leaned over the edge of the nearest hole. He pushed the torch into the hole, careful to avoid the sprinkling water. The firelight flickered in the hot wind, threatening to go out. He pulled it back quickly, deciding he could not see how deep the shaft ran, though certainly its existence, as with the others, hinted at much larger workings below.

Wincott got to his feet, wiped his mouth, and leaped across the first gap. His feet slid on the stone when he landed. His heart jumped into his throat. He cast a sheepish glance back at Sish, who nodded.

He leaped across the second hole, and Sish followed. On this went as the two thieves skipped their way across the gaps. After a dozen or so, Wincott stopped and shone the torch ahead. How much further?

The light revealed the tunnel's end. A flat, featureless stone wall a hundred feet or so ahead. Wincott cursed. It didn't make sense. There had to be a way down into the city; it was that or head back to the entrance and try their luck with the goblins.

"What is it?" asked Sish.

Wincott turned to answer the question when the younger man slipped through the floor of the tunnel in a shower of crumbling rock. He disappeared into the blackness below so quickly, there was barely a sound. It was as if the darkness reached up and grabbed him.

Wincott knelt over the edge of the hole and looked down.

"Boy!"

Nothing. Then words. A curse. He heard that clearly.

"You okay?"

"Fine," Sish called up. "Lucky, I suppose. There's another level here."

Wincott heard a splash.

"What was that?"

Sish cursed again. "I slipped. I'm standing on an angled shaft that's a bit dicey with all the water."

"How far down?"

"Hard to say," said Sish. "A dozen feet or so, probably less."

"Is there a way forward?"

"Toss down the torch, and I'll look."

"Okay, here goes."

The torch dropped and landed in a pool of water ten feet below the room with the checkered floor. He watched Sish crouch tentatively, trying not to slip while water rushed over his feet. The younger thief reached for the torch but slipped again, splashing water all over it. The light went out. Blackness. Wincott heard another splash and then a yelp as the younger man slid down the lower tunnel out of eyesight.

"Shit," Wincott cursed.

He drummed his fingers on the stone and considered going back the way he'd come. The goblins were likely gone, and there was a good chance he could slip out of the valley without raising their ire again. But he was low on provisions, and he would still have to contend with the long, cold journey to the nearest town. And, he supposed, there was his son to think about.

He sighed heavily and lowered his legs into the hole Sish had dropped through.

"Here goes," he said, already regretting it.

Wincott landed with a splash. His feet couldn't find purchase, and he went down on his ass, the stone shaft coming up to meet his backside like a hammer. The water rushed around his legs, and for a moment, he sat still in the darkness, the warm air from below tussling his wiry beard. Then the water grabbed hold of him, pulling him into the black throat of the shaft that led down into Roan. He slid for what seemed ages, his short body oscillating left to right off the smooth stone walls, spinning him around more than once, causing him to lose all sense of what was up or down or where he even was. And there was no stopping it—the shaft was as slick as a lake freshly frozen.

A circle of dim blue light appeared ahead of him, growing larger with each second, his heart thumping wildly as he careened mercilessly toward a mystery opening. The ventilation shaft spit him out high above a massive underground lake. As he careened through the air, end over fat end, he glimpsed a dimly lit city carved out of the cavern walls all around him—squat, square buildings chiseled from the heart of the mountain, cobblestone roadways, and at the top of the cavern, a great fortress. He hit the water like an arrow and disappeared into the darkness, half expecting his chest to seize up as the cold mountain water enveloped his body, but he found it to be unexpectedly warm.

He bobbed to the surface seconds later and spotted a worn-out dock jutting into the lake not far away. He struggled through the water, the soles of his feet vibrating from smacking into the lake, and found Sish standing at the water's edge, naked and wringing out his clothes.

The younger thief cocked an eyebrow as Wincott dog paddled to shore.

"I had a bet with myself that you would choose the goblins over me," Sish said.

Wincott trudged out of the water, running a hand through his thick mat of hair.

"And?"

"I lost."

"Get used to it," Wincott sniped.

"Get used to you helping me?" Sish asked, shaking the water from his shirt.

"No, losing."

Sish nodded wordlessly and went back to his chore. Wincott began to defrock as well, noticing the air in the cavern was quite warm. He stripped and wrung out his clothes and hung them off the side of the ancient-looking dock.

He turned toward the dimly lit city that rose away and above the dock behind them when a long knife *thunked* into the dock boards between his toes. He pursed his lips as a tall, square-shouldered man strode down the dock toward them. A man Wincott had hoped he would never have the misfortune to encounter again.

"Fulk," he said, shaking his head.

Sish gave him a quizzical look, but when he heard the heavy booted steps clapping down the dock toward them, he, too, turned to see the man striding purposefully toward them. Sish leaped to his feet and went for the short sword among his clothes, but Wincott held him back, shaking his head silently.

The man came to a stop before the naked thieves, retrieved his knife from the dock, and clapped Wincott on the shoulder, hard enough to nearly topple him into the water.

"Imagine my luck," said Fulk, holstering the knife at his side, his narrow, deep-set eyes flashing between the two men seated before him. "I'm *this* close to finally getting my hands on the Treasure of

Roan when I need someone small and quick with their fingers to get it for me—and *you*, you of all people, literally fall out of the sky and into my lap. What is it you used to always say a thief needed, Wincott? Finesse, focus, and *luck*. Luck, Wincott. I've always had good luck."

Fulk flashed a set of white, perfectly square teeth at him that reminded Wincott of a wolf ready to tear into its enemy. He rested his hands on his hips and laughed, a gravelly sound that brought back memories Wincott had long forgotten. He should've taken his chances with the goblins. Just then, a dozen armed men strolled up the dock behind Fulk, who turned to the nearest one and then gestured to Wincott.

"This one will do," he said, and then his eyes flashed over Sish. "Kill the other one."

Chapter Four

NEGOTIATIONS AT KNIFEPOINT

"**Y**OU WANT US TO DO what?" Wincott asked.

Almost an hour had passed since Fulk ordered Sish's execution, and Wincott had only been successful in convincing the man not to do it *yet*. Knowing Fulk, he had every intention of dispatching the young thief—and likely Wincott, too—as soon as they'd outlived their usefulness. Trouble was, Wincott had to invent that usefulness on the fly, and he was running out of ideas.

He was surprised at the level of restraint Fulk showed. Wincott had been in the man's orbit over several decades, but only once in direct contact with him, and he'd never known the old trader to hesitate about anything. Yet something had changed. Despite his wiry, muscled stature, there was a tiredness about him. A few more lines at the corners of his eyes, a bit grayer in his hair, shoulders that weren't as round as they once were.

And then there were his companions, a dozen hulking mercenaries in boiled leather and fur coats—hard men with eyes that felt menacing but unfocused, the kind of men Wincott had learned to be careful around. Their leader was a brute, with deep bronze skin that was heavily tattooed. He had a dark look about him, hungry almost, as he paced impatiently behind Fulk while Wincott attempted to convince the old trader to keep Sish alive. Sish, meantime, was on his knees between two of the mercenaries, one of them gripping his hair roughly while the other held a knife to his neck. They'd been holding that pose for about half an hour, and all three of them looked bored.

"Look, I'm not going over this again. You either come in the boat with us or I leave you here on the beach. Dead," Fulk said.

"And the boy?"

Fulk gritted his teeth and offered a curt, almost imperceptible nod.

"Fine," Wincott said. "But he's the only one I know who can navigate that kind of a situation."

Fulk eyed him carefully, his deep-set eyes boring a hole through the fat thief like hot black coffee in an empty stomach. Although relatively short and thin, Fulk wasn't the type you messed around with. What he lacked in physical stature he more than made up for in tenacity, conviction, and grit. His reputation for having an iron will—and the means to see it through—were legendary. As a chief factor of the Erdor and Expanse Trading Company for thirty years, he'd personally overseen all trade routes and the operations in each fort stretching between the Knifepoints and Alura Sea. It was a region so large the sun could set at one end while it was still only early evening on the other. Within it were several fiefdoms, dozens of towns, and more than twenty forts. Northern Erdor—the broken kingdoms, people called it—a name the priests of Sanctar dreamed up to make it sound grimmer than it really was.

Broken Kingdoms, Northern Erdor, E&E Co. territory—Wincott could care less. It was home, such as it was, and he'd long ago learned to stay away from people who spent a lot of time thinking about such things. People that had the power to name things also had the power to erase things, a reality he reminded himself of each time he fell into the vicinity of people like Fulk, who was as prudent a politician as he was a trader, and his reputation as a trader (he was known to frequently show up at remote forts unannounced in the dead of winter to conduct inspections, and if things weren't up to snuff, the fort's leaders were run out into the woods with no supplies) was the stuff of myth.

In the war with the Kingdom of Mordren's Royal Merchant Guild, he held ground at the Blackwater with only twenty men against a force ten times that number to maintain the Company's southern trade routes. Years later, with only a hundred men and a poorly stocked baggage train of riverboats, he charted a trading route to the north along the Crooked River, establishing new forts and supply lines with settlements on the far side of the mountains for the first time in generations. When the hoarfrost came down from the Knifepoints a dozen years ago, the wily son of a bitch kept the supply lines open by personally poling trade boats up and down the Ribbon to keep outposts like Fort Shatterstill stocked and their men alive. But it wasn't because he cared about them; it was because he wanted those goods moving through city markets and sold to the highest bidder.

In all that time, Fulk had been the governor of the E&E Co.'s right hand and what could best be described as the human embodiment of a fortress—his every move carefully considered, calculated, and executed to protect the governor and the Company's interests in the territory, which largely amounted to keeping profit margins high and ensuring Mordren's Guild never got a foothold in Northern Erdor. Fulk was stern, did what he said he would, and commanded the absolute loyalty of his men—at least he had.

His partnership with the governor ended abruptly when the governor appointed his whelp of a son in Fulk's place to consolidate power several years prior in a clumsy effort to establish a dynasty inside the E&E. The governor and his son were considered Company officers thanks to syndicated commissions from Erdor's fiefdoms.

Fulk, despite his accomplishments, remained a non-commissioned trader in their eyes. He was never in line for the governorship, only allowed to rub shoulders with the wealthy and powerful—the kind of people who named and renamed things—so long as the trade routes flowed.

Wincott suspected that was what triggered the old trader's violent outburst.

Fulk stormed into the governor's mansion one dinner hour and beat the man senseless in front of his wife and two other young children. Rumor had it the governor had to suck his food through bamboo shoots for months. Fulk was tossed in a cell and faced exile.

That was when Wincott officially crossed paths with him. Both had been escorted to the northern edge of the Company's trade territory at the hoarfrost line to be left to fend for themselves. The last time Wincott had seen the leathery old trader was on the shores of Cold Fish Lake, where the thief learned exile meant execution.

In a rare bit of do-gooding, he warned Fulk in time to save both their lives. Wincott figured the trader now owed him one, and maybe that would be enough to keep Sish alive. He wondered whether his son would do the same were their situations reversed.

Fulk clapped Wincott's shoulder and grinned darkly at him. "If you're saying he's more useful than you, I ought to just kill you and keep him. I'm sure *he* won't mind."

The old trader let his eyes wander to Sish, who remained naked and kneeling near the end of the dock between his captors. Fulk was right. Wincott wasn't prone to admitting his own mistakes, but Sish had been one of them. Not the thieving part—that he was okay with—but rather, what he'd done to alienate the boy and cause him to lash out so venomously. He rubbed the scar on his face absentmindedly and pushed the regret from his mind. It wasn't going to help him now, he reminded himself.

"You need us both," said Wincott. "No one has ever found what you're looking for, but a lot have died trying. I'm good with tight spaces, but the boy is magic with locks. Trust me."

Fulk snorted. "I don't trust you. But my honor won't let me gut you like I'd prefer to. Get dressed, you and the boy. We'll board the boats and cross the lake within the hour."

THE TWO THIEVES SAT ACROSS from one another again, a fire crackling weakly between them. Their clothes were still damp, but they had dressed to avoid reprisal from Fulk and his men. The fire offered little hope they would be warm by the time they climbed into the moldering rowboats Fulk and his men crowded around nearby. Sish stared into the fire, his shoulders hunched, head hung low. He looked like a man recently tossed in a cell, his grandiose plans dashed at the whim of a bit of bad luck.

Fulk shouted at one of the men who was obviously distressed about the condition of the boats. The hulking, tattooed mercenary stepped between them and eyed Fulk carefully. The old trader nodded and took a step back. The mercenary loosened the belaying pin at his belt and whipped it around against the man who had been arguing with Fulk. The weapon struck his head with a dull thump, and the man collapsed unconscious to the ground, blood streaming from the wound.

The mercenary looked among the rest of the men for any further argument. When no one spoke, he slipped the belaying pin into the leather holster at his side and nodded to Fulk.

"The boats are fine. Ready your things. We depart shortly," Fulk commanded.

Wincott turned to Sish. The young thief had formed an 'O' with his mouth, exhaling slowly through it at the sight of the dead mercenary a few dozen feet away.

"Inspires a lot of confidence, doesn't it?" Wincott said drily.

"It inspires something; not sure confidence is the word I would've used," said Sish. "Going on a boat ride, aren't we?"

Wincott nodded, and when Fulk and his men were out of earshot, he said, "Apparently, there's a series of traps on the far side of the lake that open a tunnel into the undercity. Fulk seems to think that's where the treasure is. I told him you were a wizard with locks."

"An *actual* wizard?" Sish said, his eyes suddenly wide.

"No, you dolt. A wizard as in an expert, you know?"

Sish shook his head and opened his mouth to protest, but Wincott held up a hand to quieten him.

"It was either that or he'd have his goons run you through with that short sword of yours. You're welcome."

"Not sure I should thank you. This only prolongs the inevitable."

Wincott shook his head and turned away, happy to let something less frustrating capture his thoughts for a few moments. He took in the murky cavernous grandeur around them.

They sat at the base of a rotting gray dock that reached into a large, black lake. Above, stretching away into the darkness left and right, were row upon row of squat buildings chiseled from the slate gray bones of the mountain. The rows were stacked on top of one another in roughhewn terraces that climbed several hundred feet up the cavern walls like stadium seating, disappearing into the shadows above. From the lakeside, there was no way to determine just how large the city was or how high it went. The buildings grew larger and more ornate the higher his eyes drifted, with great multilevel stone mansions and towers among them, each with scrollwork and imagery chiseled from the rock. Many of the buildings were painted in colors that were once vibrant, but in the intervening centuries of cascading dust and grime, had become dull yellows, rusty reds, and deep purplish blues.

All was silent save the quiet murmur of conversation among the dozen men dockside. The city was dead, empty of life and activity, crumbling amid fallen stones, decaying wood, and green calcium deposits that grew on the structures like moldy tumors that dripped from gargantuan stalactites. These stone fingers thrust like ancient lances from the shadowed granite ceiling far above them, leaving Wincott to wonder how deep beneath the surface they were.

The cavern, so far as he could tell, was bean-shaped, with the city at one end affording nearly every building a view of the black lake below. The lake stretched away from the dock as still and silent as an alleyway puddle, disappearing around the backside of several massive stone pillars that reached from the lake bottom to the cavern ceiling like a natural grate halfway across the water.

Wincott watched Sish as the boy's eyes wandered over the abandoned city. There was a wonder in them he hadn't seen in many years and a cool, calculating nature as well. The latter made the old thief's palms sweat.

"If you're thinking of making a run for it, think again," he told Sish. "You'll have a blade buried in your back in no time, or worse."

Wincott motioned to Fulk's hulking second-in-command.

Sish scoffed, "Wouldn't be the first group I've outrun."

Wincott leaned forward. "So, you didn't come into the valley alone?"

"I didn't say that," Sish quipped.

"You didn't not say it."

Sish scrunched his face in confusion. Mock confusion, Wincott thought, and dropped it. For a city that supposedly lay undisturbed for centuries, he found it passingly odd that so many people were suddenly converging on it in search of the treasure. And he wasn't a great believer in coincidences.

The younger thief chose to ignore him as he stood up, stretched, and checked his still-damp clothes. Wincott patted his pants, suddenly worried he'd lost everything in their watery arrival to Roan. The second set of tools he kept sewn inside his waistband were still intact. He guessed they might come in handy at some point, ideally as soon as he figured out a way to escape Fulk.

"So, what's the plan, old man?" Sish asked in a low voice.

Wincott stood and pointed across the lake to the vertical grate of gargantuan stalagmites that rose from the dark water. There were nine of them in a cluster that stretched most of the width of the lake, giving the impression of a small copse of stone trees. There appeared to be carvings in them, but from this distance, he couldn't make out what they were. The bean-shaped lake dog-legged to the left after the pillars so it was impossible to see the far end from their vantage point, though Wincott guessed something awaited them there, something Fulk knew about.

He assessed the motley collection of rowboats next to the dock and didn't like their odds. His eyes met Sish's.

"I guess we try to survive this," Wincott said.

His son only shrugged.

Just then, from high among the terraces and abandoned stone buildings, a great clanging rang out as if a metal scaffolding had collapsed. All eyes snapped toward the drab streets and causeways of Roan's bench-like levels. All was quiet again, the air still. Wincott realized he was holding his breath.

Another crash. Then a bang. A scraping noise and then a roar that rang out among the stone facades like a deep-pitched horn. The noise came from the furthest terraces of the upper city cast deep in gloom. Wincott could see—or thought he could see—a rooster tail of dust there that floated down over the drab buildings.

"To the boats!" cried Fulk, waving his arms toward the gray-roughened hulks at the shoreside.

The mercenaries sprang into action, half of them drawing weapons and lining up behind the boats to face the city, their eyes calm and collected. Men who were experienced with such things. Wincott realized they must've entered the city from elsewhere, perhaps from the direction the noise came from, and knew what it was.

The other half of the group dragged the boats into the water. Two mercenaries split off from their stevedoring companions and seized the two thieves by their shirt collars, pulling them into the rowboats.

"What the hell is going on?" Wincott yelled at Fulk.

"Start rowing." The trader pointed at him. "We're not alone."

Chapter Five

THE PRETENTIOUS PRACTICE OF DUNGEONEERING

THE BOATS SET OFF ACROSS the lake in a frenzy. Fulk was careful to separate Wincott from Sish, so the thieves traveled in separate rowboats that flanked Fulk's. The old trader's men were spread across the three boats, two in each, pulling oars as swiftly as their muscles would allow, putting as much distance between the poor man's regatta and the shore as possible. Sish was thankful he wasn't in the same boat as Wincott. The old man wasn't stupid, and a few more minutes of conversation would've forced Sish to spill the beans as to why and how he'd arrived at the city, a truth he was hoping to put off as long as possible, though his gut told him it wouldn't be long.

He watched Fulk as they pulled away from the city. The old buzzard was the only man in a boat with his eyes fixed on the far side of the lake; everyone else watched for signs of movement to explain the clatter among the cavern city's grim skyline. Sish thought he detected a hint of nervousness in some of them— the way they gripped the gunnels a little too hard or held their weapons with white knuckles. He had a sneaking suspicion that not all Fulk's men were the battle-hardened traders he was used to commanding for the E&E, but rather, thugs for hire and perhaps not very good ones at that.

"He hired a bunch of goons," the young thief muttered to himself.

"What's that?" a voice bellowed behind him.

He turned to find Fulk's second-in-command—the hulking, tattoo-blanketed brute named Kai—leering at him from his perch at the bow of their rowboat. Other than Fulk, he was the only man who looked calm and collected. The scars that carved dark canyons into his brown arms and face indicated he was no stranger to combat. Sish wasn't so bad with a blade himself, but he'd long ago made it a rule to avoid a fight with anyone who had cauliflower ears, which Kai did.

"What'd Fulk mean when he said, 'We're not alone'?" Sish asked him, changing the subject.

Kai sat back and spit in the water just beside Sish. A bit of it flecked his face. Sish bit his lip and wiped it away angrily. The fighter smiled disdainfully.

"Bit of a temper on yuh, eh? Won't live long with that," Kai said, chuckling darkly.

He spat again. He had a head like a coin safe and legs like dock pilings, with a face that reminded Sish of a beaten-up leather book bag, emphasis on the beaten-up part.

"Are there others in the city?" Sish pressed, trying to look past it.

"Not people, anyway," Kai said, his eyes briefly wandering over the cityscape they were rowing away from. "But you ne'er mind that, boy. Keep yer eyes fixed on the far shore and the job the boss got for you."

Sish turned away from him and let his eyes fall over the city again. He caught sight of a cloud of black dust that drifted down from one of the middle terraces. His stomach leaped into his throat as he watched the dust from afar, hoping it wasn't what he thought it was. Whatever was there, it was making steady progress toward the dock.

One of the goons in Wincott's boat stood and pointed toward the cloud. "There!"

Their attention turned toward it. Even Fulk pulled his hawkish eyes away from their destination long enough to watch the dust cloud roll through the terraces of the city like a barrel cascading down a series of switchbacks. Sish cursed silently. He thought he'd made the perfect escape, had even been impressed with the amount of time it had taken him to traverse the snow-laden valley above ground without aid. But then Wincott had appeared, and then Fulk, and now …

Clattering metal and hoarse yelling erupted from the ball of dust, echoing across the lake like some vengeful spirit. As it moved down the terraces toward the dock, Sish felt his skin prickle with goose bumps, his stomach clench with worry.

The shapes of several people could be made out at the edge of the dark, rolling haze. They were in retreat and fighting for each step. The largest one, a man with long, black hair, swung a double-edged sword that was as long as Wincott was tall. A hoarse yell erupted from his lungs as he urged his companions to stay behind him, the sound carrying toward the rowboats that were now almost a mile distant.

"Shit," Sish cursed.

He spotted the sword wielder's two other companions—a slender woman in green robes and a man in brown leathers, who wielded a bow. Sish knew them ... well, in fact. The tall one was Terry the Barbarian, a bag of meat that was mostly fat now that his arena days were behind him. The archer, the father of the group, went by the name Wren—a soldier turned hunter with an annoying tendency not to say much, and when he did, to be as mysterious as possible. And the girl, well, the girl was Liv Decker, a hedge mage with a sharp tongue and no love for Sish, not anymore anyway.

Then he noticed one of them was missing. Rena. The youngest member of their troupe was nowhere to be seen. A pit formed in Sish's gut. Maybe she was there and he just couldn't see her, or perhaps she'd taken another route through the city or decided not to enter with them. No, no, he knew that couldn't be it. Rena was the only reason they'd agreed to come—their ace in the hole in case things got ugly, real ugly. She was there when Sish ...

"Y'know these fools?" Kai nudged the thief with his foot, gesturing at the trio.

Sish nodded, resuming his cool. "Unfortunately."

The Dungeoneers, a small clan of do-gooders he'd been a member of until doing good had become too much of a liability.

The young thief looked in his father's direction and caught Wincott's eye. There was a mischievous smile on the man's face. The old bastard was enjoying this, Sish thought. Wincott had probably guessed that Sish had cut-and-run from the trio fighting their way toward the dock, hoping he'd be the first and only one to survive the trek to Roan to find a way into the city.

"Keep rowin'!" Fulk ordered, his voice echoing across the water toward the city.

The dungeoneers approached the dock, a swarm of black, slug-like creatures pressing against them, their oily tentacles snapping from all sides at the companions like bullwhips. Terry swung his sword in wide arcs while Wren fired arrows relentlessly into the creatures' massive, singular, cloudy white eyes.

Liv hazarded a look over her shoulder at the boats skirting away across the lake. Her eyes fell on Sish, and even from a mile away, a shudder ran up the thief's spine so cold he thought his teeth might chatter. He swore he could see her upper lip curl into an angry sneer. It wouldn't be the first time, though he guessed it might be the last if she got hold of him.

"Friends of yours, boy?" Fulk called to him from the neighboring boat. "Ha! Knew you idiots couldn't have found your way here on your own. Had some help from some dungeoneers, eh? Well, no matter. They found the mess we woke up for them."

The old trader's eyes glinted in the low light. At the mention of the trio's professional identity, there was audible whispering among the goons spread across Fulk's rowboats, notes of surprise, wonder, and fear.

"Pipe down ye mutts!" Kai bellowed, spitting into the water (more spittle on Sish's cheek). "There're only three of 'em! Got their backs to the water, a wave of Gerthulbs comin' at 'em, and *we* here have the only damn boats!"

He laughed, a hoarse, angry sound that didn't make Sish feel any better about their situation.

At one end of the lake, a certain doom awaited him, while on the other, a band of angry former companions already had their weapons drawn. If he fell into their hands, he guessed it would transform into a drawn-out process whereby, in typical fashion, they would consider one another's opinions and vote on how best to kill the wretched little turncoat that left them freezing halfway up the valley with no map. They were dungeoneers, after all, talented with blade and bow but committed to an inane and chivalric code to root out evil from the older, deeper places of the world. They weren't even in it for the money and had an annoying tendency to donate all proceeds from their adventures to museums and good causes.

Dungeoneers, Sish cursed.

Do-gooders, who high-fived their way through forgotten places, reveled in high-minded notions of teamwork and collaboration and ended their days at whatever pub would have them regaling the assembled masses with tales of derring-do.

It was downright pretentious, Sish thought, to be so privileged you could live your life drifting from one adventure to the next and never worry whether you had a roof over your head or enough food to eat. Most couldn't afford that life. Certainly not Sish. That's why he was a thief, not because he wanted to but because he had to, and even at that, he was barely scraping by. Dungeoneering? He had no time for it unless it meant he got to keep what he earned. Otherwise, what was the point?

He scanned the beach on either side of the dock for any other boats the companions could use to catch up. There were none, and he found himself smiling at the thought of the three of them stranded at the far side of the lake.

Good luck getting me now.

Sish turned toward their destination while most of Fulk's men continued to watch the raucous melee playing out on the beach. He was surrounded by goons and his father, a man he'd tried to gut three years before for being, well, a world-class asshole. He considered jumping out of the boat and swimming for it, though to where he didn't know.

He was ready to jump for it when his ears pricked to a strange gurgling, screamy sound above him. His brain registered the noise as something familiar before he knew what it was. He looked up. In the shadows above, he saw a dark, round splotch flying through the cavern's gloom toward them. No, not flying—falling. And not a splotch. It wasn't a bat. It had dark skin, legs, arms, and a rusty kitchen knife in its hand.

Meat Cleaver.

Sish looked at Wincott. The old man saw it, too; his eyes were like dinner plates. The gurgling sound became an outright scream as the goblin plummeted toward them. So transfixed by the melee between human and cavern monster on shore were Fulk's goons that they didn't notice the goblin shrieking toward the rowboats until it was too late.

The little murderer crashed into Sish's boat like a missile, his meat cleaver spinning out of his hand like a wagon wheel loosened from its axle. It found purchase in an oarsman's head while his warty little body smashed through the bottom of the moldering boat, sinking it almost instantly.

SISH'S BOAT AND ITS CREW were underwater in a flash. Wincott was on his feet. The men in his rowboat scanned the darkness around them to make sense of what had just caused their comrades' boat to vanish into the deep. Wincott caught a look of absolute befuddlement in Fulk's eyes as the old trader tried to determine if the threat was on the shore, in the water, or coming from above.

There was another gurgling scream to Wincott's right as a second mottled black body splashed into the water. And then another between his and Fulk's rowboat. And then a third when one landed on one of Fulk's goons, knocking him unconscious. The black thing, which was a goblin, spit and cursed something unintelligible and leaped to its feet, knife in hand, and started attacking the crew members. Another goblin then landed in Wincott's boat.

The thief cast his eyes toward the cavern's ceiling and saw half a dozen black shapes hurtling toward them. It was raining goblins, and Wincott knew exactly where they were coming from—the same air ventilation shaft he and Sish had navigated and ultimately fallen through.

The general confusion only lasted a moment before the glassy confusion in Fulk's eyes was replaced with that familiar iron will. He drew a bowie knife from his belt and plunged it into the chest of the goblin in his rowboat. He bellowed a command, his hand still on the knife as the creature sagged to the bottom of the boat in a spurt of black blood.

"Goblins! To arms!" he cried.

The goons were on their feet, weapons drawn almost in unison. The crew from the sunken rowboat popped above water a moment later. Wincott didn't see his son.

A memory flashed through his mind again: a woman wailing, a child submerged in frigid water.

He tore off his shirt and leaped into the lake. What he intended as a graceful dive became a bellyflop as he smacked into the water, a band of pain stretching across his stomach as he submerged.

Despite the cavern's gloom, the water was surprisingly clear. Opening his eyes, he could see the hull of Fulk's boat directly in front of him, and further ahead, the wrecked structure of Sish's rowboat drifting lazily into the murk below. Around it, several of Fulk's men struggled to kick to the surface. One had already inhaled water and drowned, his eyes wide with the sudden shock of death. All around, more goblins dropped into the water like stones.

Wincott spotted Sish a moment later. The young man's foot was caught in a part of the sinking hull. Wincott frog-kicked toward him. Sish struggled with both hands on his leg as the wreck drifted downward in a cloud of air bubbles. Wincott locked eyes with him and signaled for him to push and Sish to pull at the same time. The young thief was free a moment later, though he lost a boot in the process.

On their way up, Wincott caught sight of something large and eel-like moving through the water below him but chose to pretend he hadn't seen it. One problem at a time, he thought.

On the surface, it was difficult for Wincott to get his bearings amid the screaming, clanging of weapons, and thrashing in the water all around them. Several of Sish's fellow crew had made their way to the surface and were swimming toward the remaining rowboats. Both rowboats were in a frenzy of fighting as crewmen attempted to kill or at least dump the goblin band from their boats.

Fulk had a bowie knife in one hand and a belaying pin in the other and was almost single-handedly taking the fight to the intruders while his men struggled for their weapons or fell out of the boat into the water.

A mile away, on shore, Wincott could see the dungeoneers had retreated to the dock where he and Sish had first pulled themselves ashore after plunging from the ventilation shaft far above. The barbarian continued to sweep his sword in giant arcs, hacking black tentacles and arms away from the host of subterranean cavern creatures that pursued them to the watery edge of the city.

The one in hunting leathers had turned and was pointing toward the fray in the middle of the lake, but only the girl paid any attention to him.

Sish bubbled to the surface next to Wincott and wiped the loose hair back from his face.

"What's the plan, old man?" he asked, treading water amidst the chaos around them.

Wincott shook his head and said, "Too far to swim in either direction, so we need to get back on one of those boats."

Just then, a massive tentacle rose out of the lake next to Wincott's former boat and snapped onto it, crushing the boat and taking half a dozen of Fulk's men and as many goblins into the water.

"Guess that limits our options," Wincott said.

"To the boat! To the boat!" Fulk yelled.

He knocked the last goblin from the remaining boat with a swing of the belaying pin. There were only two goons left with Fulk. The trader dropped onto the rowing bench and began working both oars in unison. The rowboat began to pull away from the mess of white water in the middle of the lake.

Wincott saw their chance and swam for the boat. With his longer arms and strength, Sish easily outpaced him and was being helped aboard before Wincott had crossed two-thirds the distance there.

Several other goons were making their way through the water, too—the few who hadn't been pulled under, drowned, or were otherwise occupied with a goblin. As he kicked his way toward the rowboat, he hoped that whatever horror lived deep in the water had lost interest in the pitiful creatures on top.

A heavily muscled man with deep scars tattooing his brown skin pulled Wincott out of the water with one arm. Sish was already on the bench next to Fulk, rowing in his sodden clothes.

As Wincott shook off the water, he realized he was shirtless, having doffed the garment before he leaped out of the other rowboat. He cursed himself, knowing his backup set of pry tools was sewn into one of the seams of that shirt and was now forever lost to the lake.

He slumped onto one of the benches and caught Fulk's eye.

"Sure you want to keep going?" he asked, already knowing what the other man would say.

"Wouldn't have it any other way, thief," Fulk said, his ropy arms bulging with vein and muscle as he worked the oar. "We've earned that treasure now."

Fulk's second-in-command let out a big belly laugh and slapped Wincott heartily on the shoulder and then muttered something about how pitiful the dungeoneers were.

Wincott looked at Sish. The boy had to work hard to keep up with Fulk on the oar, but his body was more than up for it. He gritted through the work and kept going, a determination Wincott had known was in him since he was a boy. He saw a similarity between the boy and Fulk that shouldn't have surprised him; he just hoped the two of them wouldn't notice it.

Chapter Six

THE THIEF DOES SOMETHING GOOD FOR ONCE

Years before

INCOTT TRUDGED OUT OF THE near-frozen water with the boy cradled in his arms. He was limp and unconscious. The mother rushed to him, but the injury to her leg was too much, and she collapsed in the dirt a few feet from Wincott. Arrows whistled through the air over them as the din of battle rang out around them—the sound of a town being torn apart as a battalion of angry Guildsmen sought to push their trading territory further north and visit revenge upon the E&E and anyone who benefitted from it.

Wincott lumbered out of the twisting river. He was out of breath. His muscles ached from the cold and exertion. He carried the limp form through the reed grass and laid the boy carefully on a protected dry spot in an alcove at the base of a massive cottonwood. It smelled like wet grass, roots, and mushrooms, but at least it was out of sight of the battle nearby.

The boy was gray, his lips blue and eyes closed. Wincott wasn't even sure why he'd dived in after the boy; maybe it was a moment of weakness, or just that he'd seen enough death for one day and couldn't bear any more. Or maybe it was because some small part of him wanted to drown in that water, too. Whatever the case, there'd be time to think about it later.

He blew air into the boy's lungs the way he'd seen a field medic do once and then pumped his chest with both hands. The mother, a weathered-looking woman with a mud-streaked face and a torn dress, pulled herself from the reedy muck into the alcove by her fingernails as if she were still avoiding arrows. Her fingers were raw, split, and bloodied, but the look in her eyes told Wincott she wasn't ready to let the boy go and so he shouldn't either.

He kept pumping, occasionally stopping to wipe water or sweat from his brow, he wasn't sure which. It seemed to go on forever. More than once, his eyes wandered to the village around them, not so much looking for danger as an easy escape. The clamor around them was somewhat drowned out by the panic at their fingertips.

The child suddenly convulsed and spat up a lungful of river water. Wincott turned him to his side and slapped his back. While the boy coughed, Wincott gasped as he realized he'd been holding his breath since he dived into the river.

He wiped the sweat from his face and sat back on his shins. The mother doffed her dirty shawl and wrapped it around the boy's head and shoulders, pulling him into the alcove to rest on her stomach. She leaned against the partially exposed root ball of the cottonwood and stared, vacant-eyed into the river, which flowed swiftly past them.

The sound of mailed feet marching along the forest path above them caused Wincott to duck swiftly beneath the cottonwood's exposed roots to avoid being seen by several Guildsmen.

"We need to move," Wincott said.

The mother nodded. When he was sure the soldiers were gone, he poked his head out and looked around. The smell of charred wood and sweat was heavy in the air. The evening light cast long shadows over the village and surrounding trees, which Wincott hoped would provide them a bit of cover.

It was then he noticed a broken arrow shaft protruding from the woman's thigh, blood oozing down her torn pant leg. He thought he probably should pull it out but then worried about injuring her worse. No, it would have to wait. He'd carry the boy, and the mother could lean on him. It would be slow going, but hopefully, he could get them to the edge of town, somewhere away from the battle. He could leave them with a farmer who could look after them. And then he could be on his way, narrowly escaping yet another incursion by the Guild in E&E territory. This business was getting more dangerous by the day, he thought.

After the Guildsmen were long gone, Wincott thrust his head above the collection of cottonwood roots to survey the area around them. They were on the north side of town where the Moon River twisted through the valley with flat, murky water. If they stuck close to the river and moved between the trees, they had a good chance of escape, he figured.

He hefted the boy in his arms. The child was awake but quiet with fear, his dark green eyes surveying the bearded thief pensively. Wincott signaled for the mother to follow him.

"Stay low. Not a word," Wincott warned.

She nodded, and they moved toward the next set of cottonwoods downriver. The battle had shifted away from them an hour or so ago, so he hoped they had a good chance of getting out alive, but that didn't mean there weren't strays about ransacking homes. Like E&E men, the Guildsmen weren't well-disciplined soldiers—they were fur traders, used to traipsing through rugged terrain in all weather conditions. Strong, wiry, skilled with blade and bow but not used to being told what to do. In more recent years, raids between the Company and the Guild had turned men on both sides into something more than just mere mercantilists. They were battle-hardened and had a taste for blood now, which meant fewer places were as safe as they had once been.

They reached a second copse of trees without incident. The boy was awake now and seemed okay to move, his eyes shifting between Wincott and his wounded mother. The thief set him on his feet while his mother talked to him. She was moving with a heavy limp, and Wincott feared she wouldn't be able to get very far before her leg gave out. He took the opportunity to scout further down the riverbank.

Black pillars of smoke billowed into the sky where homes and businesses had been set ablaze. The arrow volleys had mostly stopped, but the thief could still hear the steady clang of steel as men fought in the distance. Guild raids typically didn't last long, and the raiders tended to seize land as often as they abandoned it. Wincott wasn't sure yet what type this was.

He returned to the mother and boy to give them the all-clear when a dark shape leaped down from the bank and collapsed Wincott to the ground. The air exploded from his lungs as he hit the mudbank.

"Got ye now ye dirty Company jack," a greasy voice laughed into his ear.

He rolled onto his back. A short, skinny man squatted on top of him, a hungry look on his scraggly face. He had the bright but glassy eyes of a man who'd spent too long in the bush. He stunk of fire and spilled blood, a hatchet clutched in his right hand.

"I—I'm no——" Wincott tried, but he couldn't catch his breath.

The man laughed, spittle flying between his loose teeth. He raised the hatchet to strike. The mother was suddenly behind him, swinging a heavy rock at his head. The Guildsman was dazed but not hurt. She struck again. And again. And then was on top of him, the rock colliding with his skull several more times as blood splattered across Wincott's face.

She stood on shaky legs, her breath catching, still gripping the rock. Wincott rolled the body off him. He crawled on hands and knees to the water's edge, cupping his hands in the turbid flow and cleansing his face of blood. He breathed in and out silently, gathering his thoughts before he turned and found her and the boy watching him from a few feet away.

"I guess we're even," he told her.

She nodded, "I guess so. *Are* you a Company man?"

Wincott rolled his tongue around in his mouth. "No, ma'am. I'm not."

Her eyes passed over the satchel at his side. It was brimming with stolen goods, some of them bright and shiny, glinting in the low evening light.

"A thief then," she said, not as an accusation but as a matter of fact.

He nodded. She winced, not from him but from the pain in her leg where the arrow protruded.

She spat at the dead Guildsman at her feet and said, "Well, we all need to make our way, don't we?"

"We do, ma'am," Wincott said, still on his hands and knees, looking up at her, not sure whether he should take his chances in the river or help her and the boy escape.

"What's your name?"

"Wincott," he said. "And yours?"

She hesitated a moment, a grimace passing over her face. Maybe it was just pain from the arrow in her leg, but Wincott decided it was something more. A hesitancy to trust anyone, even with something as simple as their names. After a moment, she breathed out and put her hands on her hips.

"Well, thief, I'm the local whore. One of 'em anyway," she said, looking around. "Name is Meridan. Meridan Torren. And this is my boy, Sish."

Chapter Seven

A GOBLIN AMONG MERE MEN

THE REMAINING ROWBOAT GLIDED THROUGH still, inky water in the cavern of Roan. Sish wasn't working the oar as hard as before, he and Fulk having put a lot of lake between the boat and the goblins. Also, his arms were on fire from the exertion, while the old trader seemed to be just warming up.

In the distance, he could see several men and goblins clinging to flotsam. One of them, he swore, was the same warty bastard that had sunk the first rowboat. *Meat Cleaver.*

Beyond that, the dock and shoreline at the base of the city where his former companions had mounted a defense was quiet. Sish hadn't caught sight of where those idiots had disappeared, but there was a fair-sized pile of hacked-up limbs and cavern creatures at the base of the dock, so he gathered they weren't dead.

Great. Not only did they survive, but they were likely troubleshooting a route across the lake. And despite Fulk's confidence that they would be stranded, Sish was smart enough to know the bastards would scheme up some ingenuous way across—may even beat them to the treasure. After all, that was their business. And they were good at it. He suspected Fulk wasn't entirely deaf to that fact either. And neither was Wincott.

He looked at the old thief, who sat on a bench across from him, naked from the waist up, his hairy gut spilling out over the front of his breeches, a haunted look in his eyes. He was past his best before date, that was for sure, but even Sish could grudgingly admit the old man had been a *damned good* thief in his day. He'd once watched Wincott steal a trunk of silver coins from a heavily guarded riverboat without a sound or alarm. The Company hadn't noticed until they offloaded the boat several hundred miles downriver, by which point the trunk was secreted away in one of Wincott's many hidden caches.

Too bad the old man was a greedy, lying sonofabitch, though. His better qualities weren't enough to balance out the bad stuff, so, Sish still had every intention of getting rid of him as soon as possible, which meant either leaving him behind or being the one to do him in. He was confident an opportunity would present itself sooner or later. It always did.

"Here, take over, boy," Fulk said, rising from the bench.

Sish slid over and took the second oar in hand and began to row both in unison. His shoulders ached, sagged. But he wouldn't complain; it would do him no good among this crew.

"The guardian won't come this far down the lake," Fulk announced. "The pillars mark the edge of its territory."

"What was it?" Sish asked.

It was Kai's turn to answer. He spit loudly and said, "What'chya ne'er heard of a guardian before, boy? Creature bred to keep folk like you and yer da there out. They're scattered all o'er the high country and down in the deep places of the world, you bet."

Fulk turned to face him and placed one booted foot on the bench beside Sish, his deep-set eyes boring into the thief.

"The Old Ones created and left them here to keep people like you out," he said

"And people like you?" Wincott asked.

Fulk turned on him, an eyebrow cocking.

"People like me were destined to come here, old man. Destined."

"Look!" One of the crewmen pointed up.

The boat drifted past the first of the nine gargantuan stone pillars spotted from shore. Here, the water was like glass, the cavern warm and humid. A light mist rose just above the waterline, shrouding the base of each pillar in a soft, white blanket. It smelled of wet stone and heat.

Sish looked up. The pillar was a stalagmite of rough dark brown rock pockmarked with a million divots through centuries of slow decay. It stretched hundreds of feet into the air, disappearing into the darkness above them. Carved into the front of it was the likeness of a man, a warrior clad from head to toe in plate mail, bearing a sword thrust tip-down to parallel his legs. His face was kingly, square of jaw, with a patrician nose and hawkish eyes. He reminded Sish a bit of Fulk.

As the boat drifted past the first pillar, he noticed the other eight bore similar carvings. There were two archers, both with recurve bows at their sides. And several more warriors, two women among them. And there was also a sorcerer, an elf, and strangest of all, a goblin.

"Strange to see a goblin held in such regard that it would stand tall among kings," Wincott observed.

"You don't know your history then," said Fulk. "That's Oyama. He was a castaway before he became a renowned hunter and warrior. He was the greatest among the Nine for it was he alone who held the barbican at Gauntlet Pass that kept the hordes at bay. Had he not, the Company and the Guild would've been overrun and every town with it."

Sish noticed Oyama wore an eyepatch. He asked Fulk about it, but it was Kai who answered.

The lumbering brute leaned so close to Sish he could smell the booze on his breath.

"His ma plucked it out when he was born 'cause she los' one of her own. Goblins can swap parts like that, see," Kai said.

Fulk rolled his eyes while Sish shook his head. Kai guffawed and slapped the young thief hard on the shoulder before turning away to spit again in the water.

"Land ho!" a crewman called out.

Sish reefed on the oars once more before he let the boat drift into shore at the end of the lake. It beached itself on a patch of rough dirt, rock, and sand. But as opposed to the other side of the lake, the ground here was littered with strange trees and brush.

Everywhere were stunted gray, blue, and white bushes. And behind them, closer to the cavern wall, were gnarled trees that had the twisted, fibrous trunks of cedar but were topped with almost translucent branchlets and sprays. They grew thickest at the entrance to a cave that seemingly led down to the old city.

The mouth of the cave was a great vertical gash in the rock, widest at its middle. It looked to Sish as though one of the Nine had used their stone sword to slice the rock before widening the gap with their hands like some ancient colossus.

Fulk wasted no time. The old trader was out of the boat and marching up the dark brown sand before Sish put down the oars. Kai was behind him, and the other half dozen goons soon followed, leaving Wincott alone with Sish as the boat rocked to a halt.

The two thieves exchanged a look. Wordlessly, Sish gestured for them to run the boat back into the lake, flee Fulk's party. Wincott shook his head gravely. The look on his face told Sish the old man had no desire to paddle back through the guardian's territory, much less deal with whatever creatures Fulk and the others had woken in the upper city.

"We go on," Wincott said, heaving himself over the side of the boat into the shallow water next to it. "Don't worry, son, it's only our lives at stake."

Chapter Eight

WHEN THE MAP ISN'T USEFUL

THE CAVE AT THE TOP of the beach was a strange place, smaller and narrower than the grand cavern of Roan's upper city, with a crevasse that stretched above their heads as if a giant's molten spear had been thrust upward into the mantle of the world. Within it, luminescent mineralization lined the cavern walls like a thousand eyes, bathing the strange white and gray flora in a pale blue glow.

Stranger yet was the well-appointed study built into the cavern's far wall. It looked to Sish as though someone had lifted half a library from the academy and slid it between the rocks. Stone tile floors, hardwood walls, bookcases, a rolltop desk, and a bolted green leather armchair accounted for most of the space. There was also a lavish oval door set into the wall, surrounded by hardwood panels. Yet something about the delicate script work in the stone and complex lock at its center suggested to Sish it was more ancient than the study.

Fulk's crew spotted and lit a small brick-lined firepit at the edge of the stone tile floor. Most of them were still damp from their swim. Kai moved past them toward the study, climbing a short flight of stone steps that led up to it. He looked around before setting his eyes on the oval door. He traced the scrollwork admiringly with a heavy hand.

"Your fists won't do you any good here, Kai," Fulk teased, pushing past him.

Kai paused a moment, then grunted and flopped into the leather armchair, a cloud of dust kicking up as he landed.

Fulk studied the door for a moment before lifting a book from the rolltop desk next to Kai. He wiped away a page of dust with a decisive flick of his finger.

Wincott was there next, squatting next to a bookcase, where he found a knapsack stuffed with clothes to rummage through.

Sish approached hesitantly, his eyes darting around. He was careful of any loose panels or boards, really anything at all that could be a trap, notwithstanding the fancy office. Inspecting the ornate door, he spotted a small porthole at eye level with a diameter roughly as wide as his shoulders. It looked like a massive circular keyhole. The luminescent crevasse above them closed to a point where the rock met the top of the stone door, not allowing anyone to climb over the top. The door was inlaid with flowy, interconnecting scrollwork in a language Sish wasn't familiar with. If it even was. He ran his hand over it, allowing his fingers to trace the curvature of the symbols. It looked like someone had tried to etch a message into the stone and drawn a picture of wind instead.

Fulk stepped behind him. Although the old trader was a head shorter than Sish, the thief felt as though the man was looking down on him. His gut roiled anxiously.

"Millennia or more the old city has been sealed," Fulk said.

"Why was it sealed?" Sish asked, not bothering to turn around. He didn't want to give the old trader the satisfaction, though it took every ounce of will Sish had to face forward.

"No one knows, but there are stories," Fulk said. "One tells of a disaster that struck the old city and could only be contained if the city were sealed. Another that the city's makers created a weapon so powerful they feared it would destroy the world, and so they buried it and most of their city as well."

"And another that there's a treasure so fabulous down there it'd make all the kings of the world look like paupers," Kai bellowed, picking his nails. "Mayhap there's not down there but rock, dust, and bones."

Fulk turned on his lieutenant, a rare flash of anger in his eyes. He didn't need to say anything. Kai, despite his size, withered beneath the trader's glare.

Fulk dropped the heavy tome onto the desk next to Kai. It hit the hardwood with a cloud of dust that made Kai sneeze.

"Come on, boy," Fulk said to Sish, his breath hot on the back of the thief's neck. "We need to talk about the trials."

Sish whipped around to watch Fulk descend the stairs toward the cookfire where his men crowded.

"You've a long day ahead of you," the trader called back at him. "And if you're half as good with locks as your old man claims, we'll soon find out what *is* beyond that door."

Fulk found a dusty chair made of bent branches tied together with bark. He turned it over to sit next to the fire, his goons shifting out of the way to accommodate him. The trader gestured for Sish to take a seat on a large stump across from him. Fulk drew a sheaf of paper from his jacket, carefully unfolding it and handing it across the fire to the thief.

"This is what I've been able to glean about the door," he told Sish. "As I'm sure you can imagine, there's not a lot of information about it—or Roan—in the overworld. I've only learned there are three trials that must be completed to open the door to the old city."

"Sounds stupid," Sish said bluntly, eyeing him.

When Fulk said nothing, the thief scanned the paper. It was a map of Roan that showed a second entrance through a cave system on Fang Mountain, followed by a series of tunnels that led down to the upper city, the lake, its pillars, and the guardian, which a doodle indicated was some type of octopus, not that Sish had ever seen one in real life.

So, that was how the others got into the city. They didn't lose much time then, Sish decided. But what had brought his dad into the valley at the same time? That mystery still wasn't solved.

He eyed the old thief as Wincott dug through the knapsack, sizing up a shirt he needed to cover his bare chest.

Kai lumbered from the study to join them at the campfire, his impressive bulk crowding behind Sish as the brute took a sudden interest in the map.

Laid over a large, empty section of the map was an image of the ornate oval door, with hastily scrawled notations below it about the keyhole and something about three trials. Yet beside each numbered trial was a question mark.

Shit, Sish realized. *Fulk knows nothing.*

The fact that the trader's doodle of the door looked nothing like the real thing didn't inspire much confidence in him either.

Wincott dropped the knapsack and wandered toward the fire as he pulled the shirt over his head. Sish handed the paper to him, but his eyes were locked on Fulk's. The old thief scanned it and sighed.

"This is the best you've got?" Wincott said, exasperated. "I wouldn't wipe my ass with this. It literally tells us nothing."

A few of the crewmen chuckled at the dwarfish man's reaction but were quickly stifled with a hard glare from Fulk.

Kai grunted and belted Wincott with a swift backhand. The old thief tumbled to the ground, his lip split, rage in his eyes. Sish didn't dare move.

Fulk leaned forward in his chair, elbows on his knees. He ignored Wincott, instead focusing on Sish, who, although he didn't betray it, shared his father's thoughts.

"The door wasn't meant to be opened, except by those that built it. From what I gather the hole at the center of that door is the keyhole," Fulk said, pointing at it.

"And the key is *where* exactly?" Wincott pressed.

"Your son is the key," Fulk said. He looked at Wincott and shrugged. "Or you are. The inhabitants of the city were said to be smaller than the average man, dwarf height. Like you. Which is why I found it so convenient that you landed on the lakeshore just as we were about to make our way across. I would've been forced to send a crew member, but then, two thieves fell into my lap—and you convinced me your son was the best man for the job."

Wincott wiped blood from his lip and grimaced. Kai moved to hit him again, but Fulk quietly shook his head, and the henchman stopped. Fulk's eyes lingered on Wincott a moment longer before turning back to Sish. Wincott dropped the paper in Sish's lap. The younger thief watched the old man walk to the edge of the cave, where he leaned against the wall and looked out over the misty lake beyond.

"I must admit," Sish began, clearing his throat, "I was expecting … something else."

Fulk sat back and rested one hand on the pommel of the bowie knife at his side.

"Well, if you don't like it, I could have Kai gut you both and toss your bodies in the lake, and we could all go home," Fulk said.

The assembled mercenaries grumbled approvingly.

Sish didn't say anything.

Fulk leaned forward, palm still on his knife. "Then it's decided," he said through a manic grin. "In the morning, you go in the hole."

Chapter Nine

SOMEONE'S A CON ARTIST, WE'RE JUST NOT SURE WHO

SISH HARDLY SLEPT. FULK POSTED guards nearby, ostensibly to protect the camp, but he felt it was to prevent the thieves from fleeing. The other men, while encouraged to sleep, drained a bottle of moonshine and told tales about their run-in with the goblins. Wincott bedded on a few old blankets he found, using his newish knapsack as a pillow. He fell asleep quickly, and his buzz-saw snoring shattered any hope of keeping their presence quiet. Fulk remained alert and sat at the desk poring over old papers and texts.

He wondered who had the brilliant idea to build a gentlemen's study next to a vault door in a cave. Had it been Roan's engineers? Or had other treasure hunters found their way this far before? If so, they certainly hadn't been successful, otherwise, the door would already be open. And there were no corpses or bones anywhere, so that must mean … Sish's eyes drifted toward the circular black hole at the center of the door. He shuddered.

Unable to sleep, he wandered to the water's edge, the guards eyeing him as he moved away from the camp. He slumped onto the sand and tossed pebbles into the lake just so they'd relax. He knew he could outrun them if he needed to but to where?

A heavy mist clung to the water. In the distance, beyond the nine pillars, the upper city rose to the height of the cavern, its benches of buildings stacked on top of one another, silently looking out over a black lake that was still as glass. How long had the city been abandoned? And why?

He wondered about his former companions—Terry, Wren, and Liv. And there was Rena, too, or should have been. He hadn't seen the child among them, but she had been with them when they had all set out together from town. She didn't always travel with them, mostly because Wren was incessantly worried about her. After all, she was only ten. But Liv had insisted on it—the danger lurking in Roan, she said, necessitated Rena's involvement. Sish hadn't traveled with them for several years, so he was unclear how a ten-year-old was going to shore up their defenses, but he'd learned not to second-guess Liv. He didn't like dragging a child into the valley, but it had been Liv's decision. And, anyway, Wincott had thrust Sish into plenty of dangerous situations at an even younger age, so Sish stuck to his plan.

He took the first chance he found to abandon them. His years traveling the rough terrain of the valley with his father gave him some optimism that he knew the land better than they did and that he'd have no trouble reaching the city before them. Both of which were true, but he hadn't accounted for a second entrance at Fang Mountain, the one Fulk and his goons had used.

It occurred to him then that his companions must have entered the city after Fulk, which suggested they knew what Sish planned and when he planned to do it, probably Fulk, too. Sish wasn't a big believer in coincidences. If that was the case, they'd done a superb job of keeping it from him. The only reason he'd even been part of the group was because they needed a guide who knew the nooks and crannies of the valley, and there weren't any reputable ones who didn't already work for the Company, which Liv had expressly said they wanted to avoid. No surprise there. No one liked run-ins with the Company these days. But it meant they must've had some idea what lay in Roan and that Fulk was after it, too. And they were worried enough about it to hire the young thief—a once-trusted companion—to get them there as soon as possible. Whatever they were after, they were trying to keep any information about it away from the Company. Given Fulk's breakup with the governor years prior, he suspected the outfit likely wasn't involved. But none of that explained Wincott's presence, a wild card that Sish hadn't anticipated and didn't like. He had to figure out what his father was up to.

Footsteps on the sand stirred him out of his reverie. Wincott stood behind him wiping his eyes, the black shirt he'd pulled from the knapsack at least three sizes too big for him. It looked like a dressing gown.

"Hard to tell what time it is in this place," he said.

"You've been asleep several hours, I'd guess," said Sish. "Gut tells me it's morning; at least it feels like morning."

"You know, you don't have to go. You're a bit big for that hole. It's more suited to me," Wincott said.

Sish got to his feet, dusting the sand from his trousers.

"Why?" he asked. "So Fulk can find out just how useless I am and introduce me to the business end of his bowie knife? I don't think so. I'd rather take my chances in the human keyhole, thank you."

Wincott rubbed his neck tiredly, "I'm just saying, it's ... I don't know, I guess I just—"

"Going soft on me, old man? Or is it just that you know something about that door that I don't?" Sish questioned. "You know, it's not lost on me that *if* I make it to the other side, I might be in a treasure room and have it all to myself. Why do I need to open the door at all?"

Wincott shook his head. "Then you'll die in there. There's no other way out."

Sish snorted. "Dwarfs built this city. They always put multiple ways in and out—we saw that on Fulk's map—and you seemed to find that ventilation shaft without issue, which I find convenient."

Wincott ignored the comment and said, "Dwarfs aren't real, kid, just stories old drunks like me talk about around the fire. Men built this city. And men sealed it. For a reason. If there's a treasure in here, I don't think it's anything either of us want. Old Fulk there thinks it's what'll get him back in the governor's good graces, a ticket back to his old life. But I'm with his goon on this one—not but dust and bones on the other side of that door, or something worse ... You've already seen some of what Roan had to cough up."

"And none of it seemed to surprise you," Sish shot back. "You just carry on as if it's all planned, like you know how it's going to go."

Wincott waved a hand, dismissing the comment. "Ah, that's just old thief bravado, boy. I'd be the same if we were having dinner with the queen or tucking tail from a band of marauders. I'm telling you, it ain't worth it."

"And *I'm* telling you I haven't got a choice, and I don't give a shit what you think anyway."

"Well, that much is clear. Has been for some time."

Sish puffed his chest and balled a fist. "You want to have this conversation now? Sure. Because I've been playing it over in my head for three years. Let's do it."

Wincott watched him with tired eyes and then dismissed the young thief's anger with another wave of his hand.

"I don't want another fight, Sish. I've had enough of those in my life. You want to crawl into that hole by yourself, fine. Go. I won't stop you. But if you want a hand, I'll be right there with you."

"Like you were 'right there with me' when I was a kid?" Sish sneered.

"I did my best," Wincott growled.

Sish laughed and turned away. "I know what this is. It's a con. You aren't happy with your 40 percent, and you're negotiating your way up."

"If I am, I'm doing a pretty terrible job of it, aren't I?"

It was Sish's turn to shake his head. He laughed and walked up the beach toward the camp. He wasn't quite ready to crawl into that hole in the stone door, but he certainly wasn't willing to let the old man weasel his way into Sish's affairs any more than he already had. Sish had learned that lesson once before. His father was great at playing the nice guy when he needed to, but he was always working an angle. Sish was almost certain that he was at the center of his old man's latest con—he just wasn't quite sure yet what it was.

Chapter Ten

INTO THE HOLE HE GOES

THE KEYHOLE WAS SMALLER THAN Sish remembered. He needed to cinch his shoulders to pass through the opening, and he wasn't immediately certain whether to go in feet first or headfirst. His gut told him headfirst, though he had no rational reason to trust it. But a thief often had to trust his gut. That's where he parted ways with his father's three tenets —finesses, focus, and luck—yes, those were all fine, but intuition played more than a minor role in whatever success Sish found in life to that point, and he wouldn't start second-guessing it now.

He stood at the keyhole, the parchment paper Fulk had created held loosely in his right hand. The trader stood behind him, leafing through a red leatherbound tome hoping it might contain information that would build on the barely described trials listed on the paper. He had found three words overnight that he scrawled on the parchment: allegiance, insight, and pressure. Each had a single question mark beside it, and they were in no order.

Even Fulk was forced to concede the words were rough translations from the language once used in Roan, a script long dead, just like the people who'd built the underground city.

The crewmen stood silently behind Sish, watching him. Wincott wasn't there; he'd returned to the beach under the auspices of keeping watch. The air was still, humid, and smelled like fungus after a heavy rain.

Kai cleared his throat, and Sish knew he couldn't procrastinate any longer.

He folded the paper and slipped it inside his shirt.

"I may need a hand; looks tight," he said.

Fulk gestured with his chin for the crewmen to help the young thief before he fixed his attention on the book again, giving Sish the distinct impression the old trader didn't have much faith the thief would prevail through the trials, whatever they might be. In other words, he was expendable and so was Wincott, probably each of the mercenaries, too, but did they know that?

He stepped forward and reached both hands into the keyhole and pulled his head and shoulders inside. He cinched his body inward, and a moment later, he felt rough hands grab his feet and shove him the rest of the way. He yelped as his shoulders scraped roughly against the sides, but the crewmen only laughed.

Panic tightened his chest when he got stuck and couldn't see anything but black ahead, but after a moment, he discovered wiggle room. His eyes adjusted, and he discovered the strange, luminescent blue light permeated the inside of the keyhole as well, casting a faint azure glow over everything.

His claustrophobia kicked in briefly (never a great characteristic for a thief to have), but he forced himself to close his eyes, breathe deeply for several seconds, and then push it out of his mind. It mostly worked. He opened his eyes and found the inside of the keyhole was half as wide again as the entrance, enough for him to shift sideways if he pulled his knees against his chest.

The keyhole stretched fifty yards or so ahead before it widened into another room lit in a pale-yellow glow. Metal rings lined the cylindrical shaft at regular intervals. They were a yard or so wide with gaps between each and caked in rock dust that blackened his hands. The musky cave smell had been replaced with a sterile metallic scent that made Sish think of a factory. He tried not to think too hard about what he'd just crawled inside until his heart settled.

Allegiance. Insight. Pressure. Sish had no idea which trial this was or even if it was one. Yet the three words cycled through his mind until he thought it might drive him nuts. He closed his eyes again, breathed deeply, and pushed his anxieties away.

"You see anything in there?" Fulk called to him, standing at the entrance.

"Just getting my bearings," Sish said.

"Well, get them fast."

Sish shook his head. He'd take all the time he wanted, and there wasn't a damn thing the trader could do about it. In fact, he had half a mind to curl up in this shaft and catch up on some sleep—fat chance any of them would have the guts to crawl into the keyhole or even could. He snorted, thinking Wincott and Fulk were likely the only ones small enough to fit, and he doubted Fulk would volunteer.

On his hands and knees, he crawled forward, crossing the first gap onto a metal ring and the rectangular plate that rested at its bottom. The plate was smooth and polished, almost like pewter. Nothing happened, so he carefully crossed the gap to the second ring, setting his right knee on the next plate. Nothing happened.

Then his second knee landed, and he felt the plate depress, the sound of air releasing beneath him as if it were pressurized somehow. A grinding noise like old gears being set into motion filled his eyes, and the ring began to rotate. And then a second and a third until all of them were turning, though in opposite directions. If this was the trial, it was a cinch, he thought. He moved to the next ring, depressing its plate, too, though it was a little more difficult as it was now moving. Then the fourth, fifth, and sixth. He noticed as he moved forward that some seemed to move faster than others.

He paused and caught his breath, checking to see if he was any closer to the yellow light at the end of the shaft. It was still a long way off, but there was something new there now—every few seconds, the light was blotted out. Again and again. And the darkness seemed to be moving toward him.

He watched as the rolling darkness moved down the shaft toward him, trying to decide what it was. An illusion? A sudden gust of warm air hit him in the face, and he heard something moving as the dark blot neared him. He realized at the last moment it wasn't moving toward him; it was a series of things rotating in the gaps between each ring, one after another, in a long sequence. He caught sight of it just in time: a razor-sharp blade rotating between the rings, cleaving anything caught between them.

He shifted sideways and tucked his legs in to avoid being sawn in half between the seventh and eighth rings. Now lying on his back on the eighth ring, which rotated against him, causing him to have to shift down every few seconds, he learned a new feeling: pressure.

Chapter Eleven

THE OLD BOYS CLUB

THE BREAKFAST CLUB MET EVERY second weekend in the billiard room at the Wandering Camel. The tavern master, Bart Rigby, used to let the entire restaurant to the group, but that had been when Mik Markle was its lead wizard. Mik was an E&E man, and so, by association, was most everyone else in town. Then Mik died on the job, and the club's second-in-command, Dooti Gottfried, took over. Everyone liked Dooti, that is, they liked him until he embezzled half the club's money and skipped town with Markle's widow, Francine.

That event split the group in two. The old boys (and there were mostly only boys in the club, preferably those of the white-haired type) thought Dooti's behavior atrocious and stripped him of the club presidency. The younger wizards, most of whom had been recruited by Dooti, claimed there was a lack of sufficient evidence that Dooti had stolen anything at all, and, where it concerned Francine, well, who could blame him? She was single and rather fetching. So, the young boys split from the old boys and formed a new club at a tavern across town (generally speaking, a trendier joint) and renamed their group the Conclave of Esteemed Sorcerers. Apparently, for reasons not fully understood by the older members, the younger men liked to be referred to as sorcerers instead of wizards.

Sish wasn't sure who among the Conclave was esteemed or even known to be considered esteemed in the estimation of other wizards, but he had to hand it to the young men—the name had a nice ring to it. Certainly nicer than the Breakfast Club, a name, which, according to legend, owed its origins to the practice of two very famous wizards who met each week over eggs and sausages to discuss the nature and practical application of magic.

The unfortunate thing about the split, or the Schism as it was now called, was that two-thirds of the members had joined the Conclave, leaving only the old guys to populate the Wandering Camel every second weekend for a discussion about magic. That being the case, Bart couldn't afford to give up a weekend morning breakfast service, so he moved the club somewhat hastily into the billiard room. It should also be noted that he quietly took down the once-proud sign that hung outdoors that said "Home of the Breakfast Club Wizards." Apparently, the old guys weren't in vogue anymore. Still, Bart was nice enough to provide them with a space large enough for their group and a platter of meat and cheese.

Sish hid in the rafters above the billiard room for several hours before the first of them showed up for their biweekly meeting. The doddering old fools shuffled into the walnut-lined room at half-past seven in the morning, most of them still wearing what looked like nightgowns.

The thief had it on good authority that Dooti hadn't absconded with all the club's wealth, and several artifacts of significant value remained in the club's possession, one of them a monkey carved from jade that could grant minor wishes. He had a fence in town who was willing to offer a tidy sum for it if Sish purloined it for him. The trouble was, he had to figure out how to get it. The Breakfast Club hid it using an illusion spell, which meant that between meetings, it was impossible to locate the item without holding hostage one of the wizards and forcing him to release the cantrip, which, admittedly, was Sish's style. They did, however, release the spell every two weeks at their meetings and showcase their most prized possessions, or so he'd been told.

So, partway through the night, he vanished from the squalid apartment he shared with his father to break into the Wandering Camel after it closed, climbed into the sturdy spruce rafters above the billiard room, and waited for morning when he hoped he could spot an opportunity to lift the monkey without anyone being the wiser.

Despite the actual deed of theft having not yet been completed, Sish was quite proud of himself. First, he'd managed to lift a set of picks from Wincott and departed the apartment without the old man being the wiser. Second, he'd picked the lock on the backdoor of the Camel without much issue—he was not a gifted lockpick—and managed to enter the building and reset the lock with hardly a sound.

But now, after several hours of crouching in the rafters, his legs were asleep and hamstrings as tight as a banker's sphincter. He hoped the old fools got on with it soon so he could be done. Wincott tended to sleep in on the weekends, especially if he'd been out late at the pub the night before, which he had. That gave Sish a bit of extra time to work with, but he needed the Breakfast Club to get their assess in gear, or he ran the risk of his father finding out he'd taken a job without consulting him first, and that would likely mean no cut of the profits for him.

As the wizards filtered into the room and filled their plates with meat and cheese, Bart circled the room with a pot of freshly made rosehip tea with honey and filled each man's cup, chatting with them about an issue he was having with the growth rate of the potato plants in his garden, hoping one of the wizards might volunteer to help. None did.

After everyone was settled—all eight of them—the club's latest lead wizard, Hamish Finklefunk, rose and welcomed everyone with sweeping gestures of his thin, robed arms and went through the agenda for the morning in slow, laborious tones.

"First, we shall call the meeting to order and then stand to sing the Queen's song," he intoned. "This shall be followed with the customary Tithing of Good Graces, where we each shall deposit a coin in the basket and share welcome news from our lives. Once done, we shall approve the minutes of our last meeting and move into a stimulating lecture about the transferability of earthen spellcasting to improve pasturelands for grazing cattle."

A stocky wizard in a blue robe speckled with gold stars leaned forward and said, "And who, Wizard Finklefunk, would presume to lecture *me* about earthen magic?"

Finklefunk's face was impassive, as if he was either stoned or expected such outbursts from this group. He very slowly consulted the sheaf of paper on the billiard table next to him, scanned it with a spectacle set to his eyes, and said, "Ahh, yes, there it is. The lecture will be led by Ms. Decker, a junior hedge mage employed at the E&E, Wizard Barlow."

Wizard Barlow let out a cranky breath, his bushy white eyebrows knitting together disapprovingly. "A woman? To lecture us? About *magic*?"

A fat wizard, whose round head looked like a slightly baked snowball stacked on top of another much larger and slightly baked snowball, said, "And a garden mage at that!"

There was a raucous series of comments from the eight assembled wizards. Finklefunk ignored them and took a sip of tea from the cup and saucer on the green felt billiard table next to him.

Sish was beginning to understand why the Conclave of Esteemed Sorcerers had decided to form their own club. The tone of the Breakfast Club reminded him of the litany of lessons, lectures, and tongue-lashings Wincott gave him about the most critical and important aspects of thieving. Sish had half a mind to strike out on his own just like the Conclave had. But first, he needed the means to do so, and that required the jade monkey.

The Breakfast Club meeting was soon underway, with the agenda being moved and seconded and unanimously adopted (though there was one more muttering of disapproval from Wizard Barlow about the guest speaker). Following the Tithing of Good Graces, Finklefunk invited Wizard Robillard to stand next to him to conduct the Unveiling of the Sacred Keepings.

Robillard, a stringy man of similar age to Finklefunk, got to his feet, his aged knees audibly popping, and shuffled to the billiard table. He extended his hands from his long red robe. His slender fingers danced wildly, as if he were playing a raucous tune on the piano, his eyes closed, and he said something inaudible. A green mist erupted in the air next to him. The mist quickly formed a circle that opened to reveal a hole.

From Sish's vantage point, he could see through the hole, which was only a handspan or two wide, and what lay on the other side. There was a simple wooden table there with three items on it: a giant white feather, a thimble cut from a ruby, and a jade monkey.

Robillard reached through the portal and pulled each item and set them on white doilies spread on the billiard table. Then he closed his eyes, flicked his fingers, and the portal closed. Murmurings of approval and nods of appreciation from the other assembled spellcasters filled the room while Robillard shuffled sleepily back to his chair and took a seat.

"Well done, Wizard Robillard," Finklefunk said. "Now, our guest speaker has yet to arrive, so I'd like to open the floor to a discussion regarding our former compatriots, who are now operating under a different banner."

Discussion ensued. After several hours of squatting in the rafters, Sish couldn't feel his legs. He needed to change positions and get the blood flowing, or he risked not being able to move when he needed to.

He delicately shifted his weight off one leg so he could move to the other. It was at times like these that he envied his father's short stature and guessed that he must've inherited his height from his mother's side.

The spruce beam groaned as he shifted, loud enough that the wizards below should've heard it. The thief froze, waiting for one of them to look up. But they were in a loud debate about whether they should take action against the Conclave, up to and including writing a tersely worded letter that articulated the alleged treachery.

Barlow already had pen and parchment in hand, and the fat wizard was supplying several verbal contributions to form the body of the letter. Finklefunk seemed to ignore all this, and instead, drank his tea.

Sish wiped his brow and exhaled liberally. He stretched his right leg and then did the same with the left. He moved back to a squatting position when the spruce beam groaned and then splintered with a loud crack.

The wizards heard that one.

Barlow and his fat colleague stopped their writing and looked up.

"What the devil?" the fat one barked.

Finklefunk didn't seem to notice, his rheumy eyes staring off into space as he held his steaming teacup. Sish broke into a sweat. The billiard table was directly below him.

Shit. Here goes.

Sish leaped onto the table. In truth, it was a half-fall as his left leg, it turned out, was still asleep. He hit the table like a sack of dirt, his shoulder taking most of the impact while his left leg rattled with pins and needles. He grabbed the monkey, slid it into his jacket, and took the ruby thimble for good measure, too.

As the assembled wizards climbed to their feet, Finklefunk managed to get out a word of surprise as Sish rolled off the table and hit the billiard room floor with another thud. He was up and sprinting through the Breakfast Club's ranks before any of them had a chance to get a spell off, giving him yet another inkling as to why the younger sorcerers had split and formed their own group. He guessed they wouldn't be as easy to steal from.

He was through the main room and out the front door before Bart Rigby caught sight of him. Fortunately, the young thief was wearing a black cloak and mask, so he hoped he wouldn't be easy to identify.

"Stop him!" Barlow yelled after him as he sprung out the door onto Cobble Lane.

The street was empty, save a pair of E&E guards loitering at a coffee nook nearby. Sish sprinted in the opposite direction as Barlow came out the front door, Rigby and Finklefunk behind him.

"Guards!" the fat wizard bellowed, pointing in Sish's direction. "Thief!"

The chase was on.

Sish ducked around a bend in the alley onto a narrower stone path. He heard the heavy clap of E&E guard boots not far behind him. He cursed himself. His father's never-ending lecture about finesse, focus, and luck ran through his mind. He certainly didn't have the first one, the second was questionable, and what happened in the next few moments would indicate whether he had any of the third.

He weaved past several early risers and tradesmen at work in the alley, leaping over crates and slipping around textile stalls. But he knew he wouldn't outrun the guardsmen; his left leg still wasn't fully awake, and he'd never been a particularly fast sprinter. He needed a decoy.

As he turned onto the next roadway, he spotted a figure walking toward him in an identical cloak, wearing a face wrapping against the brisk winter cold. As the figure crossed another alley skirting off to the left, Sish purposefully ran into him, sending both tumbling to the ground in a heap of clothing. He deftly slipped the statue and thimble into the stranger's inside coat pocket, rolled over, and got back to his feet.

"Sorry, sorry," he protested, pulling the figure up.

He could hear the guardsmen crashing through the stalls not far behind. As he pulled the stranger up, he realized he was a she, a young and beautiful one at that, with curly auburn hair and startling green eyes.

"Sorry ..." he trailed off, momentarily transfixed.

Surprised by the masked thief, she said nothing. The guardsmen came around the bend. He ducked into the alley. The decoy didn't work, though. The guards pushed past the girl and rounded the bend into the alley a moment later.

Sish's escape route ended at a brick wall that wasn't scalable, at least not for him. He stopped and turned. The guards slowed, smiled balefully, and cracked their knuckles. No, luck was certainly not on his side.

Chapter Twelve

BOW BEFORE YOUR GOBLIN OVERLORD

Hot wind lashed Sish's cheeks as the blades in the Keyhole whirled on either side of him. The device's high-pitched metallic scream drowned out the voices of Fulk and the others who called to him from the narrow entrance he'd squeezed through minutes before. He ignored them. They could wait. He had bigger problems on his hands thanks to some long-dead engineer who thought it a clever idea to booby-trap a tunnel instead of leaving a key behind.

He breathed, coughing as the blades kicked up little clouds of centuries-old dust that tasted like rust and smelled like metal shavings. He was stuck, at risk of being decapitated if he moved left or right, so he figured the only way forward was to sit and think.

The mechanism was a giant series of tumblers, he realized, recalling the few lockpicking lessons Wincott had bothered to give him. He spotted two embossed plates on the platform next to him. A blade spun on a steady rotation between him and the plates. There was just enough time between each revolution to get his hand in and out. Maybe.

Two more plates rested at his feet, both bare of any markings that might indicate their function. He knew better than to press random buttons, but there weren't many options, so he picked one.

Fifty-fifty odds, right?

The blade to his left—the direction from which he'd crawled into the Keyhole—stopped mid-spiral. He leaned on the second plate, and the blade started up again, this time moving so fast there wasn't enough time between revolutions to reach through and press the first plate to stop it. He eyed the next ring over and guessed it was the same—each tumbler required him to press a plate. And each time, he had even odds of getting it right.

What the hell, right?

He studied the blade as it whirred around several times more to get the timing right. A bead of nervous sweat trailing down his temple, his hand shot out to press one of the two plates in the next ring. It didn't move. He waited for his next opportunity, reached out, and tried the second plate. It slid down like a stone tumbler, but the blade only spun around faster.

"Shit."

He was either missing something or time had finally taken its toll on the ancient mechanism, and it was bungled. Now he needed something heavy to toss onto the plate next to him to see if that might work. And he only had one shot at it. He chose his boot, the only one he had left after losing the other one when the rowboat had sunk. He gingerly slid it off, aware of how close his naked toes were to the rapid incisor spinning to his right.

He watched it rotate, closing his eyes and listening to the steady whir so he better understood the timing—or hoped he might anyway.

He tossed the boot without opening his eyes.

Thunk.

The blade shimmied to a halt, and he let out a breath. A small, grim smile parted his lips as he shifted to the next ring, where his boot lay. He lifted it and noticed one of the laces had been sliced off. To his right, another tumbler spun, though not as fast. He tossed the boot again and managed to hit the correct plate this time. The blade stopped. He shifted again and picked up the boot.

Sish continued the laborious process all the way down the shaft. By the time he reached the end of it, he had counted more than fifty rings, and his guesses had been better than fifty-fifty, though wrong guesses meant the lone boot had enough chunks missing from it now that it was unwearable.

Despite his nervous sweat, his feet had grown cold. He hated cold feet and muttered the same as he reached the end of the Keyhole, where a warm, yellow light poured into the shaft ahead of him.

The young thief tossed the boot out of the shaft into the next room and climbed out behind it, landing on a smooth but ice-cold marble floor. It was so cold it burned the soles of his feet, forcing him to tiptoe awkwardly around the room, cursing every fifth step.

A series of glass lanterns lined the walls around him, their thin, yellow flames illuminating the boxy room in a chill light. Sish wasn't sure how it was the lanterns were lit, but the hair on the back of his neck stood on end thinking someone or some*thing* was waiting for him deeper into the cavern.

At the other side of the room, opposite the Keyhole, there was a series of stone figures, each kneeling away from him to face a stone dais. Atop the platform was a statue of a goblin that resembled the carved pillar they'd seen on the lake. Yet where that one had stood proud and peaceful, this one held a battle stance with weapons drawn. The statue was also quite a bit larger than the average goblin. Towering above Sish, it carried a short, curved scimitar in one hand, the length of the thief's left leg, and a dagger in the other, nearly as long as his arm. Behind the statue was a large set of wooden doors banded in iron. A series of deadbolts held the doors shut. What he couldn't see was a way to open them.

He approached the statues with a skeptical eye. There were eight in all. His eyes fell on their weapons and armor, all so carefully carved they looked real. The door behind the goblin was solid and heavy, unmoving, with no obvious way to open it. He reached out to touch the goblin's sword when a voice erupted from the Keyhole behind him, causing him to jump.

"Are you through?" the voice called.

It sounded like Fulk, but the reverberation of the steel rings made it difficult to determine. He danced back to the Keyhole and leaned his head in.

"I'm through, but don't come after me yet. I'm not su—"

He wasn't able to finish his sentence before a body slid into the shaft and started crawling toward him.

"No! Go back!" he yelled.

"Nice try, we're not letting you get too fa—"

The voice, emanating from one of Fulk's goons, was cut off as the gear system in the Keyhole coughed to life. The man must've depressed one of the plates. The wrong one. The blades started swinging at Sish's end, the rusty wind pushing him back into the statue room.

"Go back! Go back now!" he yelled over the mechanical clamor.

Between the shadows of the swinging blades, the man was still moving toward him.

Schlunk.

Sish winced, his toes freezing as sweat poured down his brow at what had just happened. He swallowed hard and peered into the Keyhole. One of the blades had severed the goon's head from his torso, leaving it spinning like a handball on the cool metal ring. *Well,* he thought, *that's one less to deal with later.* He shrugged.

With only one-way forward, he turned his attention to the room at hand, the remaining two words from Fulk's notes, *allegiance* and *insight,* running through his mind.

He tiptoed across the room, cursing the winter-like cold, and stopped behind the statues. He was about to step on the dais, where the floor wasn't so cold, when his stomach gurgled. He stopped and stepped back.

Intuition, he thought.

He surveyed the statues. Something wasn't right.

He stepped behind each of them. Moving left to right, he counted seven—a sorcerer in robes carved of stone, an elf in leathers, two archers, and three warriors. Of the warriors, two were women and one was a man clad in a cape and chainmail coif with a war hammer slung at his waist. The statues were evenly spaced with marble tiles between each, and all knelt on the frozen floor. The goblin stood on a white marble tile atop the dais in front of them.

He stopped, surveyed again, and thought back to the pillars on Lake Roan. Perhaps if he'd had more sleep, it would've dawned on him earlier—*nine!* There should've been nine. Sure enough, as he moved to the far right, there was an empty tile that looked different than the others, one where a statue should have been placed or had been and was missing.

He grinned.

"Intuition," he said triumphantly. "It's all in the gut. Fuck finesse."

He knelt on the marble tile and waited. Nothing happened at first, but after a moment, each of the seven statues to his left slowly turned their stone heads toward him, their stone eyelids peeling back to reveal blue sapphire eyes that flashed at him. The wall sconces snuffed out, plunging the room into darkness. The only light was a strange, iridescent glow that emanated from each of the seven warriors' eyes. He froze, his stomach twisting, expecting the worst. In one fluid motion, the stone warriors came alive and drew their weapons as smoothly as if they were carved of flesh, eyes still fixed on him.

He held his breath and stifled a cough. His feet were numb, the sweat on his brow pooling in his eyebrows.

In one synchronous movement, the statues lowered their weapons to rest on the dais at the goblin's feet and turned their heads toward him. In the darkness, Sish heard the groan of heavy stone. The goblin came to life, turning on its tile to step down from the dais toward him.

Its eyes flared to reveal a menacing ruby stare. It drew its weapons back. Without thought, trusting his gut only, Sish mimicked the other statues and bowed his head. A moment later, he felt a stone sword touch one shoulder and then the other. The goblin marched back to his dais. The tile beneath Sish sunk into the floor, and the deadbolts on the heavy doors snapped back with a thunderous, metallic chorus.

The seven warriors sheathed their weapons and resumed their petrified watch. The thief's heart thundered in his chest. He stood and wiped his brow, forgetting for a moment that he could barely feel his feet. He didn't move. The wall sconces erupted with yellow light once again, and one of the banded doors wedged open with a creak.

"Allegiance," he muttered to himself. "Definitely allegiance."

He tiptoed past the goblin and shimmied through the doorway.

Chapter Thirteen

SHE'S GUILD ROYALTY. HE MIGHT BE, TOO

THEY REACHED THE MEADOWLANDS AFTER nightfall. It was difficult for Wincott to see through the dark. Heavy clouds blotted out the moon, and a mixture of storm front and rancid smoke from the burning village behind them had coalesced into a pitch-black fog that forced him to feel his way forward. He stumbled in the tall grass and nearly dropped the boy named Sish. A delicate hand on his arm steadied him. The mother, Meridan. Her fingers were ice cold.

"We need to rest," she urged.

He could hear the desperation in her voice. The image of her bleeding leg ran through his mind. He guessed it wasn't any better than it had been when they'd set out from the burning village. Even when they reached shelter, he had no doubt he would be up a while longer tending to her and the boy. He groaned and shifted his arms, careful not to drop the child. He was either asleep or passed out, Wincott wasn't sure which. He rested an ear near Sish's mouth and heard faint but steady breath.

"I think I know where we are," he tried to reassure her. "There's an old trapper's hut up ahead I use as a cache sometimes."

The air cooled considerably. Wincott guessed the temperature would dip to around freezing overnight, not the type of conditions you wanted to find yourself outside in exhausted and wounded—especially with Guildsmen still in the area.

He was confident they left the soldiers behind some time ago, but he was always fearful of stumbling across the unexpected on the trail.

The meadow of tall grass gave way to a wall of thick spruce and pine that blotted out what little light there was. Meridan gripped Wincott's shirttail as they moved into the brush, no doubt afraid she'd get lost or left behind or both. Wincott was okay with it. If anything, her weight behind him steadied his own footsteps as he pushed through the needly branches.

The heavily needled spruce boughs scratched his face and arms as they stumbled precariously forward. He was forced to go slow, moving almost entirely on memory toward the small hut he hoped remained empty and untouched. A twisted or broken ankle at this point might spell doom for all three of them, so he was extra careful, even as the chill air nipped at his neck and ears and his arms burned from the weight of the boy.

After another half hour or so of careful steps, he spotted the small A-frame cabin hidden beneath a large pine. It appeared as little more than a darker shape against an already near-black forest. It was old, but the roof was intact, and he was pretty sure no one else knew about it—the trapper who'd built it was either long gone or dead, and any memory of his trapline gone with him. Or so Wincott hoped.

He pushed against the door and found it locked. It took him a moment to remember this cache possessed a lock he'd rigged up that only he knew how to properly unlatch. The fact that it was still shut was good news, indicating no one had come this way in a long time, nor had any bear taken residence up inside. The truth was, the lock wouldn't stop anyone from gaining entry, but it was enough to let him know whether anyone had found the cabin since his last visit.

He handed the boy to Meridan, who staggered beneath his weight before finding her footing. She gave him a shaky but curt nod. He would have to move fast. Wincott knelt and reached his left hand through a small, hidden hole just to the left of the door and fiddled with the mechanism on the other side. The latch clicked, and the door swung open.

An hour later, a small fire crackled in the stone hearth at the back of the cabin, the boy was fast asleep on one of the two bunks, and Meridan had washed and bandaged her thigh with cool water Wincott had recovered from a small creek nearby.

He filled an old iron cookpot with the rest of the water and found a couple of near-frozen onions and potatoes in the small root cellar near the door. Only when the light soup was ready did he notice there weren't any bowls, so they would have to share the ladle.

Still paranoid, Wincott stepped outside every few minutes to listen to the forest, cocking his head left and right to discern any unwelcome sounds. But it was silent every time. He wondered whether part of his intermittent escapes was just to give him the headspace to consider how he was going to manage a wounded woman and her son. He didn't relish being linked to anyone, much less have anyone dependent upon him for survival.

Meridan lay on one of the bunks, an arm across her eyes, her legs stretched out. Wincott stirred the soup and then took a seat on a rickety stool that required careful balance on his part to keep it from toppling over. His clothes were still damp from his swim to recover the boy, not to mention the exertion of carrying him this far. He suspected Sish and Meridan's were as well and would need to be dried, though he wasn't certain how to broach the subject, so he left it alone.

He was drifting off to sleep in the chair when Meridan sat up.

"What were you doing in Fort Wick?" she said.

"Just a little business," he said, catching her gaze.

She nodded acceptingly, but her eyes suggested she didn't believe him.

"Funny, since all the Company men left yesterday on their hunt. Not much business to be had, except thieving. In fact, it's an ideal time for that."

He shrugged and closed his eyes, leaning his head back against the chair.

He felt the cold edge of steel kiss his throat a moment later. He carefully opened his eyes. Meridan stood over him, a knife in her hand, one he hadn't known she carried.

"Girl's got to have a few surprises," she said. "Now, you're going to tell me what you were *really* doing in Fort Wick, or I'm going to shorten you by a head."

Her hardened glare told him she wasn't lying, but there was something different about her voice. Gone was the folksy rhythm of her speech, and instead, she sounded more like someone from away—a woman of higher birth and education rather than a simple whore who called a fur trading outpost home.

He considered her for a moment before answering. He wasn't a fan of answering questions at knifepoint, but it wasn't his first time either. He guessed there was little she could do with the truth at this point—they were a long way from anywhere, and her leg would hamper any getaway, and she knew it. And she'd already guessed he was a thief.

Without moving his head, he let his eyes fall over the boy asleep in the bunk next to him, then looked back at her. The message was a simple one: *Put down the knife, or this goes bad for both of you.*

She took a step back and sat on the bed opposite him, the knife in her hand still directed toward him, her jaw set.

He leaned forward, elbows on his knees, hands knitted together.

"I told you I was a thief," he said. "Fort Wick's treasury was my target. I knew most of the E&E men would be away."

It wasn't the entire truth, he admitted to himself, but enough that she likely wouldn't press any further.

Her eyes flashed wearily, but after a moment, she put the knife down and sat back, nodding.

"You're not who you claim to be either," he said. "So out with it."

"It's none of your business," she told him.

"Fine," he said. "But then, I want you and the boy gone in the morning. I've given you enough of my hospitality."

"We have nowhere to go; we wouldn't …" she trailed off, her gaze falling over the boy.

"Out with it then. I was honest with you," he lied.

"Bracewell. My name is Bracewell."

She let the surname hang in the air between him. He knew it sounded familiar, but he couldn't quite … *Lord Elgin Bracewell*, the Guild's patron and benefactor. She was nobility then.

"Meridan T. Bracewell," he said, as he came to understand who he'd brought to his cabin. "I never knew it stood for Torren."

"My mother's name."

"Elgin is your husband?"

"Yes, and not a very likable one at that," she added, shaking her head.

"And the boy?"

"Mine," she said matter-of-factly. "But his father is … well, his father is an E&E man. When Elgin found out … well, needless to say, the patron of one of the largest trading companies in Erdor wasn't about to have a son and heir who's the spawn of a Company man. It's *bad for the brand*, he'd say."

Disparate pieces came together in Wincott's mind. How could he have been so blind? It never made sense to him why the Guild wanted to raid Fort Wick this time of year. He knew relations between the Company and the Guild weren't great at the best of times, but Fort Wick was far enough out, and further north, than other, wealthier E&E trade posts. In fact, that's why Wincott had targeted it. It was an easier mark than some of the more southern forts where Guild raids were within the realm of possibility. The Guild was after its royal wife.

No, that wasn't right. It was the boy.

His gaze drifted to Sish again. The toddler was hardly old enough to walk on his own, much less make sense of any of the chaos around him. Wincott felt for him. The thief wasn't much for children or soft feelings, that had all been beaten out of him in the boarding house. But he wasn't about to abide by the murder of a boy either.

Suddenly, he was sick with guilt. He wasn't the right man to look after these two, not by any stretch. In fact, they were more likely to die being associated with the thief than were they on their own.

"They want him," Wincott said, gesturing with his chin to the boy.

She nodded silently.

"Where were you headed?" he asked.

"Fort Rivers."

"That's two, maybe three days by canoe down the Moon from here. Guildsmen will be about," he told her, quietly. "Normally, I'd suggest the overland route, but your leg …"

Sish stirred beneath the heavy wool blankets. Meridan limped over to him, running her hand across his forehead and whispering quietly until he fell back asleep.

"Best eat something, then get some shut-eye," Wincott suggested. "We'll talk more in the morning."

She nodded. He stood and went outside, careful to shut the door behind him. The cabin must've been smoking hot because the freezing air was refreshing. Steady snow fell, threading through the conifers to dust the darkened forest floor in strips of white. It was light and dry, suggesting the temperature would likely dip even further. It was unlikely anyone would be fool enough to be out searching in this weather this far from the fort, but Lord Elgin ... he had a reputation.

Wincott was glad he had chosen not to tell her the whole truth. Lying wasn't his strong suit, but a lie surrounded by the truth could often get him through a tough situation. And for now, this one had. It was true that he had been thieving in Fort Wick. In fact, he was in the midst of packing up a sack of goods when he heard Meridan's scream when Sish tumbled into the river. But that wasn't why he'd been in Fort Wick. He'd been there on the payroll of the Guild, a well-paying one at that. His job was a simple one—open the gates. And he had. He turned toward the cabin and watched it quietly, wondering what other trouble he'd welcomed to the north.

Chapter Fourteen

JUST GIVE ME THE GOLD, AND I'LL BE ON MY WAY

"**Y**OUR BOY MADE IT THROUGH," said Fulk, striding down the beach toward Wincott.

The black water lapped at the old thief's boots as he stared through a thin mist that hovered above Lake Roan to the backs of the Nine. The stone pillars cut horizontally across the flat water, forming a natural grille, a barrier to the tentacled sentinel that lurked on the far side. The mist there was heavier, concealing the far end of the lake in a soupy gray fog. Wincott shuddered, remembering the struggle on the water with the goblins and Sish's sunken boat. His mind flashed with a distant memory. He saw the boy again, this time disappearing below the gentle flow of the Moon River, the air thick with the greasy stench of fire and blood.

"You hear me, old man?" Fulk said, coming up behind him. "Your boy survived; he got through."

Wincott ran a hand through his wiry gray beard, tugged it, and snorted, shaking his head. That was the least surprising thing of all time. What the kid lacked in finesse, he more than made up for in blind luck. He may have been born to noble blood, but he had the talents of a world-class stealer-of-things if he would just put the time and effort into it.

Wincott turned toward the trader and eyed him carefully. "And?"

Fulk stopped, his shoulders squared to the lake in front of him, hands at his side, beady eyes staring into the distance.

"Thought you'd want to know," Fulk said, not bothering to look at him.

Power play. I can't believe he's still such a dickhead.

"Saves *me* from having to climb in there," Wincott said dryly. "I hear one of your goons wasn't so lucky."

"Nik, yes, hell of a fighter but not much for thinking things through. Caught up to him."

"A rather cold assessment, wouldn't you say?"

It was Fulk's turn to snort, a rare flash of emotion from the stoic former E&E man. Wincott never really had time for men like Fulk. Sure, they commanded respect among trappers and soldiers alike, but men like Fulk had a rigid view of the world that led to a monochrome view of things, a this-or-that approach to almost every situation that was often more harsh or dogmatic than it needed to be.

Life was far more fluid than men like Fulk liked to admit, Wincott thought. Yes, at times, a hard decision needs to be made, but often dogma, rules, and codes of conduct lead to zero-sum results that are as bureaucratic as they are confounding. The world wasn't a rigid place—it was organic, ever-changing, and complex and required different solutions at different times. It was true that the old thief chafed at rules and regulations (obviously), but sometimes, bending them was the only way you could resolve something without coming to bloodshed. Men like Fulk wouldn't bend. They broke. And when that happened, a man was wise to get out of the way.

"What now?" Wincott pressed.

Fulk strolled to the water's edge. The mist was thickening, and in the distance, slight ripples on the water suggested not all was quiet beneath the surface.

"You know, I figured out why your son is here," he said, eyeing the thief. "I know why I'm here. Hell, I've even got a pretty good idea how those goblins got here. But you—you I don't know about."

The thief didn't say anything. He figured the trader wasn't looking for an answer so much as he wanted to hear himself talk. Fine. Let him.

"Seems passing odd that you just happened to be at Shatterstill when your son was across the valley. How long's it been since you two fell out?"

"Not as long since you fell out of favor with your old pal the Governor," Wincott quipped. "Care to enlighten me as to why *you're* here?"

Fulk chuckled softly.

"I'm here to put an end to the reason you're thieving in this godforsaken frozen valley. I was summarily exiled from the Company. All of it. And I'm no longer sad about it. The Company. The Guild. They can't go on much longer. Forces are mounting on all sides of Northern Erdor, and they see weakness—*our* weakness."

"And you're going to what? Broker a peace deal? Excuse me while I laugh. I'm not sure that's in your skillset," Wincott said.

"Peace? Of a kind, I suppose. But I'd wager your idea of peace and my own are quite different," Fuk said. "You think the Treasure of Roan is gold and jewels? It isn't. It's something that can bring peace. Something that can make us strong again, stronger even than the great engineers who built this wonder."

"The same engineers who sealed up your treasure and abandoned the place? My guess is they had good reason," said Wincott.

"So, what are you here for then, Wincott? Last I saw you was on the shores of Cold Fish Lake. You helped me then; that's why I didn't gut your thieving belly the first chance I had yesterday. But a man needs to stand for something—what do you stand for aside from larceny?"

Wincott shrugged, allowing his lips to curl up in a slight smile.

"I'm here for the gold," said the thief. "You think there's some kind of weapon down there that'll allow you to exact revenge on the Governor and everyone who ever done you dirty? Fine. Go ahead. When we get to the basement of this place, I'll take my bag of gold and be on my way."

"And your son?"

Wincott hesitated. The look in Fulk's eyes was more inquisitive than commanding. There was something there, something he was holding back. Wincott had a feeling he knew what it was, but it wasn't the right time to press that button.

"He has a remarkable talent for getting himself out of a hot mess. I don't expect it'll let him down in here," Wincott said.

"And his friends?"

"The Dungeoneers? What of them? Bunch of high-minded idcalists with their notions of courage, bravery, and teamwork,"

Wincott said and made a farting noise. "Not for me, or my boy, for that matter. Figure he used them to get this far, and he's in it for the gold, too. You know, come to think of it, they remind me a bit of you: opinionated and intense, except without all the bloodthirsty vengeance stuff."

Fulk turned away and stomped up the beach toward his crew, who were gathered quietly around the campfire. The luminescent crack in the cavern roof cast a pale blue over them that was sad somehow, lonely. Halfway toward them, Fulk stopped and turned toward Wincott.

"Remember: the girl was with them when they set out from Fort Rivers. I didn't see her on the dock with the others, but she's here somewhere," Fulk said, his eyes scanning the misty lake. "And if *she's* here, it means they're afraid of what's in Roan, too. Very afraid. Sish is walking alone into the Old City as we speak, and you want me to believe you're here for a bag of gold?"

Chapter Fifteen

THE GRAND VALLEY OF THE LORDS OF ROAN OR SOME SUCH PLACE

THE THIRD ROOM—WHAT SISH GUESSED was the insight trial—was not what he expected. In fact, it wasn't a room at all. He found himself on a platform the shape of a semicircle with an ornately carved balustrade that provided a view of a gargantuan underground valley below, far larger than the cavern where the Upper City and lake were. He felt like he'd stumbled into a subterranean world.

Although the valley was clearly underground with a bedrock ceiling that stretched for miles ahead and to the sides, there seemed to be beams of bright light that shone through the rock and bathed the fertile valley below, allowing for vast amounts of natural sunlight that nurtured a verdant coniferous forest, meadows, and hillsides abundant with soaring cedar, Sitka spruce, and hemlock trees.

Great orange and red stalactites hung from the cavern ceiling, where swarms of bats fluttered and dangled from rock. To his left, there was a waterfall that thundered into the valley below, its white mist dampening one side of the platform. To his right was an opening in the balustrade that led to a brown tongue of cobblestones that twisted downward into the valley. The path was marked with stunted blue lamps that shone with the same strange azure mineralization that lit up Fulk's camp on the far side of the Keyhole.

Yet the strangest thing was the small man who sat atop a lone three-legged stool a few feet ahead of Sish. He wore a canonical floppy hat, moth-eaten red robes that were much too large for him, and blue felt slippers. His face was partially hidden beneath the brim of his hat, but the part that was exposed was carved with deep lines, jowls, and a knobby chin speckled with a scattering of long whiskers.

Upon meeting Sish's eyes, he hopped off the stool and revealed himself to be only three feet tall. Sish took a step back, unsure of what to do or say, wary that it could trigger another deadly trial.

"Welcome, welcome," the dwarf said. "You're the first to have come this far in quite a long time, quite a long time."

Sish shrugged. "To be perfectly honest, the first two trials were of middling quality. I'm surprised no one else has found their way here. Who are you?"

"Ruddlefunt at your service," he said, offering a lavish bow that caused his hat to slide further down his face. "And I wouldn't say *no one* has ever come this far, just very few."

He knocked back his hat, offering Sish a better view of the upper part of his face. Sish gasped. The flesh above the dwarf's nose was almost entirely gone, revealing a skull made of some type of metal. There was a series of brightly colored veins running between the metal parts. A sharp blue glow emanated from somewhere inside the skull, erupting from Ruddlefunt's torn face and eyes.

Sish had only ever seen one of the blue-eyed before, but he had heard enough tales to know their fearsome reputation and almost limitless capacity for violence. He leaped back and reached for his short sword, realizing he'd lost the weapon in the lake. He cursed and looked for something impromptu and found a large rock at his feet. He hefted it and readied for the creature's attack.

Ruddlefunt looked at him quizzically. "I'm not interested in violence," he said. "Could you please put the rock down?"

Sish hesitated and then slowly placed the rock on the platform next to him.

"Thank you," Ruddlefunt said, inclining his head in thanks. "I see you're alarmed at my appearance, but I can assure you I am 97 percent functional, and I perform my daily systems diagnostic with 99 percent efficiency."

"Is this … is this the Old City?" Sish asked, casting his eyes over the grand valley below.

Ruddlefunt turned, looked at the valley, and turned back. "You stand upon the 51st Promontory of the Second Highness in the

Grand Valley of the Lords of Roan. I am not familiar with the term you used."

"None of that means anything to me," Sish said. "What are you doing here?"

"Waiting for you to arrive," Ruddlefunt said.

"So, you knew I was coming?"

"Your advancement through the Perseverance and Loyalty trials was monitored, and so your arrival upon the 51st Promontory was a logical conclusion," Ruddlefunt said.

"Perseverance and Loyalty? I knew them as Pressure and Allegiance."

"A translation error, as the common tongue does not capture the intricacies of the language of the Lords of Roan," Ruddlefunt explained.

"And the third trial? Insight?"

Ruddlefunt lifted a finger and smiled. "There is no third trial. The Lord Engineers designed a two-system locking mechanism to access the Grand Valley. The third, commonly mistranslated as a trial, is a choice."

"A choice?"

"Correct."

"What is the choice?" Sish asked.

"You will find out," Ruddlefunt answered.

"What does that mean?"

"It's not programmed in my function to divulge the details."

"Programmed?" Sish paused.

He studied the dwarf. Intuition suggested he wasn't talking to a living creature, but rather, Ruddlefunt was something mechanical or magic-infused, but he couldn't guess how it worked. He wondered if all the blue-eyed were the same.

"What is your … purpose?" he asked.

"I am programmed as a Grade Four Expositive Sentinel," Ruddlefunt said.

"Which is …"

"I explain things."

"Could've fooled me," Sish said drily.

Sish turned and wandered around the promontory looking for any sign as to what he should be doing, but there was nothing, and Ruddlefunt just watched him. A sudden pressure in his bladder made him realize he couldn't remember the last time he'd peed.

He looked around for a location with a bit of privacy and spotted a bush a few feet down the cobblestone pathway that led away from the promontory into the valley. As he stepped off the platform and unbuttoned his trousers, he heard Ruddlefunt attempt to speak, but he was peeing against the wall a moment later and lost in the sublime ecstasy of emptying an overfull bladder.

As he enjoyed what felt like a rare moment of quiet, Sish noticed his hands were shaky and he felt a bit lightheaded. He hadn't eaten anything since he'd first set up camp beneath Roan's main gate, shortly before he'd run into his father. Nor had he had enough to drink, judging by the color and smell of his urine.

"Ruddlefunt, you got anything to eat?"

"No," the dwarf answered.

Sish cursed under his breath and did up his trousers. "That's going to be a problem."

As he turned back toward the promontory, he noticed a marked change in the colors around him. Where before the grass and bushes of the pathway had been a verdant green, now they were brown, black, and burned orange. The valley, too, had seemingly rotted in a matter of seconds.

Gone was the golden light that shone through the cavern ceiling onto the lush forest below. Instead, there was an ashen quality about everything now. The trees were leafless, twisted, and gnarled. The once rushing blue streams were swamp green and congealed. Far below were the remains of a thatch-roofed village, yet its buildings were burned and blackened—the sorry hulks of a place scorched by fire and left long abandoned. Even the rushing waterfall next to the promontory was more languid, syrupy almost.

"I don't understand," he said, looking at Ruddlefunt.

The dwarf sighed. "What you saw before was how it once looked. What you see now is how it has been for many long centuries."

"What happened? It ... how could it become this way if it's been sealed up?"

Ruddlefunt shook his head. "The Master Engineers programmed the screen on the promontory to project the Grand Valley at its most beautiful, but that was a very long time ago. A very long time, indeed. What you see is how the valley has been since the corruption."

"Corruption?"

"As I said before, it has been quite a long time since a visitor has come this far, but it's not the first," Ruddlefunt said. "There was Selena of Yarrow. She was the first after the Grand Valley was sealed. She reached the bottom of the pathway you stand upon and was promptly eviscerated by a Gerthulb. Sometime later was Maraxis Delespene. He was an interesting fellow, quick of wit and light of hand. But even he made it not much further than Selena. A bogwight of Karbold swallowed him nearly whole. And then there was Vik Tar Regare, a noted swordsman of the desert country to the south. The gerthulbs and bogwights were no match for him, but the Pelican of Sitka startled him to such an extent that his heart gave out, and he died on the fields. Strange, to come so far only to have one's body be the cause of failure. And then there was Carl. Poor Carl—"

"None of that answers my question," Sish interrupted. "Why does the valley look like this?"

Ruddlefunt scratched the scorched flesh at his forehead and looked out over the valley. "I do not recall a time when it didn't. This was the reason the valley was sealed, to keep the corruption in."

"And the treasure?" Sish asked.

"Treasure? My programming does not include any reference to treasure. However, perhaps you're referencing what has been called the Wealth of the Lords of Roan."

"Yes, wealth, treasure, whatever," Sish said, waving a frustrated hand. "Where is it? That's why I'm here—you know, the three trials, the tr—wealth, whatever you call it. Where is it?"

"The Master Engineers sealed the valley to ensure the wealth did not leave this area until such time as it could be appropriately manipulated. It is located on the far side of the valley beneath the Sixth Highness, Fourteenth Promontory," Ruddlefunt explained proudly.

Sish gave him a blank look.

"There's a castle on the far side, in the main hall," said Ruddlefunt.

Sish nodded. "Any advice on how best to cross the valley without being eviscerated by a bogwight or scared to death by a Gerthulb?"

"Correction, the bogwight uses retractive lips and an extended tongue to—"

Sish rolled his hand, gesturing to the dwarf to get on with it.

"Fine, fine," Sish said. "Is there any way you can open the Keyhole to let my friends in?"

Ruddlefunt nodded agreeably. "Why, yes, of course. You are now the candidate, and so I must obey your command. Here, let me find the switch."

"Candidate?" Sish wondered aloud, but Ruddlefunt was already busy with a panel hidden in the cavern wall near the door to the statue room.

The dwarf reached into the false rock wall, twisting his arm around and pulling harshly. The promontory came alive with the sound of heavy, rusted gears groaning to life. The doors to the statue room swung open as the goblin statue rotated to face the promontory. In one smooth motion, the stone goblin sheathed its weapons and kneeled like the other seven statues behind it.

Beyond them, the Keyhole clicked and rattled as the rock around the narrow tunnel came alive. The stone opened outward the way flower petals expand in the morning sun, each piece of rock folding back on itself to reveal the long corridor that stretched to the camp. There, Fulk and his crew stood rigid as statues, silhouetted beneath the strange, luminescent blue glow.

And there were others behind them. Three shapes that even amid the gloom Sish recognized: Liv, Terry, and Wren, each with their weapons drawn and pointed at Fulk and his goons. They marched the trader, goons, and Wincott down the corridor like prisoners toward Sish. A pit grew in the young thief's stomach as he realized what was happening.

The past had caught up to him.

Chapter Sixteen

PRISON MIGHT BE PREFERABLE

JAIL ISN'T THE WORST PLACE in the world. You have a roof over your head, a bed, and a guaranteed bowl of slop once a day, even if the occasional maggot or bit of mold appears in it. Sure, going to the bathroom in a bucket isn't ideal, and the occasional beating puts a damper on your day, but Sish also managed to reconnect with a few friends and was already planning his next caper. After all, what else would one expect from a building full of criminals with nothing but time on their hands?

But the good times came to an end when Wincott showed up. His father stood on the other side of the cell bars, his arms hanging loosely on the iron, a toothpick between his teeth. Sish could see he had started growing his beard again, which suggested the long con the old man had been working on was over. The fact that he wasn't in prison beside Sish suggested Dad had been successful, which only made him more sanctimonious as he smiled at his son through the bars.

"Did the Lady Coswell give up her secret?" Sish asked, gesturing to the fresh stubble on his father's face.

Wincott looked to ensure no guards were near—not that they cared; the guards in the Fort Rivers prison were easygoing. Sish chalked it up to it being a relatively small town—even when you let someone out, you might run into them again at the pub or in the market. Best watch your back, and the best way to do that is to avoid making enemies in the first place. It worked both ways, mostly.

"She gave up more than that." Wincott grinned and flicked his eyebrows suggestively. "So, here we are again, eh? The rate you're goin', I'll be retrieving your corpse from the gibbet one of these days."

Sish sat on the stone platform that hung from the wall that was supposed to be a bed. There wasn't much on it except a mouse-bitten wool blanket that looked like it belonged in a horse stall. Admittedly, it was better than nothing on a winter night.

"Probably right," Sish conceded. "You here to spring me?"

"What are fathers for?" Wincott lamented. "But there's a catch."

Sish shrugged, used to the quid pro quo of their relationship. "What is it this time? Lady Coswell needs another roll in the hay?"

Wincott spluttered, "No, boy! And watch your tongue; it'll be what gets you killed if it isn't your slippery fingers. Those old buffoons you stole from want their goods back."

"I don't have them," Sish said.

"No, but I know you know where they are."

"And I know you know that I wouldn't be much of a thief if I returned goods so easily, you know?"

Wincott rubbed an exasperated hand across his face. "Look, stop fooling around. They've decided not to press their claim to the gaoler—a good thing for you—if you'd just retrieve their keepsakes, something about a red thimble and a jade ferret."

"Monkey," Sish corrected. "I don't know *where* they are, but I may be able to find out."

"Good, I'll tell them to spring you," Wincott said, turning away.

"Give me twenty minutes. I just need to finish a conversation with the Pip," Sish said, jutting his thumb to a shadowy figure in the cell next to him.

"Pip? That Eddy Pippston's boy, Rutger?" Wincott said, a smile creasing his lips. "Shit, it is! How you doin', boy?"

The Pip was a scrawny teenager with big ears, arms too long for his body, and a gaunt face. His father, Eddy, had taken Wincott under his wing when he was young and remained friends with him, though Eddy's days running capers were long gone on account of losing the lower half of his left leg to a Kobold that had been trained as an attack dog.

"Nice to see ya', Wincott," said Pip, sticking a hand through the cells. "Keepin' well, I see. Me and yer boy here was jus' jawin' on 'bout a tip up in High Town might be worth a fickle or two."

"Always appreciate the tips, Pip," said Wincott, shaking the boy's hand. "But this boy's got himself up to his eyeballs in wizard shit, and I don't think a fickle or two would be enough to turn it around for those scholarly gents."

Pip nodded. "Aye, they's a right bunch of cunts, ain't they? Well, g'luck with it, Wincott. Say hallo to my da when ya see him."

Sish nodded to Pip, who stepped back from the cell door, disappearing into the shadows of his own criminal cloister. The guard turned up a moment later, jangling a heavy set of keys, and unlatched Sish's cell door.

Sish felt his head rattle before he knew Wincott had slapped him. His vision blurred, and he braced himself against the wall to avoid falling. Wincott was most of the way down the corridor on his way out of the prison by the time Sish could see straight, leaving the young thief alone with the sole guard who leered at him while he picked a rotten set of teeth. He hurried after his father, rubbing the rapidly forming welt on the side of his head.

THE JOB WAS A RELATIVELY simple get-in-get-out task, what Wincott often referred to as a Jane because there wasn't anything noteworthy about it. A few well-placed questions at taverns in the college district pointed him toward a third-floor flat off Blind Man's Alley. It was dark early this time of year, but Sish waited until well past midnight, hoping the woman he'd given the thimble and monkey to would be fast asleep. "Given" was a stretch, of course. If he'd done his job correctly, she wouldn't yet know she had them, and he'd be gone again before she did.

The trouble with wizard jobs, even if they are Jane, is you can never be sure if you have a night owl on your hands. Wincott explained that some wizards, particularly those who practiced more violent forms of magic, tended to be almost entirely nocturnal. But the waitress at the Crow's Shoulders told him the woman was a hedge mage—quite literally, a farm wizard. Her day job was coaxing the rejuvenation of forage plants to improve pastureland for grazing livestock, with the occasional bit of crop work to boost yield. She worked for the E&E, as most folks in Fort Rivers did, one way or another, which generally meant she kept daytime hours and should be fast asleep by the time he arrived.

Sometimes it's best on a Jane to go through the front door. That was the old man's approach; he liked to keep things simple. No one would question a guy walking in the front door like he owned the place, and if you were made, it was easy to make like you got the wrong address and move on. But that was Wincott's way of doing things, not Sish's. And more recently, Sish was outgrowing his father's way of doing things—it was all old hat, while the newer generation of purloiners were more adept at sniffing out trick locks and warning systems that targets were more frequently putting in place. He guessed the hedge mage likely had a cantrip on her front door, so he figured the window was the better way to go in.

She was still awake when he got there. He watched her from a shadowed alcove atop the building across the alley. The street below was empty save for the occasional drunk who meandered his way among the cobblestones searching for a path back to the bottle. Peering through the window, he didn't immediately see the small statue or the thimble. It was possible she still didn't know they were inside her overcoat pocket.

He watched her move back and forth through the apartment. It looked to Sish like she wasn't doing much of anything, except sipping from a steaming cup of tea that floated alongside her as she wandered through the apartment, consulting different books that lay open among the scattering of tables, chairs, and bookcases that squished inside the small space.

One thing he did notice was how beautiful she was. When he had run headlong into her the day before, he recalled thinking her green eyes were almost otherworldly. In the time since, he wondered if he'd overblown it because his adrenaline was up.

Nope, she was a knockout.

Long, brown hair with a slight curl framed her alabaster face, with a prim nose and full red lips. She was slender but tall, and in his opinion, had just the right amount of curves. It was the kind of thing, Sish decided, could be quite distracting if he spent any length of time around her.

Fortunately, he had no plan to. It was a Jane. In and out. Although Wincott had given him strict instructions to return the thimble and monkey to the Breakfast Club, Sish intended to sell the monkey to the fence he'd originally been working with. He'd give back the thimble, and if anyone came asking, he'd make up a story about how the monkey had vanished or been smashed beyond repair or some such thing. He'd worry about that bridge when he came to it.

The hedge mage turned down the lamp and went to sleep shortly after midnight. Sish waited another chunk of time before he leaped between the buildings and crept over the cedar shingles to the window. He paused and peered inside.

She was fast asleep in a bed littered with books, leading him to believe she didn't often have company. It was endearing, he thought, but not so much that he hesitated.

He took several minutes to slide the window open, moving it an inch at a time, careful to ensure the sound didn't wake her. It was a relatively warm night, so he didn't need to worry about a cold draft disturbing her sleep, which left him with the impression that luck was on his side.

He slipped one foot through the window, then the other, and was inside. Crouched on a bench at the base of the windowsill, he scanned the apartment. He spotted the monkey and the thimble almost immediately. Both sat atop a small desk halfway across the room.

That was easy.

He shrugged and walked over.

He was halfway there when he heard a man yell, "Now!"

Rough hands seized Sish's shoulders and slammed him to the floor, leaving him gasping for air. The lamp was turned up, bathing the room in a warm amber glow. Three figures stood over Sish as he struggled to gain his breath: a hulking plainsman, an older man, and the hedge mage.

"I'll step on his neck," the plainsman said, lifting his booted heel.

The older man held the plainsman back. The hedge mage stepped forward and looked down at him disapprovingly. She was beautiful even when she was mad, Sish thought, as he coughed and sucked in air.

"You are a *terrible* thief," she said. "You might want to consider another profession."

THEY'RE ALL A BUNCH OF LIARS

"**L**ong time no see," Elden Wren said to Sish as he nudged Fulk at sword point onto the promontory above the Grand Valley.

"Not long enough," the thief replied, a smirk curling his upper lip.

Wincott shook his head as the girl wizard prodded him forward. The kid was going to get himself killed if he wasn't careful. Ever since Sish was a child, he'd struggled to bite his lip, follow instructions, or do pretty well anything that anyone asked of him.

Wincott had taken him to the market once as a child and made the mistake of using several expletives when he saw the price of pears. When he'd gone to pay, Sish put his hand on the money before the shopkeeper could take it and told him, "My da says you can take those prices and shove them up your ass." Wincott didn't buy pears there again for a while. But he did steal them. Frequently.

Liv marched Wincott onto the promontory at Stave Point. She pushed the old thief forward to stagger him and twirled her staff to snap it against Sish's nose. He reeled backward and she push-kicked him in the gut. The young thief hit the ground like a sack of dirt.

The wizard stood and watched him writhe on the ground as she approached the balustrade to scan the tarnished valley below. With a tired look, she cast her eyes to Ruddlefunt and said to him, "How do we seal the Old City again?"

Ruddlefunt scrunched his face in confusion and said, "Seal it? You just opened it."

"No," she said, pointing at Sish. "He opened it. We want it closed."

"If we're being accurate, Ruddlefunt opened it," Sish said, wiping blood from his nose, still lying on the ground.

"Whothe Rudzlefink?" said Tring forward, fists balled.

"The dwarf," said Sish.

Terry reached for Wincott and lifted him off the ground by his shirt collar with one great, muscled arm. The old thief's legs dangled helplessly in the air. A memory flashed through his mind of watching the barbarian fight years before in the arena, besting two bears and a handful of fighters with nothing more than a net and broken javelin. He had the distinct impression Terry would need far less than that to end his life.

"You opened ith?" the barbarian said, his eyes aflame. "I'll pull you aparthe, lithle man."

"Not him, the other one," said Sish, rolling his eyes and nodding his chin in Ruddlefunt's direction.

The floppy-hatted dwarf smiled sheepishly and waved his hand at the barbarian, his moth-eaten red robe billowing about his thin arm. Terry looked at the dwarf and then Wincott. He dropped the old thief, who also hit the ground like a sack of dirt, and hefted his long sword. He wound up to cleave Ruddlefunt's head from his shoulders, but Wren caught his arm before he could follow through.

"Hell of a situation you put us in here, Sish," said Wren.

The thief got to his feet and dusted off his pants, eyeing Fulk and his goons as carefully as he did the Dungeoneers. For the moment, the old trader only watched the exchange quietly, his muscled second-in-command twisted up like a spring, ready to unload the first chance he got.

"Why are you talking funny?" Sish asked the barbarian.

"We ran into a pack of Methuro Spiders. One of them stung his face and nearly broke his jaw," Wren explained.

"It hurts," Terry said, stroking his chin.

"There are spiders here?" Sish asked.

"It's a dungeon, kid," Wincott reminded him.

Sish nodded slowly, "Well, Dungeoneering isn't for the faint of heart, is it?"

"Can we get back to the task at hand?" Liv broke in, a warning look on her face. "We need to seal the Old City again, or spiders will be the least of our problems."

"What are you talking about?" Wincott asked.

Liv ignored him and turned to Fulk, her face red with anger. "This is *your* doing, and we'll all pay the price if we don't stop it now."

Fulk was impassive. Wincott marveled at the trader's ability to remain stoic, even at knifepoint. It was never a skill the old thief had developed, tending to fold like calf's leather in similar situations.

"Why would we come all this way just to shut it again?" Wincott pressed.

Liv reared on him, "*We*? Don't you mean you and your Guild friends?"

Sish's head snapped toward Wincott as he staunched the bleeding. "Guild friends?" he asked.

Wincott's heart sank—it was exactly what he'd hoped to avoid. He wasn't sure how Liv and her cronies had found out, but they had.

"The Guild," the wizard said matter-of-factly. "You're all working for the Guild."

Sish looked at her, incredulous. "I'm not working for the Guild."

Fulk spat, "No, but you are working for the Company."

Wincott fixed his son with a glare. "You're working for those assholes?"

Sish put up his hands to protest, but he couldn't get the words out.

"Of course, he is," Fulk said.

"You're working for the *Guild*?" Sish looked at Wincott.

"Of course, he is!" Fulk said again.

Liv laughed and shook her head. "Is this for real? You're each working for opposing factions, and none of you knew?"

Both thieves shrugged.

"Then who are *you* working for?" She looked at Fulk.

"No one," he said. "I'm here on my own business."

Wren spat and crossed his arms. "So let me get this straight— you're all traveling together, but you're all working against one another? That really is something else."

But Wincott had already lost interest in the Dungeoneers' musings. He was so enraged he couldn't get the words out of his mouth, just a series of curses, spittle, and stamping of his feet. He wanted to strangle Sish then and there. How could the boy be so stupid as to trust the E&E for anything? It would only get him tossed in cells, or worse—a first-class ticket to the gibbet care of the Company.

He looked at his son, an irrational part of him hoping that his body language alone would get his point across to Sish, but he knew that wouldn't be the case. The boy was too proud, too stubborn. He was in deep, and *this* time, Wincott couldn't help him out.

Sish lunged for Wincott, catching the old thief by surprise. The two toppled to the ground in a tangle of limbs, Sish's arms around his father's neck.

"How could you?" the younger thief yelled. "After what you did to her. I should've killed you when I had the chance."

Wincott tried to push Sish off him, but the boy was too strong for him. He struggled helplessly for air. It was like the last time the two of them had fallen out. There had been a knife then and just as much anger. The Guild. It was always about the Guild.

Terry intervened, peeling Sish off Wincott with one leathery hand. The old thief rolled over and coughed until he caught his breath. He struggled to his feet after a moment and realized everyone was still arguing about what should happen next.

The Dungeoneers had the upper hand, Wincott knew. But a needle prick of intuition in his gut suggested things were about to shift.

Fulk was trying to rationalize with Wren. Liv was studying the mechanism near the door to the statue room with Ruddlefunt, probably trying to figure out how to reverse engineer the device. The dwarf looked befuddled. Terry was talking Sish down a few feet away, the boy's eyes still staring daggers at him.

But the Dungeoneers had forgotten about Kai and the remaining half dozen goons Fulk had hired to get him to the treasure. The old trader's lieutenant stood near the doorway and when no one was watching, drew a knife from his belt and quickly seized Liv, holding her against his chest, the knife pointed at her neck.

"Okay, y'all stop yer yammerin' now. Kai gunna tell ye how it's goin' to go," the man said, calling everyone's attention away from their individual arguments.

Sish pushed past Terry and charged toward Kai, but the goon saw him coming and pressed the knifepoint in the wizard's neck a little deeper, drawing a droplet of blood that oozed down her neck.

The young thief cursed him. Wincott knew then that his son's feelings for the wizard weren't completely gone, no matter how much things had gone sideways in their past.

"One move and she's dead," Kai told them.

Sish stopped. Fulk took a step forward but was held back by Wren. The trader looked at the Dungeoneer and said, "Tables have shifted on you now, haven't they? Men, tie these buffoons up so we can be on our way. We're close to the goal."

The goons took a step forward to follow Fulk's command, but Kai held out his free hand and told them to stop. "Not so fast. We don't need you now, Fulk. I think we'll just take the girl and be on our way without you."

The old trader's face turned ashen as the mutiny hit him.

Kai shifted around the group and walked Liv toward the pathway that led down from the promontory into the valley below. Each goon had their weapons drawn and were ready to fight. While Fulk and Sish vibrated with anger, Terry and Wren wore expressions that suggested they weren't intimidated by Kai and his entourage. Wincott suspected Terry could take out half of the mercs with a single sweep of his arm but likely not before Kai would kill Liv.

"Let her go," a new voice said.

It was a girl's voice.

Wincott followed the childish sound to spot a nine-year-old girl with short, almost spiky hair, a cherubic face, and eyes as black as night strolling out of the statue room. Rena. So, the summoner accompanied them. Things were about to shift again.

Everyone shifted their attention to the girl who strode through the standoff onto the promontory. She wore a simple pair of faded blue traveling pants with a white collared shirt and dark leather overcoat, all of which made her appear older than she was. Despite being only slightly taller than Ruddlefunt, she walked with the air of a woman three times her age. It was impossible to tell what the black orbs she had for eyes focused on at any moment, but Wincott felt a shudder run up his spine when she spotted him.

"Who's this then?" Kai stopped, a confused and slightly sarcastic look spreading across his face.

"Rena, don't do anything," Liv told the girl, the knife pressed to her neck.

Kai wrenched her hair, causing the wizard to cry out. Sish pushed forward, but Terry held him firmly.

Rena balled her fists and turned toward Kai. "I said *let her go.*"

"Rena, it'll be okay," Wren cautioned, taking a step toward her, his eyes wide as dinner plates.

Kai threw his head back and laughed. "Shut it, girl. We're takin' yer friend with us."

He moved off the promontory onto the path. Rena fell to her knees and looked skyward, her mouth hanging open like a clam, wider than Wincott could've thought possible.

"Cover your ears!" Wren yelled.

Everyone but Kai and his goons held their hands to their ears as the girl let out an earth-shattering scream. Wincott felt the pressure of the noise in his head as it reverberated through him as though it shook the very muscle that clung to his bones. The pressure in his head was immense, as if his eardrums might burst. He held his hands so tightly to his skull that he thought it might crack it.

The rock walls of the Grand Valley vibrated.

Kai and his goons collapsed, writhing in pain. Liv was suddenly free. She stumbled toward her companions. Rena's scream stopped.

"We have to go back," Liv urged as soon as the noise cleared. "It's not safe now."

Fulk was still as a statue, a dazed look in his eyes, as his former mercenaries struggled to their feet, blood dripping from their ears, eyes, and noses.

Wren grabbed Wincott by the sleeve and urged him back through the door to the statue room. The old thief looked at Sish. The boy looked intent on carrying out his mission into the valley— he wanted that treasure, whether for the E&E or himself, Wincott couldn't say. But he knew that stubbornness when he saw it.

A great bestial roar emanated from the valley below. The ground shook as if tons of rock had slammed into it. Pebbles and rock dust rained down on the promontory from the cave ceiling above them.

"It's coming. We have to go!" Liv urged.

"What's coming?" Sish asked, confused, his back to the balustrade.

A gargantuan serpentine head emerged behind him a moment later, and with it, two great reptilian arms that gripped the stonework, crushing it beneath talons that were as long as spearpoints.

The creature roared again and came into full view. It had the head of a cobra with a long snake neck, a scaly body consisting of two massive arms and legs, and a tail of serpents that snapped hungrily over its back like a scorpion's pincer. The creature, which was easily four times the height of Terry, roared again, its neck flaps spreading outward.

The stone balustrade crumpled beneath its weight. Wincott felt the once-solid rock promontory start to shift and crack beneath his feet, as if it couldn't bear the creature's weight.

Its venomous tail snapped wildly, colliding with Kai and his goons. The big man managed to duck in time, but his men were snapped up in the jaws of the writhing snakeheads attached to the tail, their screams muffled as the monster ingested them like a sword swallower.

Liv yelled something, but the thundering crack of the rock giving way beneath them made it impossible to hear. The promontory gave way.

Wincott was closest to her. The old thief reached for her and dived into the statue room just before the ground sloughed beneath them. He managed to reach back and grab the strange dwarf by the collar and pull him through the door as a plume of rock dust rolled into the chamber after them. When the dust cleared, the promontory was gone and everyone with it.

Chapter Eighteen

A DIFFERENT KIND OF BOAT RIDE AT A DIFFERENT TIME

ERIDAN STRODE THROUGH THE FOREST like a hunter in pursuit of wounded game. By midmorning, she was a quarter mile ahead of Wincott, the boy meandering among the alder and spiny devil's club between them. She moved as though she weren't wounded, though Wincott knew that wasn't the case. And he gathered she wouldn't be able to maintain her pace for more than a day before her leg gave out.

Two days had passed since they'd felt their way through the dark to the trapper's cabin east of Fort Wick. Meridan wanted to get moving immediately, but Wincott could tell from the pallor of her face that she was in no shape to travel, and he had no desire to shoulder her and the boy to Fort Rivers. Truth was, he wanted to be rid of them as soon as possible. A woman and her child were a nuisance he didn't need, and he worried the longer they were with him, the more likely they'd find out he was working for the Guild.

The thought crossed his mind to turn the twosome in to her husband, Lord Elgin. It wouldn't be too difficult to create a smoke signal or leave a series of blazes in trees marking their route. But the Guild was just as crooked as the Company, and he had no reason to believe they wouldn't shut him up with a knife to the throat as soon as he handed Meridan and Sish over, much less pay him for the convenience. Elgin wouldn't want to leave anyone alive who knew he'd be cuckolded.

But if he ingratiated himself enough to Meridan … well, the Chief Factor at Two Rivers might see fit to reward him. And Wincott had debts that needed to be paid. The paltry amount the Guild had paid him to sabotage Fort Wick might buy him some time with a few unfriendly faces he owed money to in Fort Rivers, but he'd have to make a score almost immediately or he'd be gutted there, too, or at the very least, run out of town. A reward from the Company, though? That might finally turn things around for the thief who had been down on his luck and calling in favors to keep food in his mouth for the better part of two winters.

But first, he needed to get to Fort Rivers. The way Meridan was hiking through the snow and trees, he wouldn't be surprised if they made it there in less than three days. But her pace wasn't sustainable, and the longest part of the route was via the Moon.

And now he was worried about Guildsmen picking up their trail, or worse, stumbling across something more formidable on the way there. The forests were not safe to travel, with all manner of unsavory creatures prowling the unyielding wilderness. And when winter struck and food was short, well, those things got hungry.

The thief shuddered and rubbed his hands together to warm them up. Meridan had disappeared over a short rise ahead while Sish trudged up the hill following her path. The snow was patchy, but there was enough of it that they could be tracked. Wincott picked up the pace.

Before they left the cabin, he told Meridan that the plan was to pick up a canoe he'd stashed a ways down the river where the Moon flowed into the Ribbon. From there, they would float to Fort Rivers. It meant a longer hike through the woods than originally planned, but a better chance of avoiding any prowling Guildsmen near Fort Wick, and it was unlikely anyone else would be on the water this time of year.

Wincott figured the Guild knew Meridan and the boy had escaped and were likely looking for her. If any one of those men had an ounce of brains, they could hazard a guess that Wincott had something to do with it. After all, a thief never wastes a good opportunity.

The boy stumbled a few hundred yards ahead of Wincott. The thief quickened his pace to help him back to his feet. He'd ground some dirt and small pebbles into the knees of his pants and his palms but was otherwise okay. Wincott dusted him off and sent him forward. Meridan had stopped to watch the thief look after the boy, but when they were up and walking again, she turned away without a word and continued her march through the woods.

"Your mom's on a mission, kid," said Wincott.

The boy didn't respond. He plodded alongside the thief. Wincott guessed he was probably already tired. There hadn't been much in the way of food to take from the cabin, and there was still another several hours before they reached the canoe, if it was still there. Wincott hoped to fish a couple of trout out of a productive pool next to the launch point, which would hopefully see them through until the next day. It was late in the fall, but he may even get lucky and pull a salmon out.

He licked his lips thinking about seared trout baked on hot rocks next to the river and nearly missed the speck of blood that dotted an alder branch he and Sish strode past. He looked ahead. Meridan was still moving, but the distance between them had shortened considerably and she was clearly favoring her wounded leg. It must have reopened, he thought. He hoped they would make it to the canoe before she needed to rest, or worse.

"Your mom good to you?" Wincott asked, more out of a desire to break the silence than anything.

The boy didn't say anything, just nodded slightly.

"Seems like a good lady. Tough as nails," Wincott said.

The boy nodded more vigorously.

"Lord Elgin, your fa—dad. How's he?"

Sish was quiet, his eyes fixed on the trail ahead of him. If what his mother had said was true, Wincott knew the house Sish had known was a stern one. Lord Elgin had a reputation, and the thief gathered that he didn't look kindly on children, much less one that wasn't his own.

He tried several more times to make conversation with the boy, but Sish never gave him more than a nod or a shake of his head. He gave up when he saw Meridan stop on the path ahead.

"What is it?" he asked as they reached the top of a small rocky hill.

She sniffed the air. "Do you smell that?"

He did. His eyes widened with alarm.

Slitherers.

He lifted the boy up and grabbed Meridan by the hand, dragging her off the narrow path to cut through a fern grove before skidding down a coarse, gravelly hill.

"What is it? What's that smell?" she pressed as they slid to a stop.

"Nothing we want to meet," he told her, hurrying them up the next rise.

Once they were inside a thicket of blue spruce, he stopped and gestured for them to crouch low.

"Slitherers," he told her. "Not very bright, but they hunt in packs, and if you get surrounded …"

A few minutes went by, and the smell grew worse. He pinched Sish's nose shut as Meridan covered her face. The aroma was like wet meat left to rot in the sun, sour and cloying. Their proximity suggested the creatures had caught Wincott's scent and weren't far behind them. They would have to move quick or … he considered leaving the duo. The thief watched them quietly as they peered through the spruce boughs searching for their rank pursuers.

He knew *he* could get away, but he wasn't sure he would survive with Meridan and the boy in tow. He looked at her, and she returned his gaze. She wore a vacant look, almost waiting to see whether the thief would betray them. Did she know what he was thinking? He turned away. Sish didn't say anything, but his shoulders were visibly shaking, and he was biting his lower lip hard enough to draw blood.

Wincott picked him up and readied himself to sprint down yet another hillside, hoping they could make it to the canoe and river before the slitherers caught up with them.

"I'm going to need you to ignore the pain in your leg," Wincott whispered to Meridan as he hefted the boy. "We need to run. Fast. Can you do that?"

She nodded wordlessly.

"Okay, let's go."

He was up and out of the copse of trees in half a breath, Sish dangling from his hip as he pushed his way through the spiny brush. Meridan was a step behind him. The brush ended abruptly at the top of a steep hill, but Wincott had been moving too fast to stop himself. He stumbled and then partially rolled down the hill, mindful as they tumbled to keep the impact on his body instead of the boy's. At the bottom of the hill, he sat up, dazed. When his eyes cleared, he realized their luck had run out—a pack of slitherers formed a circle around them.

The creatures reminded him of half-melted globs of butter with toothy slits for mouths that stretched across their bulbous body-heads. Dozens of ropy custard-colored tentacles flapped in every direction from their bodies. Although slitherers were blind, Wincott knew they could be lightning fast when their tentacles latched onto something.

He carefully got to his feet, hefting the boy higher on his hip. Slitherers surrounded him on three sides; behind him was the hill he'd just rolled down. Meridan was atop it still, her thin, half-bent body casting a dark shape against the iron-gray sky behind her. She called down to him. He winced as the creatures sloshed toward him.

He turned and tossed Sish up to her. The boy flailed through the air, but his mother managed to catch one little hand and hold on, pulling him up. He heard her groan beneath his weight as her leg gave out.

Wincott could try running back up the hill, but it was steep. He risked sliding back into a waiting mouth, which he didn't relish. The knife in his belt would be enough to fend off one, but there must have been twenty of them oozing around him now.

A handful of ropy yellow tentacles sprang toward the thief. They wrapped around his legs and pulled him to the ground. Instead of inching him toward the slitherer, the creature leaped into the air, its toothy grin hinging open as it sailed ravenously toward him.

He reached for his knife and tried to pull it free, but the hilt was caught on his belt. He reefed on it, but it was stuck. Time slowed as the monster came toward him. Suddenly, a knife flung through the air and buried itself in the slitherer's open mouth. The creature gurgled and landed on top of him, oozing its yolk-ish oozy into his face. He grabbed hold of the knife in its mouth and pushed it further into the creature's gelatinous cranium. Its tentacles relaxed, allowing him to toss the monster to the side.

He got to his feet and looked up the hill. Meridan was there, her arm stretched forward from the knife throw. She continued to surprise him. He felt a wave of heat through his gut as he remembered how, only moments prior, he'd considered abandoning them.

Wincott held her knife in one hand and drew his own a moment later, ready to face off with the other nineteen slitherers that inched toward him.

A sudden gust of hot air from his right caused him to wobble back. He knelt to recover as the trees around him began to crack and splinter. A massive shadow slithered among the conifers just out of sight. Wincott fell back and crab-walked into the hill behind him, an irrational fear catching his breath as his chest tightened. He realized what he was looking at.

The Hag.

No one knew it by its rightful name, nor did they know how old it was. Stories about the Hag spared detail, save three things: it was ancient, indestructible, and could best be described as a giant slitherer that devoured anything in its path.

It looked to Wincott like a giant black octopus, one that was at least four or five times the size of the largest grizzly bear he'd ever seen. It moved through the forest with the grace of a spider, its tentacles wrapping around tree trunks one after another as it pulled itself through the spaces between jack pine and blue spruce.

The Hag hovered at the edge of the trees, facing Wincott for a moment that seemed to stretch for hours. Was it looking at him? Its tentacles snaked around two trees, and it retreated among the trees.

Woosh. Splat.

The Hag shot out from the trees and landed on the pile of slitherers like they were ants, a gnashing, crunching noise coming from beneath its body as it sucked the butter blobs into its belly.

Nineteen slitherers would have been a hard-fought battle for a dozen well-armed soldiers. Even the Company's best hunters would be hard-pressed to fight a pack that large. The Hag devoured them in an instant.

The octopus snapped several spruce trees in half while it did so, its tentacles batting the trees out of the way like matchsticks. When it was done, it turned toward the thief and pulled itself through a narrow gap between the two closest trees at the base of the hill. Its glassy black eyes came within an arm's length of Wincott's face; hot, earthy breath cloyed at his face. He heard Meridan cry out above him, but something about the Hag's eyes made it impossible to look away.

The creature surveyed him for what seemed like hours but was likely no more than a minute. Then in a flurry of movement, its rear tentacles latched onto trees behind it, and the Hag snapped through the trees away from him and was gone. In its wake were a dozen stumps, overturned conifers, and a few custardy masses that leaked across the forest floor.

Wincott breathed out slowly. Then in again. And then out. He did this for several minutes, his hands working their way around his body to make sure all his limbs were intact and that he hadn't shat his pants. He was surprised to discover he hadn't, and strangely, felt a small bit of pride in that.

Meridan slid down the hill, coming to a stop in a cloud of dirt and dust, the boy held against her chest. Anger twisted her face. No. It was worry. And fear.

The boy, on the other hand, grinned like he'd just had his first trip to the baker's.

"That was the best thing I ever saw!" he blurted out.

Wincott exhaled. He shared a wry look with Meridan, and both began to howl with laughter.

THEY REACHED THE CONFLUENCE OF the Moon and Ribbon rivers in the middle of the afternoon. The sun was already starting its precipitous drop in the southwest sky. There was a brisk wind, but it was warm and came from the west. That was good news. Western winds were carried in on the ocean currents and generally signaled warmer weather. It would also be at their back as they made their way downstream, meaning a shorter travel time.

It would be dark in two hours, maybe less, so Wincott planned to fish for dinner, make camp, and head out in the morning. The river was low and shallow. Although it was almost entirely flat water, he worried about paddling in the dark and striking a rock that would dump them into the river with no ability to see.

Meridan wouldn't be much help anyway. She limped her way to the river shore, one hand holding her wounded leg like it was a bag she was forced to carry. Her pant leg was stained crimson. She'd bled through the bandage, and it would need to be changed quickly.

A soft mat of dry pine needles beneath a large tree looked as good a place as any for her to rest. Wincott helped her down. She winced and sucked in a breath each time her leg moved. The boy watched her carefully, worried. Wincott eased her against the trunk of the bushy pine. It wasn't a proper chair but about the most comfortable thing you'd find outside of a town or city.

He checked the canoe he'd stashed to make sure it was still river-worthy, and once satisfied, sent Sish to fetch firewood while he tended to Meridan's wound. She was pale. Her was brow speckled with cold sweat. Her skin was hot to the touch, suggesting a fever.

"How you doin'?" he asked her.

"Just peachy," she said with a small chuckle that turned into a racking cough, "What's the doctor's opinion?"

He gingerly rolled down her pant leg to get a better look at the wound. The white gauze was soaked red. He peeled it off, trying to ignore the fact that her nails dug into his shoulder like needles as he did so. Nearly all the stitches he'd tied at the cabin had come apart. He didn't have a needle or thread, so the best he could do would be to wash it out, let it air overnight, and bind it again in the morning. Once they got her to Fort Rivers, he could find a doctor.

He remembered her telling him her family name was Torren. A glimmer of recollection flickered in the back of his mind—he'd heard that name before but couldn't quite place it.

"Not much I can do but keep it clean. Need to get you to a doctor," he said. "You know one at the Fort?"

She grimaced as he washed her leg with a rag torn from his undershirt. It was the cleanest thing he could find, so it would have to do.

"I did when I was a girl," she said, her voice breaking with the pain.

"Torren, right?" Wincott quizzed her.

"Right. Dad was a hunter. Kept the blue-eyed ones at bay so the traders could keep the lines open."

It dawned on him then. Edgar Torren was one of the most senior hunters among the E&E ranks, a near legend. He'd spent more time in the northlands than anyone else and had the trophies and scars to prove it. If she was Edgar's daughter then … well, given how well she handled herself with that blade, it wasn't actually any real surprise, Wincott realized.

"Edgar," Wincott said.

"You know him?"

"*Of* him. Everyone does. How did it come to pass that you married Lord Elgin? Edgar's got a reputation for being independent, but he has no love for the Guild."

Meridan grunted as Wincott reapplied the bandage. She shimmied against the tree as if trying to get away from the pain, the sweat dripping down her temples as she gripped his shoulders the way a hawk seizes a mouse in the field.

"Well, he didn't approve, if that's what you're asking," she said, gritting her teeth.

"And you didn't care?"

"I was younger," she said flatly. "Dad was a good hunter, not a great father."

The thief nodded knowingly. He had no real idea about fathers or being one. He had never known his dad, and at this point, didn't care to.

Wincott helped her pull her pants up and then cast his eyes on the boy, who had returned with an armload of firewood.

Wincott never had a great relationship with his own mother, though if it weren't for her, he wouldn't have survived being a baby. She'd come down with an illness when he was ten and died after a short sickness. With no siblings and no other family, he was sent to a boarding house before he eventually ran away and turned to the streets to feed himself. He learned to thieve by running errands for some of the heavies in Chicken Town.

He'd weathered a few romantic relationships along the way, none of them ever lasting very long, certainly not long enough to consider marriage or children. All that was to say Wincott had no real concept of what it was like to love someone the way Meridan loved Sish, to put your life on the line to give someone else the chance at a better life. But there was a part of Wincott, a very small part, that could kind of understand it. And he almost envied it, though he pushed the feeling out of his mind as quickly as it had come.

He left the woman at the tree and found the fishing pole he'd stashed some months before. He rigged up the line and set a large black hook on the end with a small red indicator.

He pulled his shoes off, rolled up his pants, and waded out to his knees in the freezing river. The rocks were slick, and his feet were numb after a few minutes. He hated having cold feet, but he would have to suffer through it because the only way to access the pool where the trout so often lurked required him to get a bit wet.

He cast the line out. The clouds had parted, and the sun was low in the sky, casting a pale pink glow across the underside of the flat gray ceiling that became a deep blue and purple toward the eastern horizon. A perfect time of day to fish, and no breeze either.

He had a few nibbles and reeled in but had trouble getting one on. After a few minutes, he felt a solid tug and reefed on the rod to set the hook. A breath passed before he felt the vibration in his hands that told him the fish was on. He let it tire itself out and then reeled it in, walking it onto the shore, where Sish watched with rapt attention. It was a twelve-pound sockeye on its way to spawning grounds. It would feed them well that night, with maybe some leftovers for the next day.

Meridan limped over to him and took the fish. "I'll gut and cook it," she said.

"Make sure to toss the guts in the water. Don't want to attract bears … or worse," Wincott told her.

"I wasn't born yesterday," she said, rolling her eyes.

The fire crackled. The stones beside it sizzled with freshly filleted fish. Wincott didn't need to fish more, but it wasn't quite dark yet, and he was still twitchy with adrenaline from earlier in the day, so he thought it best to keep fishing until the moon was up.

He went to get his rod and found Sish holding it. He reached for it and then stopped himself.

"Want to try?" he asked.

The boy looked at his mother. She nodded.

"Take your shoes off, and let's roll up your pants," Wincott told him.

Wincott took the rod in one hand and Sish's hand in the other and waded into the river with him. He found a safe spot where the water was slow moving and gave Sish a few pointers. It took the boy a few tries, but on the third attempt, he sent out a nice cast, and the hook and indicator dropped into the center of the trout pool.

Within minutes, he had a fish on. His eyes were wide as dinner plates, and he was unsure what to do. Wincott coached him, showing him where to place his hands, offering encouragement and a little extra muscle when he needed it. They carefully walked the fish onto shore and discovered Sish had reeled in a nice four-pound rainbow trout.

"I'll hold it, you pull the hook out—then it's yours," Wincott told him.

The boy twisted the hook and popped it out of the trout's mouth. Wincott handed him the still-flapping silver fish. The boy mooned over his first catch. He sprinted to Meridan beneath the tree.

"Look! Look!" he told her.

Meridan smiled and congratulated him. Her brow was thick with sweat again, her skin gray. She looked at Wincott and mustered a thankful smile. Sish turned toward the thief and did the same. Wincott realized it was the first time he'd seen the boy smile, and it warmed his heart so much he forgot how numb his feet had become.

THEY WERE ON THE RIVER shortly after the sun crested the eastern horizon the following morning. A weak light spread across the pale blue sky that suggested winter was at hand. A chill breeze from the north was in the air, causing their breath to escape in little puffs of steam. The weather was changing. If they were lucky, they'd reach the fort before the snow started to fly.

Wincott steered the canoe from the stern while Sish sat cross-legged on the floor between him and Meridan at the bow. She held the paddle but swirled it lazily in the water as if struggling to stay awake. She didn't look good. She was deathly white, and her fever was so bad she was drifting into delirium. Sish had gone quiet when he realized his mother was rambling incoherently.

The thief paddled hard toward the fort but, at best, they would be there by nightfall. He stopped regularly to cool her fever with a wet cloth and provide water and strips of salmon, but she couldn't keep anything down. She heaved over the side of the canoe several times, and by midmorning, had given up paddling altogether.

The boy's shoulder drew inward, hunching, as the day wore on, his head sunken, not even bothering to watch the landscape drift past. After a while, Wincott pointed out interesting things along the riverbank to distract the boy, but it was half-hearted, and he was roundly ignored.

Midway through the day, they stopped to relieve themselves and refresh. Sish played with a stick on the shore while Wincott tended to Meridan's wound at the canoe. She couldn't even climb out of the boat.

"He can't … he can't find out about us," she told him, her pupils dilated and upper lip slick with sweat. She was hallucinating.

"I just need to check the wound," Wincott told her. "This might hurt a bit."

"Keep it from him, don't … don't let him …" she was saying.

Wincott soothed her with a cool rag on her forehead and checked the wound. It was bleeding again and smelled musty, like dirty feet. Not a good sign. The infection was burning through her body. She didn't have long.

"We need to get moving," he urged, wrapping her wound again.

"Don't … Fulk … don't let him find out," she said between rasping breaths. "He can't know … can't know you're his—"

Her eyes closed, and she fainted, rolling limply into the boat. Wincott knew the man she mentioned. Everyone did. Fulk was the deputy chief factor of the Company, a well-respected and notoriously strict commander. And no fan of thieves.

Wincott wasn't sure what he would do when he got to Two Rivers. Knowing the trader was likely the boy's father didn't give him any more confidence about a reward; in fact, there was less. Their affair had obviously been a secret until Lord Elgin found out. Wincott guessed she'd escaped with the boy by then, fleeing her husband's ill temper. Would Fulk be any more welcoming? Especially to a thief who showed up on his doorstep with a bastard in tow.

Wincott shook his thoughts away and propped her upright in the belly of the canoe, bunching up a shirt that he slid beneath her head for a pillow. His best option was to get to Fort Rivers as soon as possible and keep her alive. That *had* to be his focus for now. He told Sish to get in the front and handed the boy a paddle.

"Your mom is real sick," Wincott said. "I need your help now. You know how to paddle?"

He suspected the boy didn't, but Sish nodded all the same and turned away, setting the wooden blade in the water. They set off, finding an earnest but steady rhythm within minutes, hoping the lazy current would help get them there in time.

By late afternoon, they reached a short canyon where great sandy cutbanks rose on either side of the Moon. Meridan moaned intermittently but said nothing coherent. Sish would glance over his shoulder every so often to check on her, but Wincott would remind him to keep his eyes on the river and look out for stray rocks and sweepers, though, really, he didn't want the kid to watch his mother suffer.

As they rounded a bend somewhere west of Fort Rivers, Wincott's eyes were drawn to a dazzling sight. The river channel narrowed, and a great stone dragon spanned a gap over the river between two rocky cliffs that soared above them, forming a short, narrow canyon.

"Look, the great wyrm—Myrrhmyth," Wincott pointed, "This was his territory before the traders arrived. The statue marks the gateway to the dragon's old lands, stretching from here to deep into the mountains to the east, where it's said he still guards his hoard."

Meridan moaned, shuddered, and choked quietly, her struggles masked by the quiet trickle of water as Wincott dug his paddle in and out of the water. Sish was so enraptured by the statue he didn't hear her.

Wincott was thankful for it because she had let out her last breath.

As the canoe drifted beneath Myrrhmyth's stone wingspan, the thief checked her pulse. She was gone. The boy watched the dragon in awe as the canoe slid east through the quiet water toward the fort. As afternoon drew to dusk, Wincott was able to make out the faint amber glow of Fort River's lights against the ashen sky. They were close. So close. Not close enough.

Wincott knew the boy would turn around any moment, and then he would have to tell him his mother was gone, that he was on his own. The thief's heart sank as he savored the boy's final few moments of innocence, a passing few seconds before the reptilian indifference of life reared its ugly head and shattered it forever.

Head held high, shoulders back, the boy had lost himself in the discovery of something magnificent in the world. How long had it been since Wincott had felt that way about anything? Yes, magnificent. And also awful. Two feelings that too often came together.

That's the world we live in, boy.

Wincott made a decision then, one that only a few days prior would never have entered his mind. He would tell Sish that his mother had died, but he would also tell him he wasn't alone. He could stay with Wincott as long as he liked. Maybe together, they would have a better chance beating back the awfulness out there. Maybe together, there would be a little more magnificence.

Chapter Nineteen

OF PEELERS, BITERS, RAVENERS, AND A COLLEGE-EDUCATED BARBARIAN

SISH AWOKE TO A MOUTHFUL of dirt. The dust had settled around him, but the murky gray daylight cast strange shadows that moved and shifted all about him. For a moment, he forgot where he was—half expecting to awaken in Fort Rivers or in a frigid bedroll halfway between here and there, wherever here was.

He rolled onto his hands and knees and spat out a clump of rock dust. It tasted like more rocks than dust. Blood and saliva dribbled from a split lower lip, and a sharp pain on his right side when he breathed in suggested a cracked rib or two.

Great.

He breathed shallowly, resting on his backside while he got his bearings. The air was warm and humid and tasted of mold. He was at the edge of a black pool of water, which lay at the bottom of the now-languid waterfall that had been next to the promontory.

His eyes widened

Grand Valley.

He wiped the grime from his eyes and caught sight of his feet: they were bare, toenails cracked and broken in a few places, with more than a few scrapes. It all came back to him. Wincott, Roan, the lake, the Keyhole, statues, and then *it* climbed up the promontory and sent them cascading into the valley below.

The Treasure of Roan.

Sish surveyed the valley around them. He gathered they had fallen into the pool after the rock ledge crumbled. His clothes were still damp but dry enough that some time had passed. How had he made it to shore?

A hulking shadow approached him.

"You're alive," said Terry, standing over him.

The barbarian looked no worse for wear, still clad in little more than a loincloth and fur sash that stretched diagonally across his chest and doubled as a scabbard for his great sword on his back. His knee-high fur-lined boots were also perfectly intact. Frankly, he looked ridiculous.

The thief got to his feet with the barbarian's assistance and dusted his clothes. "Take more than that to kill me. You, too, apparently."

The barbarian shrugged and said, "The other one is awake, too. I built a small fire over there so you can dry out your clothes."

The barbarian pointed to a flickering campfire a dozen yards from the water's edge. Fulk sat naked on a log next to it, his beady eyes fixed on the dancing flames. His clothes were organized across a series of rocks near the fire, drying in the heat.

Sish looked at Terry again. "Your mouth—you're talking okay?"

The barbarian nodded, rubbed a scratch on his jaw, and raised his eyebrows, "Hmm, guess the fall fixed it."

Sish nodded wordlessly and wandered toward Fulk. For the second time in two days, he stripped naked at a campfire and laid out his clothes to dry. He sat on a stump across from the trader and asked him what he planned to do.

"Keep going," Fulk answered.

He eyed the promontory above them—there was nothing left to climb up to and no visible exit from the valley, at least not the way they came.

"Can't go back," he whispered, almost to himself. "And we're close. *So close.*"

Sish rested his face in his hands and massaged his eyes and forehead with the tips of his fingers, as if trying to push away the sheer exhaustion of it all. He did not relish the idea of traipsing deeper into the Grand Valley alongside the trader, especially after Ruddlefunt had indicated there was no shortage of gerthulbs, bogwights, and terrifying birds hanging about, not to mention the snake-tailed giant that had climbed up the side of the valley for them.

He shuddered, remembering how it plucked Fulk's men from the cliffside and swallowed them whole.

But then he thought about what the dwarf had told him: *The Wealth of the Lords of Roan.* What was it? A treasure horde? Multiple treasure hordes? Some kind of weapon?

Then again, he hazarded a guess, glancing around, given the presence of such obvious corruption in the valley—and the fact that it had been sealed—that there wasn't going to be a room full of gold coins waiting for him at the end of this pathway.

"You know it was a mistranslation," Sish told Fulk.

The old trader raised his eyebrow and stared quietly at Sish. "What do you mean?"

"The dwarf. Ruddlefunt. He had no record of a 'Treasure of Roan,' only the 'Wealth of the Lords of Roan.'"

Fulk cracked a smile and licked his lips. He leaned closer to the thief over the fire. "I know. That's what I'm here for. The question is, *Company Man,* what are you here for?"

Sish leaned back and crossed his arms. It felt awkward doing so when he was naked, but it was such a natural movement he wasn't sure what else to do with his arms. But Fulk was right, what was he doing here? The Company hired him to open the gates of Roan. They paid him handsomely but had not told him much. He surmised they planned to get the treasure and use it to fund a major trade route expansion that would tip the balance of Erdor to their control.

When he thought back on his brief conversation with the deputy chief factor in Fort Rivers, he remembered the urgency in the man's voice. They must've known the Guild was interested in the abandoned city and its secrets as well, which was now clear in that Wincott was working for them.

The thief's stomach twisted thinking about it. He had scant memories of his mother, but what he did remember was them fleeing from Guildsmen in Fort Wick. Lord Elgin had been a bastard of a stepfather, abusive, and so the thief had no love for the Guild or anyone who associated with it. Sish was a liar and thief, of that there was no question, but he still had standards—and working for the Company was a lot different than helping sleazy Guildsman to Northern Erdor's bounty.

It shouldn't have surprised him his father was working for the Guild, though. The old man had been run out of Two Rivers for too much debt, and the Company wanted his head. And well, he had a history there, didn't he? The thief recalled their last encounter before they parted ways for several years. It felt good to cut that nasty scar into his father's face; he only wished he'd finished the job.

But he also knew he didn't have it in him, at least not then. For all that Wincott was a traitorous bastard, he was still the only family Sish had. The old man kept him alive as a boy and had saved his life more than once since. It was why he didn't gut him when he watched Wincott climb unawares into the gate of Roan. Killing wasn't an easy thing most times, and Sish had learned it was downright impossible when it came to family, at least for him. He wondered, though, whether that assumption would get tested before their journey through Roan was through.

"We need to move," Terry said, urgency in his voice.

The barbarian's eyes flicked left and right, scanning the gnarled trees and dead bushes around their campsite. Sish saw a flicker of movement to his left. Something small and dark leaped toward him from the rusty brush. Terry's sword swung as he tore it from its scabbard and cleaved the creature in two. Its severed body landed at Sish's feet. He wasn't sure what to make of the sloppy carcass near his bare feet, though he knew it looked bad, like a furry black maggot with a round mouth full of teeth.

"Peelers," Fulk said, as if it were a swear word.

Sish had never seen one until then, but he'd heard of them. A lowlife named Ludge from Chicken Town picked one up in the sewers one time; it stripped his arm off in the blink of an eye. *It wants you to shake it off*, Ludge told them later.

"There'll be more," Terry said, "Larger ones. In the water. Get your clothes on. We need to move."

Fulk was dressed and fleeing with Terry before Sish had his shirt on. The thief half-ran, half-stumbled out of the camp as he pulled on his pants. He realized then he was still weaponless, not a great position to be in given the peelers.

They bolted through the tangle of trees away from the swamp, Terry in the lead, his sword drawn. Sish was amazed at how deftly the barbarian weaved through the narrow spaces and overhangs between the trees, his sword twisting and turning as the gaps allowed, avoiding every trunk and branch as if it were just a soft bit of satin ribbon trailing behind him.

Fuck, do I have a crush on him?

The thief had heard tales of the barbarian's prowess in the arena, none of which he'd initially believed. But then he'd had the good fortune—or misfortune depending on what side of Terry's blade you found yourself on—to watch him fight.

Sish had run with the Dungeoneers on a few jobs the last few years, first because he had no choice and then because he needed the money and they needed someone with slippery fingers. Dungeoneering as a profession required a variety of skills that caused even the most morally stout individuals to occasionally compromise their stance on things.

The problem with this set of Dungeoneers was that they didn't ever want anything from the dungeons they raided. In fact, Wren would say the whole point was to explore, identify the nature of the danger lurking within, and then make that information available to anybody who wanted it. Occasionally, the danger was so high the group would seal off the dungeon, cave, fortress, or haunted house in question.

It was idiotic. How do you pay rent on that kind of work? It was a waste of potential wealth. Just think of all the loot those stupid fucks left behind.

And that's where Sish and the Dungeoneers parted ways.

But before that happened, he'd witnessed Terry cleave his way through more than a few monstrous hordes, and the barbarian had even saved the thief's life once.

As they moved away from the swamp, Fulk, it seemed, had no trouble keeping up with the barbarian, and neither did Sish, once his pants were on and buckled. His feet were a little worse for wear, with more than a few rocks and twigs stabbing into the soft, exposed flesh, but those were lesser problems compared with having his skin stripped off by a worm.

They ascended a rocky hill dotted with burned trees. Sish wondered how a forest fire could start in a cavern but decided he didn't want to know. The valley stretched in every direction outward from them and felt larger from below than it had looked from the promontory. And whatever sickness infected it, it was evident everywhere.

Not only were trees burned, bare, twisted, or dead, but large pulsing fungi attached themselves like tumors to trees, rocks, and earth. Mottled with purple and dark yellow spots, the growths seemed to sweat. The thief guessed the jungle-like humidity of the cavern and the fungi were related somehow, but he didn't care to find out why. He had only two goals: to get to the treasure and get out alive. Neither would be easy, judging by his surroundings and the Company.

At an arched stone bridge that forded a languid stream, the barbarian gestured for them to halt their jog and crouch behind the spindly brush. The big man pointed ahead. At first, Sish couldn't see what the barbarian was indicating with his finger, but Fulk was nodding and whispered something low to Terry that the thief couldn't overhear. The barbarian grunted in agreement.

"What is it?" Sish said.

"You blind, boy?" Fulk scolded him. "Raveners. A group of them squatted on the underside of the bridge, made it their home, looks like. We'll have to find another way around."

"We could ford the stream; it looks shallow there," Sish pointed down a ways from the bridge.

Terry shook his head. "Full of peelers, probably biters, too."

Sish snorted. "I have to say, we're not very creative when it comes to naming these things, are we?"

Terry considered his remark a moment and then said, "Those are the colloquial names. I believe the proper name for a peeler is Platyhelminthes Caro. One of the few naming systems left over from the old people."

Sish and Fulk exchanged a look that was somewhere between surprised and confused.

"How do y—"

"I fought in the arena to pay my way through college. I planned to be a hedge mage like Livinia, but, well, things happened ..." he trailed off.

"Interesting. So you have a college degree?"

The barbarian pumped his head once and opened his mouth to explain, but Fulk cut him off.

"This little trip down memory lane is nice, but we have more pressing matters—we need to get to the far end of the valley as soon as possible, or we'll be eaten alive down here," said Fulk.

"You want that treasure," Sish said, reading between the lines.

Fulk fixed him with a glare. "Yes. And I don't want to die down here, otherwise, it's useless to me. I say we go over the bridge."

"I say the stream," Sish countered.

The barbarian considered both options and rubbed a callused hand across his mouth.

"The bridge," he decided. "If we're quiet, we may just be able to sneak past them. No chance of that in the water, and the sound of us fleeing the peelers might garner the attention of the raveners anyway. Sish, you're the nimblest on your feet—you go first."

The thief's eyes widened. "And if they're waiting for me? I'm defenseless."

The barbarian reached into the fur sash that stretched across his chest and pulled out a penknife, handing it to Sish. The thief chuckled, knowing it would be more useful to use it to slit his own throat than face a pack of raveners. But that's how the day was going. That's how it always went with the Dungeoneers.

Chapter Twenty

LISTENING TO THE PLAN WOULD HELP

THE DUNGEON WAS SMALL, MAYBE only five or six rooms and as many corridors. Wren traded a set of lynx furs for a map, though Liv had already expressed doubt over the veracity of the layout. Terry didn't care, suggesting it was better than nothing and the rumors about this particular dungeon—a half-dug mine-shaft-cum-lair for a troublesome lich—were enough to justify risking life and limb to explore it.

Sish had tuned out the details of the conversation, being completely distracted by the young hedge mage as she flitted about the room, making plans and preparing spells to deal with whatever they found once they were inside. It was the way her auburn hair tussled like a stream of brown gold every time she second-guessed herself that did him in. He could watch that all day, he decided.

They were gathered at Wren's flat in Chicken Town, a dense little borough of Fort Rivers, hemmed on one side by the Ribbon. It was best known for the rancid smell of poultry-processing factories that butted up against the riverbank. Most of them were shut down and had been turned into housing for the last wave of colonists to the area, but the name had stuck.

Wren's quarters consisted of a large open room that housed a sitting area, a small study, and a half-kitchen. There were two bedrooms at opposite ends of the flat, but other than that, it was sparsely decorated, reminding the thief how little time Wren spent in Fort Rivers, preferring the wilderness and traplines over the commotion of a large town.

"Sish? Sish, you paying attention?"

Wren's voice drew him out of his reverie. The thief nodded. In fact, he hadn't been and had no idea what he'd just agreed to, but if his experience with the Dungeoneers so far was any indication, he'd have the most uncomfortable job.

Six months had passed since the group had caught him trying to steal the jade monkey and thimble from Liv's apartment. Being the moral people they were, he'd been forced to return both items, a fact his fence wasn't too happy about. Wincott pressed him for the details when he learned the Breakfast Club had been made whole again, but Sish left out the part about being caught in Liv's apartment.

He'd participated in a couple of raids with them since. Turns out, even the righteous have need of a thief or thief's skills occasionally, though even Sish had to admit he wasn't as slick as his father. But what he lacked in finesse, he more than made up for in sheer determination. Plus, there was more than a little luck.

But the truth was, he didn't need the work. Wincott turned over a decent score some months prior, and pickpocketing at the market paid decent most days, both of which kept them fed and warm at night.

He stuck with the Dungeoneers because he had a major crush on Liv and no idea what to do about it. He was almost certain she didn't feel the same way, but a part of him hoped that just by hanging around, she might one day take notice of him. If nothing else, just being in the same room with her felt better than the rush he got lifting wallets and coin purses in the market. So, when she approached him about the Morvid Lake dungeon job, he agreed before she had a chance to explain what they wanted him to do.

He caught himself staring at her again while Wren went over the final plan and quickly averted his eyes as she turned toward him.

"Sish, you okay?" she asked.

He struggled to find words and nodded instead.

Stupid. Stupid.

Every time she looked at him, he grew flustered. He didn't understand—any other woman, even the ladies in Madame Hawk's brothel, he had no trouble with. But Livinia Decker? He froze up like a hummingbird in a hard frost.

"Let's go," Wren announced.

Terry was the first out the door, Liv directly behind him. As Sish left the flat, Wren put a hand on his shoulder and held him back.

Once the others were out of earshot, he said, "You're not foolin' anybody, least of all her."

"What do you mean?" Sish shot back, playing stupid.

Wren pursed his lips and raised his eyebrows.

Morvid Lake was half a night's hike southwest of Fort Rivers. The lake rested silently at the bottom of a large natural bowl, with several creeks that trickled into it from the approach. It was early summer, the birch and cottonwood trees thick with fresh foliage that whispered in the gentle nighttime breeze. A warm, clear night with a fabric of twinkling stars above was perfect for adventuring, Sish concluded. As they approached the lake, the only sound was the steady rustling of the trees overhead.

A pale lunar glow lit the narrow, rooty forest path ahead of them. As they reached the edge of the trees above the lake, Wren pointed to a narrow, rocky path that wound along the left-side ridge and ended at the mouth of a squat but wide cave on the far side of the lake.

"Sish, do your thing," Wren told him.

The thief paused, not sure what "thing" he was supposed to do. He guessed he should've spent more time listening to the plan than daydreaming over Liv, but it was too late now. And he wasn't about to let on that he didn't know what the plan was. Liv would judge him poorly for that.

"Okay," was all he said before sauntering onto the rocky path.

A heavy hand seized his shirt collar and pulled him into the trees. "No, down. Go down," Wren lectured, pointing to the lake, where, in the distance, he could see another rocky opening far below the cave.

He shrugged as if he'd known all along and then picked his way down the ridge beneath the moonlight, careful to stop and crouch every so often to listen for anything out of the ordinary, but all he could hear was the breeze.

The opening at the base of the lake was directly below the cave entrance above but only as wide as his shoulders. Sish wasn't a fan of tight squeezes; they made him claustrophobic. Not great for a thief, really.

He breathed deeply and pushed his way into the tiny entrance, finding it widened almost immediately on the far side and was tall enough for him to walk with only a slight stoop.

The cave stretched before him a dozen yards before it ended at a stone ledge that overlooked a wider corridor below that stretched perpendicular to his own. Flickering torches lined its walls, which burned a greasy black smoke that smelled of cedar pitch. He guessed the lower corridor led back to the main entrance. To his right, it led downward and ended with a series of rusted, narrow-gauge ore cart tracks that stretched out of view into the gloom.

Sish hadn't listened to Wren's plan, but he guessed his role was fairly simple: drop into the lower corridor and work his way back up to the main entrance, where he would let the others inside, assuming there was a door that blocked their access. He didn't rightly know. He hoped he was right; otherwise, he'd already botched the job.

He dropped lightly onto the cavern floor below and turned left, climbing up the steep path to the main entrance. At the top, he found a wrought-iron metal gate between him and the forest and Morvid Lake beyond. He drew his lockpicks and worked the mechanism, the door swinging open on a rusty iron hinge.

A whistle brought Terry, Liv, and Wren into view. Once they were inside the dungeon, Wren looked at him and said, "That was quick. How many are there?"

"What do you mean?" Sish said, giving him a funny look.

"You were supposed to scope the place out and find out how many of those skeleton things are downstairs. Did you?"

"Nope," Sish admitted. "Forgot that part."

Liv shook her head. "You really are the worst thief."

Terry's face darkened. He drew his great sword and proceeded down the incline without another word. Sish clucked his tongue awkwardly. The barbarian clearly wasn't pleased. Shaking his head, Wren drew his short sword and lifted a torch from the wall sconce and followed Terry. Liv drew a wand from inside her long, green overcoat—it was her preferred instrument to channel spells these days, Sish had noted, though he had, on occasion, seen her toy awkwardly with a staff.

Deeper in the dungeon, they passed a handful of abandoned ore carts knocked off their rails. Littered among their rusted iron and wood ruin were the bleached bones of miners, the long-dead victims of some horrid accident. No one knew what had been mined at Morvid Lake, and Sish had the distinct feeling it was best not to find out.

Several small storage rooms branched off the main shaft, where the iron tracks remained in decent repair. Sish guessed they were areas that had been mined, and once the veins were tapped out, had been turned into storage areas. Now they were abandoned bunk rooms, supplies rooms, and one served as a makeshift library of sorts. Everywhere, there were bones, mostly human, but some animal he couldn't make out as well. Whatever they were, they were bad, judging by the serious look on Wren's face as he crouched to inspect them.

But nowhere was there anything of value.

Directly ahead, Terry halted in front of a set of square double doors that hung ajar. A strange red light emanated from behind them, which, typically, wasn't a good sign as far as dungeons go.

Wren's map showed the final room—where the lich resided— just beyond the doors. It was supposedly a small, square room with four natural rock pillars interspersed through it. The goal was to deal with the lich so that … well, Sish couldn't quite remember the reason the lich needed to die, if liches could even die. But his companions had decided as much, and so, here he was.

Terry quietly gestured for them to get ready. Sish drew his short sword and held it in a sweaty palm, rotating it nervously to find a better grip on the leather handle. He just hoped it wouldn't slip out of his hand when he needed to use it.

The Dungeoneers burst through the door with a roar, the barbarian charging across the room, sword drawn back. The lich was ready for them.

The creature was roughly the same height as Wren and clad in long, torn purple robes. It was human; except, the flesh and muscle on its hands and face were almost entirely gone, leaving only dry yellow bone wrapped in black corded sinews. Hands outstretched, the lich fired a barrage of fireballs at the foursome as soon as they were through the door.

Terry spun around mid-stride, narrowly dodging one. Wren dived for the ground and kept safe from another. Liv took refuge behind a stone pillar one of the fireballs crashed into, showering her in orange embers. Sish wasn't so lucky. One of the fireballs struck him square in the shoulder and knocked him back against the cavern wall near the door.

Not missing a beat, Terry surged forward and swiped at the undead. It dodged his first strike, but the second took off one of its arms. The lich screamed in rage and cast another spell. This time, a blue streak of light erupted from its remaining hand and shot into the cavern beyond the doors.

Liv got to her feet and waved her wand to conjure a root system out of the floor that wrapped around the lich's legs, binding it to the floor. The creature sagged. Wren cleaved its head from its shoulders, and the lich collapsed in a heap of rotten robes.

Terry stopped and breathed.

"That was close," Wren said.

Liv nodded and chuckled, slipping her hand into her robes.

Sish got to his feet, rubbing his shoulder where his shirt had been scorched and the flesh grayed with a nasty burn. He grunted and stumbled forward when he heard something like bones rattling outside the doors they had come in through. He poked his head through the doors and found a dozen skeletal miners shambling toward him, pickaxes and hammers in their hands.

"Guys, we have a small problem," the thief said, jutting a thumb toward the door.

Just as he said it, a pickaxe bit into the heavy wood behind him, proving the point.

"We'll fight our way out then," Wren said.

"Wouldn't have it any other way," Terry announced triumphantly.

"Just let me check for anything arcane," Liv cautioned. "I wouldn't want this lich reawakening as soon as we leave."

Sish rolled his eyes at the bravado. It was all … a bit much.

The Dungeoneers cut their way out of the Morvid Lake dungeon with a fervor the young thief had come to expect. He even managed to cut down one or two miners himself, earning an approving nod from Terry as the barbarian led the way up the torchlit corridor to the forest beyond.

Outside, Wren sheathed his short sword and breathed in the night air. The huntsman was the most down-to-earth of the group but staunch in his worldview. Sish always felt Wren watching him, never fully trusting. The thief gave him credit. Sish wasn't one of them, he didn't feel like one of them, and he had no plans to become one of them. Adventuring wasn't in his bones that way, and each time he went out, he always felt out of place. Strangely, it was in those moments that he most missed Wincott and their life together. Although his father made him want to pull his hair out, Sish felt a lot more at home with him than he did with Wren and crew.

"Well, another job … done," Wren said, eyeing him carefully.

Sish caught his breath. The early summer air filled his lungs and left the scent of pine needles in his nose. Liv and Terry had already started on the trail to Fort Rivers. Wren waited with Sish a moment longer, as though he wanted to say something. He cleared his throat and then started down the trail wordlessly.

THE SUN CLIMBED ABOVE THE eastern horizon as they strolled into Chicken Town, providing a weak gray light behind the heavy cloud cover. The borough clanged with the sounds of early morning shopkeepers and stable hands starting their day, and the smell of freshly baked bread in the air indicated the baker was already halfway through his own.

Sish's stomach rumbled as they reached the stairs that led up to Wren's flat. He realized he hadn't had anything on the trail. He tended not to eat when the adrenaline was pumping through his system as it made him sick.

Wren and Terry said their goodbyes and trudged up the stairs without another word. A light mist started to fall, decorating buildings and cobblestone streets in a million dull raindrops.

Sish loitered at the base of the stairs a moment to see if Liv might invite him back to her apartment for a bite to eat.

"Well, I best catch up on some sleep," she told him. "I need to be on the fields early this afternoon to deal with some pasture that a herd has mucked up pretty good."

Sish nodded, not sure what to say. What *do* you say to that?

"Why do you stay with him?" she asked, her brows knitting together as she looked him over.

His stomach knotted at the sudden change in her tone. He met her eyes and immediately knew who she was referring to.

"He's my father," he said simply.

She cocked her head to one side, raising her eyebrows. She knew, as they all did, that Wincott wasn't his actual father. Apart from the fact that they didn't look anything alike, the thief had confessed to her one drunken night that Wincott had saved him and his mom's life when he was a boy.

He shrugged. "I guess it's what I know."

"When my father found out I was adept, he threw me out. My mother protested, and for a year or two, I went back and forth. Then she grew ill and died and ... well, he's gone. And I'm alone. And better for it," she said, pursing her lips.

His face burned. He felt judged but was unsure what to say. Sish had never heard her talk about her past ... or really anything personal in that manner. It was a common characteristic among the dungeoneers—none of them talked about their pasts, and no one pushed them to do so. And now, she was, obviously, trying to get a point across that he didn't want to hear or wasn't ready to.

"Wincott is an excellent thief," she commented. "The *best* if the stories are true."

Sish half-smiled, a bit of pride welling up in him. A bit of jealousy, too, always living in the shadow of his fath ... dad.

"But you're not and not ever going to be," she told him, her eyes leveling at the thief.

It was difficult to look away, but her green eyes made him twitchy. He shifted uncomfortably in his shoes and looked everywhere but at her.

"The sooner you realize that the better," she said. "You'd make a good dungeoneer, Sish. But you can't be both, and sooner or later, you'll have to decide, like I did."

Sish didn't have a response. A part of him, one he didn't want to acknowledge, felt she was right. But thieving was what he knew, *all* he knew. How would Wincott feel if he …?

He didn't finish the thought, suddenly growing angry and jealous at the thought of his father again, a great thief who always put himself first. What did it matter what he wanted?

This is my life. My choices. The old man be damned.

Liv turned to walk away but stopped a few paces down the laneway and reached into her coat. She drew a small red jewel and tossed it to him. He caught it and realized it was the ruby thimble he'd nicked from the Breakfast Club and been forced to give back.

"They gave it back?" he asked her.

She shook her head. "I found it on the lich. Identical, isn't it? It's either an amazing coincidence or our mutual friends at the Breakfast Club have more going on than sausage and eggs at Bart Rigby's. Might be worth following up on."

She turned and walked away, disappearing into the shadows and mist of the alley, her heavy green cloak gathered about her thin frame. Sish rolled the thimble around in his fingers for a moment and thought about it and other things.

Chapter Twenty-One

THE PENKNIFE ISN'T MIGHTIER THAN THE SWORD, BUT IT'LL DO

SISH INCHED DOWN THE DUSTY hill toward the bridge on his stomach. He knew it looked ridiculous, and both Terry and Fulk were likely shaking their heads watching him, but they weren't the ones creeping toward certain death with no shoes and a penknife, were they? Plus, his feet needed a break—if he made it across the bridge alive, his first order of business was to find a pair of boots; even a set of sandals would be welcome at this point.

The bridge was in poor repair. Carved from some type of granite, half of its width had collapsed mid-span, leaving only a narrow path by which to traverse the highest point of the arch. That made it the perfect place for an ambush.

He lifted his head to scan the streambed again, looking for said ambush or even an easier way across. But there weren't any. It was the bridge, or he'd be stuck on this side of the valley until something other than a pack of raveners killed him.

He sighed, got to his knees, and then his feet, crouching low. His feet were caked in muck and small cuts so moving slowly was his best option. He crept toward the bridge. The raveners, which were just large, hairy goblins, huddled beneath the stone structure, jabbering incoherently amongst themselves. He hoped their mutterings would mask whatever noise he made.

He tiptoed until he reached mid-span, where most of the rock had fallen away. The gap in the bridge was larger up close; the intact portion of the structure was barely wider than his hips. It afforded him a view of the lazy stream below and the small encampment the raveners had made on the mudflat next to the water. They had a cookfire, several tents, and crude furniture. Were it not for the fire, he wouldn't have seen them at all, their hair and skin being so dark.

He stepped carefully along the bridge, his eyes flicking between the creatures below and his foot placements above. He was a step away from safety on the other side when a chunk of mud sloughed from his heel and landed on the campfire below. The jibber-jabber halted; the creatures looked up. Sish leaped out of view and rolled hard down the stone bridge. But the raveners were already shrieking and snorting, a sound not unlike a stuck pig.

The first ravener ambled onto the bridge a moment later, its black, lidless eyes fixing on the thief in front of it. Without thinking, Sish leaped forward and jammed the penknife into one of its eyes. The creature threw its hands up in panic and tumbled off the bridge with a startled scream. It hit the mudflat with a loud thump, and the others joined the cacophonous chorus.

Sish knew the rest would swarm in any moment. He sprinted down the far side of the bridge barefooted and unarmed. A glance over his shoulder revealed Fulk and Terry coming up the other side of the bridge. Fulk held what looked like a sharpened tree branch, which, the thief supposed, was better than nothing. Terry was ready with his broadsword.

The raveners scrambled onto the bridge from all sides, scurrying up the worn stone edges like hairy cockroaches sniffing out carrion. There was half a dozen of them, one of which was easily more than eight feet tall, with hulking arms and legs. It wielded a spiked flail and wore a strange helmet made of crudely stitched leather and bones. If its size didn't indicate it was the boss, the stupid hat certainly did.

Two of the raveners split from the group to pursue Sish, while the others turned toward the barbarian and trader as they came onto the bridge. The thief didn't have time to see the barbarian do his thing, but the sound of steel ringing and screams of pain told him the man had wasted no time.

Sish darted onto a dirt path on the far side of the bridge, penknife in hand. His feet hurt like hell, and his sole kill felt like luck. Two raveners tailed him now, one with a club and the other with bare but clawed hands. Even ill-equipped, they were more than a match for him. He scanned the path and gnarled brush around him for something—anything—that would give him the upper hand. The best he found was a collection of stones on a small outcropping. He scooped half a dozen of them into his hands and started pelting the creatures with rocks. His aim was terrible. All it did was cost him time.

On the bridge, Terry made short work of most of the raveners and was dodging the heavy swipes of the big one's flail. The barbarian slipped around the spiked head of the creature's weapon with ease, but the flail crashed into the bridge deck each time, scattering chunks of granite in every direction.

Fulk ducked around the barbarian and sprinted toward Sish, stick in hand. The old trader was the thief's best chance for survival.

Sish leaped around the raveners as they climbed up the steep path toward him and landed hard on the ground near the base of the bridge. Fulk was already there. The trader hefted the stick and launched it like a javelin at the creatures, spearing one in the chest. He leaped on top of it and drove the stick further, his boots pressed on its sternum and neck as it wailed in agony beneath the trader's wiry frame.

The remaining ravener charged toward Sish, swinging its club at the thief, who dodged around it easily. He lunged forward with the penknife, but the club caught him in the ribs on the backswing, pushing the air out of his lungs. He fell onto the path sucking air, the ravener's club raised above its head to finish the job. But Fulk was there, stabbing the ravener in the chest with a bloodied stick-spear and kicked it off the bridge, where it landed in the water and sank with a gurgle.

The trader stuck out his hand and helped the thief to his feet.

"Father never taught you to fight?" Fulk asked.

"Not in his repertoire," Sish replied.

The two turned toward Terry, who was battling the large ravener on the bridge. The creature swung the flail again. This time, it collided with the granite railing and lodged itself in the stone. Terry placed his foot on it and used it as a lever to leap at the monstrous creature, sword raised above his head as he catapulted through the air. The sword cleaved the ravener's skull in two, and the creature dropped off the bridge into the water below. The barbarian landed easily on the far side of the gap and walked toward the two men, shaking the blood from his blade.

"Not exactly as planned, but it'll do," he said.

"We probably woke everything up doing it," Fulk said, scanning the twisted, dead forest near the base of the bridge for any signs of movement. "We better get a move on,"

"Where are we going?"

"Sixth Highness, Fourteenth Promontory," Sish cut in, recalling Ruddlefunt's words.

"What?" Fulk asked.

"Something the dwarf said. That's where the Wealth is kept," Sish said. "Sixth Highness, somewhere up above, Fourteenth Promontory."

"That could be anywhere," Terry groaned.

Fulk nodded. "We need a map or an indication of some type."

Sish pointed to where they had entered the valley. "That was the Fifty-Sixth Promontory on the Second Highness, the dwarf said."

"That doesn't make this any less confusing," Fulk said.

Terry scanned the valley around them, his sword resting on one shoulder like a woodcutter's axe. "I've seen a lot of dungeons in my day, and not once was the treasure located near the entrance," he said. "I bet if we head to the exact opposite side of the valley, we'll be close."

Sish's eyes widened, and his feet suddenly ached. "That's a long walk," he said.

Terry shrugged.

Fulk spat, an impatient crease marring his forehead. He considered it a moment and then said, "There's nothing for it. We go on or we die—the barbarian's suggestion is as good as any."

Without waiting for agreement, the trader marched away up the hill. Sish shared an uncertain look with Terry, knowing Fulk was just as committed to his goal as he had been the moment he set foot inside Roan. For the moment, Sish was confident the three of them could work together to survive the valley, but each of them wanted something different.

Terry trudged after Fulk, sheathing his broadsword as he paced behind the older man, leaving Sish alone at the bottom of the hill, just steps from a dead pack of raveners, and no shortage of peelers nearby. He knew the partnership among the three men was, at best, temporary, if it could even be called that. Terry wasn't the type to stab him in the back, and he didn't think Fulk was either … more of a stab-you-in-the-front kind of guy. He would stick with them for now, if for no other reason than he had a better chance of staying alive that way.

However, another feeling gnawed at the back of his mind that he couldn't quite articulate, the way you forget a word but know the right letters are on your tongue. Maybe it was the lack of food, the constant near-death experiences, or the stinging cuts on his feet, but Sish was … tired, tired of always looking over his shoulder, thinking that everyone was waiting to plunge a knife into his back. He was tired of holding that all in until he found himself at a place where he had no one.

His life had been unexpectedly saved on the last day. Twice, by men he had no reason to trust except that they'd done that for him. Neither of them had, too. And it didn't mean he suddenly trusted them, but the speed with which he walked up the hill to catch up with Terry and Fulk was not nothing either.

Chapter Twenty-Two

SHHHH, WHEN YOU'RE IN THE LIBRARY

WINCOTT SLID TO A STOP on the cool marble floor beside Liv, his arms wrapped around the dwarf, who was lost in a tangle of dirty red robes. The statue room's massive iron-banded doors clattered like storm shutters behind them. As the dust settled, the old thief wiggled his fingers and toes to make sure everything still worked. He shifted the dwarf off his chest and sat up. The stone goblin and his seven petrified guards stared down at him from their perches, seemingly unperturbed by the cobra-headed colossus that had ripped part of the cavern down and destroyed the promontory moments before.

Sish. Had the boy survived the rockfall?

Wincott ambled to his feet and tugged on his beard as he approached the great doors. He pulled one open to find a scrap of rock ledge that extended a foot or two from the doors down a sheer cliff to the bottom of the twisted, brown valley. The promontory was gone, and there was no way to get to what remained of the path that led down. And there was no sign of Sish or the others.

Wincott's heart thumped. Had the kid bitten it?

He pushed the thought from his mind. He scanned the valley below, but it was impossible to see through the thick canopy of twisted trees. Finesse and focus were not Sish's strengths, but the kid always had luck on his side, as if the gods at times intervened on his behalf. Wincott had to assume the young thief was at the bottom of that valley somewhere.

And likely already up and after the treasure, too.

"Shit," Wincott swore. "He's going to have a head start."

Wincott wiped the grime from his brow and considered how a simple job for the Guild had turned into this mess. He'd taken the work to keep from starving; there simply weren't many jobs left for him in Fort Rivers. All those bridges had been burned. Decades of bad decisions and associating with the wrong types. That left one client, one he didn't relish getting back into bed with. But a man has to keep a roof over his head.

The Guild paid him to chart a route into Roan, map it, and turn it over to the Guild traders at the Yellowhead Cache. The trip to Fort Shatterstill was a side hustle slid into the journey upon hearing a rumor that the vault there had been abandoned with its goods intact when the E&E fled years ago. Had he gone straight to Roan, he might have beat Sish to the entrance and found the route in on his own, sparing the boy all this.

Then again, the kid had his own reasons for being in Roan, apparently at the E&E's behest. Not for the first time, Wincott wondered why the E&E and Guild were suddenly so interested in a long-abandoned city in a valley neither had paid much attention to before. The Treasure of Roan, whatever it was, whether it even existed, was a high priority it seemed, which sent shivers up his spine. He had a long-held rule never to be interested in anything that the Guild or E&E also were—that's how you wound up at the long end of a noose.

He turned away from the door as Liv helped Ruddlefunt untangle himself from his billowing red robes. The hedge mage glared at the old thief, obviously not pleased to be stuck with him under the present circumstances.

"Are we going to talk about it?" she pressed him.

"About what?"

She sighed. "The fact that it's always your fault. The last time I saw you was shortly before he called off the wedding. I *know* it was you."

Wincott snorted. "Sish makes his own decisions. I had nothing to do with it."

"Right," said Liv, rolling her eyes. "So it was just a coincidence he called it off after you had your falling out. Just like it's a coincidence that you showed up at Roan's front door when he did, three years after you two stopped talking."

Wincott lifted his eyebrows. "Well, yes, it is. An amazing coincidence, I'll admit. Now can we get back to the problem at hand? My boy is in the bottom of that valley, and that snake-thing might be hunting him as we speak."

"Yig," said Ruddlefunt.

"Pffft," snorted Liv. "You don't care one wit about him. Never have. You want that treasure."

Wincott's face grew red. He pointed a finger at her and said, "You're wrong."

The thief turned away from the pointless conversation and searched the room for another doorway or passageway out, anything, really, that might make it easier to get to the valley bottom.

Liv stood still and watched him quietly, her arms crossed.

"They're probably all dead; that *thing* wasn't taking prisoners. We need to seal the cavern off and get out of here," she said.

"Yig," Ruddlefunt said again.

"Flee? Are you kidding?" Wincott questioned her, an incredulous look on his face. He took on a mocking tone. "But I thought you were a *Dungeoneer*—sworn to protect the weak, fight evil, and uphold justice! *Flee*. Are you kidding me?"

"It's the only rational thing to do," she said evenly.

"A wizard would say that," Wincott shot back. "What is it you want to keep hidden down there anyway? Want to keep it just for yourself?"

Liv scoffed, "No, you old fool. The Grand Valley was sealed for a reason. The Wealth isn't some trunk of jewels you can carry out of here and cash in at the market. It's dangerous, and the people who built this city knew it. That's why they protected it and it's been locked away all these centuries. If it gets out ... well, that snake-thing will be the least of our worries."

"Yig."

Wincott and Liv turned toward the dwarf and yelled in unison, "Stop saying that!"

The dwarf's eyes widened in surprise. "Its name ... its name is Yig not *snake-thing*. I see the people of the world have grown more crude with time. Perhaps the Masters were wise to seal me in here."

"What's a Yig?" Wincott asked.

Liv stepped toward the dwarf and crouched in front of him, her hands on his shoulders. "Are you ... did I hear you say *Yig?*"

The dwarf nodded. "An ancient guardian. The Masters created it, as they did me. Though I must say, Yig is far more dangerous, so it was logical they sealed him in the city when they left. Others … other guardians were not sealed. The dragon, for one."

Liv nodded and looked at Wincott. "We need to seal the valley. If what he says is true … if Yig or others like it were to get out … nothing could stop them."

"Myrrhmyth," Wincott breathed, nodding slowly.

Ruddlefunt nodded. "Yes, the dragon. You know it?"

"No, no one has seen it in generations. It's said to haunt the mountains east of here, blocking the old trade routes. The Company and the Guild have been trying to expand their territories to the east far longer than I've been alive, but a long time ago, they gave up—most these days say it's because the paths are nonexistent or too rough to make trade profitable. But it's the dragon."

Ruddlefunt looked at him quizzically. "This Company and Guild you mention. I have not heard of them. Do they work for the King?"

"The Erdor and Expanse Trading Company—the *Company*—is owned by the Queen. The Guild is independent—a merchant network formed by former Company men some two hundred years ago before it was taken over by Mordren's royal family," Wincott explained. "How long have you been down here?"

"As I told the candidate, a very long time."

"Candidate?" Liv inquired.

"Yes, the young fellow, tall, a bit gangly, no shoes. What did you call him?"

"Sish," said Wincott. *My son.*

Liv eyed the old thief inquisitively and then turned to the dwarf.

"Why do you call him the candidate?" she asked.

"He successfully traversed the first two trials to gain entry to the Grand Valley of the Lords of Roan. He is now the candidate. If he can traverse the valley safely to the Storeroom, he may access the Wealth."

"And he's the only one?" Wincott pressed.

Ruddlefunt nodded. "Yes, but no candidate has ever survived, and I daresay he likely hasn't either. Yig doesn't crawl out of his cave for nothing. Which reminds me, that girl you brought with you: I've never seen anyone quite able to do what she can do."

"That's because no one has," said Liv, "She's gifted. What we call a summoner."

Ruddlefunt pumped his head knowingly.

Wincott turned to Liv. "I know you want to leave, but if Sish survived and Fulk with him … well, I wouldn't bet against the two of them getting to that treasure. And if they get there, it won't matter if we've sealed the valley from this side."

The wizard nodded, grudgingly. "Fine. We go."

The thief turned to the dwarf. "Is there another way into the valley?"

"Yes," Ruddlefunt said.

He drew a set of large keys on an iron ring from inside his robe and strode across the marble floor of the statue room to the cavern wall. He felt his way along the wall for a moment until he found the spot he was looking for and then inserted a key into a hidden slot and turned it.

The goblin statue twisted in place with a grinding noise and then slid backward, revealing a spiral staircase that descended beneath it into the darkness below.

The dwarf started down the stairs, pausing partway down to look up at the dumbfounded thief and mage.

"Are you coming?"

THE GLOOM AT THE TOP of the stairs became a suffocating darkness as they worked their way down, spiral after spiral. Wincott could only hear the metal tapping of Ruddlefunt's feet on the stairs below him to indicate that there were in fact more stairs ahead as he felt his way through the pitch-black, his left hand white, knuckling a cold iron railing thick with dust.

Occasionally, he felt Liv's hand brush over his shoulder, making sure he was still there. He stuck his arm out once and touched the cavern wall. It seemed the staircase had been bored out of a vertical shaft. As they made their way down, a faint breeze tussled his hair and a smell like … musty books filled his nose.

Just as Wincott's knees began to ache, the dwarf told them to be careful.

"This next part can be a bit disorienting," he said.

Wincott wasn't sure what that meant, but a moment later, he found out and nearly toppled over the railing to his death. Instead, he crouched and pasted his body against the stairs as an overwhelming wave of vertigo washed over him.

The pitch-black tunnel opened into a gargantuan cavern beneath them that stretched away into the darkness in every direction. It was so large that everything looked miniature, as if he were looking down upon a colossal dollhouse.

The spiral stairs were little more than a thin cylinder of structure that plunged from the cavern ceiling to a dozen or more levels below, each lined with impossibly high bookcases and an intricate series of ladders and platforms between them for access. The ceiling glowed with the pale blue luminescence they'd first noticed at Fulk's camp, casting a ghostly light over book stacks, tables, chairs, and artwork below. The sheer scale of the room was like nothing Wincott could have ever imagined. It was a library, with more books, scrolls, and precious artwork than he ever thought had been produced.

"There must be ..." Liv said breathlessly, her eyes filled with wonder.

"Millions," Wincott finished. "How is this possible?"

Ruddlefunt smiled in satisfaction. "The Masters were committed to the idea that all knowledge and creativity should be preserved for future generations, and so, the Library of Roan was built."

Wincott sniffed. The decay of old paper cloyed his nose.

"And it's protected from the valley?"

"No, the corruption exists here, too. Look at the platforms ... closely." Ruddlefunt stopped on the stairs and pointed.

An open corridor bathed in indigo light stretched away before them, either side lined with large bookcases, interspersed by old fabric chairs covered in cobwebs and dust. Wincott didn't see anything ... and then, the shadows shifted near one of the bookcases, as if it were made of greasy smoke. There, he spotted something in the dark—a robed figure with an octopus head and short tentacles extending from its mouth, lapping melodically at the inky darkness around it.

"Mindflayer," Wincott breathed.

Ruddlefunt pumped his head. "The Librarian doesn't go looking for books anymore. There are several of them hereabouts. Careful."

"And where is this Librarian? I'd like to meet her," Liv asked.

"I am the Librarian," Ruddlefunt said proudly.

They continued down the spiraling stairs until Wincott's legs burned from the stress on his knees and hips. They slipped past a dozen or more floors, stopping twice to let mindflayers glide silently by, hoping to go unnoticed amid the gloom.

By the time they reached the bottom, Wincott was out of breath and his knees ached something awful. There was a plush set of oak Chesterfields he found nearby, clearing the cobwebs with his hands so he could stretch out on one. He feared if he closed his eyes, he might never wake—he was so exhausted—but it was the first bit of comfort he'd enjoyed in weeks, mindflayers be damned.

Liv wandered to the closest bookshelf and thumbed through several titles.

"I can't understand the language in most of these. What are they?" she asked.

"That is an old-world language," Ruddlefunt said. "It's been millennia since anyone spoke it, but we've preserved the volumes and codices necessary to translate it all the same."

"Is there anyone else here ... you know, to help you?"

Ruddlefunt sighed. "There was once. But they all ... they died some time ago." He rubbed reflexively at the burned flesh on his forehead, the metal plates beneath it scratched and charred. "It's been me ever since."

"Do you ever get lonely?" she asked.

"I'm not programmed to experience what you would call loneliness," he said. "But I do miss conversation. The candidate was the first person I've spoken with in more than two hundred years, by my count."

Wincott turned his head and studied the dwarf. Ruddlefunt's blue eyes were a dead giveaway that he was a blue-eyed one, also known as a Warden, but the thief had never come across one quite like him. Wardens generally appeared like any other person, except their eyes glowed blue in the dark. In fact, that was the only way to tell them apart from any other person, other than their vicious behavior.

The Company and Guild strictly avoided them as they were considered incredibly dangerous and aggressive. Just as intelligent as humans, Wardens were faster, stronger, and trained to fight. They each claimed to be a protector of Erdor, but it was never clear who or what they were protecting it from. Typically, they traveled alone, but Wincott witnessed small bands of Wardens grouping together at times, though they seemed to avoid towns and cities altogether, preferring the wilderness.

What made Ruddlefunt different was that he was a dwarf and had a metal skeleton beneath his skin. He looked … he looked like something made in a factory.

"Ruddlefunt, are you a Warden?"

"I'm not familiar with that term," he said.

Wincott thought carefully, sat up, and leaned toward him. Perhaps he needed to be more direct. "Your blue eyes, metal skeleton, you're not like us. What are you?"

"I am a Grade Four Expositive Sentinel. For the purposes of this city, the Librarian," the dwarf said simply. "I was manufactured elsewhere, though, if that's what you were asking. I am not organic like you, but rather, an artificial lifeform."

"Artificial?" Liv said with a gasp.

"Yes, there were many like me once, but I believe I am the last. Later versions were organic, like you."

"Was this city filled with ones like you?" Wincott asked.

"Yes," Ruddlefunt answered. "The Masters programmed our size, characteristics, and abilities to match a life spent primarily underground. Your people would call us dwarfs, a silly name that stems from old-world stories, though I will concede it is rather apt."

"What were the instructions the Masters gave you regarding the candidate and the Grand Valley?" Liv probed.

"The Masters did not provide any instructions other than to welcome the candidate to the valley and provide a way to the Upper City should the candidate wish to do so, though no one ever has," Ruddlefunt said.

"And that was it?"

"Well, no," Ruddlefunt said, looking a little sheepish. "I was also informed that once a candidate entered the valley, it would be impossible for them to leave it alive."

Wincott sprang to his feet. "The third trial."

Ruddlefunt nodded quietly.

Liv looked at the dwarf and then at Wincott. "Third trial? What do you mean?"

Wincott tugged on his wiry beard, his eyes darkening. "I should've known. Fulk had assembled a cheat sheet on the city—what he thought was a way in, but it was a trick. He had three words: pressure, allegiance, and insight. They were translations, and I bet that's not what they mean, is it Ruddlefunt?"

"You are correct. The correct translation is perseverance, loyalty, and wisdom. The third trial is a choice."

"Of course," Wincott said knowingly. "And since you opened the way to the Upper City, the choice was a simple one—turn back or keep going, but if Sish kept going ..."

"He will be executed," Ruddlefunt finished. "Like all the candidates before him."

Chapter Twenty-Three

TRADER IN A BOTTLE

THE KID DROVE WINCOTT BATTY. He wanted constant attention, something to eat or to play. Even after all three were done, Wincott was lucky to find twenty minutes to himself before Sish started up again: he was bored, or something was scary, or he was hungry again. If he left for work, it was even worse. Wincott was guaranteed to come home to a mess, plus, the kid was hungry, bored, and he'd probably broken something while Wincott was gone, or the landlady downstairs, Ms. Burbidge, would complain about all the racket.

Of course, that was before Sish figured out how to escape the flat. Once that happened, the kid got up to all manner of trouble—nicking pastries from the bakery, chasing cats, throwing rocks at well-dressed people. Wincott caught him tailing the thief to work and had to drag him back to the flat by his ear.

One truth he couldn't get away from was that he wasn't the kid's father, despite what he told everybody, Ms. Burbidge included. She had a thing about morals, so he told her he married the boy's mother and came to the city to find work after she passed away. A tragic tale that was … partially true, like all the best lies, not that he was very good at telling them.

In the six months since they'd arrived in town together, the fact that Wincott wasn't a father figure had become more painfully obvious with each passing day. Finally, he'd decided he simply wasn't cut out for the job, and that, in his opinion, the boy would be better off with someone else. And that someone else was his real father—Fulk Dundurn, deputy chief factor of the E&E at Fort Rivers—a real son of a bitch, if reputation held.

Wincott told himself it was the right thing to do. How could a thief raise a boy anyway? He'd starve to death or end up dead. Certainly, he wasn't any shining example of moral high ground, which he understood as being an important part of being a parent. Fulk, on the other hand? Well, it was said the deputy worshiped every week, started work before sunup and often wasn't done until sunset, and was firm but fair with his men. There was a whole bunch of other tall tales about him doing battle with creatures in the wild, defending bosomed women in distress, and generally being everything that Wincott was not, though the thief had been alive long enough not to believe half of them, though he found them just as entertaining as anyone else. But as far as father figures go? He was certain Fulk was the better man.

The Company's territorial headquarters were in a building known as Rivers Factory, a broad, whitewashed three-story wooden structure that sat atop a large hill in the middle of town, affording it a 360-degree view of the bustling trading enclave. Rivers Factory was surrounded by a series of palisade walls that protected it from invasion. Through the main gate was the headquarters building, several warehouses, trader bunkhouses, stables, a blacksmith, a pub, and a water tower.

When he told the guards at the various gates that provided entrance to Rivers Factory that he had a meeting with the deputy chief, they let him pass without issue. If he'd known it were that easy to get into the factory, he would've robbed the place blind years ago.

Of course, he didn't have an appointment with the deputy chief; he'd only recently heard the man was back in town following a lengthy trade mission into the uncharted northwest and so decided it was now or never. He didn't even know what he would say, hoping the words would come to him when the time was right. And that the man would receive them well. That last part was important, because it had also crossed his mind that he might just as easily be clapped in irons for his effort.

At the headquarters building, a servant in red and white livery ushered him into the main hall, which was lavishly furnished in hand-carved cedar furniture and the walls lined with oil paintings. The pictures depicted traders on the so-called frontier, hauling their goods through dense forest, trading with locals, battling strange creatures.

The servant raised a set of bushy eyebrows at the thief, as if doubting the man had any legitimate business inside the fort. Wincott explained who he was there to see. The man's eyes widened, as if it brought him no pleasure to call on the deputy chief, before he beetled down a long hallway, leaving Wincott alone to consider what he'd say.

Servants, traders, and officials strode past him without a second look as he loitered in the main hall. The only sound was the steady tick of a grandfather clock that had obviously been imported to Erdor at great expense.

A few minutes passed, and he began to inspect the art and decorations, almost breaking a miniature porcelain canoe that had been turned into a candy dish. After a half hour, he decided he'd been entirely forgotten about. A wave of excitement stirred in his belly as he considered the sudden and unexpected opportunity to purloin one or two things.

A long, wide corridor lined with rich carpets led him further into the fort's main building. To his right, a steady series of tall, narrow windows afforded a view of the courtyard, where a group of soldiers practiced drill to the harsh report of a whistle. To his left were smaller hallways with offices branching from them. And above his head, as regular as the windows, were luxuriant silver and gold chandeliers heavy with dried candle wax.

A red-coated servant appeared from a hallway to his left, his arms overloaded with books and letters to the point that he didn't even notice the thief standing near him. The man shuffled away quickly, his attention focused on not dropping anything, allowing Wincott to duck into the corridor and poke his head into several of the offices.

They were all empty. The first was a shared office with several desks. Across from it was a storeroom of some kind, and a little further on, he found a small library, and across from that, a different sort of storeroom with shelves bursting with artifacts.

Wincott slipped inside and gently latched the door behind him. The room was windowless, but a small desk lamp afforded a flickering amber glow. He carried the lamp and strolled between the shelves, inspecting the strange items stored there.

There were wands, ornately inlaid daggers, a hatchet that was frozen to the touch and the shelf it lay on, from the look of it. A great floppy cattleman's hat decorated in wolverine claws stood out on a shelf above him. Next to that was an eyepatch made of a strange black stone with a small hole in the center of it, and beside that was a series of books wrapped in what Wincott guessed was human flesh.

He pulled one off the shelf and opened it. An immediate pressure like someone had pumped twice as much air into the room as it could handle froze him in place, and then, pain vibrated behind his eyes as he scanned the strange, almost violent, black scrawling etched onto each page. He slammed the book shut and put it back on the shelf, wiping his eyes involuntarily.

Next, he lifted an intricately crafted miniature toy trader in a bottle off the shelf and held it in his hands. The figurine was held inside a glass bottle, like a ship-in-a-bottle, but someone had turned the inside of the bottle into a diorama of a campsite, complete with cedar trees, grass, tent, and a small, flickering campfire. Wincott guessed it was enchanted because the flames looked to be truly burning.

The hunter was fast asleep against a log next to the fire, a wide-brimmed hat pulled down over his face. Wincott withdrew the cork from the bottle, and the hunter sprang awake, leaping to his feet, bowie knife in hand. The miniature hunter turned toward Wincott, spotting the giant through the glass, and yelled at him.

"Hey! You! Let me out of here. I'm trapped!" the trader pleaded, his voice tiny and high-pitched, almost like listening to a mouse talk, if mice could talk.

Wincott replaced the cork and returned the trader and his campsite to the shelf, walking away. As he neared the far wall of the storeroom, he heard muffled voices talking heatedly on the other side of the wall.

He pressed his ear against the cedar finishing and heard two men. Above him was an air vent. He dragged a stool to it and ambled up, pressing his ear against the vent.

"Well, I don't care what they want—they don't make the decision. I make the decision," a throaty voice argued.

"Yes, sir, but ..."

"But what?"

"There are too many injuries, sir, and it's causing unrest among the ranks," a smaller voice explained.

"Unrest? We'll stamp it down. Why do you think I carry this belaying pin? Unrest is a symptom of men with too much time on their hands. What they need is more work."

"But it's not the work that's the issue, sir; it's the toll on the children. They were only ever meant to be a stop-gap workforce to keep the mines running until more men arrived. It's been three years, and we've lost half of them to—"

"I *know* what we've lost them to, and it's because our soldiers were lazy and didn't listen to my instructions. The mines need to keep running, and we don't yet have the manpower to relieve those boys," the heavy voice replied.

"But, sir, the conditions are worsening, and if we leave them in there we'll … I'm afraid most won't survive."

"That's the cost of doing business, Langan," the heavy voice explained. "Most of those boys are orphans anyway, the result of a whore rutting with a tradesman out of wedlock. We could do with a few less of *those* types running around."

The conversation ended, and Wincott climbed down from the stool. He wasn't surprised by what he'd heard. The Company put on a good face in the public as the main source of work for most of Fort Rivers, but behind the scenes, they were as ruthless as their counterparts at the Guild, interested only in wealth and power.

He departed the storeroom and wandered back to the main hall. A moment later, the red-coated servant he'd talked to earlier came back and informed him that the deputy chief would be with him shortly. The man then slipped away like a shadow.

Fulk Dundurn strode into the main hall a moment later. Wincott had heard of him but never laid eyes on him. He was bald, with deep-set dark eyes, a small, wiry frame, and he wore a blue and white overcoat with gold buttons, black trousers, and a button-up shirt. He looked every ounce the stern Company man Wincott had expected.

He walked to Wincott and took in the thief with a barely contained sneer. "Yes? What is it?"

Wincott recognized the gravelly voice immediately. This was the man he'd been listening to through the wall. His stomach churned. The thought of handing Sish to him made him sick. He'd wandered up to Rivers Factory absolutely convinced it was the right thing to do but suddenly found himself unable to go through with it. Images of Sish toiling away in the mines, the conditions eventually killing him, made his stomach churn and the skin on the back of his neck turn hot with anger. Wincott still didn't think he was cut out to be a father, but he knew enough about being a decent person that you don't knowingly put a child in a situation like that.

"Are you daft, man? I asked you a question—speak up!"

Wincott smiled through thin lips and told a lie.

"Yes, sir, I was told by Mr. Gravely to come up here and inform you that a shipment of goblin skins has been returned due to spoiling on the river. The shipper is at the dock now if you wish to speak with him."

"Spoiled? That's ludicrous. The Company's products are packed to the highest standard in the world, and those goblin skins will fetch a pretty price in the southern markets," Fulk protested. "You tell this … Mr. Gravely to stay where he is. I'd like to have a word with him.."

Fulk spun on his heel and strode away without so much as a goodbye. Boy, would he be pissed when he walked all the way down to the docks only to find out there was no shipment of goblin skins. Wincott chuckled to himself as he walked out of the main hall into the courtyard.

The trip to the deputy chief hadn't yielded the results he'd hoped for, but it hadn't been a complete loss either. At least he'd been able to inflict some frustration on the man—it was a small win but felt like an important one. That and he'd purloined the trader in the bottle. Wincott patted his coat pocket, where the glass was safely stored. He'd fetch a few coins for it at the enchanter's market, enough to keep food on the table for a while yet to come. But first, he'd show it to the kid. He might even tell him how he came across it.

Chapter Twenty-Four

ONE CORPSE'S GARBAGE IS ANOTHER MAN'S...

THE GRAND VALLEY DIDN'T LIVE up to its name at ground level. Ruddlefunt led them through a series of doors and passageways that connected the library to the valley through the cavern wall. They emerged into a meadow of rotting thistles, limp fireweed, and prickly grass. Ahead of them was a forest so thick with tangled, naked branches that it was impossible to see more than a few feet inside it. And there was no way around it.

"Ruddlefunt, I don't suppose you know a safe route through the valley?" Wincott quizzed him.

"There isn't one," Ruddlefunt said.

Liv tapped her staff against the ground and shrugged. "Well, no time like the present."

Wincott nodded and followed her into the forest. Ruddlefunt didn't move.

"Coming?" she asked.

"I'm the Librarian, I'm not sure …" he trailed off.

"Well, you're free to stay, but I suspect your librarian knowledge might come in handy. Plus, stick with us and we can promise lots more interesting conversations," said Liv.

The dwarf perked up and ran over to join them.

"I don't suppose you have any weapons we might use?" Wincott asked. "I'm not sure that staff will be enough to get us across the valley."

Ruddlefunt put a finger to his chin and said, "No, but if I recall, Vik Tar Regare died not far from here, and we may be able to recover his belongings, assuming they weren't already taken. Would that help?"

The thief stared at him evenly. "That would help."

THERE WAS NO PATH THROUGH the forest, but the sheer number of bare branches and dead trees meant they could chart their own course. Yet it was slow going, bending back branches to pass between thick trunks and ducking around razor-leafed holly and gigantic bristly thistles. That wasn't too bad, all things considered. The real problem was keeping their eyes peeled for dangers.

Ruddlefunt was helpful in that regard. The dwarf was able to point out deadfall pits, leaf beds crawling with venomous cockroaches, and more than one Methuro spider poised above their heads. It made Wincott wonder why none of the previous candidates ever bothered to ask the dwarf for help or directions; perhaps one of them may have had a different outcome then.

"They didn't see value in it, I suppose," Ruddlefunt mused when asked.

Although there was no sun to speak of in the Grand Valley, there was a perpetual gray light that drifted in from the cavern above. The openings led him to believe there was a way out onto the snow-laden valley above, but if that were the case, why hadn't the corruption spread to the broader world beyond Roan?

They took a break at a small creek that ran through the forest at what felt like midday, though it was impossible to tell. Wincott was sweaty from all the walking, and even Liv looked a bit worse for wear. The dwarf showed no signs of fatigue.

"I guess you don't get tired, do you?" Wincott asked him.

"No, sleep is not a necessary function," he said.

"I wish," Liv groaned.

She pulled off the heavy green cloak she wore and hung it on her staff against a tree. Beneath, she wore fitted black leather pants and a vest over a loose blouse, and he was suddenly self-conscious about the loose black shirt he'd pulled from a knapsack on the other side of the Keyhole. Probably a dead man's shirt, come to think of it.

He turned his attention to several baubles that hung from a key ring on her belt.

"What are those?" he asked.

"Tools of the trade," she smirked.

"Going to turn me into a chicken?" he teased.

Hands on her hips, she fixed him with a tired stare. "You never had much patience for magic."

"I have a lot of patience, just not much in the way of trust," he said. "I've met more than a few of your kind in my years and never one that I could rely on."

"And you're trustworthy?" She eyed him.

"As far as thieves go, yes," he said, straight-faced, rolling up the loose-fitting sleeves of his shirt. Despite the sad gray light and gnarled trees, the air was hot and moist like a jungle, and he was covered in a thin sheen of sweat.

She smirked and shook her head. "You know, I still don't know why you did it."

Wincott hesitated. He had good reason not to trust Liv, but more than that, she was wrong for Sish. The boy was too young to settle down and have kids; he could barely fend for himself. Wincott had watched her tease Sish for years, then draw in his affections, and rope him into getting engaged.

"You weren't right for one another," he said after a minute. "You Dungeoneers ... you're all ... Sish wouldn't ... shit, I don't know. I just know the boy, and I know it wouldn't have worked."

"And it's your place to decide that?"

"I'm his father," Wincott said, though that reasoning felt less relevant as time went on.

"He loved you, you know," Liv said, her voice softening. "I'm not even sure he truly loved me in the end. The idea of me, maybe. But you? Everything that he is because of you. Strange as it may sound, he was proud of that. And you showed him that what he thought, what he wanted didn't matter."

"Enough," Wincott snapped angrily.

Liv pursed her lips and turned away from him.

"Where to, Ruddlefunt?"

"The Second Highness, Fifty-Sixth Promontory," the dwarf said, pointing to the far end of the valley, beyond a long, black lake that stretched ahead of them. "As well, I believe it was right around here that … yes! Here it is."

The dwarf bent and cleared a bed of blackened leaves to reveal a skeleton. The bones were clad in rotten clothing and a rusted set of armor and helm. Ruddlefunt lifted the visor on the helm to reveal a skull, darkened with time and rot. A dusty but ornately crafted scabbard clung to the skeleton's belt, a sword still in it.

The dwarf unclipped the scabbard and handed it to Wincott. The thief rubbed the grime from the sheath to reveal purple scrollwork inscribed down its length. The pommel of the sword was made of amethyst that glittered in the low light. He drew the weapon to reveal a long, thin but slightly curved blade that was still sharp to the touch and free of rust, despite the obvious years it had lain beside the decaying corpse of its former owner.

"The weapon of the celebrated swordsman Vik Tar Regare," Ruddlefunt said, a bit of awe creeping into his voice. "I believe he named it Raspberry."

Wincott turned the weapon over in his hand. It was lighter than it looked but solid and felt natural to him. Perhaps he wasn't as good a swordsman as Regare had been, but he felt more confident having it at his side than walking around a murderous valley with nothing but his wits and bare hands.

"Raspberry?" Liv asked.

"Yes, he had a peculiar sense of humor, I recall. Before he descended into the valley to meet his doom, we had a long conversation. Well, he spoke, and I listened, and the strangest thing about it was he just told jokes. One after another. Imagine that?"

"How did he die?" Liv asked.

"The Pelican of Sitka surprised him, and his heart gave out," Ruddlefunt said.

"Guess the bird got the last laugh," Wincott remarked, chuckling lightly to himself. He was pleased with that one. Buckling the sword at his side, he said, "Shall we go?"

THEY REACHED THE LAKESIDE THAT evening. Wincott's legs were ready to give out, but he was thankful the dwarf had navigated them along a route that let them avoid the worst of the valley's horrors so far.

There was a small dock at the water's edge with a rowboat tied to it. The lake was long, narrow, and calm as glass. The thief didn't like the look of it, and the decision over which route to take quickly turned into an argument with Liv.

"The lake will be faster. If Fulk has already reached the far end, it may be too late. We must move quickly," Liv argued.

Wincott held his hands up to calm her. "I get that. But the last time I was on a lake in this city, there was a giant octopus in it that nearly killed all of us. I say we walk around. They can't be that far ahead of us."

"Dragorath," Ruddlefunt said.

They looked at him and nodded.

"Fine. Dragorath almost killed us," Wincott said. "Lord knows what's in that water, but it's probably worse."

"Let's ask the Librarian," Liv said. "What's in the water?"

"Well—"

A raucous chorus of jabbering voices cut the dwarf off. Wincott turned and spotted a dozen short, black figures running toward them, several holding torches and brandishing weapons. There was a single goblin in the lead, and Wincott immediately recognized the weapon in its hand—a meat cleaver.

"Goblins," he said. "Persistent ones."

"You know these goblins?"

"They've been chasing me since I killed their chieftain at Shatterstill. I thought they drowned in the Upper City, but I guess I wasn't so lucky," Wincott said.

Liv offered a wry smile. "What is it you used to always lecture Sish about? Finesse, focus and … what was the third?"

Wincott fixed her with a glare. "The third was something I appear to be short on these days. We better get moving."

"The boat then," Liv urged. "It's the only way to put any space between them and us."

Wincott cursed beneath his breath and agreed. The goblins were close, and he swore he saw a gleam of manic satisfaction in

Meat Cleaver's eyes as the goblin sprinted through the tall, brown grass toward them. The thief lifted Ruddlefunt under one arm and followed Liv to the dock.

170

Meat Cleaver's eyes as the goblin sprinted through the tall, brown grass toward them. The thief lifted Ruddlefunt under one arm and followed Liv to the dock.

Chapter Twenty-Five

ILL-CONCEIVED TRAPS AND BAD LUCK

Terry spotted Kai and Rena before the others. The burly goon had tied and gagged the girl and carried her over his shoulder in a crude net he must've found in the valley bottom. He was half a mile or so ahead of them, hiking along a ridgeline that ran parallel to a long, black lake.

"Is she alive?" Sish asked.

"Yes," Terry said.

"How do you know?"

Fulk chimed in, "Because why would he bother to carry a dead kid in a net all that way?"

"Maybe he wants to eat her. Could be a cannibal."

"He's not a cannibal," Fulk said. "An asshole, yes, but not a cannibal."

"We must move faster," the barbarian said, ready to sprint after Kai.

"Hold on," Fulk said, laying a hand on the big man's shoulder. "He's more dangerous than he looks. Kai sailed with Captain Reeve along the Outer Coast; he knows his way around a blade."

Terry scoffed, "No match for me."

Fulk wasn't convinced. "Careful. I hired that man for a reason, and though I now regret that decision, I'm confident in saying he's a problem we can't overcome through sheer brawn. We need to outthink him."

"And how do you propose we do that?" Sish asked.

Fulk thought for a moment and then surveyed the landscape. Sish noticed the ridge Kai hiked along had several undulations and low points, spots that would be perfect for an ambush. He was also easily visible.

"We get ahead of him," Fulk said. "Set a trap."

"And Rena?"

Fulk nodded. "She's important. We'll make sure she's unharmed."

THE FIRST TRAP WAS A sure thing, Fulk told them. The trio followed the trader's lead and ran parallel to Kai's route to get well ahead of the mercenary, cutting into the forest once he was well behind them to find a spot to lay a trap. They quickly located the narrow, root-laced path that twisted among the conifers toward the far side of the valley, guessing they had not more than a half hour before the big man would be on them. At one of the low points, between two rocky outcroppings that shouldered the route, Fulk instructed them to dig a hole.

Terry hesitated a moment, not a fan of taking orders from a man who just recently had been their adversary. But after a moment, he nodded quietly and went to work, no doubt deciding the enemy of his enemy was something close to an ally for the time being.

"How deep?" Sish asked.

"Deep enough to slow him down," Fulk answered, not bothering to look up as he combed through the leaves and brush for loose branches.

Terry and Sish worked like dogs to get it as deep as possible while the trader kept a nervous watch and sharpened each end of the branches he found. When it was four feet deep, Fulk dropped into it and drove stakes into the ground to create a hasty-but-nasty-looking deadfall.

"We agreed she wouldn't be hurt," Terry challenged him, puffing out his chest.

Fulk met his gaze and offered a half grin as though he were talking with a simpleton. "She'll be fine. We need to hide."

They hastily covered it with thin branches and leaves and then hid themselves and rehearsed the crude plan: the mercenary would stumble in, gore one or both of his legs, immobilizing him. Then Terry would swoop in, cut off his head, and Sish would rescue the girl. Sish wasn't much of a planner, more of a by-the-seat-of-your-pants kind of guy, so he wasn't in any position to voice doubts, though he had some.

They heard Kai coming from several hundred yards away. The big man clearly wasn't worried about the creatures in the valley because Sish could hear him whistling lumberjack tunes as he strode along the wooded ridge toward them. As he neared the deadfall, a squirrel ran across the path in front of him, directly over the deadfall, and collapsed it. The creature tumbled into the hole with a squeak. Kai stopped, looking at the sprung trap, lifting one dark eyebrow.

"That was close," the big man said to himself.

Terry placed a hand on the pommel of his sword, but Fulk stayed him. The barbarian pinched his lips together in frustration. What the barbarian had in strength, he lacked in patience.

Kai hefted Rena over his shoulder, stepped carefully around the deadfall, and kept walking.

"This will work," Fulk assured them sometime later, without an ounce of doubt.

What the trader had in confidence, he lacked in delivery, Sish thought.

The second trap was slightly more complex. The trio sprinted ahead of Kai again, lucky to have not alerted him as they weaved through the naked, dead trees in the silent forest. Along the way, the barbarian pointed out a large pelican atop a spindly needle-less spruce a quarter mile further.

Sish regurgitated what Ruddlefunt had told him, that it was likely the same pelican (how many could there be in an underground valley?) that scared a swordsman to death. The pelican happened to be in a tree directly in front of Kai's path—the plan was to hit it with a rock just as Kai came near it. The bird would shriek, and the mercenary would be momentarily stunned, allowing Terry to move in and cut his head off and Fulk to rescue Rena. Admittedly, the plan had some obvious flaws, but neither Sish nor Terry could come up with anything better, so they agreed to it.

The bird was massive, three or four times the size of an average pelican, with dirty gray feathers and a long, flaming red beak. Kai continued a jaunty whistle as he came over the rise, Rena thrown over his shoulder like a sack of potatoes. Sish was selected to be the human atlatl. He found a mostly round hunk of granite slightly smaller than his fist among a matt of blackened leaves.

"Don't miss," Fulk told him as the thief drew back his arm.

Sish paused. "No shit," he said, looking at the trader.

He threw the rock and hit the pelican square in the head. The bird groaned and fell out of the tree, collapsing dead on the path at Kai's feet.

The mercenary halted his rhapsodic lumberman's tune, shifted Rena to his other shoulder (the girl was awake and looked bored), and gave the dead bird a nudge with his foot. He bellowed a great laugh and carried on.

The third trap was Sish's idea, or that's what he led everyone to believe. They needed to get Kai to drop the sack, freeing the girl to immobilize him herself, which would give Terry time to cut his head off. Sish wasn't fussed about whether Terry killed him with a stab wound, a slash, or a decapitation, but the barbarian insisted it be the latter. Fulk only listened and nodded, obviously unhappy that his first two attempts had been duds.

The plan was this: Terry would step out in front of Kai and challenge him to a fight, forcing the mercenary to put Rena down. Sish would sneak out, free Rena, and the girl would do her thing; Terry would then kill Kai, and they'd all congratulate one another with hearty claps on the back when it was all done. It was simple, and therefore, gave Sish some confidence it would work. Fulk crossed his arms tightly, chewing his lip thoughtfully. He added nothing, and Sish couldn't figure out whether the trader was sore about being left out of the plan or plotting something else altogether.

At the top of a high, scrubby ridgeline bare of trees, Terry stepped onto the path and waited for Kai. Sword drawn, eyes fierce, the barbarian waited. The mercenary strolled into view with the girl several minutes later and greeted the barbarian with a crooked smile. He carefully put down Rena and drew a large belaying pin from his belt.

"I'm going to enjoy this," he said.

The barbarian hefted his sword and charged Kai. They were similar in size. Kai easily dodged Terry's first swipe and struck the barbarian in the ribs with the pin.

Sish jumped onto the path and helped Rena out of the sack. The girl was yelling something, but he couldn't make it out because of the gag in her mouth. Her eyes fixed on something behind the thief. He turned around in time to see Fulk's arm coming down toward him with a rock in his hand.

The trader struck him, knocking Sish to the dirt. The world spun. Bright circles of light flashed in his eyes, and he was unable to get his hands to work to pull himself up. In the distance, Kai and Terry battled. Terry missed another swipe, and Kai hit him with a three-part combo, knocking the barbarian to the forest floor. The barbarian dropped his club and hefted Terry's sword, ready to end the barbarian's life.

Fulk took the penknife from Sish's belt and strode up behind Kai while the mercenary was focused on the barbarian and thrust it into the back of the big man's head. Kai collapsed to his knees and then fell dead to the ground.

The trader marched back to Rena and grabbed the girl. She struggled, screaming with the gag still in her mouth. Fulk slapped her hard, dazing her, and shoved her back into the net Kai had used as a sack to carry her. The trader turned toward Sish and planted a boot in his ribs. He knelt, spat, and watched the thief for a moment.

"Too trusting, boy," Fulk sneered, his voice, like wheels rolling over gravel, reverberating painfully between Sish's ears as the world spun to black.

Chapter Twenty-Six

ROW AT THE TOE

SISH WAS DRUNK BY THE time the music started. The band at the Werewolf's Toe that night were out-of-towners from Fort Ox. He didn't care for the musicians or the fort, having been snowed in there with Wincott once on a Jane that proved to be a waste of time for them both. Even though the drumbeat made his ears feel like they were going to rupture, he wasn't leaving the plum seat he'd scored at the bar, so he ordered another round and settled in.

The Werewolf was shoulder-to-shoulder and smelled of sour beer, sweat, and roast meat soaked into the sawdust that covered the floor. He'd been drinking since noon, which was how he'd been able to score such a good seat on a normally busy night, and he was at least a dozen drinks in. Normally, he enjoyed a crowded bar at the end of a long week but not this time. It had been a long week but not in a good way.

To start, work was hard to come by since the E&E governor ordered the guard to root out all the thieves and grifters around town. So, he was down to pickpocketing to keep food in his mouth, which was fine if not particularly laudable. But a bone-chilling storm had blown in out of the far north and brought with it two feet of snow, sending everyone indoors. Not great conditions for pickpocketing. On top of that, the rent was past due, Sish was penniless, and Wincott had vanished to chase a baggage train to the south on a rumor of a score of jewels.

In truth, though, his run of bad luck wasn't new. Things had been going sideways since he and Wincott had it out over the Dungeoneers. The old man thought it a waste of good talent for Sish to spend his time with a bunch of do-gooders who couldn't turn a profit selling water in a desert.

"We need to pay rent, boy," Wincott would remind him. "And beyond that, get ahead. Tough out there these days; no time to be messin' about with your friends."

With the old man gone south and not enough money to pay Ms. Burbidge, Sish decided to shirk his responsibilities and blow a few pennies down at the pub. Not, strictly speaking, a good idea, he could admit, but it did create opportunities for other things. One thing was the ability to pickpocket the drunks that were stuffed inside the Werewolf's Toe on a cold winter's night.

Sish had already lifted a small coin purse full of coppers and two wallets thanks to well-timed piss breaks. At this rate, he may have enough to pay Ms. Burbidge before the night was out, but he also had to be careful he didn't get too drunk and slip up, or he'd be back in the cells before dawn. Or worse.

The thirteenth pint of ale—or was it the fourteenth? — went down as fast as all the others. The music was blaring by that point, Sish was sweating in his shirt, jacket, and pants, and all the women that an hour before hadn't seemed remotely attractive were suddenly not so bad and might even be worth a drink or two. Certainly, he had enough money to stay in his cups until dawn. So, he ordered more.

An hour later, the pub seemed to be orbiting on its own axis. He entered an arm-wrestling competition he lost several times, managed to convince a couple of girls to dance with him, and even co-sang one of the songs with the band until he was applauded offstage or taken offstage, he wasn't quite sure which. He ordered more drinks.

On a piss break, he snatched a purse and necklace and puked his guts out in the back alley. He got back to his stool, hung his jacket over it so he could cool off, and ordered another drink. By that point, he was confident no one would figure him out, so he relaxed a bit and bought a close-knit group of a dozen strangers around him another round.

More dancing, singing, arm wrestling, and dart throwing ensued, two more piss breaks, and he started to sober up another hour or two later. Or at least he felt more sober than he had been and was finally able to see straight.

That was when Liv walked into the Werewolf, a tall, broad-shouldered man with a dimpled chin holding the door open for her. Sish's stomach sank. He hadn't seen her in months, avoided her, in fact, and not bothered to explain why.

Wincott had made the conditions of Sish's continued tenancy in their flat perfectly clear, and one of them was no longer running around with the Dungeoneers. Not that Sish had joined them to fight evil in the first place—he was interested in the girl. The problem was, he was certain she had no interest in him despite his best efforts.

The man who followed her in was a head taller than Sish, with shoulders that looked armored, and a lean, well-muscled physique beneath a loose-fitting, open-collared white shirt. He was handsome, had a perfect set of white teeth, and oozed confidence. Sish immediately hated him.

The thief sunk into his seat, shoulders hunched, and took a long pull of his ale. He hoped they wouldn't notice him, but that hope was erased when he felt the firm tap of a finger on his shoulder. He turned and found Liv standing there, one hand on her hip, her head cocked sideways as if to say, "Where the hell have you been?"

He flashed what he hoped was a confident grin, but he was still too drunk to know whether he came off the way he pictured or was a sloppy mess. He feared it was the latter but would carry on with the ruse anyway.

"Hi, Liv."

"Don't '*Hi, Liv*' me. Where have you been?"

Her expression darkened, a look Sish was all too familiar with. He wilted like a late summer pansy. He hadn't seen her in half a year, and yet, his heart thumped at the sight of her, his words catching in his throat like a dry cough. His feelings for her hadn't abated one wit. So, he had another drink.

"Around," he finally managed to say, trying to sound casually confident.

The look on her face told him it hadn't worked. A moment later, Liv's handsome companion sidled through the crowd toward them and placed a comforting hand on the small of her back. Sish's stomach twisted.

"This guy giving you trouble, Liv?" the man asked, surveying the thief with his stark blue eyes.

"No, he's … an old friend," Liv said, not moving her eyes from Sish.

The man nodded and extended a meaty hand, Sish shook it reluctantly.

"Davin," the man said. "Davin Faithguard."

He let the name hang in the air, his eyes waiting for a response. Sish said nothing but took another drink, his eyes flashing questioningly at Liv. She shook her head ever so slightly.

Davin let out a perturbed sound. "My friend, it's polite to introduce yourself. What is your name?"

"Sish Torren."

Davin's eyes changed, suggesting he knew who the thief was. Did that mean Liv had talked about him? *Still* talked about him? He wondered.

"The *thief*," Davin said. The last word sounded as if it had left a bad taste in his mouth. "Come on, Liv. Let's find more *agreeable* company."

The man guided her away with a hand on her waist, but she resisted.

"Are you going to explain yourself?" she pressed Sish.

"What's to explain?" the thief said, a dumb look on his face.

"Come on, Liv. He's not worth our time," Davin sneered.

Sish felt hot. His hands grew clammy. The cloying stench of sour beer was suddenly overwhelming. Who did this asshole think he was anyway? And what kind of name was Faithguard? Frankly, it sounded made up or an epithet purchased at the market for a few coins.

"Piss off, pal," Sish said. "This doesn't concern you."

Faithguard's eyes darkened, and several people around them stopped their conversations and turned toward the brewing confrontation. Davin's chest puffed, his back straightening.

"You, sir, have no honor. I invite you to make the same remark to me outside," Davin said, his hand shifting toward the pommel of a sword slung at his waist.

"Outside? Why not just settle it *here*?" Sish said.

Without thinking, the thief balled his right fist and cranked it across Davin's jaw. The big man stumbled backward, his hand going to his mouth where he'd been struck, but he didn't go down. Sish's hand vibrated with pain. There was a chorus of "oohs" from the assembled crowd. Liv yelled something at Sish, but he didn't hear what it was. His blood was up so much it drowned out all sound except the beating of his own heart. He jumped off his stool and took a step toward Davin.

Faithguard smiled wickedly, the look on his face reminding Sish somehow of a cat about to lash out. There was a bit of blood on his lower lip and front teeth, his tongue wiping it away. An image of the man's hand on Liv's waist flashed through his mind once more. He swung again. And missed. It was Davin's turn.

The big man sunk a heavy fist into Sish's gut that felt like being hit with a battering ram. The thief doubled over in time for a second fist to come up under his jaw and snap his head back like an oyster opening to spit up its pearl. His vision blurred. Two heavy hands grabbed him by the shoulders, lifted him up, and threw him across the bar.

Sish landed like a sack of potatoes on the far side of the bar. He expected Davin to be on top of him a moment later, but he wasn't. Through his daze, he heard a commotion from where he'd been sitting.

"My wallet!" he heard someone say.

"That's my coin purse!" another shouted.

"Thief! He's a bloody thief!"

Sish's skin prickled. He struggled to get up, his arms weak from being hit.

I'm not going to get out of here alive.

He pushed upward again, shaking his head as the arguing became an uproar on the other side of the bar. Yet no one came after him. The crowd seemed to have forgotten all about the drunk thief who'd been tossed over the bar. He inched onto his knees and then his feet, his vision still jarred, his jaw throbbing. Across the bar, a handful of angry patrons rifled through his coat while a second crowd was in a full-on fistfight with Davin. They thought *he* was the thief.

The pub still orbited at an odd angle around him, yet he allowed himself a small chuckle at the man's misfortune and then immediately regretted it as pain danced down his face. He brought his hand up to ease the feeling and caught Liv standing still, staring across the bar, her eyes aflame with rage and … there was something else he saw there too—humor. She shook her head, her lips doing their best to suppress a smile.

Sish grinned, wincing against the pain, and mouthed, "Luck," recalling Wincott's lectures.

Half a dozen people rifled through the thief's coat, extracting purloined money and wallets, a necklace.

He had an idea.

"Hey!" he yelled at them. "That bastard took my coat!"

The handful of angry victims looked up and then to where Sish pointed, shifting their eyes angrily toward Davin who, by that point, was in a full-on melee with four of the Werewolf's burliest patrons. One member tossed Sish the now-empty coat, which he caught and very gingerly donned, patting down the pockets to see if anything was left behind and found a wallet no one had claimed. It was surprisingly heavy, with perhaps enough coins to pay Ms. Burbidge after all.

"Well, I best be off," he announced, rubbing his jaw, though no one heard him.

He drained his pint of ale and slipped through the crowd out the front door.

Chapter Twenty-Seven

ALACOST METHURO, REST IN PEACE

SISH SQUIRMED LIKE A DESPERATE merchant during Wintertide in the alley below Wren's flat later that month. He needed work. He'd paid rent to Ms. Burbidge, but then two unfortunate things happened: he was robbed at knifepoint in Chicken Town one night, making him suddenly poor again, and Wincott came home empty-handed before he promptly ran into a couple of Uncle Frank's heavies who said he owed "taxes." Uncle Frank, one of Chicken Town's old-time gang leaders, was likely feeling the pinch of a hard trading season as the Guild encroached on E&E trapping territory and disrupted trade routes. Now the surly bastard sent his goons out to shake every street thief and brigand's pockets loose.

That sent Wincott into a spiral. He ordered Sish to spend extra time in the market pickpocketing while he stayed behind and dreamed up a better-paying scheme. So Sish spent three days lifting wallets and purses in the marketplace before the E&E guard got one too many complaints and posted more watchful eyes.

"You're going to have to go out there yourself," Sish told him one night, slumping onto the moth-eaten Chesterfield that doubled as his bed in the apartment they shared above Ms. Burbidge's cottage. "They're going to nail me next time I'm there; I know it."

"You were made?" Wincott cast a stern eye toward him as he poured a healthy dose of whiskey into his nighttime coffee. "How many times have I told you to finesse it?"

Sish cocked an eyebrow at his dad. "What does that even mean? Anyway, I wasn't made, but there are a dozen guards there now that weren't before."

Wincott scoffed, waving off Sish's worries. "I didn't raise you to be a weak-kneed sop from High Town—get out there, boy, else we're both done for."

Sish nearly exploded out of the Chesterfield, his spine straightened, fists balled as his face reddened with anger. "I wouldn't have to be out there if you actually brought some income in."

Wincott swallowed, winced, and put his mug down, turning toward the younger thief. "What did you say, boy? Weren't for me, you'd be dead. All this—the roof over your head, the table with food, clothes on your back, and even the way you earn money—*me*. It's all because of *me*."

There was truth in that, Sish knew, but he was old enough by then to also know it masked a harsher truth—Wincott wasn't the thief he'd once been. He didn't take basic jobs that kept the money rolling in, instead preferring long cons he wasn't very good at and racking up debt with people who weren't very forgiving, like Uncle Frank. Sish was carrying all the weight now. Worse yet, the old man was judgy about everything Sish did and how he did it.

"We need a bigger score," Sish told him, flexing his fingers, knowing he had to keep his cool if he were to convince Wincott of anything. "Lifting wallets in the market and running Jane jobs won't get those heavies off your back or keep Ms. Burbidge happy. We need a long con. Bring me in on one. I can do it."

Wincott was thoughtful for a moment before he tugged his beard and shook his head. "No, too young. You don't have the skills yet. Get us both killed. Get back to the market."

Sish mumbled angrily beneath his breath, grabbed his things, and left, slamming the door behind him. He had intended to go to the market, he really had, but found his footsteps carrying him into Chicken Town, and before long, he knocked on Wren's door.

The fact was the Dungeoneers always had a job on the go, and although dangerous, there typically was some loot to find along the way he could fence for a decent profit. Plus, it would piss Wincott off to no end if Sish paid off Uncle Frank's heavies from loot made on a job with those "do-gooders." He could see the old man gnashing his teeth now, and it filled him with a little too much excitement.

Plus, there was Liv.

There was only one problem. Davin was a member of Wren's crew these days, and the young thief hadn't seen the man since the brawl at the Werewolf's Toe.

"Look, I won't cause trouble," he told Wren, the two of them standing in the alley beneath the staircase that led up to the older man's flat.

Mid-autumn rain was pouring from the sky, soaking everything below in a refreshing mist. It dripped from eaves and railings, draining into small streams that filled the mossy gutters between the cobblestones at their feet.

Wren cradled his elbow in one hand, his other hand tiredly wiping down his face. He wasn't keen on having the thief around. No doubt he knew about the incident at the Toe.

"I've heard that from you before," Wren said. "What sort of trouble are you in now?"

Sish softened his face, trying to look as honest as he could. "None. Just want a change of pace."

Wren eyed him suspiciously. "I don't believe that for a second. But ... your timing is good. We have a job that needs some slippery fingers, and I don't trust Terry or Davin to pull it off without things getting ... loud."

"What is it?" Sish asked.

"There's a tower, north of here, on the river past the trading post at Summit Lake—well, the ruins of one anyway," Wren said, suddenly thoughtful.

"Lone Butte," Sish said knowingly.

A great stone tower once stood there, high atop a natural butte that rose almost a thousand feet above the forest around it, affording a lookout point for all trade along the Crooked River. It was a wild and unsettled area with a reputation for increasingly bitter winters, dangerous predators, and thick, nearly untraversable forest.

The King always ensured the tower was manned to protect the E&E's interests, back in the days when there had been a King. But blue-eyed sentinels slaughtered the guardsmen years before and set it aflame, most of it collapsing into a heap of stone rubble and charred joists. Little remained, save charred beams and a half-collapsed tower atop the butte.

Yet it remained a vital trade route, and the recent appearance of a particularly large and ancient Methuro spider named Leoressa was yet another reason business was flagging for the E&E along its northern supply lines.

"Shouldn't the Company send a battalion to deal with that?" Sish asked.

"They're tied up with a fight down at Shatterstill," Wren explained. "Goblins, apparently. Anyway, they've asked us to deal with it. Decent pay, too."

Knowing the speed at which the tower had burned and how fast the spider had taken over, Sish also wagered there were one or two things in that rubble worth stealing. He agreed.

"What about that rubbernecker, Faithguard?" Sish asked.

Wren nodded. "He's coming, too. He's excellent with a sword and knows his way around this sort of business, so you two will just have to … tolerate one another."

"And Liv?"

"She has her own mind about things; might punish you, might not," Wren said with a shrug. "But that's her business, and I learned some time ago to stay out of it. Terry will be there, too, and Rena."

"Rena?"

"We may need some extra oomph if things get out of hand," said Wren.

THEY DEPARTED THE FOLLOWING DAY. The weather was warm but blustery for late fall, the trees clinging to rust leaves, bathing the forest in a blanket of flaming color. They took the trader's road north to Summit Lake, which was a daylong hike, camped for the night, and set out in three canoes the following morning.

The lake drained into the crooked river, and from there, it was a few hours of paddling a low, gentle stream downriver to Lone Butte. Wren and Rena were in the lead boat, Liv and Davin in the middle, and Sish found himself with the barbarian in the rear. Liv hadn't acknowledged his presence since they'd set out and avoided making eye contact the entire way. Davin, on the other hand, had taken the exact opposite approach—questioning why they needed the thief at all, explaining to anyone who would listen that thieves were essentially untrustworthy and brought more trouble than they were worth. He was also far too handsy with Liv, making a very public point that he and the mage were some type of an item.

It was the last part that bugged Sish the most. He'd been called a thief, liar, and braggart before—that was nothing new. But when you had feelings for someone, watching them laugh and carry on with someone else was ... difficult. At least the barbarian was annoyed with it, too, he noticed. The big man paddled and swore irritably under his breath every time the warrior said something, reminding him more than once to keep his eye out for sweepers along the riverbank.

"Guy couldn't guard a chicken coop," Terry mumbled.

Lone Butte came into view by midmorning. The ruins squatted atop a lone thumb of rock that jutted above the forest like a cork. Atop the hill was a ring of stone battlements, mostly collapsed, and above that, the ruins of the watchtower itself. It was a stone cylinder missing half its diameter, leaving Sish to think it looked like a long, sharp fingernail rising above the knoll that the slightest breeze might cause to curl over and scratch the rubbled ground beneath it.

Wren steered the lead canoe into a rocky shore at the edge of the forest. A small game trail cut through the bushes at the edge of the rocks and twisted away from the river toward the foot of the butte.

The hunter was on his feet first, splashing in the ankle-deep water as he dragged the canoe onto the rocky shore. Rena sat at the front of the boat, bundled in fur against the morning chill. Wren helped the girl to the shore and then dragged Liv and Davin's canoe to a stop next to his own. Davin then guided Terry and Sish's canoe in, but after the barbarian got out, the warrior let go of the canoe, causing Sish to half tumble into the chill river water as he climbed out.

Boots and clothes sodden, the thief trudged out of the river to take a swing at Faithguard, but the broad-shouldered man was already on the game trail, heading toward the tower. Sish shook his head and squeezed the water from his pants and boots as best he could, muttering angrily under his breath.

"You coming?" Wren asked, standing at the forest's edge.

Sish stood up and met the hunter's eyes as he ran his tongue over his lower lip, considering exactly how he'd exact some kind of revenge on Faithguard the first chance he got.

Feed him to the spider.

He unconsciously cocked an eyebrow and chuckled at the thought. Wren gave him a strange look, trying to figure out what the thief was on about, but Sish only nodded and gestured for the man to take the lead, following the others into the dense spruce forest.

The path was narrow but hard-packed and easy to follow. Part of what made it easier was that this far north of town, the forest was mostly conifers peppered with some birch and aspen that had already shed their leaves, affording a more expansive view once they were in the understory.

It wasn't a long walk to the tower, but it was a gloomy one. A bank of steel gray clouds had pushed the morning's blue sky into memory, and a sharp northern wind whistled among the cold, arthritic trees. That combined with his damp clothes sent repeated shudders up Sish's spine as he pulled up the rear of the group, growing more miserable with each step, new and interesting ideas as to how he might visit revenge on Liv's new boyfriend rattling around in his head.

At the base of the knoll, Wren found a small clearing where he crouched and drew a folded paper from his leather vest. Unfolding it revealed a crude sketch of the tower, complete with floor plans. He explained the layout of the tower, what was in ruins, and what was likely still intact.

"The problem is, we don't know where the matron spider is—that's your job Sish." Wren pointed at him.

"You sure we want to trust this kid to find out? He's about as graceful as a pig in a mudflat, just as likely to get us killed as find the spider," Davin sneered.

Wren ignored him. "The kid's up to it," he said, leveling a gaze at Sish that said, *"You better be."*

Wren went on for a few minutes, explaining how Sish would sneak in, spot the matron, steal an egg, get her attention, and exit through an archway in the tower that likely remained intact.

Likely.

Sish shivered.

The plan was that the matron spider would get stuck in the archway and be easier to deal with. Liv's job was to use whatever spells she had at her disposal to slow or trap it while Terry and Davin cut it to pieces. Rena was backup if things went wrong.

Sish cast a sidelong glance at the girl who stood at the edge of the circle, her big, round blue eyes flitting around the forest in wonder, seemingly uninterested in the dangerous plan laid out in front of her. If you didn't know her, you'd think she was any other kid: she didn't talk much, hardly ever looked anyone in the eyes, and was never particularly enthusiastic about much of anything.

But Sish had been around long enough to know that below that quiet, diminutive façade was a thriving intellect, deep emotions, and a power unmatched by anyone he had ever met. Rena was a summoner—natural born, not taught, which meant she could call on incredible forces that manifested themselves in creatures mightier than a legion of soldiers when needed.

Sish didn't know the full story as to how she'd wound up with the group, but like Terry and Liv, she had no family and had been informally adopted by Wren. The hunter had a talent for attracting lost causes. The thief had hardly ever spoken with her, but he'd be lying if he said he didn't have a soft spot for her. Another outcast, just like he was, raised by someone with enough humanity to take an interest in her, just as Wincott had with him long ago, though Wren was far more adept at fathering than the old thief ever had been.

"Good luck, Sish," Wren said as he folded the map and replaced it in his vest.

"Yeah, try not to get us all killed, okay, kid?" Davin added.

Sish rolled his tongue around in his mouth, ready to let fly several insults, but decided against it. He caught Rena's eye. A small, knowing grin parted her lips, her eyes aglimmer as if she could read his mind. Sish wondered if, in fact, she could. He nodded quietly and proceeded up the trail alone.

THE SPIDER WEBS BECAME NOTICEABLE near the top of the butte. At first, Sish thought they might just be the remains of cottonwood shedding in the summer, but the stickiness and distinct stranded patterns within it were more evident with each bit of hill he ascended.

Sish didn't like spiders, much less Methuros, so named for Alacost Methuro, a textile mage who bred them with the hope of cornering the clothing market with ultra-strong spider silk. All he wound up doing was getting killed and unleashing an invasive species of giant arachnid that could spin that silk.

Swallowing hard as he trudged up the path, Sish did his level best not to think about the fact that he was walking into a nest of them and that if they managed to get a hold of him, they'd eat him alive. Instead, he considered how he might win the day with some kick-ass thief moves, leave Davin in the dust (or better yet, bound eternally in spider silk), and get the girl.

Finesse, focus, and luck.

Ugh. Thanks, Dad.

The last thing he wanted was the old man's advice ringing through his head, reminding him he'd never be as good a thief. He switched his mind to Wren's instructions and the worn parchment map the hunter had shown them. He noted a detail in it the trader had failed to mention—a storeroom. If there was any place left in that tower with treasure, it was that room.

Sish intended to make a pit stop there before he got on with the business of luring the matron Methuro out. Leoressa. He stopped and shuddered, a chill wind blowing up his back as the spindly black spruce trees creaked eerily around him.

From what he remembered, the room was in a sub-level of the tower. He figured he could sneak in, fill his pockets with any valuables, and then find an egg to steal. Lickety-split.

Sish reached the base of the tower a half hour or so later, his legs aching from the climb. He really needed to get into better shape.

He crept behind a short, crumbling stone wall and held his breath before summoning the courage to poke his head high enough to look beyond it. The base of the tower was on the other side, except now, it was halfway open to the elements like a poorly designed amphitheater and blanketed in thick patches of moss and webbing. Broken masonry, charred timbers, and rubble formed a junkyard of shit strewn everywhere, and there seemed to be passages into the tower complex branching off in several directions, though he couldn't be sure which were real passages and which were false caves formed as the structure decayed through the years.

High above soared the remains of the watchtower. It looked even more precarious up close, shadowy, hollow, and leaning toward him like a cloaked phantasm ready to envelop him in labyrinthine robes.

"It is a bit like a fingernail," he muttered to himself, absent-mindedly scratching at his three-day-old beard.

In fact, it leaned over so much, Sish wondered how it could possibly still be standing. But then he saw the Methuro webbing, which was strong about it like gossamer steel cables propping up the ruined masonry through some mad blend of physics and arcana.

Everywhere, there were webs and spiders. Thousands of pale-yellow juvenile spiders dangling here and there, filling every nook with ghostly silk. There were larger ones, too—as big as Sish's hand or even his head, suspended in doorways, above arches, or in the high ceilings. Nowhere did he see the Methuros, though, which were larger than a man, sometimes as large as a grizzly bear. The matron, Leoressa, was also not visible, yet a burning feeling at the nape of his neck suggested she was there somewhere.

His eyes found a set of curved stone steps that wound their way from the courtyard up into the ruins of the tower. He guessed that was the way to the matron, but first, he needed to find the storeroom. He spotted a square hole with a series of crumbling steps that led downward a few strides to the other side of the wall from him.

The thief deftly slipped over the bulwark and down the steps without a sound. It was pitch-black inside, but that only gave him an excuse to use the ruby thimble Liv had given him some time ago. She said it was a type of wand, but as far as he could tell, it had only two tricks: giving off a few sparks to start a fire when needed and helping him blend into shadows, both of which were extremely handy in his line of work. Liv had rolled her eyes when he told her how handy the device was, noting that it probably did a lot more than he was aware of, but since Sish wasn't a magic user, it was pretty much lost on him.

A small torch flickered to life thanks to the thimble, lighting the moist stone walls in a flickering orange light as he crept deeper into the tower. He ran the palm of his hand over the pommel of the dagger at his side as he moved deeper into the basement of the tower, hoping the weapon might chase away the gnawing fear that had taken hold in his belly. It didn't.

The basement was a series of rooms and corridors, most of which were collapsed or filled with debris and pools of musty-smelling water. Fortunately, the way to the storeroom was not. But it was choked with cobwebs.

A set of heavy wooden doors that had fallen together when their hinges rusted away blocked access to his goal, but there was enough space between them for the thief to hunker down into a puddle of watery slop and crawl inside. On the far side, he found two things: unopened chests and large, milky-white spider eggs. *Very large* milky-white spider eggs.

They clung to the stone walls and ceiling like uncooked dough balls and littered the floor like bloated bowling pins. Each were about two feet in height and half as big around.

Methuros.

He really wished Alacost hadn't been so enterprising. *Sometimes it doesn't pay to have an idea,* Sish thought, shuddering. He guessed the storeroom was Leoressa's nest, though she was nowhere to be seen.

The chests were large, banded in iron, and locked. He very carefully laid the torch in an old sconce on the ground next to him and reached into his coat for a set of picks. Gingerly stepping between the first two eggs, he picked his way toward the first chest. The lock was surprisingly limber, and he was able to pop it without too much work, though he winced at the loud click that broke the moist silence of the egg room as it came unlatched.

Lifting the lid, he found a set of leather armor, their gild hidden beneath a thick coat of dust. The second chest was more promising. It held a small purse of silver coins and several E&E trade notes, each worth as much as the bag of silver, he guessed. The third chest, found on the far side of the storeroom, was the jackpot. It was full of rare gems, a small leather satchel with rough gold nuggets, a smaller box of coins, and several books.

If the Dungeoneers were successful in killing Leoressa—and he had no reason to believe they wouldn't be—word would travel fast that the spider was gone, and adventurers would descend on the tower within days to rob it of any leftover riches. He had to get what he could now.

He pulled the satchel on and stuffed his pockets with coins and gems. He made sure to fold the trade notes and slide them into his shirt alongside the purse of silver coins. He wouldn't be able to take it all, but what he already had would be enough to keep him and Wincott comfortable for years, if they wanted. Or maybe just him. Did Wincott *need* to know? He wondered. Something to consider more deeply later.

He turned to make his way back through the storeroom when he spotted a broad-shouldered dickhead standing at the doors. The man held Sish's torch high enough to cast a greasy light over the egg room, a sneer blemishing his otherwise perfect face.

"I knew we couldn't trust you," Davin said.

Sish froze halfway toward the warrior, several coins and a sapphire jingling from his pocket onto the stone floor.

Davin didn't say anything. Instead, he lifted the torch and looked up.

Sish suddenly realized how Leoressa had managed to get into the storeroom without knocking the doors down. Directly above them was a massive black hole that gouged upward into the ruins of the watchtower. Crouched in that hole was a spider large enough to make a full-grown grizzly bear look small, its glassy black eyes flashing coolly in the flickering torchlight.

"Davin ..."

"Don't you dare try to talk your way out of this," Davin shot back. "I told Liv you weren't worth her time. Anyone's time. Just a bloody thief through and through. No honor."

"Davin ..."

Leoressa's mandibles twitched slightly as their heated whispers rose toward her, signaling she was about to move. Sish was ignoring Davin completely now, his eyes glued to the gargantuan tarantula hanging above him.

"Oh, I knew she was there," he said. "Have fun."

The dickhead tossed the torch upward, striking the spider in the face with a shower of sparks that rained down on the eggs, singing their delicate yolk sacks. The warrior slipped back through the doors. Leoressa chittered and fell hard on the floor, right on top of Sish. The thief narrowly avoided her fangs by ducking behind a stone pillar but found himself pinned between the stone column and a hairy leg.

He squeezed out of the way, got back on his feet, and made for the doors, using the muck puddle to slide under them at a run.

Finesse.

Dozens of coins and jewels jingled from his pockets onto the eggs as he moved. He swore under his breath, wiping a cold sheen of sweat from his brow as he started toward the stairs that led out of the tower. Patting his pockets, he was pleased to find the satchel of nuggets still intact.

Davin sprinted up the stairs ahead of him to the courtyard. The doors to the egg room exploded outward toward Sish as he gave chase. Leoressa was there, snapping at him as she struggled to squeeze through the too-narrow passage between rooms. He stumbled. More coins and jewels jingled. He ignored her, never stopping to look back even as he felt her rancid breath on his neck, keeping just ahead of her mandibles as she reached out to seize him.

Focus.

He was up the stairs and in the courtyard a moment later, but there was only more danger there. Davin was surrounded by Methuros, his sword drawn. He pierced and swiped at them, but for each spider he killed, two more took its place.

Sish rolled from the passage into the gloomy daylight just inches free of Leoressa's angry mouth. He felt a heavy leg pass over the top of him and drew his dagger, swinging wildly. He felt it nick something and heard the creature nicker angrily at him. Banking on intuition alone, he rolled again, narrowly dodging another swipe.

Luck.

A green flash of light filled his vision, and Leoressa was blasted backward by something hard. The air smelled of brimstone and burned meat. Sish scrabbled backward from the wounded arachnid. Liv stepped over him, wand in hand, and sent another jet of coruscating green energy toward the spider, but Leoressa had recovered and artfully dodged out of the way. She came around the wizard's side and snapped at her, taking Liv out at the knees.

With her hind legs, she brushed Sish back, throwing him hard against the outer wall of the tower and spraying a jet of ropy webbing toward him that glued his left leg to the tower wall.

The spider crouched over Liv and readied to strike. From the corner of his eye, he spotted Davin. The warrior was free of spiders, but he was drenched in loose webbing and black spider blood. He looked at Liv—he was within striking distance to help—but there was fear in his eyes. He turned and ran.

Leoressa raised her abdomen to strike, the black stinger dripping with venom. Sish struggled to peel himself from the wall. He couldn't look away. And then a blade flashed, and Leoressa shrieked. Another flash, more pain.

Terry was beneath the spider now, the barbarian's great sword cleaving its bristly legs like a machete through bamboo stalks. Leoressa collapsed to one side. Terry grunted and drove his sword into her abdomen. He put all his weight behind the thrust, the veins popping out on his rippled arms. He caught Sish's eye and ... was he *actually* grinning?

The barbarian lifted the massive creature over onto its side before pulling his sword free with a wet *schlunk*. Leoressa shrieked and curled over onto her back, where she died.

The barbarian slew several more Methuro spiders as he lifted a terrified Liv from the ground. The remaining arachnids scattered, retreating into the shadowy hollows of Lone Butte as the melee ended.

Sish unstuck himself as Wren and Rena came through a narrow stone arch that served as the sole intact remaining entryway to the tower courtyard.

"Where's Davin?" Wren asked, out of breath from sprinting up the hill.

Rena appeared completely fine.

Terry and Liv shook their heads. Only Sish had witnessed the man's cowardice. His hands shook with a mixture of fear and anger, a rage so deep he couldn't control himself. The thief ignored them and sprinted through the archway after Davin, leaving everyone behind.

He caught up with the warrior at the canoes. Davin was halfway into the boat when Sish came out of the trees.

"Leaving without saying goodbye?"

Davin twisted toward him and smiled darkly. "Ahhh, you lived. Too bad."

"I could say the same for you."

"Don't trifle with me, kid. You'll get hurt. Now be gone back to your *Dungeoneers*."

Sish fingered the dagger in his hand. "You're not going anywhere. She was almost killed because of you."

"Oh, that's what this is about? The girl. I knew you had a crush on her, but I didn't … No, I didn't know you cared for her that much. Does she know? I doubt it. You were the farthest thing from her mind when she was in bed with me."

Sish took a step forward. Davin drew his sword.

"Didn't like that much, eh?" Davin teased him. "Yes, she was with me. Many, many times. While you were … where? Lifting purses in the market for dear old Dad? Pathetic."

Sish lunged forward. Davin easily parried him, knocking the dagger from the thief's hand like he was a toddler, sending him stumbling into the bed of river rocks. Davin turned and placed a muddied boot on his neck and the point of his sword against the thief's chest. The blade bit into Sish's skin.

"I'm going to take my time with this, make you feel it … like she did," he said, smiling.

"Davin, no!" Liv called out.

He turned toward her. Liv stood at the edge of the woods, Wren, Terry, and Rena behind her. A pleading look in her eyes.

"Let him live? This whelp?" Davin protested with a laugh. "You know he's madly in love with you, Liv. Was jealous of us. That's why he chased me down here, to kill me."

"Leave him be," Liv said. "He's just a boy."

The words rang through Sish's mind like alarm bells. *Just a boy. Just a boy.* The rage built inside him. Davin's sword point lifted a bit, giving the thief enough room to move. He reached out and lifted his dagger from the rocks next to the canoe and plunged it into Davin's spine when the man wasn't looking.

The warrior dropped his sword, collapsing to his knees with a sudden inhale of breath cut short as the shock surged through him. He fell unconscious, blood dribbling from his lips onto his dimpled chin, leaving Sish on his knees, panting. Liv turned and walked away.

Chapter Twenty-Eight

THE BEST LIES ARE WRAPPED IN OTHER LIES

THE CAMPFIRE CRACKLED WEAKLY. SISH lay on the ground on his side in a fetal position, dirt in his mouth. He spat and swished his tongue around his gum line, checking to see whether any teeth were loose or missing. He didn't mind scars, bumps, and bruises so much, but a missing tooth would really mess up how he looked. When his mouth seemed okay, he sat up, and his head exploded in pain so intense he nearly fainted.

"He knocked you pretty good," said a voice from across the fire.

Sish cradled his face for a moment. When his vision cleared, he found Elden Wren sitting on a rock across from him, the old hunter resting his elbows on his knees and watching the young thief with kind but intense eyes.

"You survived," Sish remarked, sitting up, running a heavy hand through his matt of unruly brown hair. It was clumped and crusty where Fulk had hit him. Dried blood.

In his mind, he saw Fulk's hand hurtling toward his skull with a rock, then the trader sauntering away with Rena in a sack slung over his shoulder. It infuriated him so much that his head hurt all over again and his vision blurred. He spat more dirt, his vision blurring.

"I did," said Wren, "and you have as well, though by rights, you should've died."

"Yeah, well, not the first time I've been told that. Probably won't be the last either. Where'd he go?"

Sish climbed to his feet, weakly dusted dirt off his pants and shirt. And noticed he was still barefoot, his toes caked in grime and more than a few scrapes.

They were hidden in a shallow knell, surrounded by thumbs of rock capped with twisted trees and moss that offered shelter from the broader valley and anything that lurked nearby. Wren's campfire burned on a small patch of river stones that had been assembled for that purpose, causing Sish to wonder how he'd got there and where the barbarian had disappeared to. His question was answered a moment later when the big man lumbered into the camp carrying a brace of rabbits, a pleased look on his face.

"You lived," Terry remarked, his eyes surveying the young thief. "You look like hell."

"Feel like hell," Sish groaned. "Fulk's ahead of us. We have to get to him."

Wren stood and gestured for Sish to sit. "We will. First, you need to rest. And answer a few questions."

Sish ignored the older man and took a step forward to pursue Fulk, but a spell of dizziness caused the world to gyrate and his stomach to roil with nausea.

"You need something to eat and a bit more rest," Wren told him. "That's why I sent Terry to scrounge up some food."

Sish considered the rabbits. They were dark-furred and had the normal number of feet and ears, but he worried about eating anything from the valley. His stomach thought differently and grumbled loudly. He decided he'd wait for the barbarian to have the first few bites, and if he didn't die, then he might eat, too.

Sish sat and gently probed the wound on his head with the tips of his fingers. It had already crusted over. Wren eyed him carefully and then sat on a stump across from him.

"Why'd you take off on us?" Wren asked.

Sish ignored him at first, his eyes falling on the barbarian, who quickly gutted and skinned the rabbits. He speared both of them on a long, sharpened branch and then hung them over the fire to cook, turning them every minute or so to ensure more even roasting.

Wren didn't press Sish, while the thief ignored him, preferring to wait him out, knowing the young man had nowhere to go. Typical Wren, Sish thought. The hunter had more patience than … well, something with a lot of patience, anyway. More than once, he'd goaded Sish into spilling the beans simply by not saying anything at all.

Why did it matter that he'd ditched them before they got to Roan? He hadn't ventured out with Wren's Company in some time, and last he heard, there was no love lost between any of them. And he'd been with them against his will in the first place, but that was the nature of the job.

Eventually, he sighed and said, "I didn't need you anymore."

Wren nodded silently to that and said, "So, what? You used us for … ?"

"To confirm what I thought was the case: you were headed into the valley to locate the city and seal it before anyone else could get in."

"And you didn't want that?"

"I wanted the treasure," Sish said.

Wren clapped his hands against his thighs, raised his arms to the cavern ceiling above them, and gestured all around him. "And what a treasure you've found—not but corruption, monstrosity, and death here."

"We haven't reached the end yet," Sish countered, wiping the dirt from his feet and between his toes. He was surprised to discover the soles of his feet were mostly intact.

Wren leaned forward, elbows on knees, fingers knitted together. His eyes darkened. "You're still convinced there's actual treasure in the vault the dwarf told you about?"

"Storeroom," Sish corrected. "I'm not sure, but I'm going to find out. And I want to find out before Fulk does, so can we go?"

A dollop of rabbit fat dripped and sizzled on a blackened river stone in the campfire. Terry yanked off a charred leg and bit into it tentatively. His jaw worked the meat for a moment before his eyes brightened, and he gestured for Sish to do the same. The thief tore off another leg and gnawed on it.

"But it's not you you're here for, is it?" Wren pressed. "You're working for the E&E. The governor sent you down here for something. What exactly?"

Sish swallowed. The meat was greasy and overcooked, but at that point, it tasted like the best thing he'd ever eaten. He tore off another leg, stripped it of meat, and tossed the bone aside.

"I guess it doesn't matter at this point," said Sish, "But, yeah, he sent me down here."

"Why?"

"Wants the treasure for himself, why else?" Sish said. "Hand me another leg."

Terry tore off another chunk of meat and tossed it to the thief. He offered some to Wren, but the hunter shook his head. The barbarian shrugged and kept eating.

"Damned fool will get us all killed," Wren grumbled. "So then, why come with us? Why not just go yourself?"

"The chief factor heard you had left town already and asked me to work my way into your group, slow you down if I could, buy him some time."

"Asked?" Wren looked at him questioningly.

"Told," Sish corrected. "It was that or the gibbet for me."

"Got caught again?" Terry asked him.

Sish nodded matter-of-factly. "Yup. Would you believe it was for pickpocketing of all things?"

Terry flashed a small grin and shook his head.

"So, you took our maps, ditched us partway here, and figured we wouldn't find Roan without you or the map," Wren said, filling in the details.

"No, I figured you'd find it, just not so fast. I'm guessing you came in the way Fulk did?"

Wren nodded. "There's a cavern in Fang Mountain."

Sish nodded. "Didn't know about that."

"You expect me to believe any of this?"

Sish laughed, his head throbbing slightly, cutting the chuckle short. He tossed another bone aside and wiped his greasy hands on his pants. "Of all the unbelievable things that have happened in the last two days, my story is the most believable thing that's happened yet."

"The best lies are wrapped in truths," Wren said.

Sish made a crude noise with his mouth, suggesting he disagreed with Wren's statement. "You got it wrong. The best lies are wrapped in other lies. That way, no one can untangle them. Anyway, doesn't really matter now, does it? We're here, and Fulk's ahead of us. So, let's go."

"Except that the Company is right behind us, aren't they?"

Sish's stomach twisted. His head pounded. It was true. The governor had sent a contingent of soldiers from Fort Rivers to track and follow the Dungeoneers to Roan. When the thief stole Wren's maps and made the decision to approach the city from the main entrance, he'd hoped it would slow them enough that the Company would catch up and neither group would find its way to Roan. But Sish miscalculated—he'd forgotten Wren knew the roads, paths, and game trails of the mountains east of Fort Rivers better than anyone alive. It dawned on him that he'd never seen Wren consult the maps, nor anyone else, even though they'd been visibly prominent since the five of them had left Fort Rivers.

He shook his head and cursed himself. "It was a ruse. The maps were a ruse."

Wren smiled. "I had a hunch you weren't in it for our benefit."

"Better than a hunch," Terry piped up. "We knew you were lying."

Wren nodded triumphantly. "It was Liv's idea. She figured you couldn't resist a map. Guess you haven't changed much since she dumped you."

Sish was about to protest, but it was true, even the part about Liv.

"But you didn't know about the Company," Sish said.

"Not until now. How many of them are there?"

"I don't know. The factor never said, and I never saw them. My guess is they followed you, so they may be lost somewhere in the Upper City."

Wren exchanged a worried look with Terry. "We cut our way through the city; wouldn't be hard to follow. If they can get across the lake …"

Wren left the thought unfinished, but Sish knew what it meant. The E&E soldiers were somewhere inside Roan already, likely not far behind. Fulk would do everything in his power to ensure his former employer didn't get to the treasure first, and that presented a renewed danger for Rena. It wasn't just for themselves they were exploring the city but to keep whatever was in it out of the hands of greater powers.

Sish cursed himself for being such a fool. How could he not have seen it? The maps were a clever ruse, but the game wasn't a simple treasure hunt in a forgotten city—it was a struggle that had been playing out in every port, fort, and town across Erdor for decades. The Erdor and Expanse Trading Company and the Royal Merchant Guild were at it again, and Sish found himself unwittingly at the center of it.

He could explain Fulk's part in all of it. The man was a piece of work, but Sish suspected he was being truthful about wanting the Wealth of Roan for himself, to tip the balance against the Company and the Guild. Would that be so bad? Perhaps, Sish thought, it might finally put an end to all the violence, the same violence that had killed his mother.

His thoughts drifted to Wincott. He was still enraged that the old man was working for the Guild, but he didn't find it surprising. He wondered then if the Company wasn't the only group that had sent a contingent of soldiers to protect its interests.

Chapter Twenty-Nine

THROWING SHADE

WINCOTT WAS SLICK WITH SWEAT, his heart thumping loudly in his chest by the time they paddled far enough from the moldering dock to avoid the crude arrows and slings the goblins used. The creatures grumbled loudly from shore, gesturing angrily with their arms and weapons, but after a few minutes, the lead goblin—Meat Cleaver—signaled for the others to follow, and they disappeared into the forest that ran alongside the water.

That meant the little runts meant to outpace the thief, Liv, and Ruddlefunt to the far side of the lake, where, no doubt, Meat Cleaver and his pals would be waiting. Yet the lake stretched away into the gloom toward the far end of the valley, so it was impossible to discern whether that was even possible. If nothing else, it gave him time to think through a plan to deal with the creatures that had been dogging him since his piss-poor attempt at thievery in Fort Shatterstill. That felt like an age ago, but it was only a couple of days, right?

He shook his head. It was impossible to tell how much time had passed since he'd entered Roan. A part of him wished he'd demonstrated a little more finesse when he'd decided to rob the little buggers at Shatterstill. Was he losing it?

He stopped paddling and flexed and shook his fingers, wondering quietly whether they were as nimble as they had once been. He refused to admit they weren't, truth be told, which was an admission in and of itself.

The old thief shook his head wearily and continued rowing. When they were halfway down the lake, he stopped for a breather. Liv cocked an expectant eyebrow at him.

"All tuckered out?" she teased.

He offered a wry smile. "Would you like to take over?"

The wizard laughed scornfully. "Not on your life. It's your fault we're in this mess."

Wincott scratched his beard and lifted the oars once more, rowing more slowly this time. "How do you figure that?"

"Where do I begin?" she shot back. "No, you know what? It's not worth explaining."

Her eyes drifted away from him over the lake. The water was still, like glass, and inky black, similar to the lake they'd made their way across in the Upper City. He shuddered, thinking about what lurked in the water and decided to fix his eyes and thoughts on something else.

The Grand Valley stretched around them in every direction. High above, stalactites of all shapes and colors gouged downward from the cavern ceiling. On either side of the lake were gently rolling hills and rocky outcroppings, carpeted in twisted, barren trees and yellow witchgrass. There was nothing pleasant to the eye in the Grand Valley, Wincott decided. His nostrils filled with the heavy musk of rotten leaves and fungus that left a stale, almost acrid, taste in his mouth that reminded him of a home that hadn't seen a spring breeze in many years.

"Ruddlefunt, what do you know about the lake?" Wincott asked him, breaking the heavy silence in the boat.

The dwarf sat on a bench across from him, his little legs dangling above the hull like a child's.

"Mirror Lake," Ruddlefunt said. "It's said to show us the worst version of ourselves."

Liv scoffed, "Wincott doesn't need a lake for that."

The thief muttered something incoherent under his breath and kept rowing. "What does that mean, exactly?"

Ruddlefunt shrugged. "I don't know."

Liv, kneeling behind Wincott at the bow of the small boat, peered over the gunnels into the water. She made a disappointed noise and turned her gaze back to the horizon. Wincott leaned over and investigated the water, its inky blackness reflecting a perfect image of his face. He was taken aback at how old he looked, the deep lines in his forehead, crow's feet at his eyes, and wiry tuft of gray beard that jutted from his chin making him feel as though he was staring at someone he didn't really know. Wincott knew he wasn't a young man anymore, but the image shocked him.

He thought about the choices he'd made, the path that had led him to this place. He hadn't had a father to set an example for him as a child, and his mother had died young, like Sish, leaving him in the care of his aunt, who had quickly shoveled him into a workhouse. That's where he'd first started working for the Guild and learned that if he didn't want to starve, he'd have to lie, steal, and connive. Thievery hadn't been a calling, it was a requirement, and he didn't regret that part of who he was.

But as he got older, it became a choice. There were times when he could've gone another way but chose not to. He grew comfortable with it, and worse, a part of him felt he was entitled to it—to take from others what he'd never had himself. No one had ever looked out for Wincott, so why should he bother to care about anyone else?

That line of thinking had led him to take the Fort Wick job for the Guild, which had led him to Sish. He didn't know if it was guilt or something else that caused him to take the boy in and raise him. Perhaps loneliness, he considered. Or maybe it was that no one else seemed to teach their kids how awful the world really was, that to survive, a person had to lie, cheat, steal, and do whatever was necessary to see the next day. And he wanted Sish to know that. Or maybe it was that he wanted himself to know that, to believe it, because the older he got, the less certain he was that any of it was true.

He peered over the side of the boat and caught his reflection again. But this time when he went to look away, the Wincott in the water smiled queerly at him. The old thief felt an icy tingle run up his back.

"Liv ..."

The boat rocked, first to one side, then the other. Water kicked up on either side, splashing over the gunwales into the bottom of the boat. The oars jutted out of Wincott's grip, one of them knocking Liv onto her back into the bottom of the boat. They slipped out of their oar locks and vanished into the water. The boat gave a great heave and flipped over, dumping them into the water.

There was a great swoosh of water that soaked everything and a dizzying feeling as if they were tumbling down a river, until suddenly, the boat settled and Wincott found himself in the open air. He opened his eyes to a murky blackness all around them. The boat was dry. Ruddlefunt was on the ground next to him, and Liv was across from him, her legs tangled up in his.

"What was that?" she asked, sitting up.

Wincott looked around. The Grand Valley was gone, replaced with a pitch-black lake that felt … empty. It was as if they were floating in a half-formed world, where only the three of them, the boat, and the water existed. There was nothing else except a deep, heavy darkness.

Wincott found that even his clothes were dry, as were the others. He pulled himself to his feet and looked around. He was completely lost. The oars were gone, and the boat seemed to drift lazily in one general direction in the water. The only source of light was a faint gray glow that came from the water below them.

He looked over the side of the boat and was startled.

"Liv, you better look at this," he said.

In the water below them was a mirror image of the rowboat, except, it was gliding upside down in the lake they had just been on. Below that version of the boat was the Grand Valley, complete with hills, trees, and cavernous ceilings stretching away from them as if he were looking into the bottom of a lake.

Liv swore. "Well, this place sure lives up to its name, doesn't it?"

Ruddlefunt nodded agreeably. "The Masters preferred simplicity for their creations."

"Indeed," Wincott said, peering over the side of the boat, unsure of what to do.

The mirror version of himself peered back at him. Suddenly, the mirror Wincott shoved an oar straight into the water, and the paddle slammed into the real Wincott's forehead, sending him sprawling backward, pain lancing his face. A great deal of muffled laughter bubbled up from the mirror rowboat below them. When his head cleared, he looked at Liv.

"Got any ideas?"

"Ruddlefunt?" The wizard looked at the dwarf.

The dwarf shrugged. "That's all I know."

"Nothing else about this lake in that gargantuan library of yours?" she asked.

"Not that I'm aware," he said.

"Not helpful," Liv said. "Well, it's definitely magic."

"I'm aware it's magic," Wincott snapped at her, "but how do we get back to the other side?"

She peeked over the gunwales. Another oar slammed through the water, but she deftly moved her head aside and ignored a second round of laughter that followed it.

"Our boat seems to be moving with theirs like we're attached somehow," she observed.

"A shadow," Ruddlefunt said. "Yes, yes, now I remember. Mirror Lake was designed as a testing ground for a new form of magic known as Shade Magic. The Masters engineered the lake so that practitioners could flip to the Shadow side and test their spells without damaging the Grand Valley. Quite ingenious if you think about it."

Wincott ignored the dwarf's enthusiasm, instead focusing on the fact that the Grand Valley felt increasingly like some madman's laboratory. Not for the first time, he wondered who these supposed Lords of Roan had been and what they were up to. He also wondered if there was truly anything of value at the far end of the valley at all and was beginning to think that if the valley had indeed been created by madmen, then the Wealth of Roan might be just as ridiculous as everything else they'd uncovered. Either way, the mirror images of themselves were making a beat across the lake below them—above them, whatever—and they needed to figure out how to flip things back around, or they might be left in the shade forever.

"If we're their shadow, then they can't leave us behind," Liv said, thinking aloud.

"Or at least they can't so long as we're all on the lake," Wincott countered. "I'm not sure I want to test that theory once we … they … reach the other side of the lake."

Wincott peered into the water again and could see all three of their mirror selves, each bearing twisted, haunting grins. The shades slammed their oars into the water and howled with laughter like rioting prison inmates. The thief fingered the pommel of the sword at his side. Raspberry. Stupid name, yet … he wondered.

He drew the weapon and waited. After a moment, he leaned over the gunnels and waited to catch eyes with his shade. When he did, he made a taunting face. The shade exploded in anger and drove the oar into the water. The device popped out of the lake on Wincott's side, and he swiped at it, slicing a neat line of wood from the tip of the oar. The shades wore shocked expressions. Muffled yelling could be heard through the water.

"There's some link between them and us," Wincott said.

Liv nodded, drumming two fingers against her lips thoughtfully. Frustration darkened her complexion.

She cursed and said, "Shade magic. I've never heard of such a thing—give me grass, give me trees, give me earth, those I can deal with but not … *this*."

Wincott cocked an eyebrow. "I guess your pals at the Breakfast Club aren't the wise and all-knowing wizards they claim to be."

Liv chuckled ruefully. "The only thing they're wise about is the consistency of breakfast sausages."

"Well, we have to do something. The end of the lake is in sight," Wincott said, pointing.

The reflection in the water showed a forested shoreline fast approaching. The shades rowed faster, so the boats on both sides of the water picked up speed. Wincott felt the hair on the back of his neck prickle at the thought of what might happen to them if the shades got out of the boat and left them behind. Trapped.

His thoughts drifted to Sish. There was no way to be certain, but Wincott felt the boy was still alive.

Luck.

Curse him though for working for the E&E, Wincott thought, but he knew he wouldn't have done anything different were their situations reversed. He smiled to himself, thinking, in fact, *he hadn't* done anything different. He was working for the Guild. The apple didn't fall far from the tree.

Wherever Sish was, he was likely intent on finding that treasure, and Wincott could only guess that Fulk was either with him or ahead of him—the old trader wouldn't die so easily. And neither the boy nor the trader knew their relationship to the other. Wincott remained the sole keeper of that knowledge, and he wondered whether that was right. Maybe it didn't matter. Maybe who your dad is isn't so much about the blood that runs through your veins but the guy who stuck around to patch you up when you spilled some.

He didn't know. Hadn't known it as long as the boy had been his ward, and he didn't expect that anything that might happen in the depths of Roan would provide any additional clarity for him. But what was becoming clear was that he had no intention of living out his days trapped in shadow while his son sought out that treasure alone. Maybe it was because Wincott couldn't accept the boy landing a score bigger than anything he ever had, or maybe it was because he wanted him to. It didn't matter, he decided. What mattered was that he'd decided he would see his son alive again, one way or another.

The thief began to rock the boat.

"What are you doing?" Liv said, bracing herself against the gunwales.

Ruddlefunt went still, an alarmed look crossing the dwarf's strange blue eyes.

The thief nodded to the reflection in the water. The shore was only a few hundred yards below them.

"I'm going to flip this thing over before they get to shore," Wincott said.

"I'm not sure that will work the way you think it will," Ruddlefunt observed, his eyes gleaming.

"Got any better ideas?" the thief challenged him.

The dwarf thought about it, and after a moment, said, "No, but a suggestion: Get them to stick an oar into the water when we're rocking. When it comes through, grab it and pull as hard as you can."

It didn't make sense to Wincott, but then again, he was in a mirror universe with a mechanical dwarf and a wizard, so he was willing to take it on faith alone.

He grabbed Raspberry and stuck the blade in the water, probing the other side with a swirling motion to capture the attention of their shades. Liv rocked the boat with him. It heaved side to side. Muffled yelling bubbled up from the water. The shore was only a few dozen yards away now. Blue-black water splashed over the gunwales onto their feet. An oar came through the water.

Ruddlefunt yelled, "Now!"

Liv grabbed it and pulled as hard as she could.

Chapter Thirty

IT WAS MORE OF A JANE, AND NOT WORTH THE TROUBLE

THE JOB WENT BAD FROM the get-go. It was a Charlie, so named for Charles Mickmore, who did more to perfect the art of using tunnels to access highly secure areas than any other thief in known history. Wincott was not a tunneler but had worked with a guy, oddly enough also named Charlie, who was pretty good and had taught him one or two things some years before. Unfortunately, *that* Charlie died when one of his tunnels collapsed and buried him. Of course, no one knew about it until three years after he died when a fire reduced the jewelry shop Charlie had been trying to rob to a pile of ashes, revealing poor Charlie's blackened bones beneath. There hadn't been a funeral, but a few of the fellas down at the Wandering Camel raised a toast to him, nonetheless, and forever named a tunnel job a Charlie.

This Charlie was a solo job. He was in trouble with Uncle Frank again and needed to pay a debt. Word had it that the museum in High Town was in receipt of several crates cleaned out of storage after one of the Breakfast Club wizards died, and in those boxes was a map, and that map led to a fabled treasure. Wincott was down on his luck and hoped he could get his fingers on the map, fence it, and get Uncle Frank off his back. He also fully intended to memorize the map and go looking for the treasure later.

The problem was things weren't going well. First, he had to do the entire job alone—no one he trusted was looking for work, and he didn't think the map would fetch him much coin, so he had no real desire to split the profit among multiple people. That meant he had to scout and dig the tunnel by himself. It took him the better part of a week. In that time, he hoped the Fort Rivers Museum of Natural and Arcane History didn't decide to suddenly become ambitious and inventory the dead wizard's belongings, which might result in the disappearance of the map before he could get to it. He was confident they wouldn't. Museum curators tended to move at a pace like civil servants.

He dug the tunnel from a side alley that few frequented, covering the entrance with well-packed snow. Winter was handy at times but tough in other ways. The ground was frozen solid, and he nearly froze to death on the second night as he chipped away at the dirt and rock below High Town. The good news was the tunnel was more likely to be stable, or so he hoped. Of course, he didn't forget the most important thing Charlie had told him: *Make sure you have roof supports.*

Wincott used discarded lumber he found at the docks for that. Sish asked why he had come home with so much wood, but all the older thief told the boy was that he had a bit of work to do. Sish insisted on helping him. The boy was nearly a teenager and had proven to be a quick study, but he was also gangly, clumsy, and loud, qualities that didn't lend themselves to a Charlie.

"No, you keep the hearth warm and food at the ready. I'll need it when I get home in the morning," Wincott told him.

"Uncle Frank was here earlier," Sish said, wincing slightly.

Wincott's heart almost burst from his chest. He'd been doing his best to keep Sish separated from the ugly reality of his work, but he knew the boy was wise to it by now. Still, Uncle Frank was a menacing character, and he didn't have a habit of making house calls unless he intended to send a message.

"What did he say?" Wincott asked tentatively.

His eyes searched the room, watching the windows and doors for movement.

"Nothin'," the boy said, shrugging. "Said he'd come back for you later."

Wincott nodded carefully. He needed to move faster. He would have to chisel through the night, break in, get the map, and fence it by morning or he risked both his and Sish's lives.

"I'll be back by sunup," was all he told Sish, hoping the creases of worry on his face weren't visible.

THE TUNNEL WAS ROUGH BUT serviceable. Wincott reached the wood foundation below the museum an hour before dawn. He needed to move quickly. He chiseled around the support beams until the age-blackened underside of the museum floor revealed itself in the lamplight. He guessed he had come up under a storage area, but it was difficult to be certain.

He dropped the chisel, picked up a small hand saw, and cut into the floor above him to create an opening wide enough to slip through. That's when the tunnel behind him collapsed in a shower of dirt, rock, and ice. Once he cleared the rock dust from his eyes and mouth, he realized his avenue of escape was gone. He'd also lost most of his tools.

"Well, shit," he said, half-chuckling at his poor luck.

Time to focus.

He worked his way into the museum, emerging through a gap in the floor into one of the exhibits, this one depicting the founding of the Erdor & Expanse Company and its traders as they built a merchant empire atop the ruins of much older kingdoms. It was all hogwash, but the museum's primary benefactor was the governor.

He found a mammoth-skin rug on the floor nearby and dragged it to cover the hole as he got his bearings. It was dark and quiet, the air thick with a stillness that unnerved him. He brushed the dirt from his pants, focusing on little things to ignore the thread of anxiety weaving through his intestines. He had a half hour before sunup when escape would be a lot more difficult. The curators lived upstairs, so he had to tiptoe to the storeroom and hope they weren't early risers.

Shelves lined with artifacts filled the room at the back of the museum. Dusty old trunks and cobwebbed crates lined the walls from floor to ceiling. It smelled like old books and rat droppings, forcing him to put a hand to his mouth to stifle several sneezes.

Near the backdoor were several newish boxes filled with a variety of what appeared to be old wizard junk, or what he guessed an aging wizard might have that would be junk to anyone else: floppy hats, strange carvings in semiprecious stones and unusual hardwoods, mini-statues, quill pens, books, and bottles filled with many-colored powders and liquids.

He stashed a pair of bright green and deep purple powder bottles in his coat, recognizing them as spell components that, in isolation, made for fun pyrotechnics. He and Sish might have fun playing with them later.

At the bottom of the lowest box was a leather satchel full of rolled-up parchments. Wincott opened the first and found a map of Northern Erdor, the second showed a map of High Town, and the third was a map of a small dungeon at a place called Moon Lake. Wincott had never heard of it, but it looked promising.

He folded it and slid it into his coat pocket. Just then, a puff of red smoke erupted in the storeroom, and a wizard blinked into existence in front of him. The man was old, with long, straw-colored hair, sunken cheeks, and deep, dark eyes. His lips curled back in a smile, revealing a menacing set of long, thin, browned teeth clinging to black gums.

"It worked," the wizard said with a thin, pleased voice.

The mage doubled over with a hacking cough that Wincott was pretty certain would wake the curators. The thief winced, waiting for the sound of footsteps upstairs.

"Who are you?"

"Graetius Hallow," the wizard introduced himself, with a small bow. "And those are my things." He pointed to the boxes.

"You're supposed to be dead."

"Faked it," Graetius said.

"Why?"

"The same reason you're here: to steal something from the museum," the wizard said through a toothy smile.

Wincott had half a mind to throw one of the boxes at him, but caution stayed his hand. Most wizards needed an implement to cast spells, such as a wand, orb, or staff, but some could cast with hands and thought alone. Wincott didn't want to risk finding out what kind Graetius was.

"Couldn't you have just magicked your way in here and taken it?" Wincott retorted.

The wizard laughed and said, "Because I am dead. The undead, anyway. Soon I'll have the Catalyst of Nerjammer, and nothing will stop me."

"So, you faked your death and hid in a box until … wait, I'm missing something here …" the thief trailed off.

"Until a thief showed up to steal my things that I could then blame for taking the catalyst, and no one would be the wiser," Graetius said.

Wincott sighed. It wasn't his first run-in with a haughty wizard. Erdor was full of them. In his youth, Wincott had taken a few basic jobs at the academy in town and discovered wizards were very much like professors: overly educated, socially awkward, and generally unaware of their own shortcomings. Even in death, Graetius appeared to carry on that fine tradition.

He opened his mouth to reply when the wizard turned and glided out of the room into one of the exhibit halls. Wincott fingered the map in his coat to ensure it was still there and followed him out. Graetius appeared lost for a moment, scratching an open sore on his scale thoughtfully, a chunk of gray flesh sloughing off onto the floor next to him. Wincott's stomach lurched.

The wizard spotted what he was looking for and let out a little cry of joy, steering his rigid undead body to a glass case next to the far wall. In it, the thief saw several jeweled implements.

Wincott ignored him and headed for the front door, having obtained what he'd come for. He had no intention of sticking around long enough for the wizard to frame him for stealing some magic artifact he had no interest in.

Graetius rattled the padlock on the case a few times before smashing the glass case with a bony fist. Wincott turned to notice the wizard had lacerated his hand in several places, but no blood emerged.

The mage reached through the broken glass to take hold of a ruby thimble, raising it above his head in long, skeletal fingers and screeching with laughter. Wincott rolled his eyes, but his stomach lurched when he heard footsteps pounding across the floor upstairs.

The thief rushed to the front door and tracked the doorknob, but the lock clicked shut on him. He turned to see Graetius wearing the thimble on an index finger pointed toward him.

"Enjoy, thief," the wizard sneered.

The wizard offered a deep, courtly bow and vanished in a puff of red smoke and laughter. Wincott swore. With the door jammed and his tunnel collapsed, he had few options to escape.

Footsteps on the stairs told him he had only seconds before he was caught, and if he was caught, he'd be back in the cells with a one-way ticket to the gibbet. And the gods only knew what Uncle Frank would do to Sish to settle Wincott's debts.

His eyes darted around wildly, but all the windows were too high for him to reach. A mild panic set in as he felt glued to the floor. Stuck. Caught. At a dead-end.

Focus.

"Dad, here! Up here!" a small voice drifted down to him.

He looked up. Sish lay on one of the rafters, his legs wrapped around the beam, a long, skinny arm extended toward Wincott.

"What are you doing here?" Wincott snapped at him angrily.

"No time, come on!"

The curators were downstairs now, the light of their oil lamps moving through the adjoining room toward him. He cursed under his breath and jumped, reaching toward his son's hand. Sish caught him, and with surprising strength, pulled the thief into the rafters as the curators entered the exhibit room.

Sish put a finger to his lips and pointed to a small opening in the wall at the end of the beam behind him that led onto the roof outside. Father and son crept along the beam and slipped out of the museum without a sound.

They made their way across the snow-laden roof, tracing Sish's steps to a low point, where a collection of large crates afforded a short jump and climb down to the same alley where Wincott had tunneled in. It wasn't lost on him that the boy had found a way into the museum, which suggested the job was more of a Jane than a Charlie, but he said nothing.

Once they were free of the alley and the museum was a few blocks behind them, Wincott pulled the boy aside and lectured him about being out at night.

"I thought you could use a hand," Sish said, his eyes wide and watery.

Maybe it was the adrenaline or the sheer panic, or maybe it was knowing he'd been outsmarted and saved by a twelve-year-old, but Wincott's hand moved without another thought and cuffed the boy hard across the head.

Sish staggered back, falling to the cobblestones in a scrawny heap. Tears leaked from the corners of his eyes. Wincott immediately regretted what he'd done. He thought he'd console the boy, but a hardness in him stayed his hand. No one had ever consoled Wincott as a child or comforted him after he'd been beaten black and blue. The thief told himself he needed to raise Sish to be a survivor, tough and resilient against all the horrors of the world. He needed to learn some lessons the hard way.

The thief turned and walked away, leaving the boy crying and alone in the alley. And he never stopped regretting it.

Chapter Thirty-One

THIS PLACE KEEPS GETTING WEIRDER

SISH MANAGED A DECENT SLEEP next to the campfire Wren had cobbled together in the Grand Valley, waking only once when the hunter dropped a pair of gently used boots on the thief's chest. Apparently, Terry stumbled across them while hunting for rabbits, the barbarian explaining in detail how he had to peel them from the maggoty feet of a long-dead corpse wrapped in a bramble bush. He was convinced the bush killed the man, swiping at its spiked tendrils for good measure.

"But I guess they're better than nothing, right?" Terry prompted him, ever the optimist, as Sish picked the remaining larva from the boots.

He was pleasantly surprised to discover they fit almost perfectly.

"Maggot boots." Terry nodded to the thief while chewing overcooked rabbit. "There's your Treasure of Roan!"

The barbarian erupted with laughter, slapping his knee at his own joke. Wren smiled. Sish only shook his head but promptly stopped when his vision blurred from the pain. Fulk had hit him hard. Any harder and he probably wouldn't have woken up. He gently probed the goose egg at the back of his head with the tips of his fingers. It hurt to the touch. Best leave it alone until it went away or killed him, he figured.

He got to his feet, wobbling dizzily before steadying and walking gingerly in the maggot boots. They really did fit perfectly, he marveled, supposing a bit of leather over his soles wasn't a bad thing in a place where everything was trying to kill you, even the plants.

He sucked in a teeth breath and looked around. Roan's warm almost swampy air erased all memories of the frozen world outside the abandoned city and the long trek he and the others had endured from Fort Rivers to get here. Had it all been worth it? Probably not, though he was experienced enough to know the answer to those types of questions was only gleaned long after the events in question passed, assuming you survived them. So, it was a mug's game to wonder about it now. Best get on with it.

"Ready?" the thief asked, drawing a surprised look from the two men.

They exchanged a glance of muted respect and nodded quietly. The hunter kicked out the fire. The barbarian sheathed his sword, turned, and started jogging away, Wren right behind him.

"Come on, Maggot Boots, let's see what you can do," Sish said to himself, starting after them.

Sish wasn't in the best shape of his life, but he was able to keep a decent jog going through the morning, and by noon, the end of the valley was in sight.

The end of the Grand Valley rose in front of them in the form of a gargantuan rock wall with a castle carved into its face. A seemingly endless number of spires climbed up along the cavern wall above a crenelated fortress that sat like a squat house on a plain of yellowed witch grass and bush. Many of the towers were in ruins, their inside staircases exposed to the elements like rotten mouths spitting crumbling stone teeth, yet enough form remained that it appeared scalable to a large promontory that jutted from the cavern wall at the top of the highest tower. Sish guessed he was looking at the Sixth Highness, Fourteenth Promontory. The half-melted dwarf was right then. They were close.

It all seemed like such a long time ago now, but the thief hadn't forgotten one detail that had gnawed at him ever since he entered the valley: the supposed third trial. Fulk's notes said there would be three trials, and Ruddlefunt said the third was a choice, not a trial. Sish wasn't sure what that meant; he only hoped he hadn't yet made the choice, whatever it was. And that when the time came to make it, he'd see it coming.

His palms sweated thinking about it, like he was forgetting something. That worry grew into a ball of anxiety in the pit of his stomach as he jogged up a grassy hill after Terry and Wren.

At the top, despite the general rotten aspect of the valley, the view was something to marvel at. To his right, at the bottom of the slope, was the edge of the long, black lake they'd paralleled up the valley chasing Kai, which drained into a river closer to the cavern that forked into several smaller rivers that cut through a knotted wood. Sish couldn't see very far into the wood on account of its thick brush, which told him all he needed to know about going that route to reach their destination.

There were still several miles ahead of them before they reached the field at the base of the fortress far below the promontory. The thief followed Wren's eyes to the lake, where, in the distance, a small boat plied the water. He guessed that wasn't Fulk, and if not the trader, then it was likely Wincott or Liv. But there was also a chance it was Company men, and if so, they didn't have long.

Yet Fulk left no sign of his passage along their route. Even Wren was forced to admit the old deputy chief factor was a talented bushman.

"We'll take a break," Wren said, out of breath.

"I worry Fulk is too far ahead of us; we may not be able to catch up," said Terry, not out of breath at all.

Sish was doubled over, catching his breath, sweat streaking down his temples. But his feet didn't ache at all. He was beginning to wonder whether the boots weren't in fact a treasure.

"He's carrying Rena," the thief told them. "It'll slow him. He can't be that far ahead. We'll catch him or die trying."

Wren cast the young thief another look of surprise, and even the barbarian could barely contain his mirth.

"You're starting to sound like a Dungeoneer," Wren teased.

Sish wiped his brow and shook his head. "I lied and cheated my way into this forsaken dungeon, and I'll be damned if some old bureaucrat is going to take what I've earned."

"Earned," Wren said, as if rolling the word around in his mouth. "Funny concept for a thief."

Sish ignored him and started jogging down the hill toward the forest. He didn't expect them to understand how he was feeling; doing the right thing came naturally to people like Terry and Wren. For Sish, it was a struggle. Everything he'd ever cared about had been taken from him or turned on him, from his mother's death to Wincott's treachery and Liv dumping him hours before their wedding.

But Roan—this, *this place*—he'd made happen for himself. Despite the efforts of the E&E, the Guild, the Dungeoneers, his father, Fulk, and a host of monsters, he'd come this far. The treasure was up there somewhere, and Sish intended to get his hands on it, *steal* it, if necessary, and only then would every one of them realize he'd outsmarted them all.

He imagined what it would look like, how it would feel, the moment he got his hands on it, whatever *it* was. The excitement, the elation, the achievement. It spurred his legs forward as he ran down the hill toward the fortress and a gnarled forest ahead of it, all feelings of fatigue washed away. And his feet felt pretty darn good as well.

THE FOREST WAS A MAZE of twisting, interlocking branches and boulders. Little streams trickled left and right, some wide enough to step across, others deep, wide, and placid, tumbling over stone gullies that foamed with steam above deep trout pools. It would have been beautiful if Sish wasn't cautious about what lay beneath the water's surface. Everything in the Grand Valley seemed programmed to kill, so he stuck to the trees, even when they had to crawl on their hands and knees at times to work their way through the brush. It would have been beautiful if it wasn't so frustrating.

Sish was in the lead, but more than once, he had to glance over his shoulder for advice from Wren on how to navigate the next collection of brambles or walls of rocks. He was halfway along a narrow path above a foaming stream between two high rock walls when he heard voices. At first, they were hushed, and the thief wondered if an ambush awaited them, but then he heard laughter, and his nerves calmed.

The rock walls ended as if he'd stepped through a doorway emerging into a glade of tall grass and fiery orange and red paintbrush flowers. There, he spotted three creatures seated comfortably around a campfire at the base of a crumbling barbican. It looked as though it was once part of an outer perimeter wall that stretched through the forest, but the rest of the wall had long since been eaten by the cavern.

The creatures were nothing like Sish had ever encountered. A short man, with goat horns atop a head of soft brown hair and goat's legs, perched on a flat-topped boulder. Next to him was a middle-aged woman with greenish skin and snakes for hair, who sat cross-legged, examining her fingernails as if she were waiting for an appointment at the salon. And across from them was a large brown spider with a man's head. Yet the most alarming thing about them was the eerie blue tinge in their eyes. Blue eyes. Sentinels, like Ruddlefunt. But these three were far too … relaxed maybe? Yes, too casual to be the menacing loners that stalked Northern Erdor's wilderness between towns and trading forts.

An idea took shape in Sish's mind, a nascent understanding of what he was looking at—what the Grand Valley truly was or intended to be—but it slipped away as quickly as it came, like a warm spring breeze that teased summer fragrance before vanishing in a gust of north wind.

"Who goes there?" The goat man stood up, a battle hammer in one hand.

Sish raised his hands defensively as he trod across the glade toward them, "Just a traveler passing through."

"No one passes the Alteri Gate without permission," the goat man announced, a menacing look in his eye. "We three guardians shall smite you where you stand!"

The goat man raised the hammer menacingly and growled. Terry went for his great sword, but Wren stayed his hand, waiting to see what the creatures would do. When the men didn't move, the goat man dropped his hammer and broke into peals of laughter. The snake-headed woman and spider did the same, snakes bouncing, arachnid legs clicking.

Sish stepped closer, his hands still raised. There was a cookpot slung over the fire and something bubbling within. His stomach growled hungrily at the smell, but part of him worried about what the three creatures might find appetizing that he would not.

"Wh—who are you?" he asked.

"*Who* are *we*? Why, we three are the guardians of the Alteri Gate—entrance to the Great Fortress of the Lords of Roan," the lady answered, one eyebrow cocked, lips twisted mischievously.

"Forgive me, but I've never heard of an Alteri Gate or Great Fortress," Sish said.

The spider turned toward them, his deep blue eyes flashing playfully, "Well, of course, *you* haven't. The Great Fortress has been abandoned these thousand years! Not but us and bogwights in the Grand Valley now."

"And the Pelican of Sitka," the goat man added.

"And raveners, lots of those," the woman chimed in.

"Oh, and Yig."

The woman nodded knowingly, "Yes, Yig. Where has he gone?"

The spider pointed with three legs to the far end of the valley from where Sish and the others had come, "Went screaming to that end of things. Suspect it was when this lot came through."

The goat man turned back to Sish. "Who are you that should be so bold as to traverse the horrors of the Grand Valley?"

"Would you stop talking like that," the woman snapped at him.

"Okay," the goat man said, his little shoulders slumping.

"I'm Sish Torren, this is Elden Wren, and that's Terry," said Sish.

"I am Dalla," the woman said, standing and introducing herself with a short bow, the snakes on her head flowing like liquid as her head dipped. "This is Petr," she gestured to the spider, "and that's Seygan the satyr."

"What's a satyr?" Terry wondered.

Seygan stood up and gestured proudly to himself with his hands and said, "A woodland creature of ancient mythos, one part man, one part goat, and a dash of ribaldry."

The creature and its companions laughed, but Sish, Wren, and Terry weren't sure what to do, so they stayed silent. Terry's hand brushed the pommel of the great sword strapped to his back, ready to murder all three of the guardians if he got so much as a whiff of danger from them.

"Of course, I'm not actually a satyr, nor is Dalla a gorgon, or Petr a Methuro spider. But the Masters engineered us to look that way, and so we have ever been," Seygan explained.

"How long have you been here?" Wren asked.

"Come, sit by the fire," Dalla suggested, sliding on a wooden bench to make room for the newcomers. "It's been a long time since we had visitors, and our days of being fearsome guardians of this abandoned city are … well, behind us, wouldn't you say Petr?"

The spider clicked its legs in agreement and shuffled aside to make room for the newcomers. Sish shrugged and sat next to the gorgon. The food in the pot smelled better than ever, and it was all he could do to keep his eyes off it.

"We have been here since time immemorial," Seygan said, his voice oddly normal for an arachnid. "We were created in the high age of machines, when humans graced the moon and stars, mastered the air and water, and shaped the land as they saw fit. This was the time before the Reclamation, before magic returned."

"The Reclamation?" Wren asked.

"The dismantling of the world," Dalla answered. "A purposeful retreat by humans to return the world to its virgin state, a time before machines. But it, too, was corrupted, and from that …"

Her eyes shifted to the spider, who shuddered uncomfortably.

"It was a long time ago," Petr said, head bowed to reveal the full extent of his magnificently curled black horns. "Why have you come? Certainly not to learn a history lesson."

"We're pursuing someone," Sish said. "He might've come this way with a girl in tow. Have you seen him?"

The guardians exchanged a bewildered look and said no. Sish guessed Fulk had sneaked past them, which likely wasn't that difficult. The guardians didn't seem too interested in guarding much of anything.

"He must already be past us," Sish mused, looking at Wren and Terry. He got to his feet and asked for directions to the Sixth Highness.

The creatures gasped at the mention of the name.

"The storeroom," Dalla said. "Why do you seek the storeroom?"

"It's the man we're after," Sish lied. "He's heading there now. And others, too. He has our friend."

Wren cast a sidelong look at Sish, highlighting the glaring omission in the young thief's story, but he said nothing. And neither did Terry. The barbarian was a ball of taut muscles, ready to snap into action, either to kill the guardians or sprint to the fortress or both. Sish grinned inwardly, thinking Terry was likely tired of talking things through.

"Then we shall accompany you!" Seygan announced.

He drew a horn from his belt and blew on it, but instead of a loud, triumphant blare, it sounded like a weasel being stepped on. The satyr broke into peals of laughter again, as did the gorgon and spider.

"We won't be much help," Dalla said. "None of us have fought a battle in … well, ever."

"But we know the way," Petr chimed in. "Follow me."

The spider stamped out the cookfire and scurried through the ruined barbican. Terry and Wren followed, both keeping their hand close to their weapons apprehensively. The Dungeoneers didn't have a great track record with spiders.

"Follow them," Dalla said with a smile.

Sish fell in behind the hunter, the gorgon at his side.

"And I'll follow you," Seygan said, giggling as he skipped along behind them.

Chapter Thirty-Two

APRIL WIND

A HIGH-PITCHED SCREAM ERUPTED FROM THE alley next to the marketplace. It was after dark, the cobblestone streets and laneways mostly deserted, but Sish chose to ignore it. Screams were not uncommon in this part of Fort Rivers, and it was none of his business anyway—he had a coat full of wallets that weren't his, and the last thing he needed was to be entangled in some domestic dispute that would bring the E&E guards down on him. But then he heard it again, a high-pitched cry of pain. There was something familiar about it, an inflection in the voice that made his heart stir … *Liv!*

He spun on his heel and sprinted down the alley in the direction he'd come, following the noise. He heard it again and veered onto a narrow street to his right, past boarded-up shops and merchant booths, a cool breeze wafting over the cobblestones toward him.

He made one more left before he found her in a heap of torn green robes in a shallow puddle of rainwater. She wasn't moving. A light mist cascaded from the night sky, falling sporadically between the A-frame cedar-shake roofs of the three-story shops and buildings that loomed darkly above the alley, not a single lamplight on in any of them.

"Liv?" he asked, kneeling at her side.

She stirred, a soft murmur parting her lips. Sish turned her over and brushed back her long, auburn hair to reveal a gash across her forehead and down her cheek, blood trickling down her flesh to swirl with the rainwater beneath her. She moaned again, only semiconscious.

The alley was silent. Whoever attacked her must have fled, and nothing led Sish to believe the guards were coming either. His flat was a few blocks away, near the market, a place he'd secured on the cheap after he'd unceremoniously decamped from his and Wincott's home above Ms. Burbidge. Wincott shrugged it off, muttering something about not pissing where you eat, but Sish had ignored him, a behavior he'd become more accustomed to as the old man grew more irritable, jealous, and filled with contempt each passing day.

Sish squatted, slid his arms under her, and pushed up on his heels, lifting her into his arms. He hadn't laid eyes on Liv since the incident at Lone Butte, his last job with the Dungeoneers, which he'd never collected on. He shuddered thinking about what he'd done to Davin. He woke up some nights, his teeth clenched, hand flexed like he was holding a knife. He remembered how it felt, how easily the blade had parted the man's flesh and ended his life. Like nothing. *Too* easy.

If it was mere chance that he happened upon Liv this night, then it was a strange one at that. The thief had just finished his last day pickpocketing at the market in Fort Rivers. He'd secretly booked passage aboard a riverboat the next day, intent on heading south to the desert country and warm weather, where he'd ply his trade in a place where no one knew his name or his father's.

Wincott didn't know he intended to leave. He didn't think the old man deserved that, having cut Sish out of all the meaningful jobs, forcing him to continue jobs that were simple for a street urchin while he drank the rent money away at the Werewolf's Toe, buying rumors and gossip that amounted to nothing,

It would've been one thing if the old man just ignored him, but most days, he came back to their flat drunk and angry and took it out on Sish. The old man had grown all too comfortable raising a hand against him, and sometimes, a belt. Until one day, Sish decided to hit back. He was strong enough to hurt Wincott and had, getting one good punch in before Dad laid into him like a battering ram and left him on the floor with a broken rib and bruised jaw. That was it. Wincott had never been supportive of Sish finding his own way and was getting worse and worse about it with time. So, he moved out, got his own flat, and did his best to avoid the parts of town where he thought he might run into him.

Discovering Liv in the alley was the first familiar face he'd seen after months of solitude. He wasn't sure if he should be elated or worried. One part of him was strangely excited to see her, to talk to someone from that part of his life that seemed so long ago now. But another part remembered the look on her face when he killed Davin. It wasn't hatred, but something almost too difficult to bear … disappointment. Heartbreak.

His arms were gassed by the time they reached his flat. The hike up three sets of rain-slicked stairs in the dark left his legs shaky, but he managed to squeeze through the narrow, poorly hung door and lay her down on a sunken Chesterfield that had been there when he moved in. He lit the lamps and coaxed a gentle fire to life in the blackened brick hearth and waited for his muscles to stop aching while he watched her sleep.

He couldn't lay claim to a nice flat—a pickpocket income didn't buy much in a Company town. He lived in a poorer stretch of town on the top floor of an old building with a sagging, moss-ridden cedar-shake roof and a set of rotten stairs that bent and creaked beneath his weight. The neighbors kept to themselves—an old lady on one side who boiled turnips into soup every day that made his nose curl, while on the other side was a butcher who worked one of the chicken houses a few blocks over. Neither seemed to notice the young man living between them, just the way he liked it. And although he had no plans to stick around, the place was dry and warm, and he didn't have to worry about whom he came home to.

He slung Liv's robe over a clothesline near the fire to dry and filled the kettle to make tea. He'd stowed a couple of satchels of peppermint in his bag for the riverboat journey but decided she would enjoy them more than him.

She awoke shortly after midnight. He'd washed the dirt from her wounds and laid out a cup of tea next to her, which had long since gone cold. He was half asleep on a ratty velvet chair next to the fire.

"Sish?"

He opened his eyes as she wiped the sleep from hers.

He nodded quietly and offered a guilty, closed-lip smile. "Are you okay?"

She nodded slowly, sitting up to sip from the mug next to her. "It's cold," she said.

"I thought you would've woken long before now," he said. "Sorry."

"How did I get here?"

Sish explained where he found her and the long walk back. She thanked him and remarked on the coincidence of him being within earshot exactly when she'd been attacked.

"Do you know who it was?" he asked.

"No," she said, shaking her head thoughtfully. "Not exactly."

He looked at her, his brows knitting together questioningly.

"Guildsmen, I think," she murmured.

"What are Guildsmen doing in Fort Rivers?"

She shrugged and said, "The same thing E&E men are doing in Fort Sage: undermining the competition."

"But why would they target you?" he wondered.

"It's a long story," she said between sips. "Anyway, where's Wincott? How come I don't recognize this place?"

Sish rubbed his palms over his pant legs and tossed a couple pieces of wood on the fire while he thought through an acceptable answer or just ignored the questions entirely, he wasn't sure which. She said nothing, using the silence as a weapon to make him uncomfortable enough to spit out an answer. It worked.

"I wanted to go out on my own," he said, "the old man was a bit … stifling."

Liv pursed her lips and nodded quietly, then sipped her tea again. She didn't press any further, instead letting her eyes wander over the sparsely furnished flat. There was a bed, a rough table and chairs next to a small galley kitchen, a chamber pot room, and two empty bookshelves that flanked the small brick hearth.

Rain tapped loudly against the thin glass window that looked out over the stairwell and dirty garbage- and horseshit-strewn alley below. A heavy spring wind moaned through a narrow gap in the front door, leaving Sish to think it was not a good night to travel. As a child, he had trouble falling asleep most nights and often woke up with nightmares about his mother or strange creatures in the woods chasing him. On the nights when Wincott was home, his father would often sit with him and tell him fairy tales until Sish fell asleep.

One of those tales was the story of the April Wind, which was a heavy storm of warm air that would blow out of the south every spring and chase away the spirits of winter, melting snow and ice, and the ghouls and ghosts that haunted darker times of the year. It was called April Wind because it always came at that time of year, and once it had, the leaves would be on the trees within a few weeks.

It had been a long, cold winter this time around, a pattern that seemed to be a trend in recent years, causing more than a few sky mages to predict a coming ice age. They might be right—shorter summers, colder temperatures, and heavier snows were commonplace. The E&E traders who prowled the wilderness beyond the city told tales of glaciers expanding at an alarming rate.

Yet as Sish listened to the steady tattoo of rain on his window and the heavy, almost tropical wind that blew out of the south, he rested comfortably knowing, for this year at least, winter had come to an end.

"April Wind," he muttered, staring out the dark, rain-streaked window.

Liv offered a knowing smile. "I was just thinking that."

"You should stay here tonight," he told her, "You can have the bed."

"Kind of you, but I should be getting on my way," she said, setting down the mug.

She got to her feet but wobbled weakly and quickly fell back onto the couch. An embarrassed giggle parted her lips as her eyes rolled drunkenly around in her head. She traced her fingers across the gash on her face, wincing.

"Or maybe not," she pronounced.

"Whoever is after you probably knows where you live and might be waiting," he told her, "You're safe here. In the morning—"

"In the morning, I'll leave," she said matter-of-factly, as if there were no room to negotiate.

"Now tell me about these Guildsmen," he pressed.

"First, *you* tell *me* where you're going," she said, meeting his eyes with an even glare before looking at the packed bag that lay next to the door.

Sish chewed his lip and said, "South. Start fresh. I leave on the morning boat."

Liv's eyes widened. He detected something there, but he couldn't quite put his finger on it. Surprise? Anger? Disappointment? He wasn't sure. Maybe all three, but Sish had never been particularly good at reading a woman's face, especially hers.

"Does your father know?"

"He's not my father," Sish said, a slightly churlish tone in his voice.

She looked at him impatiently.

"No. He doesn't. He doesn't even know I live here," he told her.

She sipped her tea quietly and looked thoughtful for a moment. After a minute or so, she said, "Good. I know he's meant well at times, but I'm not sure he—"

"Let's change the subject. Back to the Guildsmen. What's going on?"

She sipped her tea again, as if she wasn't sure where to start. After a moment, she leaned forward. "It's Rena. One of the Guild's merchant princes learned about her … abilities … and is convinced she can turn the tide of trade in their favor."

Several questions popped into Sish's head. In his time with the Dungeoneers, he'd come to respect and care for Rena, as had the others, but she remained a mystery, and he little understood the nature of her power, only that she was a weapon of last resort. At times, Sish wondered if Wren adopted her simply to strengthen his own hand, but he had long ago put that thought aside. The hunter was stern and gruff, but the people he chose to have in his life were those he genuinely cared for.

One question did bubble to the surface, though, and a prickly feeling at the back of his neck suggested he knew the answer before he asked it.

"What was this prince's name?"

"Lord … hold on … Edwin? Elgard? Elgin. Lord Elgin Bracewell," Liv said.

A cold finger traced up Sish's spine. It was a name he hadn't heard in many years. The Guild's patron. His mother's married name. Lord Bracewell was Sish's real father. Wincott was the only man he considered a father, though he wasn't a very good one at that. He'd not thought about the man since his mother had fled north with Sish to find a better life. But he remembered him, mostly the back of his hand and the ever-present bruises on his mother's face.

Elgin Bracewell wasn't just a merchant prince; he was the benefactor of the Guild in the territory it controlled to the south. The very territory Sish planned to travel to on the morning boat, though admittedly, he had no intention of looking up dear old Dad for hugs and kisses. More to the point, Sish was old enough to know—and probably knew better than some others—that if Bracewell was after Rena and bold enough to send his own men into the heart of E&E territory, he was a real threat.

"Has Wren warned the Company? Surely, they would be more friendly to us if they knew the Guild was here," he said.

"Us?" she said, raising an eyebrow. "No, the governor has lately replaced his long-time right-hand with his son. I'm no fan of the E&E, but whatever semblance of professionalism it had has been buried beneath a mound of nepotism and corruption. We've done a good job keeping them ignorant of Rena's existence, and I intend to see that continue. What I don't understand is how the Guild found out."

Sish kept mum about … well, mum, believing if she found out he would become the prime suspect in outing Rena. After all, you can't trust a thief, right?

"What is it about her?"

Liv was hesitant for a moment, her shoulders stiffening unnaturally. She looked at him. "Do you still have that thimble we recovered from the lich at Moon Lake?"

He reached into his waistband, where he kept an extra set of picks, and withdrew the ruby thimble. He had no idea why it had been so important to the lich; as far as he could tell, it was nothing of importance. But it had been a gift to him from Liv, the first time he felt she'd noticed he was even alive, so he'd kept it. He tossed it to her.

"This is a catalyst," she explained, "specifically the Catalyst of Abdul Faisal Horux Nerjammer."

Sish knew catalysts were implements that wizards and their like used to focus and channel their magic; without them, most wizards couldn't light a candle without a match.

"I always found it odd the lich had *this* catalyst. The books suggest it was never actually functional but rather an experiment gone wrong when an apprentice of Calibre—you've heard of him?—okay. When his apprentice, Abdul, attempted to duplicate his master's ability to create life. The story goes the experiment went awry, killing Nerjammer and leaving only this catalyst and a pile of ashes behind as evidence. No one since has been able to make use of the device; in fact, it's widely considered little more than a valuable curiosity."

The idea that Sish had been carrying around a valuable but useless ruby emblem in his pants for years made him laugh inwardly. If he'd known, he probably would've fenced it.

"What does any of this have to do with Rena?" he asked.

"Wizards like me need catalysts to do their work. I prefer a wand or staff, others an orb, and some choose thimbles. Rena ... Rena doesn't need a catalyst. In fact, her form of magic is so potent I fear what might happen if she tried to use one."

"You mentioned in the past she's a summoner. What is that?" he asked.

"Well, for starters, she's the only one I've ever met—that anyone alive in Fort Rivers has ever met, except maybe that old fart Hamish Finklefunk. Truth is, we can describe what she can do, but we don't *know* what she can do or how she does it. It's said in the ancient world there wasn't any magic, that people ruled it with machines and advanced technologies. When the world was dismantled, magic began to return, but in some places, it was combined with that ancient knowledge and used to create ... well, create the world we live in today with all manners of beasts, creatures, and monsters. Over time, magic has grown stronger, changed ... mutated in unexpected ways. I believe that Rena is exactly that, a new evolution of magic that we don't understand. In the wrong hands, she's a weapon."

"And Lord Bracewell knows it," Sish finished.

The thief got to his feet and wandered to the window, suddenly paranoid someone might be listening in on their conversation. He looked through the rain-streaked glass to the shadowy alley below but saw no one. The wind howled and beat against the frame, the faint aroma of fresh, warm southern air hinting at the changing season. April Wind.

"Where is she now?" he asked.

Liv turned toward him and hesitated, the look on her face revealing she wasn't sure she could trust him.

"Some place safe."

He nodded quietly and turned back to the window, watching her blurry reflection in the darkened glass. The look on her face reminded him of that day at Lone Butte. He heard the strange hollow *thunk* the knife made when he slid it into Davin's back. His fingers twitched uncomfortably at the memory. He clasped them in his other hand to steady them.

"I'm sorry, Liv," he told her, his eyes looking beyond her reflection into the murky night beyond the flat. "That day, at the tower ... I ... lost control."

"I know," she said, "After ... Terry told me what he did, how he treated you. I never saw ..."

"You didn't want to see," Sish snapped at her.

She said nothing. The thief stepped toward the hearth, his eyes fixed on the flickering amber light. He couldn't look her in the eye.

"I shouldn't have said that. It's just ... I feel like ... like no one ... no one gives a shit, no one ever has. I'm just a nuisance to Wincott and to you guys? A tool to be used when the job calls for it. You weren't in that tower. Davin left me to die, and when I didn't and chased him to the canoes, he tried to kill me there, too. If I didn't ... if I didn't kill him, he would've killed me. That's all there was to it."

He exhaled deeply. A strange feeling washed through him like a great weight had lifted from his shoulders, the shroud of the lie he'd been telling himself ever since that day cast off. The thing he struggled with most was that murdering Davin hadn't really affected him at all. Deep down, he believed his actions were just. And it terrified him. Was he a monster? Hard and emotionless like Wincott? Or worse, like his father? He hoped not. Was there a pathway back to the person he hoped he could become? He didn't know.

He cast his eyes over the backpack on the ground next to the door. In it was the ticket away from Fort Rivers, from this life, from what people thought he was. In Fort Sage, he could become something else, start anew. Was *that* what he wanted?

"I know," Liv said, after a moment. "Terry told us. He saw what Davin did in the tower, but he couldn't get in to save you himself. And he saw how Davin ... fled when I was cornered."

Sish met her eyes. He wasn't sure how to feel. He bit back tears of vindication and screams of rage. She knew and let him go? Let him feel this way all that time? And yet, somewhere deep down, Sish knew he had needed that time alone, to part ways with Wincott, wrestle with what he'd done, and find a way to keep going, regardless. He stepped toward her.

"You knew? All this time?" he said, his voice tight with emotion, eyes watering.

She stood. "Is it true, what Davin said about … how you felt about me?"

"You know it is," he told her.

She kissed him then, and he let her. Their mouths locked warmly in a moment of pure bliss that felt like infinity, and he came to feel then that he knew how to kiss her, as if he'd always known and had just been waiting for this moment to find out. They stumbled across the room and fell together onto the bed. Warm tropical rain lashed the window through the night while the wind moaned, heralding a new season.

Chapter Thirty-Three

MAYBE GOBLINS AREN'T SO BAD

THE BOAT FLIPPED IN THE nick of time. Wincott, Liv, and Ruddlefunt were pulled through the water by their shades as the bow slid onto the rocky beach. Their mirror selves vanished into the inky lake with an angry gurgle. The old thief launched across the bow onto the shore with a thud, the dwarf landing heavily on top of him. Liv, meantime, stepped lithely out of the boat and helped both to their feet.

"Not an experience I'd like to repeat," Wincott said, dusting off his pants and sheathing Raspberry at his side.

"But very informative!" Ruddlefunt added.

"Where to?" Liv asked, looking around.

Ahead of them was a tangle of forest: stunted trees, brambles, rock, and overgrown grass sliced into fingers of land by several small rivers that drained from Mirror Lake. To their left were more hills, sparse trees, and the gods only knew what horrid creatures, yet beyond all of that was the end of the valley and a great spiraling fortress carved out of the cavern wall that rose away above them to impossible heights.

"The Fortress of the Lords," Ruddlefunt announced, following Wincott's eyes. "We're nearly there."

Wincott's thoughts shifted to Sish. He had no way of knowing whether the boy had survived, but he found himself silently praying that he had. The thief suspected Liv felt the same. He knew she still loved Sish, and he did her, despite what happened between them.

Wincott shouldered some of the blame

there, probably a lot of blame. If they survived this mess, maybe he'd get the chance to correct some of it, or at the very least, cede that he'd been wrong. But all that hinged on finding Sish before the boy got the treasure.

What Sish didn't know was that the moment he stepped passed the promontory, he would fail the last trial. There was no way out of the valley alive for anyone who sought or laid hands on the treasure, or so Ruddlefunt had explained. That might mean none of them would survive the strangeness of the Grand Valley, which, to Wincott, seemed entirely designed to kill a person at every turn. In the remote chance that Sish somehow survived getting to the treasure, Wincott hoped the murdering part of the trials didn't happen until the boy laid his hands on the treasure, which might lend Wincott a bit of time to stop him.

But there were a few issues to sort out between then and now, not least of which was the fact that a surly battalion of Guildsmen were likely already in Roan and may already be as deep as the Grand Valley. When he took the job that led him to Fort Shatterstill, he received intel that a battalion of the Guild's best soldiers were camped at the southern end of the valley on a narrow spit of pine flat between the Sage and Ribbon rivers. The agreement had been he would map out Roan and send word when it was safe to enter.

Truth was, he never planned to send word, not until he located the treasure and decided for himself whether it outweighed his payment from the Guild. He was also certain they wouldn't bother to pay him. A thief was an easy thing to dispose of, especially this far into the wilderness. The bastard commanding the legion was a stuck-up noble, the type who believed his privilege was a divine right.

The old thief decided to roll the dice and forsake the mission at the abandoned fort. He'd heard a rumor some years ago from a hunter in Fort Wick that there was a second secret entrance to Roan hidden beneath Fort Shatterstill, on the opposite side of the valley. That was why Wincott had gone there first. Perhaps no one had ever gained entry to the city because it was properly sealed, leaving the only remaining access through Shatterstill.

Of course, that hadn't turned out to be the case. Shatterstill was overrun with goblins, and when he reached Roan, it hadn't been that difficult at all to find a way in. Nor had it been for Fulk and his goons or Sish's friends. The city wasn't hard to get into; it just killed everyone who did.

"Ruddlefunt, what's the shortest route to the fortress?" Wincott asked.

The dwarf scratched at the metal plate on his right cheek where his flesh was burned away, the faint blue glow of his eyes pulsating as he considered.

"The Alteri Gate is heavily guarded by three creatures I wouldn't want to cross, but there is another way," he said.

"If it's by water, I'd rather take my chances at the gate," Wincott grumbled, fingering Raspberry nervously, his eyes drawn to the lake they'd barely escaped.

"No, no water," Ruddlefunt said, dismissing the thief with a shake of his hand, "Bridges. Rope bridges. Several of them span the river. They were not built by the Masters, but other things that have made a home in this valley since it was abandoned."

Liv rolled her eyes. More monsters. Wincott admitted he didn't like the sound of that, but after two lake trips gone awry and a forest full of horrors, he was willing to take a chance on some bridges. He looked at Liv for an indication of preference, but the wizard pursed her lips and shook her head tiredly.

They set out for the bridges with Ruddlefunt in the lead, which meant slow going as he tripped over the billowy edges of his crimson moth-eaten robes. Wincott suggested he carry the robes for the Librarian, but the dwarf wouldn't hear it.

They hiked alongside the little river that drained lazily from Mirror Lake, waded through a shallow portion of it to a long, thin, rocky island, and hiked along that until they came to the first of several suspension bridges made of rope.

They were unusual in that there were only two ropes each, a top for your hands and a bottom for your feet, and each hung rather loosely over the water.

"Not exactly bridges then," Liv remarked.

More like high wires, Wincott thought.

Ruddlefunt didn't seem to notice the danger and quickly inched along the first one and was across to another small island filled with trees in a few moments.

Wincott gestured for Liv to go next, but she insisted he go ahead. The thief shrugged and climbed on. He was halfway through when he lost his footing, and his legs went into the water, soaking his boots. The icy cold water stung his toes, and he was suddenly reminded how cold feet made everything else more miserable. He clung to the top of the rope bridge with both hands, attempting to pull himself up, but the river pushed hard against his legs, threatening to suck him into the water.

He felt a hand grab the back of his shirt and heave him upward. His feet scrambled numbly for the lower rope, and he found purchase, settling back onto the bridge. The wizard was beside him, a small grin on her face.

"Nearly lost you there," she said, smirking.

Wincott tried to think of a quick retort but thought better of it given the circumstances and said thank you instead. Liv gestured for him to carry on, and they made it to the other side without issue.

They forded two more bridges before they reached another small treed island between three branches of the river, where the clang of steel on steel rang out ahead of them. Wincott motioned for them to crouch, which meant only he and Liv knelt while Ruddlefunt continued walking like normal. They crept toward a large boulder close to the commotion, from which they could gain a better view.

On the other side of the rock was another long bridge with a dozen soldiers working their way across the ropes to the far side. Ahead of the soldiers was a small group of goblins firing arrows at them from a copse of trees. Wincott felt his heart leap into his throat. One of them was fending two soldiers off with a meat cleaver.

Wincott was surprised at the creature's ability to fight, though perhaps the grubby creature's persistence since Shatterstill should've indicated he was no mere monster. The pair of soldiers attacked the goblin together, but Meat Cleaver was able to hold them at bay with parries and counter-slashes.

The goblins were badly outnumbered, and Wincott's initial elation at seeing Meat Cleaver meet his end was dampened when he recognized the markings on the soldier's mail coat: a stylized coat of arms with a falcon and a dragon flanking a red sword on white—the Erdor & Expanse Trading Co.

Something burned in Wincott. An emotion or realization he hadn't felt before. He began to see things differently. He didn't see a dozen men valiantly beating back a horde of monsters, but rather, a dozen poachers preying on a badly outnumbered and poorly equipped group of defenders. The thought shocked him, paralyzing his movements as he peered out from behind the boulder at the bloody melee.

Since when were goblins worth anything at all? But seeing the Company there, and knowing what it could do, what it had done to the people and creatures of the Northern Erdor, changed the thief's way of thinking.

"Sish," Liv cursed as she recognized the E&E emblem.

"He's not with them," Wincott said.

"But he brought the Company here."

"What's the Company?" Ruddlefunt asked.

"They're a problem, that's what they are," Liv spat.

"Don't worry, I have an idea," Wincott said.

He snuck crept past the boulder into the long reed grass closer to the rope bridge. Meat Cleaver was doing a praiseworthy job of keeping the soldiers held up on the ropes, but even Wincott could see the goblin growing tired. Behind him, the other goblins were out of arrows and had drawn rusty knives and short swords, ready to battle if their leader fell. The creatures were grim-faced but determined, and the thief recognized in that look something he'd never seen in goblins before, perhaps because he'd never bothered to give it a second thought or because there was something different about these goblins. There was determination there, a commitment and loyalty to something unspoken. Certainly, it explained how tenacious they'd been in chasing him across the valley to Roan. He thought back to the nine pillars in the lake and the statue of the goblin the other eight knelt before through the first two trial rooms.

Meat Cleaver and his companions wouldn't give up until they were dead, he knew, reminding him of the Dungeoneers.

"Damn do-gooders," he whispered, pushing down the pride he felt. "I can't believe I'm doing this."

He drew Raspberry and started sawing the ropes that held the bridge up. The sword cut through the bottom rope easily, sending three of the soldiers into the river with barely a yelp. They sank like stones beneath their heavy mail.

Two more turned to Wincott when he started on the upper rope and scrambled toward him, reaching for his head with gloved hands. Meat Cleaver caught sight of the thief and fought with renewed vigor. Wincott cut as fast as he could. Raspberry made short work of the heavy rope, and the bridge collapsed a moment later, taking the remaining soldiers into the river with it.

He watched the cold, dark water, waiting for a soldier to surface, but not even one came up. Out of breath and clammy with near-death sweat, the thief climbed to his feet and sheathed his sword. Across the river, Meat Cleaver stared at him, a soldier dead at his feet, the other lost to the river. The goblin's sharp yellow eyes met Wincott's, his knobby black chin held high. If he recognized the thief from Shatterstill, he didn't show it. He nodded once and turned away, vanishing into the woods with his companions.

Chapter Thirty-Four

HE'S A COLD FISH

THE ROAD TO COLD FISH LAKE was little more than a goat trail that climbed through a heavy spruce forest between snow-capped peaks. It was late summer, but already an autumn chill was in the air and the snow line was halfway down the mountains. Wincott seemed to think winter was coming earlier each year, but he wasn't a sky mage that studied such things, so the only evidence he had was his own experience, which he had to admit was questionable.

What was also questionable was the march to Cold Fish Lake. He was exiled from the operating area of the E&E for repeated offenses against the exchequer, which was a fancy way of saying he'd been caught one too many times stealing important things from important people, or people who thought they were important anyway, among them the chief factor of Fort Rivers.

Wincott considered his exile a badge of honor. The man next to him—Fulk Dundurn—didn't see it that way. The story was all over the city. Fulk's reputation was nearly legendary, and the chief factor felt threatened by him, so replaced him with his son as deputy, getting rid of any perceived challenger and securing his own legacy in one fell swoop. Wincott was grudgingly impressed by the man's gumption, but the story went that Fulk had been decidedly less impressed.

So unimpressed had Fulk been, that he stormed into the factor's bed chamber one night, pulled the man out of bed with his wife, tied him to a chair, and proceeded to give him a lecture about honor, integrity, and leading by example. Apparently, it fell on deaf ears because the factor's wife screamed loud enough to wake the guards, and a fight ensued. Fulk won and beat the factor nearly senseless in the process and proceeded to drag him out into the fort courtyard and conduct a trial at half-past midnight for high crimes and misdemeanors against the Company. Only the crows bore witness.

A backup team of guards arrived a while later and managed to wrest control of the situation from Fulk before he lopped the factor's head off (though it was said the man pissed himself in front of several dozen men). He was thrown in the cells, and although the governor should've executed him, he feared reprisals from Fulk's loyal traders and exiled him instead.

Bit of a wuss, the governor was.

Fulk was clamped in irons in a cell next to Wincott's. The two had never met, but Wincott knew very well who the man was, not just by his reputation for being a tenacious Company man but also because he was Sish's real father.

The journey to Cold Fish Lake, the very edge of the Company's territory, of any Company's territory for that matter, was a fortnight via canoe and pack horse. Wincott had been thinking of a way to tell the man he had a son since they were in jail together but could never quite get the words together.

He hadn't forgotten that he'd tried to tell him years earlier, and it wasn't lost on him that if he told Fulk now, the man would likely want to know why he'd taken so long to tell him. Wincott could lie, but eventually, the truth would be out. So, he hadn't said anything. It was a lie by omission, he knew, but lying never bothered Wincott the way it did Sish.

Besides, he and Sish were on the outs. The boy was reckless, didn't listen to a thing Wincott had to say, and invited all manner of danger into their lives. He'd gotten mixed up with that crew of treasure hunters and disappeared with the young farm wizard somewhere to the south. There didn't seem much point now in telling Fulk he had a son, yet he'd come to know one thing about life—very few things were true coincidences.

There was a pattern to life, something unexplainable, that knitted everything together, and it was no accident the thief had found himself chained to the former deputy chief factor along a pack train to the edge of the wilderness. He had no idea what would happen to them when they reached the lake, but he hadn't known the Company to be particularly trustworthy over the years, so he doubted they'd just let them go free. And even if they did, what then? Would he and Fulk partner and start a new kingdom in the wilderness?

He choked back a laugh. He didn't know what the other man had planned, but Wincott fully intended to lie, cheat, and steal his way back to Fort Rivers and resume life as a purloiner of other people's things. And if there were no jobs for him there, maybe he'd go south, where he still had contacts with the Guild, and find that idiot kid and his girlfriend.

They were two days from Cold Fish Lake on a narrow mountain path when Fulk finally said something. Wincott had attempted to engage him in friendly conversation more than once, but the best he'd achieved in response so far was a low grunt. The other exile, a former banker turned fraudster named Cotswold Carlish, had been more amenable to conversation, though everything he said amounted to a plea for his life.

"You know, they're going to kill us," Wincott told Fulk.

The three exiles marched beside one another up the path. It was late afternoon, and he knew their retinue would halt soon to make camp, which was the exile's job to set up. The weather was fair, the sky dotted with large, white clouds that glided aimlessly overhead, and the forest was still full of birdsong.

Fulk looked at him but said nothing. Cotswold, on the other hand, went straight into panic mode.

"Kill? What do you mean *kill*? They can't kill us. We're exiled. Set free. Exiled, that's what that word means. Look it up in a dictionary," Cotswold protested, his round, pudgy face filled with fear. "I can't be killed, don't deserve to be killed. I only made one mistake, a few rounding errors, no harm done. No, not killed. Exiled. Right? Tell me I'm right!"

Wincott smiled but didn't say anything. He liked watching the fat man squirm.

Fulk elbowed the banker in the ribs and said, "He's just trying to scare you. You won't be killed. This is the E&E; we have more honor than that. You'll be a free man."

Wincott shook his head in disbelief. How could he be so blind to what was obvious to the thief?

"He talks!" Wincott announced, teasing him.

Fulk grunted. "And you talk too much."

"Q-quiet, they'll hear us a-and—" Cotswold stammered.

A whip lashed bit into Wincott's shoulders, tearing at the skin beneath his overcoat.

"Shut up, or I'll gut ye all right here and leave yer bodies for the Blue-Eyeds!" a heavyset guard yelled at them from atop a horse behind them.

He was one of the leaders of the pack train, with massive arms and dark skin etched with deep scars and tattoos that suggested a life spent at sea. Wincott had caught the man's whip more than once and his eye as well, and the look in it suggested he was just waiting for an opportunity to lay into the three exiles.

That night, after the three men raised the tents and watered and brushed the horses, they gathered around a small fire with shallow bowls of stew and ate in silence. They were still manacled to one another, but the guards had long since ignored them and were gathered around a larger fire nearby, where they had plenty of food, drink, and conversation.

"The big one said there are Blue-Eyeds here," Cotswold said, his eyes darting searchingly between Wincott and Fulk. "You think so? I heard they tear any man they come across limb from limb and eat children."

Wincott rolled his eyes.

"Might be," was all Fulk said between mouthfuls of his stew.

"What do we do if they come? You guys get any tips? I'm just a banker. Not a fighter," Cotswold said.

His hands were visibly shaking, his eyes as wide as saucer plates. Wincott almost felt bad for him. Almost.

"You're not a banker anymore," Fulk told him, his deep, intense eyes fixing on Cotswold's like a leopard eyeing a mouse.

Cotswold lowered his eyes, his shoulders slumped. He ate in silence.

"Seems strange to travel all this way for three exiles," Wincott observed. "They could've easily sent us on a raft south or marched us a few miles out of town."

"Expansion," Fulk said. "This is a reconnaissance mission. Some of my men mapped this area as far as Cold Fish Lake several years ago, looking for new, rare pelts, blood, and mineral deposits. Some promising spots, but they saw signs of a guardian and turned back. The Company wants this area before the Guild gets it."

Wincott nodded. "And you're the man for the job?"

"Maybe," Fulk said, a tone of hopefulness in his voice. "If I can prove myself."

Wincott shook his head ruefully. "Don't know why you bother, friend. All the Company cares about is profit. The Queen has never even visited these lands—just enjoyed the goods they produce off the backs of people like you and the banker here. They don't give a shit about any of us so long as we make them money."

Fulk carefully set his bowl on a flat rock next to his feet. Then, with the speed of an osprey, backhanded Wincott across his cheek. It wasn't hard, but it stung and sent a message. The Company man leaned so close to the thief he could smell the onions on his breath.

"Now, you listen to me, you little worm. None of us would be here were it not for the Company. After the kings abandoned us, this land was plunged into a dark age, and the Company pulled us out—ended the famine, the pox, and the endless poverty and death. We control these lands now; the roads are safe, and people don't have to worry about what might crawl into their huts at night and eat their children, all because of the Company. You're alive right now because of the good grace of the governor, so mind your tongue."

Fulk picked up his bowl and resumed eating without another word. Wincott's cheek burned, but he refused to show any weakness in front of the trader, so he clenched his teeth, pursed his lips, and kept eating.

THE WEATHER WAS GLOOMIER THE next day. A heavy cloud straddled the mountains on either side of them, and the trees grew tall and thick, their heavy needle branches providing a canopy over the narrow dirt trail that led deeper into the wilderness. A slight breeze blew down from the north, a faint whiff of decayed leaves and frost signaling the change of season.

Cotswold complained about chafing on his legs by midmorning, but there was nothing Wincott could do, so he ignored the man and plodded along in silence. The manacles bit into his wrists, but otherwise, he was in fairly good shape for nearly two weeks of paddling and walking through rough terrain.

The bruiser that lashed them kept at the rear of the train that day, and Wincott was happy for it, knowing it meant less chance that he'd feel the lash of that whip. Midmorning, when they were stopped at a mountain creek that rushed with aquamarine water, Cotswold asked why the guards weren't wearing the bird and dragon emblem of the Company.

"Because they're not Company men. They're mercenaries," Wincott said.

Fulk looked marginally impressed as the thief figured it out.

"But they still follow Company rules," Fulk added with an air of authority.

Wincott wasn't so certain, but he also knew they would find out one way or another. He successfully purloined a small bit of metal that he could use to pick his manacles when the time came, but he was waiting to determine when the best time was to do that, and he hadn't yet found an opportunity that wouldn't bring several skilled hunters down on him.

Just then, their tattooed torturer galloped past them astride his mare.

"Lances at the ready!" he yelled.

His gravelly voice boomed through the forest. Wincott hadn't heard or seen anything, but he noticed the forest was silent—there wasn't even birdsong. A stiff, cool breeze blew past them as they waited in anticipation for whatever the guards saw coming.

A moment later, a dozen men and women burst through the edge of the forest next to the pack train, swords, axes, and staves raised for battle. They screamed loudly, but it was a guttural noise. One of them—a woman, her face torn, leaving gaping holes around rotten teeth—surged toward Wincott with a machete. Fulk yanked him out of the way as the machete thunked into the wooden cart behind him, sticking there.

The woman, who had noticeably blue eyes, moaned as she attempted to pull the weapon free. Wincott noticed then that there wasn't any bone beneath her torn flesh but plates of metal and whirring gears. He had never seen one of the so-called sentinels before, but they more than lived up to their reputation for fierceness.

Fulk kicked the woman in the gut, then came behind her, wrapped his chains around her neck, and strangled her until something heavy snapped in her neck. The sentinel collapsed on the ground. Next, he wrenched the machete from the cart with ease and turned as a second sentinel with a spear lunged to gut Cotswold. Fulk kicked the banker out of the way before he was gored and leaned in with a heavy slash that decapitated the sentinel, its mechanical head spinning as it sailed to the ground several strides away.

More of the blue-eyed attackers spilled from the trees around them. The tattooed mercenary wielded a club that he used to great effect against a number of the attackers as he charged his horse up and down the line.

Fulk pulled Cotswold and Wincott under the cart, where they would be safe, and kept alert while the melee raged around them. After a few minutes, most of the sentinels were dead, and the remaining fled into the forest. The mercenaries went to chase, but the lead guard halted them.

"That's their territory, this here is ours," he barked, pointing at the narrow path. "Form up, be ready. Leave the bodies. We make for Cold Fish Lake."

THEY MARCHED THROUGH THE NIGHT and reached the edge of the water before dawn the following morning. The lake was long and narrow, occupying a thin strip of land between two mountain ranges. It lay on the eastern edge of a territory known only as the Spats, an ancient word for where the mountains were said to be dusted in minerals that far surpassed the wealth of all the kings that had ever lived.

A fanciful tale, Wincott thought, but one with enough staying power that he believed it had caught the interest of the Company and men like Fulk. Maybe they would survive all this.

The rest of the march had been uneventful, aside from Cotswold's constant complaining about how raw his thighs were. As they neared the lake, Wincott smelled the moisture in the air and said as much to Fulk. He grunted in agreement. Cotswold started to panic again, asking over and over whether the mercenaries meant to kill them.

They made a camp at the lakeshore, and at dawn, the lead mercenary had the exiles lined up at the water's edge, their backs to the lake. The heavyset mercenary pulled a folded piece of paper from his leather jerkin and read from it.

"The chief factor gives you a choice," the man read. "Admit your guilt and pledge allegiance to him and his son, and he'll allow you to remain here to establish a new fort and expand the Erdor & Expanse's trading territory, but you will be forever banned from entering Fort Rivers or any of the Company's other settlements. Here you must live and here you must die, Company men."

Wincott thought it was a raw deal, but if it meant he could live another day, he had no problem doing what they said—he'd figure the rest out later. He stayed quiet, waiting for Fulk or Cotswold to answer, but the trader seemed deep in thought and the banker was so scared he couldn't muster any words.

Wincott stepped forward. "I admit guilt."

The banker was next. "I, too."

"I'm really guilty," Wincott said, pouring on the emphasis with a dose of sarcasm.

"Super guilty," the banker said.

"No!" Fulk yelled. "This wasn't the agreement. I was not in the wrong, and though I can accept exile, I can't swear allegiance to that … that … whelp!"

Wincott slunk his head. *Here we go.* The big mercenary shrugged and pulled a knife from his belt. Cotswold turned toward Fulk, his cheeks streaming with tears.

"What are you doing? Just say it; say it and we'll live!" he pleaded.

But it was too late. The mercenary's dagger sunk into Cotswold's neck, and the banker dropped to the ground in a pool of blood and shock. The mercenary went for Fulk next, but Wincott had another idea.

He slipped off the manacles he had picked overnight and swung them like a flail at the mercenary, knocking him to the ground. The dagger spilled out of his hand onto the ground. Stunned, Fulk looked at the thief and froze.

"Grab it! Grab it, or we're dead!" Wincott pleaded.

Fulk, still chained, picked up the dagger and booted the big mercenary in the face, knocking him out. Three more mercenaries came at him with swords, but the trader bested them in a whirl of parries and thrusts that saw all collapse dead on the shore.

He dispatched several more before the remaining guards fled down the path the way they had come. At that point, the big mercenary was up and on horseback some distance away, his mare pointed toward the trail they had traveled on.

He laughed heavily, and his horse reared.

"You've got balls, Company man!" the mercenary yelled, a grin splitting his face. "Balls, I'll give ye that! If you make it outta here, look me up—I'd fight with ye anytime! *If* ye make it."

"What do I call you?" Fulk called after him.

"Kai," the mercenary said and laughed again.

He slapped his horse and sped down the trail, leaving Fulk and Wincott alone on the beach surrounded by bodies and empty tents and supply boxes. The trader turned toward the thief, the bloody dagger in his still-manacled hands. He breathed heavily, his muscles taut beneath his clothes. He dropped the knife and walked to Wincott, holding out his hands. The thief picked the lock and freed the man's hands. Fulk rubbed at the tender skin and eyed the thief carefully.

"You saved my life," Fulk said, "I owe you for that. A debt I'll repay should we ever cross paths again."

Wincott shrugged and said nothing. Fulk stuck out his hand, and the thief shook it, a single heavy pump. With that, the trader turned on his heel, unloaded several supply bags and camp supplies, and carried them to a canoe on the lakeshore.

He pushed the boat into the water, tested its buoyancy, and climbed in, paddle in hand.

"Where are you going?" Wincott asked, wandering over to him.

"The Company taught me today what it really stands for," he said. "It's lost its way. It's time to chart a new way, one I expect to find out there."

Fulk looked down the lake, his eyes glittering with adrenaline and adventure. He stuck an oar in the water and paddled into the water.

"Wait!" Wincott called after him.

The trader backpaddled and turned the canoe toward him expectantly.

"I never told you—there's a boy. I knew his mother. She claimed he's your son," Wincott called over the water.

Fulk was quiet for a moment and then laughed, a skittering, manic sound that made Wincott uncomfortable.

"Maybe! Who knows? Many a woman in Northern Erdor have claimed I've sired their bastards," he said, still laughing. He thumped a fist against his chest and said, "This blood—the Dundurn blood—is *mine* and mine alone, thief. I bid you farewell!"

He hooted loudly at the sky and stuck his paddle in the water. Soon, he was a tiny, dark spot on the lake that stretched westward into the pink and blue morning sky. And then, he was gone.

Chapter Thirty-Five

WE'RE ALL GOING TO DIE

THE GREAT FORTRESS OF THE Lords of Roan was a ruin. The grass field at the base of its grand staircase was littered with weapons, blackened bones, and blood-stained stone. Banners hung limply in the moist cavern air, mildewy and rotten from centuries of neglect. It unnerved Sish as he picked his way through the detritus toward the castle entrance, as if the victors had simply evaporated after the battle had been won. *If* it had been won.

A massive arch framed in a square block squatted atop the staircase. Its brutalist design reminded him of the cold entrance to Roan, like a black mouth frozen in a perpetual yawn. Where the gateway to Roan had been open to the elements in the valley above them, great wooden doors littered the stone entranceway of the fortress, their splintered remains piled high with the desiccated corpses of soldiers who had taken their last breaths fighting to gain entry to the castle.

"What happened here?" Terry asked, looking at the guardians who led them into the fortress.

"Rebellion," said Petr the spider, and hung his head low.

Sish ambled over the ruins, doing his best to turn his eyes away from the eyeless skulls that stared blackly into the fortress. Once-rich carpets and tapestries lined the inner walls, torn, charred by fire. Furniture was turned over and in shambles, walls streaked with soot as if a conflagration had torn through the structure in the distant past. A fireball that had started inside and incinerated the army trying to breach the castle walls.

"Not everyone agreed the valley should be sealed," Dalla said, her small voice dampened by the heavy, still air. "There was a battle to control the Lords' creation sealed away in the storeroom far above. An invasion force fought their way through the Upper City and into the Grand Valley. The battle waged for days across the valley until it reached the fortress …"

Her voice trailed off, sorrowful.

"Until they were repelled," Petr finished for her, "and the valley was sealed."

"And you were tasked with guarding it?" Wren pressed.

The satyr nodded. "We were, though we were not guardians or sentinels like others of our kind. We were knowledge keepers, initially created as experiments that were only half successful, and left behind when the valley was abandoned. How strange is it to leave us three to defend a broken fortress?"

The satyr giggled uneasily as though he felt he'd said something he shouldn't have. Sish watched the gorgon and spider for their reactions, but both looked sad, guilty almost.

Terry wandered through the room, his eyes searching the shadowed corners for danger. Sish was surprised at how empty the fortress was given the hordes of dangerous creatures that filled the valley. It was Wren who found the first evidence someone had been through it ahead of them—the net Kai had used to hold Rena captive lay unraveled on the floor at the base of a wide set of stairs leading deeper into the fortress. There was no sign of the girl, but Sish thought that might not be a bad thing.

"Fulk must've tired," Wren said, kneeling next to the net, grimacing. "They went on foot from here, but there's no way to tell how far up they may be."

"We should go. There may not be much time," Terry urged.

Both men looked at Sish for his thoughts. It was an uncomfortable moment for the thief. He wasn't used to being the center of attention, much less getting any attention at all, unless it was the bad kind. He always thought of himself as the cat of any group, aloof, noncommittal, and slippery. There was pride in that. Now he was a bloodhound on a scent, and the source of that scent waited a thousand feet above them in a room no one had laid eyes on for a millennium or more. His shoulders ached suddenly, as if he'd been carrying water pails all day. Maybe it was just the knowledge that the next step was to hike up a seemingly endless stair. He was mentally exhausted, his shoulders and back aching, his feet … his feet felt fine. Better than fine, as if they *wanted* to run.

Maggot Boots.

Not bad. Not bad at all.

He wasn't sure what to do or say, so he rocked on his feet and nodded silently. Apparently, the enthusiasm he'd shown at the Alteri Gate to pursue Fulk and recover Rena had inadvertently placed him in a leadership position, but he wasn't certain the others understood the reasons for his enthusiasm. It wasn't that he'd decided to throw away his life as a thief or ignore the treasure of Roan. It was more basic than that. There was a man controlling a child against her will, and his actions might very well get her killed. He could sympathize with that. He *felt* that in a way he didn't feel other things. It wasn't something he was going to stand by and watch.

Sish took the lead, winding his way over and around the debris down a long corridor past a series of doorways that flanked them. Some were open, their stone frames crumbling to reveal destruction and debris similar to what they'd seen outside, while others were closed and appeared perfectly intact. The thief wondered what was behind those doors and if there was anything of value. He shook his head against baser urges and continued, Wren and Terry at his side, the three creatures a few paces behind.

At the end of the corridor, a wide, shallow-stepped spiral staircase led up. It was cast in shadow, save a faint gray light that cut through the darkness from above. As they climbed, circling around the fortress, they found it was one of the towers that had its outer wall torn away, affording a view of the valley below.

Up they went, one step at a time, twisting round and round, the valley falling away below them until Sish and Wren were out of breath, even if his feet were just fine. The thief was glad he wasn't the only one. The barbarian looked no worse for wear though, and in fact, had a bit of an impatient look on his face, his arms crossed as he waited for the other two men to stop puffing.

Sish wiped his brow and looked out over the Grand Valley. From this end, it seemed even larger than when he had first looked down upon it standing next to the dwarf. He remembered how lush and healthy it had looked, an illusion that was pulled back like a curtain the moment he'd stepped off the promontory.

Ruddlefunt had told him the third trial wasn't a trial but a choice. Had he made it then? Was all this the result of such a simple, avoidable decision as taking one footstep forward when he should've stopped and turned back? And yet, what would he have turned back to? At the other end of the Keyhole was a man who would've killed him as easily as anything else, and in fact, had been the one to compel him into the narrow shaft of spinning blades in the first place.

Perhaps Sish should've stopped and stayed on that promontory forever, and all this could have been avoided. But that was no choice either. He sighed and accepted the reality that there never is any going back in life, any ability to undo what you've already done, and often, the choices laid out in front of you aren't really choices at all, more like the next turn in a slide that tumbles ever downward, and the best a person can do is slow down here and there and enjoy the ride before it comes to an end, not knowing when or where or how that end will come about.

A great shifting mass of bright colors in the valley below caught his eye. He wasn't certain how he hadn't seen it until now, but it was plain as day and moving toward the fortress with a slow but steady rhythm. A marching rhythm. Men. In lines. Hundreds of them, wearing bright blue and yellow uniforms.

Guildsmen.

Sish clenched his jaw and cursed Wincott. Liv was right, the old fool had been working for them all along. The anger burned hotly in Sish, and though he, too, had been working for an opposing faction, he couldn't separate that fact from the knowledge of what the Guild had done to his mother.

"We're running out of time," he said, pointing at the column of men below.

They were halfway across the valley, working their way along a scraggly pasture that ran alongside the black lake.

Terry swore. Wren shook his head and looked up the next set of stairs, gauging the distance they still had to climb. It was the gorgon's reaction that shook the thief the most.

"It's happening again," Dalla said. "This time, there won't be any stopping it."

"Stopping what?" Sish turned toward her.

The snakes on her head writhed as if mirroring her chaotic thoughts.

"What's in the storeroom? What is it for?" he pressed, leveling his voice.

She looked at the satyr and spider, and both nodded to her quietly. "Creation. Chaos. This. All of this. It comes from there. It was sealed so that the horrors of this place would not trouble the people of the Overworld."

Wren looked at her, a knowing look spreading across his face. "You mean the thing that created you ... that's what's locked away in there?"

She nodded.

The hunter looked at Sish impatiently. "Now do you understand why we came here? What we were trying to stop?"

The thief ran a clammy hand through his hair and turned away from him, his eyes taking in the valley again. When in doubt, stare across the landscape; it buys you time to think. If the Guild and the E&E were here, he wasn't sure how any of it could be stopped. They simply didn't have the manpower. Worse, Fulk had Rena, and although the thief knew little of her abilities, he guessed mixing her with whatever was in that storeroom probably wasn't a good idea.

"Look, I was just trying to get rich," the thief conceded after a minute.

Wren nodded and patted him on the shoulder. "I know, kid. I know. But we've got bigger problems."

The sound of Terry's greatsword being unsheathed echoed off the stone walls. The barbarian stood next to them, sword in hand, his brow knitted together fiercely.

"Can we get moving? My sword hand is getting itchy."

Sish looked at the satyr, gorgon, and spider. "You don't have to come any further, you've done enough. This ... whatever this is ... it's on us now."

The gorgon and the spider looked thoughtful, but the satyr only smiled and said, "I haven't had this much excitement since I had the Pelican of Sitka chase Yig halfway across the valley. Let's go!"

The group raced up the tower, Terry in the lead this time. The barbarian took the steps three at a time and was quickly out of sight. As they climbed higher, the stone wall remerged, providing a bit more safety from a slip and fall that might cause any one of them to plummet hundreds of feet to the top of the fortress below, though Sish wouldn't trust the stone enough to even lean on it.

Atop the first spiraling tower carved from the cavern wall was a curtain wall of brown, crenelated stone that afforded yet another view of the valley. Far below, three small figures darted across the war-torn field at the entrance to the fortress; behind them was Yig, big, lumbering, and angry. The army of Guildsmen, meantime, made steady progress, though a section of men had fallen behind and appeared to battle a large pack of raveners, slowing the column's progress. Sish could only hope the monstrosities of the valley slowed everything down a bit.

The walkway along the curtain wall led to another spiral tower that led even further up. They clambered up that one as well, Terry still in the lead, not showing so much as a sheen of sweat for his effort. Sish's lungs felt like they were burning, but his legs were fine. It was a strange mix he wasn't sure how to reconcile, so he heeded the part of his body that hurt the most.

At the top, more views of the valley were afforded, and another wall led away from them, this one set into the cavern, which connected to yet another tower. They climbed that one as well.

As they climbed, Sish counted the number of platforms and stairs carved into the cavern walls around them. Most seemed to simply be viewpoints, but several had doorways that led into other towers or straight into the rock wall, and he wondered how many tunnels and secret places Roan and its Grand Valley kept to itself.

At the top, which he assumed was the Sixth Highness, Fourteenth Promontory, they found Fulk and Rena standing alone in front of a large glass door that had no handle or discernable way of opening and was free of holes, cracks, scratches, or markings of any kind. Behind it was only shadow but it was large enough for Yig—or perhaps even the great dragon Myrrhmyth—to walk through if opened.

The barbarian was there first; he inched forward, sword in hand.

Fulk turned and grabbed Rena, putting a knife to her throat.

"I wouldn't," the trader warned.

Sish and Wren were behind the barbarian a moment later, Seygan, Dalla, and Petr just behind them. Fulk's eyes fell on the creatures, but if he was surprised by them, he didn't show it.

He looked at Sish and laughed grimly. "Beyond that glass door is what you came for, thief."

"There's no treasure there, Fulk," Sish told him. "Don't open that door."

Fulk cast his eyes beyond them to the Grand Valley below to where the army of Guildsmen marched in their direction.

"What lies beyond that door is our only hope to break the corruption and suffering caused by the Company and the Guild. With it, I can reset the stage, open new pathways for trade, perhaps even through the mountains and past the dragon."

"You're a fool if you think that," Wren told him.

"Doesn't matter if I am or I'm not; we're going to open that door," Fulk said.

"So, open it," Sish said.

"He can't!" Rena yelled, her voice loud and firm.

The girl was unharmed. In fact, she didn't even look scared, but Sish didn't know if that was because she didn't fully understand the danger she was in, didn't care, or knew something the rest of them didn't. Sish hoped it was the latter.

"Rena, are you okay?" Wren asked, stepping forward.

Fulk tightened the knife against her throat. "Not another step, hunter, or she's gone."

"If you kill her, then what?" Sish shot back.

"Then maybe we all die. Her blood will be on your hands, boy. Now open the door."

"I can't open the door!" Sish protested.

"Actually, you can." It was Wincott, emerging from the final tower, Liv and Ruddlefunt in tow. The old thief was red-faced and out of breath. "This is the choice, Sish. You survived the trials. The valley was designed so that only the person who survived the trials could open the storeroom. But if you do it, we all die."

Sish studied his father's face, looking for a trace of a lie, but he saw none, and neither was there any there in Liv or Ruddlefunt's faces. The wizard looked broken and the dwarf concerned.

Sish considered his options. Do as Fulk said, and Rena lived, but maybe they all die. Ignore the trader, and Rena dies, and maybe they still all die. He glanced over the side of the promontory; it was a thousand-foot drop to the valley below. He could jump and kill himself, he considered, and then no one could get into the storeroom. But they might all still die.

Despite all the warnings and portends, Sish decided none of them knew what was beyond that door, not even the guardians or Ruddlefunt. There might be nothing. Or there might be a horrible evil none of them could contain. In the end, he decided none of it really mattered anyway because there was one possibility he couldn't accept: watching Rena die for another man's selfishness.

It wasn't a rational choice, he knew, but neither was the situation, and if they all managed to live through this thing, the one future he couldn't accept for himself was one where he let a little girl die. A person must draw a line somewhere, he decided. It was a choice as simple as putting one foot in front of another.

He held up his hands and walked toward Fulk.

"Fine," was all he said.

Not knowing what else to do, he walked to the glass door and placed a hand against it. It was so cold it burned his skin. A red light like a single eye flicked to life behind the glass directly in front of him. It flashed, momentarily blinding him. He held his hands to the glass now, refusing to pull away despite the freezing cold that crawled up his fingers into the bones of his hands. A soft chime like a piano's high notes sounded, and the door pushed back several inches and retracted into the ceiling.

Chapter Thirty-Six

APPARENTLY, HE'S BECOME HONEST

THE RIVERBOAT GLIDED TO A gentle stop in the warm spring breeze, the deckhands leaping onto the dock to tie it up. Sish waited, backpack in hand, taking in the familiar chatter of riverboat men, hucksters, and stevedores that bunched up against the Ribbon just below Chicken Town. A year had passed since he'd set out from Fort Rivers for warmer climes and new adventures. He'd found both and had the scars and stories to prove it, but he was glad to be home. Where before he had seen a city of rank smells, corruption, and zero opportunity, now Fort Rivers greeted him with the fragrant nostalgia that only time away from a place can conjure, a small pinhole of excitement in his belly at how he might do things differently this time. He shouldered his pack and stepped onto the gangway; his lungs filled with the dewy spring air.

"Going to wait for me?" A familiar voice came up behind him.

He turned and found Liv standing behind him, an expectant look on her face, her pack in hand, green eyes glittering in the morning light. Her eyes matched the verdant shade of spring leaves that filled out the birch trees in the hills around them, announcing the arrival of summer.

"Of course." He held out his arm, taking her hand.

They walked down the gangway onto the dock and bid the captain farewell and thanked him for a safe journey up the Ribbon. It had been Sish's decision to come home, though Liv hadn't been opposed to it—she missed friends and familiar places.

"Where to first?" she asked.

Sish shrugged. He had no idea what he would do with himself in Fort Rivers, though he hadn't ruled anything out. They had enough money to see them through the summer without working, if needed. He suspected Liv would want to see Wren and the others as soon as possible, and Sish even had to admit he wanted to know what his father was up to.

"Let's get a drink at the pub and figure it out," he told her.

"The Wandering Camel?" she suggested, as if savoring the sweet sound of the strange public house's name as she said it.

He looked slightly sheepish. "Not sure I'm welcome there. The Werewolf's Toe?"

"You're definitely not welcome there," she said.

"The Widow's Pecker?"

Liv burst out laughing. "Nice try."

Sish looked incredulous. "I'm serious. It's over on Cottonwood Lane. Good wings."

She punched him playfully in the arm and said, "Shouldn't that be Widow*er's* Pecker?"

"Come on," he told her with a grin, shouldering his pack.

They walked arm in arm along the dock into Fort Rivers. The city was bustling. Rope was stretched overhead between buildings crisscrossing each street. Brightly colored paper lanterns dangled, tussling in the light breeze as if awaiting the arrival of a party. Bakers, chefs, tradesmen, and others wandered the streets with trays of food and drink they handed out to anyone who wanted something. The streets were shoulder-to-shoulder packed with people and smelled of freshly baked bread and roasted, salted meats. Street performers in multi-patterned outfits and floppy hats performed music, plays, and miming on street corners, and there was even a trio of sisters who deftly juggled flaming swords back and forth between two balconies on opposite sides of a street.

"It must be Leaftide," said Liv, taking in the festival.

Leaftide was Fort Rivers's largest annual festival, held on roughly the same two days each year when the leaves were finally fully sprung on every tree and the E&E's chief factor could declare winter officially ended for another season.

There was a ceremony each year leading up to the declaration, wherein the chief factor would travel to High Town Park at midday each day and inspect an ancient stand of birch trees ringed in stones. A botanist from the academy and a farm mage from the Breakfast Club would typically accompany him, and the three would inspect the size, color, and tensile strength of the leaves, sample the soil, and conduct a wind check. If the leaves reached a certain size, the soil wasn't too sodden, and the wind blowing from the south, they would declare the start of Leaftide to a great hurrah from the assembled crowd. If not, the botanist would threaten that everyone better think warm thoughts or winter might soon return. Of course, within a day or two, the festival was always declared open, and the nonstop eating, drinking, dancing, and merriment commenced.

For all the bleak memories Sish had of growing up in Fort Rivers—the poverty, endless, bitter winters, and danger at home and elsewhere—Leaftide was a source of fond memories. Even Wincott would soften each year during the festival, ensuring he and Sish had a few days away from their work to take in the sights and sounds and stuff their faces with as many sweet treats as they could find.

He also knew it was a special time for Liv, who had studied and practiced as a farm mage, and at one time, had hoped she might one day be the wizard who accompanied the chief factor to ring in the start of the festival. Of course, she'd proven to be a more adept wizard than even she expected, and life took her in a different direction.

He caught her eye as she stuffed a sweet chocolate roll between her lips, laughing as she swallowed it in chunks, half of it spilling out onto her green robe. He kissed her, lifted a shot of gin from a tray passing by, and toasted their return to the city.

THAT NIGHT, A KNOCK CAME at the door shortly after midnight. They were asleep in Liv's flat, which she had maintained with regular payments to the landlord via mail boats while they were away.

Leaftide was still raging. The steady notes of a harpsichord dragged on in the street below, filling the air with raucous laughter and conversation, but both were so tired from their travels that the noise didn't bother them. Sish got to his feet, half asleep and slightly alarmed, but he breathed carefully, reminded himself no one knew they were back, and opened the door without fear.

A huge lumbering mass sprang toward him and wrapped him in a hug so tight he heard his spine crack. He was suddenly enveloped in the barbarian bone-crushing but familiar musk.

"Liv!" a girl's voice screamed.

Sish heard the pitter-patter of small feet as Rena darted through the door past him and wrapped her arms tightly around the wizard's legs. Terry let go a moment later, still cradling Sish in his hands, a grin spread from ear to ear across his face.

"We saw the light on and figured you were back," he told them.

The barbarian stepped aside, and Wren entered the flat behind him, sticking out a hand to shake and greeting him and Liv with a smile.

"We're glad you're back," Wren told them, "The letters you sent kept us all on the edge of our seats—especially the engagement. Congratulations. When is the big day?"

"We haven't set it yet; I'm leaving it to her," Sish replied, poking a thumb in Liv's general direction.

She crossed her arms and said, "And I told him it's his job since he asked. Why should I have to plan it?"

Sish's reddened with embarrassment, but he only grinned stupidly and welcomed them inside, shutting the door behind them so they could carry on a conversation without the noise of revelry outside disturbing them.

Liv drew an old kettle from a shelf and brewed tea on the wood stove while Terry caught them up on the goings-on in the fort over the past year. Rena sat quietly and nibbled on cookies she had stashed in her pants while Wren listened patiently and sipped his tea.

Sish was suddenly restless. He tried to sit and listen but found it difficult to focus his thoughts. Maybe it was exhaustion from the travel or the chorus of celebration ongoing outside, but something nagged him. He wandered to the window while Terry regaled them about a fight with the E&E traders in some far-gone fort. Even in the middle of the night, the streets below were filled with bodies dancing, drinking, and carousing between long log picnic tables that filled the streets.

He was glad to see the group, but it also gave him a pang of anxiety being in a room with them, as if their year away had never really happened. But there was something else, too—a feeling that if Liv could pick up as easily where she had left off, how would it go for him? Had anything changed with Wincott? Was there any point in finding out?

He stood, drank, and listened quietly to Terry's stories. Apparently, he, too, had departed Fort Rivers, heading north for a year by himself to explore the edges of E&E territory.

"You're timing is impeccable," Wren broke in after a while. "Terry and I were just packing up to head west on a job and were feeling a bit short-handed."

Liv leaned forward with immediate interest, asking for more details. Sish was a bit more circumspect, not sure he wanted to jump back into that life right away or at all. He'd done a fairly good job the past year, keeping his hands clean and out of jail, and one thing he'd told Liv he worried about coming back to Fort Rivers was falling back into the old lifestyle. Thieving was fun, and he was good enough to make a living at it, but it was also dangerous and not consistent with any type of stability. There weren't many thieves that lived past thirty; in fact, he could think of only one.

"We just got back ..." Sish started to say, but Liv held up a hand and shushed him. He cocked an eyebrow, annoyed, but she wasn't paying attention. Terry looked at him and shrugged while Wren went on.

"A galleon washed up in the headwaters of the Serpentine. Well, I shouldn't say washed up, thawed out is more like it. Rumor is it's been locked in hoarfrost there for years. One of Captain Reeve's armada from the Whitewater Rebellion."

Sish had heard the tale of Captain Reeve from Wincott when he was a boy. He was the most feared privateer on the coast for years and balked at the growing influence of the E&E and Guild in his backyard. When the two teamed up to eliminate him and privateers like him, Reeve raised an armada and fought back.

For a year or two the Whitewater Raiders grew quite wealthy and kept the trading companies at bay, but the might of foreign powers eventually overpowered Reeve and broke the armada up in Crone's Strait. It was said the battle happened during a horrendous winter storm, and only Reeve escaped alive, taking shelter in the group of islands to the west that few explored. All the other ships, heavy with booty and weapons, sank to the bottom of the strait.

"How do you know it's one of his?" Sish inquired. "I was told all the ships sank."

"Some have it that way, yes," Wren said. "Others say that a few managed to escape into sheltered coves or upriver."

"It could be any ship," Sish replied. "Long way to go on a rumor."

Wren hesitated and then turned back to Liv. "A fellow hunter—a man I served with years ago and trust—brought me the news. This ship, the *Talon*, was said to carry a magic weapon that formed the backbone of Reeve's strength in the first place. If the Company or Guild got their hands on it ..."

"And you need a wizard to understand it," Sish finished for him, not bothering to look away from the window.

"And light fingers might help," Wren answered, looking at the thief. "In fact, two sets of light fingers would be even better."

"I don't like it," Sish said.

Wren lifted his eyebrows in surprise. "That southern climate make you softer?"

"Smarter," Sish replied, looking evenly at Liv.

She sighed awkwardly. "We just got back. Give us some time to think about it?"

Wren looked at Terry, and the barbarian nodded. "We were meant to leave at sunup, but a day or two won't make a difference."

"We'll let you know tomorrow; right now, we just need rest," Liv said, taking Wren's hand in both of hers and squeezing it warmly.

Sish scoffed. "We don't need time. The answer is no. No, we're not going."

The room went silent. Liv blushed with embarrassment, her eyes fixed angrily on Sish. Wren ignored the outburst and thanked them for their time as he and the barbarian made for the door. Rena finished her cookie and gave Liv another hug, whispered something in her ear that caused the wizard to smile, and left with the other two men.

"What the hell was that?" Liv stood, her hand gesturing to the door.

"What?" he said, playing ignorant.

"You don't make decisions for me. We make decisions together."

"Fine," he shot back. "Then let's make the decision together not to go."

She ran a hand tiredly through her hair. "You know that's not what I mean. Things were easier down south for us—there was work, and it wasn't the kind we're used to. But we talked about this. We're back now, and you know things are different here."

He stepped toward her, his hands gently caressing her shoulders. "But they don't have to be. We don't have to go back to that. We can do something else."

"Like what? Start a bakery? Serve drinks at the Widow's Pecker? Did you ever think *I* might like this kind of work?"

"Of course, but—"

"No, Sish. It's not your decision to make. At least, not for me. Now, let's get some rest. Tomorrow, you need to find your father."

Chapter Thirty-Seven

A LONG CRANKY JOURNEY TOWARD ... NOTHING

WINCOTT WAS LOOKING FORWARD TO being released from jail when Sish showed up and ruined it for him. The old thief turned himself in at the start of winter on a number of outstanding warrants. He figured it was a good idea to clear his record and also get three square meals a day, a roof over his head, and avoid the cold, all at the same time. That way, he'd be back in fine stealing form in time for high summer.

But then Leaftide rolled around, and his traitorous son showed up to buy out the remainder of his time, armed with a pack of lies and some cock-and-bull story about a magic treasure on a pirate ship. He hadn't seen the boy in nearly two years, only heard that he'd run off with the she-witch to Guild lands to make a better life. Apparently, neither had made him smarter.

Father and son sat over two mostly full pints at the Werewolf's Toe, enjoying a protracted silence, when Sish decided it was time to talk about things.

"Dad, I left because ... I just needed to figure some things out," he said.

Wincott sipped and wiped the beer foam from his beard and said, "So what'd you figure out? That your old man isn't so bad after all?"

"No, I ... I figured out I wanted something different than ... this, something better."

Wincott spat his beer. "Better? That's what you're calling it? You want *better*, boy, march up to High Town and play a long con on one of them rich ladies, and you'll find better. That she-witch and her high-minded friends ain't going to bring you any sort of better than what you had with me."

Sish was silent. He drank his beer and looked around the pub, his eyes drifting between the other patrons, conversations, musicians, food … everything but Wincott. The old man stared at him, not sure what to say or how to get through to the kid. He just didn't *get it*, did he?

"And if things are so much better, why are you back here? Sitting across from me? Asking about a job?"

Sish changed the subject. "How'd you get back into town anyway? I heard the chief factor exiled you to Cold Fish Lake."

Wincott drained his mug and signaled for another, telling the waitress that his son was paying for it. "He did. But I know how to keep my head low and have enough friends to keep fed. You a Guildsman now?"

Sish shook his head vehemently. "Never. They're worse than the Company. You know what they did."

The old thief eyed him carefully. Still naïve.

"You might find things aren't so black and white as you get older, boy," he told him. "Now what's this you want from me?"

Sish explained the job. The hunter Elden Wren had a fix on one of Reeve's lost galleons and wanted to extract a bauble from it before someone more powerful did. Wincott always thought the hunter was a bit small-minded about these things. There was far more profit in getting the bauble and then trading it to the highest bidder, likely the E&E or the Guild. Let them fight over it and walk away a wealthier man, he figured. But the damned fool probably planned to destroy it, bury it, or toss it in a bottomless lake. Wincott bet there were other things in that ship, though. Captain Reeve had a renowned eye for gold.

"So, it's a Reuben then," said Wincott.

Sish choked on his beer. "It's *not* a Reuben. They're my friends. We do the job their way."

"Except they need me—so we're going to do it my way."

A Reuben was another name for a double-cross job when the thief goes along with the main plan, but near the end, goes ahead, takes what he wants from the rest of the group, and leaves, often to die. It's best when the others die first as it avoids nasty reprisals. Wincott had pulled a couple Reubens in his time and had one pulled on him that he managed to survive. Sish knew what a Reuben was, but the kid couldn't tell a lie to save his life, Wincott knew, so best not to press it too far, lest he cause him to blather to Wren and screw everything up.

But a Reuben would certainly test the boy's loyalty and tell Wincott whether he was worth having around again.

"So, Wren's got word of a ship at the headwaters of the Serpentine, but he's never been there himself?" Wincott mused.

Sish motioned for him to be quieter, his eyes shifting left and right to ensure none of the other patrons overhead. Wincott rolled his eyes.

The boy leaned forward and whispered, "You've been there?"

Wincott took another sip. "Near there. Cold Fish Lake isn't far from it. But I know the way. Long walk, Blue-Eyeds about."

Sish nodded quietly and finished his drink. He paid the waitress as she lowered two more mugs onto the dirty table between them. He got to his feet and buttoned his coat to leave.

"Where you going?" Wincott asked, eyeing him.

"Home," he replied. "And you should, too. We gather at the Moon River launch at sunup the day after tomorrow. We'll see you there ... or not,"

Wincott only grunted and then ordered another drink. Sish lingered a moment as though he wanted to say something. He sighed and left without another word.

Wincott wanted to say something, too, but he wasn't sure how, or maybe he really didn't think it was necessary. He was once told that time heals all wounds. He laughed at that, sipping his drink. He had hoped if he ever saw his son again, that might be the case, that he could get past the fact the kid moved out without a word and left the city altogether without saying why or even goodbye. But it turned out that all it did was open those wounds again.

SISH FOUND THE TRAIL TO the top of the Serpentine long and boring. They paddled up the Moon River as they could, before portaging overland into the narrower Runny and onto the wide, glassy expanse of Fortide Lake. From there, it was a rough hike overland via a goat path that hadn't seen fur trading traffic in many seasons, making it difficult at times to discern the path from game trails that forked away from it through thick scrub oak and alder underbrush. More than once, Wren stopped, scratched his forehead, and used his dirk to bat lazily at the foliage to remind himself which way to go. Sish would only shake his head, grumble beneath his breath, and wait for the hunter to figure himself out. Liv usually gave him an impatient look if he grumbled too loudly, but he wasn't impressed. *A man ought to map things out before he takes on a new job,* he thought, and he was increasingly wondering whether Wren really knew the way at all, which undermined the extent to which Sish had any confidence in their venture, to begin with. Which he didn't, in all honesty. Not because Wren was inept, far from it. But he had a nagging feeling that something was off about this one, as if he'd given in too easily to Liv when he'd agreed to go and roped his father into it as well.

But at least the scenery was gorgeous. Spring was in full swing, with summer on its heels, the air filled with birdsong from sparrow, robin, and jay. Occasionally, a bald eagle was spotted on the hoary limb of an old fir or cottonwood or circling above a forgotten lake pockmarked with fish circles that suggested good eating. Wren pointed out deer and bear tracks, the occasional moose and elk, and a large pack of wolves that had moved through some days before.

They rested a night at an abandoned trading post at the top of Runny Lake. Its darkened windows and the generally derelict condition of the stout log house suggested the E&E traders had been gone some time, despite Wren promising they had a warm meal and good company to look forward to. The deeper they hiked into the wilderness, the lonelier the forest around them felt, as if the trees had inhaled a great breath and were holding it, waiting for them to pass.

They spent a quiet night amid cobwebbed furniture and a small, crackling fire in a stone hearth. No one said much, and even Liv seemed anxious. Terry watched the windows nervously, oiling his sword, his eyes peering through the leaded glass into the gloom beyond. But nothing happened, the forest held its breath, they managed some sleep, and carried on at sunup.

After a while, the sense of adventure, beauty, and the welcome warmth of the spring sun gave way to trail fatigue, muttering, and general crankiness. The worst part of the lot, so far as Sish was concerned, was Wincott.

The old thief frequently lagged, complained about the dry rations, and did as little as possible to guide their way. Occasionally, Liv would fall back to keep him company and ask for stories about his life in a valiant attempt to keep him from growing so morose that he tanked an already challenging mood among the group. He would talk lively for a bit, but the tales always ended with the same bitterness or curses toward someone else whose actions resulted in Wincott's poor luck. Each story ended with him spitting a wad of phlegm onto the trail beside him and muttering angrily, and then Liv would drift back toward Sish, raising her eyebrows at him, and carry on in silence.

Sish mostly ignored him, which Liv openly questioned at first and made him feel bad, but after a while, let it go. Sish figured the best way for the two of them to survive one another was to stay separated, so he always made sure to keep a liberal distance from his father while they progressed along the trail each day, and at night, he would often set up his and Liv's tent and blankets away from Wincott. Only once did Wincott utter words about it, choosing to mutter something unflattering about the wizard and how his only son had been stolen away from him. Most of the others didn't hear, though Sish knew Liv had. She winced on hearing it but said nothing and was just as pleasant to Wincott the following day as if he'd never said anything at all. Sish admired that in her, but he also worried she was starting to force it and would eventually blow up at him.

They reached the upper reaches of the Serpentine in two weeks' time. It was a beautiful, mountainous country, filled with alpine meadows on high glacier-capped mountains where cold blue ice scraped against low-slung, puffy white clouds. Fragrant beds of wildflowers stretched like carpets of color ahead of them, sliced up by little meandering rivers of glacier-fed water that meandered through the untouched landscape like some natural-born irrigation system.

They reached their destination on a clear, sunny day at a time of year when the wilderness was alive with the brightness of spring. Sish had seen few things more beautiful in his life, and yet, at its center, was an object that marred the vibrant reds, oranges, blues, and pinks like a coal stain on fresh canvas—the *Talon*.

She was a two-masted square-rigged ship that looked as though some monolithic cyclone had lifted it from the sea and dumped it hundreds of miles inland. While the valley was bright and cheery with spring flora, a murky pall was cast over the *Talon* as it lay amid a muddy reef, listing forlornly to one side, its gunports empty and black, sails torn and tousling weakly in the afternoon breeze.

Wren pointed to a flat section of meadow above a pot-shaped lake that afforded a closer view of the ship, where they could make camp. They were quick about setting things up, having had a fair bit of practice over the last couple of weeks, but as Sish hoisted the heavy canvas tent he shared with Liv, he paused, staring into the black eyeless gunports of the *Talon*, wondering whether any of this was a good idea. Maybe the past year in Guild territory had softened him. Warm weather had a tendency to do that, he'd been told. But they had no idea what lurked in that ship, only rumors of the undead.

Seeing the unsure look on his face, Wren stopped what he was doing and said, "I know a cut-and-run is generally the safer approach to a job like this, but we're the only ones here, and we have time on our hands. I want to send an advance party to inspect the ship and learn more about what we might be in for before we go in."

Sish nodded quietly and ignored the confident look on Liv's face. Sometimes, she trusted the hunter too much, he thought.

They ate dried beef and pemmican for dinner, a taste that all the others were tired of by now but accepted with a quiet resolve. Except Wincott. The old thief tore at it like a buzzard feasting on raw meat and complained bitterly between every bite.

"You're a bloody hunter, Elden. Go fetch us some deer or even a rabbit," he suggested, tossing the last piece of beef in the fire between them.

Wren offered a patient smile and sipped his tea. After a bit, he told Sish that he and Wincott would be the advance party.

"See if you can get a sense of the layout, the condition of the ship, entrances and exits, and where the captain's cabin might be, though I suspect it's aft," Wren said, nodding to the ship.

"And if there's anything moving inside," Terry added as he oiled the great sword stretched across his thighs.

SISH SAT UP NEXT TO the fire that night with Liv and Wincott. It wasn't planned, but Wren and Terry had long since turned in. The lumbering barbarian snored loud enough to wake whatever still lurked in the *Talon*, Sish thought, while the hunter rested on his back, arms folded over his chest like a man about to be nailed shut in a pine box. Sish envied the pine box at the moment as the air was thick with awkward silence between Liv and Wincott and he was too tired to play diplomat between them.

He wandered away from the firelight, where he was afforded a better view of the valley below and the clear night sky above. A dusting of blue, purple, and pink stars stretched in a band across the sky above his head, flanked on either side by pinholes of light that seemed to poke through the vast black fabric of the heavens.

Below, there remained a hint of deep blue light bordering the southern horizon, a marker of the time of year when the days were long and the night weren't quite as dark. The slim light silhouetted the mountains with a deep blue luster, set against the ebony skyline, allowing him to peer into the valley below, where different shades of blue and black coalesced into a dark pool that formed the headwaters of the Serpentine.

It was beautiful. And calming. Yet a pang of anxiety scratched at the back of his neck. Maybe it was the typical nervousness he felt the day before a dungeon job, but as he turned it over in his head, he realized that wasn't it at all. Even though the galleon he planned to waltz into tomorrow morning was teeming with the undead, it didn't bother him the way it might have a year or two before—or at least it didn't worry him quite as much as something else. What that something else was, though, he wasn't sure. He felt as though he were standing on the precipice of something … a change that was unavoidable.

"Never should've come back," he grumbled quietly to himself.

After a while, Sish turned back for camp. As he came through the trees, heated whispers from the campfire reached through the forest toward him. Peering through the thick boughs of the cedars, he spied Liv and Wincott arguing. His father was on his feet, hands on his hips, face twisted in anger. Liv sat on a log, her face leaning in toward the older man, her cheeks red.

He supposed he shouldn't have, but old habits being what they were, Sish listened in. She was pressing the old man hard about something, but Sish couldn't make out what it was. After a few minutes, the argument died down and Sish stepped into the firelight and asked what was going on. Wincott turned away from him and stomped away into the woods. Liv opened her mouth but couldn't find the words. After a breath, she offered a close-lipped smile, put her arm around his shoulders, and guided him toward their tent. He wanted to ask her what the conversation was all about, but he didn't want her to know he'd been eavesdropping. But there also remained a pinprick of unease in his gut that he couldn't overcome. He chose to ignore it.

Wincott had never been to sea, and he was glad of it. When he set foot on the *Talon*, he felt the immediate oppressiveness of its shadowy, confined spaces. For whatever reason, the old thief never had a problem with tight places anywhere else. In fact, he was used to them. But there was a cell-like quality to the galleon that unnerved him, and it wasn't long before his fears started to run away with his thoughts, and the only thing he *could* think about was what it would be like to be trapped in a lower deck as the ship drowned in icy seas. He shuddered and closed his eyes, trying to push the thoughts from his mind.

"Why are we stopped?" Sish whispered behind him.

His son was crouched behind him in a partially collapsed part of the hold, his eyes searching Wincott's for an answer the older man didn't have. After a moment, Wincott managed to push the fog from his brain, and tugging on his beard, grunted and crept forward.

They entered the *Talon* from a man-sized hole torn into the port-side hull, either from being dashed against a rock or rot. Based on what little information Wren had, Wincott thought it made more sense to comb through the sloop from bottom to top rather than the other way around, though none of them were sure what state the

Talon was in, so their expedition to get a sense of the interior layout and possible locations of the gem was touch-and-go.

So far, there was no sign of anything living or otherwise inside, or at least nothing that moved. That didn't mean they were in the clear, but it suggested the possibility there were no phantoms in the ship after all. Of course, if that were the case, it was also possible there was no loot either and the whole trip had been a waste of time. He wouldn't put it past Wren to operate on poor intel. He was a hunter, after all, not a scholar or even a well-established thief like Wincott, who knew the difference between good information and bad. If it turned out there was nothing in the *Talon*'s hold but rotted timbers and cobwebs, the thief had half a mind to clobber the man as soon as he was outside, or worse.

Violent images raced through his mind. He saw himself beating the hunter to death with a heavy club. He even felt the weapon in his hand, though there was nothing there when he flexed his fingers. He stopped, winced, and tried again to clear his mind but had trouble doing so. Ever since they had come within proximity of the *Talon*, he'd felt … different. He felt numb all over, and beneath that, a rage bubbled up like smoldering coal beneath a rain-dampened fire, ready to burst into flame at any moment. He had the misfortune to experience a fair bit of magic in his life and knew what that felt like— the goose bumps raised on the flash at the uttering of a cantrip, the sharp electric feeling of the air as if right before a storm strikes. *This* wasn't *that*. It was something he'd never felt before, as if everything around him had at once grown heavier and hotter.

He wiped the sweat from his brow, grunted, and moved forward, doing his best to ignore the feeling. He heard Sish's quiet footfalls behind him and wondered whether the boy felt the same but decided not to ask. The last thing he needed was Sish questioning his sanity. His son already thought the old man was past his prime. Why give him any additional confirmation?

They clambered into a larger section of the hold that allowed both men to stand upright, though their heads were bowed. Wincott lit a small oil lamp he'd brought along, its greasy flame pushing back the dark. There was not much around them but debris from broken crates. The floor was blanketed in mud, sand, and sword ferns that had taken root since the ship washed up at the headwaters. To

Wincott's left was a narrow, steep ladder, missing a few rungs, that led to the next deck. He climbed and poked his head through the hole, but the darkness was so complete he needed the lamp to get a sense of the space.

He was in a large, open deck lined with hammocks, tabletops, and barrels suspended from the ceiling on dust-thickened ropes. There were no signs of lichs, skeletons, zombies, or other undead dwellers, for which he breathed a sigh of relief, but what he did spot were a set of rooms at either end of the deck, each with their doors closed. He suspected one of them was a magazine where the powder for the guns was kept and the other might be the captain's quarters. What little he knew of ships suggested the captain's berth was often at or near the stern. He decided that was the direction he'd go first.

Sish popped his head up beside him.

"Not enough room on the ladder for the both of us," Wincott growled.

Sish snorted. "You could fit in a medium-sized trunk. I'm sure we'll be fine. That must be the captain's cabin, eh? We should search there."

"Way ahead of you," Wincott said.

Sish rolled his eyes. "Then why are we just standing here?"

Wincott fixed him with a glare and then climbed the rest of the way up, the lantern bouncing in his hand to cast sharp shadows across the rotted walls. They picked their way carefully through the hammocks and tabletops, careful not to disturb anything. As they neared a cabin, they found a faint trace of orange light framing the doorway.

Sish reached for the handle, but Wincott slapped his hand.

"Are you crazy? You don't know what's behind there," Wincott scolded him.

Sish gave him an incredulous look. "Then what are we doing here?"

Wincott breathed, pressing the bubbling rage down inside him. He reached for the handle. If anyone was going to open that door, it was him.

Inside the cabin, they found the captain sitting quietly at his desk beneath the warm glow of lamplight, scribbling notes with a quill pen as if he were making daily log entries.

The two thieves froze, Wincott's mouth hanging open.

The captain looked up at them, his flesh mostly rotted away, revealing bones, sinew, and black eye sockets that glowed with a pale blue light. He wore a tattered overcoat with epaulets that marked his rank but had long since been stained black, either by time or blood or both. He paused his scribbling, placed the quill in its holder, and sat back in his chair, his cavernous eye sockets assessing the visitors as they came through the door.

"Oh, hello," he said, his voice perfectly gentlemanly, as if he'd just run into two friends at the market.

Wincott and Sish exchanged a glance. Sish looked surprised and unsure of what to do. For his part, Wincott was immediately frustrated.

Why must there always be *something*? He cursed inwardly.

He'd expected ghosts. He'd expected a lich or two, heck, even a pack of acid-spewing slugs. But an undead skeleton captain with his wits about him? What was he supposed to do with that?

The old thief rolled his eyes. The weight he'd felt before—the numbness and deep-seated rage—boiled to the surface, and he found himself talking before thinking.

"Where is it?" Wincott demanded.

The skeleton assessed them coolly. "The curse is on you, I see. Nasty bit of enchantment that."

Wincott pulled the short sword from his belt and waved it threateningly. It did not have the intended effect. The captain didn't flinch, and for the briefest moment, Wincott wondered whether a skeleton could flinch. He decided it probably could, and it was more the case that his hasty attempt to threaten a man made of bones wasn't well-thought-out.

Sish raised his hands defensively and took a step forward. "What curse?"

"The one I assume you're here to procure," the captain said. "Perhaps we should start with introductions. I am Captain Reeve, and you are on the *Horus*."

Wincott's eyes shifted toward Sish's again. He screwed up his face in confusion. "I thought this was the *Talon*. And Captain Reeve was … missing …"

"And to whom do I have the honor of speaking?" the skeleton pressed.

"I'm Wincott, this is my son, Sish," the old thief indicated, jutting his thumb toward the boy.

"Pleased to meet you, and to answer your question, Captain Reeve *is* missing and is also dead, as you can see," the skeleton said, indicating his face. "The guns backfired."

"Backfired?" Wincott asked. "Look, I think we'll be going now."

The old thief felt a mounting wave of dread descend on him with each second longer they spent in the dead Captain Reeve's cabin and had a sudden and overwhelming desire to turn and flee. He tried to move his legs, but they felt stuck to the cabin floor.

"The *Horus* and everything on it is cursed," Reeve said.

"We're here for—" Sish started but was quickly cut off.

"The weapon that was the secret to my fleet's success?" Reeve asked. "Yes, it's here."

He opened a heavy wooden drawer in his desk and extracted what looked like a hand-sized golden hourglass, except, instead of a figure-eight-shaped glass filled with sand, there was a solitary violet gem that pulsed with a shade of black.

"Cursed gem," Captain Reeve announced proudly, letting his hollow eye sockets pass over it fondly. "Found it far to the south. Rough country. Wouldn't go back. We used it to maraud."

"What does it do?" Sish asked.

"Curses things," Reeve replied matter-of-factly.

Wincott tried to move his legs again but couldn't. He found himself sheathing his sword and taking a seat across from the skeleton. Again, not his choice. Sish did the same, as if the trio was called together for an everyday meeting of sorts. Against their will.

"Let me elaborate," Reeve told his captives.

He set the object on the desk between them and leaned forward, resting his bony elbows on the edge of the desk, his joints cracking like sticks snapping in an icy wind.

"A curse is a form of chaotic magic," he went on, "You never can tell what it will result in, and it's different for everyone. Think of a curse like a living thing, a demon trapped in this tiny crystal. For my fleet, it meant we brought bad luck to any other ship or settlement we came across, which, since we're privateers, gave us a distinct advantage.

"Yet, it had disadvantages as well. At first, it meant we ran into heavy gales often. After a while, it meant that as soon as we'd win treasure, something would happen, and just as quickly, we'd lose it. There was sickness and death among the crew, at first on the other ships, but then ours as well. Eventually, we turned on one another during a great storm. I believe most if not all the other ships sank. We were blown inland, and the ship made its way here, where it busted up on the beach, and here I've been ever since."

"And you're stuck here?" Sish asked.

Captain Reeve nodded. "It would appear that, after all this time, the curse has rendered me unable to depart the confines of this ship. I've tried to end my life on several occasions, but that's not possible either. So here I wait, until either the ship disintegrates around me and I can disembark for good, or I can give the curse to someone else."

The skeleton smiled grimly, his rotten, bony teeth seeming to angle sharply outward toward them.

The suggestion in Captain Reeve's words was not lost on Wincott. True, they had ventured far to recover loot from the abandoned galleon, but Wincott knew that neither he nor his son had any desire to depart with Captain Reeve's cursed gem.

"I think we're good, actually," Wincott said.

Suddenly, his legs were freed, and he was able to stand. Sish did the same, and the two headed to the cabin door.

"We'll show ourselves out," Sish said.

"Nice to meet you," added Wincott with a wave of his hand.

Captain Reeve rose to his feet and leaned over the desk. "I could kill you, you know."

"Are you going to?" Wincott asked.

"No," the captain answered, almost petulantly. "I've grown numb to such vices. You may go, but I should warn you that you've been exposed to the curse now. It may not afflict you so deeply as it has me, but you won't be free of it either. Neither of you. Who knows what it might do?"

Chapter Thirty-Eight

THIEF AND ... FAILED ASSASSIN

BACK AT THE CAMP THAT night, Wren was incredulous. Wincott had been in a black mood ever since they departed the *Horus* and had gone on a long walk in the woods after supper. Sish stayed behind and did his best to recount their story for the others. He, too, was feeling down and more than a little angry about the entire episode, especially when he factored in the time it had taken for them to travel this far and the knowledge they would have to travel the same path back.

"Last time I agree to a job with Wren," Sish mumbled to Liv partway through the evening.

She didn't share his irritability, which only annoyed him further, instead pestering him with question after question about who said what, when, where, in what tone, and what was around them at the time, few of which he could rightly remember or answer twice the same way. Then she would cross-examine him with the inconsistency of his answers, which only made him more frustrated, which, when she noticed, she would backpedal and say she was only trying to understand better.

Bullshit, she thinks we're full of shit and that Wincott's pulled a Reuben.

"We should go back and talk to Captain Reeve," Wren said to Liv.

She nodded lightly, half-committal. Sish's face twisted in anger.

"Have you not heard anything I said? The whole damn place is cursed. You go in there you'll be cursed, too."

"Like you," Liv replied, leveling her eyes at him.

"You don't seem cursed," Wren observed.

"He's right. You look normal to me," Terry added.

"You think we're making this up?"

"No, it's not that," Liv said, rubbing a hand consolably across his shoulders.

"It just might not be exactly as you remembered it," Wren chimed in.

"So now I'm forgetful? We both told you the same thing. There's a skeleton captain in there and a curse. Don't. Go."

The Dungeoneers ignored him, turning back to their debate about the ship and how best to get inside and eliminate any threat, curse, or no. Sish sighed heavily, stretched, and wandered out to where he had looked up at the stars the night before. He found Wincott sitting alone on a rock, his chin resting in his hands, eyes unfocused as he gazed over the valley below.

"Dad?"

The old thief shook his head and turned around. A small smile parted his lips. "Those idiots still arguing about whether we're liars?"

"We are liars," Sish answered with a grin.

"S'ppose so," Wincott said.

A long silence passed between them. After a while, Wincott asked whether Sish planned to follow them back aboard the *Horus*.

"Not on your life," Sish answered.

"What if she goes?"

Sish opened his mouth to answer but couldn't find the words. No, that wasn't right. He could find the words; he just knew Wincott would know he was lying. If Liv decided to go, what choice would Sish have? He opened his mouth to answer again, but still, he couldn't muster the words. After a while, he sighed, sat next to his father, and cupped his chin in his hands, elbows on his thighs, eyes cast out over the wilderness beyond.

"People," Wincott mused. "We all look relatively the same, sound relatively the same, breathe air, eat food, walk on two feet, and die, but not one of us is the same. And what pushes people— what gets them out of bed in the morning, causes them to do what they do, make the decisions they make? Well, that's different for everyone, too."

"Might look similar on the outside, but we're all a bit different up here," he said, tapping his temple. "Those friends of yours? Different than you and me. See the world differently. I bet they're up there right now thinking how best to destroy that curse so it can't hurt anyone else. That's fine. The world needs people like that. But you? Me? We're not made that way. I bet the only thing you want to do is put as much space between you and that curse as possible and keep her away from it, too. Am I right?"

Sish met his eyes but said nothing.

"Yep," Wincott said. "You and me, we ain't blood, but we're family just the same."

Wincott got up and left. Sish sat there for a long while, turning Wincott's words over in his mind, challenging them from every direction he could think. But there were truths in there he didn't like to say aloud or even admit to himself. Not for the first time, he had the suspicion the old man was mostly right, but it only left him wondering whether a person could change who they are, become something else, over time, if they wanted it bad enough. But how bad do you have to want it? And what does that feel like? Sish didn't know, and he wasn't sure he wanted to.

THE FOLLOWING MORNING, WREN, TERRY, and Liv were ready to go before breakfast. Sish awoke to the clatter of equipment and voices outside their tent, Liv's spot beside him empty and cold. He pulled on a shirt and stumbled outside, where he found the three of them going over their plans next to a cold fire.

Sish didn't need to ask what they were planning to do, so instead, he launched into all the reasons they shouldn't. It was quite the speech, or so he thought, but as ineffectual as Captain Reeve's attempt to get them to take the curse from him.

"It's no use, son. These woolheads are hell-bent on do-goodery, and it'll be the death of them," Wincott said, hopping out of his tent and pulling on his boots.

Liv gave the old thief a baleful glance, but her words were for Sish, her green eyes leveling with him as she shifted her gaze to the young man. "We can't leave it here. If the wrong sort were to find it…"

"It could be disastrous," Wren finished.

"It needs to be destroyed," said Terry, sheathing the greatsword in the scabbard across his back.

Wincott only shook his head and busied himself dismantling his tent. Sish could see his bag was out and he was packing up to leave.

"You're going?" he asked.

Wincott nodded. "Not waiting around to watch these three go up in a puff of black smoke. Besides, Cap'n Reeve says you and me are cursed already."

Sish looked at Liv. "Don't go. We can leave this one alone. There's not a town within a hundred miles of here, and no one nearby, not even Company men. Let's just forget it."

His pleading fell short as she straightened her back and stiffened her jaw.

"This is what we do, Sish. You knew that when we got involved," she said.

Wincott cursed and said, "Let the boy make his own decisions."

She turned on him, eyes narrowed. "Like you made a decision for him in Fort Wick?"

Wincott's eyes widened. Wren shook his head, and Terry sighed. The air was thick with things unsaid, and that pinhole of anxiety Sish had been fighting for days was quickly becoming a gaping chasm.

"Don't," was all Wincott said.

"Don't what? Tell him the truth? Come on, old man. You're all for telling *us* what you think we need to hear. How about we flip that around?"

Wren took a step forward. He placed a hand on Liv's shoulder to calm her, but she shrugged it off.

"Liv …" the hunter urged.

She ignored him. Wincott's face was red. He stuffed the roughly folded canvas tent in his backpack like he was murdering it. The pit in Sish's gut grew wider. He looked from Liv to Wincott, but both ignored him as though he weren't there, and neither Wren nor Terry would look him in the eye.

"Come on, Sish, we don't need these people," Wincott said, tying closed his pack.

"What is she talking about?" Sish asked him.

Wincott shook his head and told him it was nothing. Liv scoffed. Wren tried to urge calm again, but his voice was lost in the tension.

"Nothing? It's nothing that you were hired by the Guild to help them take control of Fort Wick?" Liv pressed.

She turned on him, her eyes wild with anger and frustration. An image of Captain Reeve's violet, pulsing crystal appeared in his mind, and for the first time, he was very aware of how close their camp was to the *Horus* and its accursed cargo.

The words halted Sish in his tracks, hitting him like a hammer to the chest. The air burst out of his lungs, his jaw dropping open. Everything was silent, still, and thick. Sish locked eyes with her. Gone was the warm and playful shade of green he'd first seen there when he'd literally run into her years before while on the streets of Fort Rivers. All the color seemed to have bled out of them at that moment, leaving only dark irises wrapped around violet pinpricks of pupils. In the distance, he thought he could hear the screaming laughter of the mad pirate from the deck of his ruined galleon, but it sounded so far away and mattered so little in that moment. All he could do was look at Liv and feel the pit in his stomach widen into a yawning black hole that threatened to swallow him whole.

He heard the thud of a bag drop and footsteps head toward him. A thick-fingered hand seized Liv by the shoulder and spun her away from Sish. Wincott cursed, and his fist rammed into her jaw. She collapsed to the ground.

Sish moved without thinking. He drove his booted foot into Wincott's stomach, driving him back to land hard against the grass. A knife was in his hand. He gripped his father by the shirt collar and slashed, drawing a stream of blood from a deep gash that stretched from the bottom of his right eye to his jawline. He went to plunge the knife into Wincott's chest, but Terry intervened, batting the weapon away and holding his arms in a lock.

Blood poured from the wound on Wincott's face, his eyes fierce with rage. Liv moaned in pain on the ground, a hand to her jaw, Wren knelt next to her. Wincott got to his feet and wiped away the blood with a bare hand, smearing it like a menacing tattoo across his skin. He walked to Sish and spat in the young thief's face.

"No son of mine," he growled.

"I ever see you again, I'll finish the job," Sish screamed at him.

Wincott wiped more blood away, lifted his pack onto his shoulders, and marched out of the camp.

Wren helped Liv to her feet. Her lower lip was split, and Sish could already see a bruise forming where Wincott had struck her. Terry released Sish when his breath calmed. The young thief looked sadly at her, but he didn't approach her. Angry, bitter thoughts raced through his mind. He chewed his lip, searching for something to say that would articulate how he felt, how she had made him feel. Like a fool and a child. Embarrassed.

"You knew? You knew all this time, and you didn't tell me?" he hissed at her.

Her eyes hardened. The violet was gone, replaced with the familiar green he had fallen in love with, but there was no playfulness or warmth to be found there. Just a cold, hard truth of who they were, how different they were.

She wiped a speck of blood from her lip and lifted her staff from the ground. She looked at Wren and Terry and asked if they were ready to go. Both men shrugged awkwardly.

"Are you coming?" She looked at Sish.

She was going into the *Horus*, and there was nothing he could do to stop her. Maybe they were cursed already, Sish thought. Maybe this is what it looked like for them. Wincott's words from the night before rang through his mind.

Those friends of yours? Different than you and me.

Sish wasn't sure he was like any of them, Wincott or the Dungeoneers. He didn't think he wanted to be, not anymore.

"If you go, you go without me," Sish told her.

Liv pursed her lips. Her eyes drifted to the galleon and then back to Sish. Jaw set, back straightened, she sniffed and walked away without another word.

Chapter Thirty-Nine

NOT WHAT THEY WERE EXPECTING

ULK FORCED THEM AT KNIFEPOINT to march through the massive door into the storeroom ahead of him. Sish was first, with Terry and Wren at his sides, followed by Wincott, Liv, Ruddlefunt, and the curious three creatures his son had picked up along his journey to the fortress. Fulk held Rena close to his chest, weapon at the ready, and was the last to enter the long, square corridor that led to the alleged treasure each had come to Roan for.

The old thief eyed the young girl as he walked past her into the storeroom. She looked calm and collected, as if her thoughts were somewhere else entirely. The stories about the girl were little more than rumor, but Wincott knew she was more powerful than any of the other Dungeoneers by a long shot, which was saying something because Liv was no pushover and Terry could make short work of a handful of the E&E's most elite soldiers with little more than a spoon if he wanted. Some part of him was waiting for her to burst into a monstrosity or bring the walls down around them as she had at the other end of the valley, but she did and said nothing. For now.

As Sish moved down the darkened corridor ahead of him, the floors, walls, and ceilings came alive with stark white light. It was bright but not blinding and filled the perfectly cut square panels that lined the walls around them as though they strode through a strange subterranean gateway to the afterlife.

Wincott brushed a hand against the wall and was surprised to find that although bright, it was cold to the touch, and the walls weren't stone, but rather, some type of flawless composite the world had long since forgotten how to make.

At the far end of the tunnel was a wide, shallow staircase made of the same composite. Each stair sprung to light with an ivory glow as they descended into a massive open room.

Stretched before them was a grand warehouse filled with thousands of armored knights that stood at attention, kite shields in one hand, lances in the other. They stood unmoving, their eyes closed, and in such perfect formation that if a person were to stand directly in front of one column, they would see only the first lancer. The columns stretched away into the shadowy reaches of the storeroom until Sish reached the bottom of the short stairs and laid foot upon the floor.

A chime like a deep piano note rang out, and the floor came alive with pale blue light that shone upon the mailed leggings of each soldier, slicing the lines between the tile floor, where normally, dusty mortar would have settled. Yet there was nothing dusty at all about the storeroom. It felt clean, as if the last person in there had polished everything to a sparkle and left only moments before, careful to turn off the lights and lock the door behind them.

As the party fanned out at the bottom of the stairs, each with their eyes wide with wonder or mouths agape, Wincott noticed a different set of knights toward the back of the warehouse. Some bore leather armor and longbows instead of shields and lances, and still others were taller even than Terry and bore heavy two-handed maces. At one end of the room, there were no knights but a contingent a robed dwarfs that looked identical to Ruddlefunt, and elsewhere, Wincott could see raveners, bogwights, great bears, mountain lions, and even replicas of the reptilian monstrosity the dwarf had called Yig.

"What is this place …" the old thief breathed.

The spider with a human head clicked along the composite floor tiles and came to stand next to Wincott.

"The storeroom," it said matter-of-factly. "This is where the Lords planned, designed, and left their creations. It is where I," the spider's eyes fell over the satyr, gorgon, and Ruddlefunt, "where *we* were born."

The dwarf stepped in front of one of the soldiers, his delicate fingers reaching out from his billowing red robes to touch the flawless silver plate mail. Then touched his own face in wonder, his fingers tracing the curvature of his face upward and over the scorched flesh to the exposed metal plates of his skull, where gyros whirred quietly amid an identical blue glow.

"I … I was not programmed to … I don't remember," the dwarf said, his eyes searching between Wincott and Liv for an answer.

The gorgon stepped forward and laid a calming hand on his shoulder. "The Lords erased your memory so that you couldn't give anything away should anyone enter the Grand Valley. We guardians were allowed to keep that knowledge. Our purpose was different than yours, though all that was so very … long ago."

Wincott wandered among the columns of soldiers and could not find a nick or scratch on their armor. Their faces were made of flesh, their eyes closed, as if sleeping, but there was no movement in their bodies, no breath or heartbeats that he could detect. He wondered if, beneath that flesh, there were the same metal plates that Ruddlefunt was made of, or were they muscle, bone, and sinew, like the vicious sentinels he'd come across in the wilds of the Northern Erdor? He couldn't recall any of them wearing such exquisite armor, but perhaps they had once.

A shudder traced up the thief's spine like a cold fingernail as he considered that, at any moment, the soldiers could wake and gore him on the end of their razor-sharp lances. He stepped out of the line, and his eyes fell on Fulk as the trader strode down the stairs into the storeroom, Rena's left forearm firmly in his grasp, a hungry look in his eyes.

"At last! The Treasure of Roan," he called out, his heavy voice echoing through the silent warehouse.

"What do you mean to do?" Wincott turned toward him.

The trader fixed him with a look, his eyes glazed over as though he suffered from some strange fever. "What I was meant to do. Awaken this army, take charge of it, and forge a new power in the Erdor, one strong enough to overcome the combined might of the Company and the Guild, strong enough to challenge even the great Myrrhmyth."

Terry drew his greatsword and took a step toward the man. Fulk clucked his tongue and stuck the tip of the dagger against Rena's throat. The girl didn't seem to notice, and Wincott was beginning to wonder why, if she was so powerful, did she not simply burn the trader to a cinder where he stood?

Wincott fingered the pommel of Raspberry at his side but thought better of it. His eyes passed over Sish, who looked thoughtful more than anything. Wincott was pleased to see the boy alive, but if Fulk was successful, none of them would get out of Roan alive. He wondered whether Ruddlefunt's prediction was true—would it be some danger this late in the game that killed his son and the others or Fulk's madness?

The trader stepped carefully past the assembled group and led Rena through the seemingly endless columns of mailed statues to the far side of the storeroom, where a small platform made of composite blue tiles the color of Ruddlefunt's eyes rose above the room. Atop the platform was a collection of metal tables fitted with rectangular devices that were nothing like the old thief had ever seen before.

"Stay and watch if you want," Fulk called after them as he dragged the girl onto the platform. "I'll only need your summoner a moment, but if I were you, I'd flee."

Chapter Forty

A THIMBLEFUL OF A CHANCE

SISH WATCHED THE OLD TRADER disappear amongst the columns and wondered what to do. Wincott looked as dumbfounded as he was, and neither Wren nor Terry seemed to have a plan either. His eyes fell on Liv. She looked exhausted, her hair in a tangle and a generous helping of dirt and mud smeared across her robes and face. Her staff was missing, which would make it nearly impossible for her to channel any spells. Yet still, she was resolute, her jaw set. He knew that look, had been on the wrong side of it more than once. She meant to go after Fulk and likely get killed in the process.

His hand strayed involuntarily to the waistband of his pants, where he found something he'd forgotten he had. A worthless trinket, perhaps, but a meaningful one. The thing he'd traded back and forth with Liv for as long as they'd known one another. It created only sparks for him, but in the hands of a wizard …

He reached into the secret pocket that held the trinket along with a second set of picks and drew the ruby thimble. The Catalyst of Nerjammer. It was dull, dirty, and less impressive-looking than he remembered, but at this point, anything might help.

"Liv," he called.

She turned, and he flicked it at her. She caught the device in surprised hands, turned it over once or twice before she realized what it was. Her green eyes met him.

"You kept it," she said, her expression softening.

He shrugged. "Thought it might be worth a few bucks one day if I was down on my luck."

"What is it?" Wincott asked, curious.

She held it up for the assembled group to see. "The Catalyst of Nerjammer."

Wincott's eyes went wide. "That stupid thimble I tried to steal from the museum … how did you come by it?"

He looked at Sish, who grinned and said, "Long story, but Liv can use it to channel a spell or two. With that, we might be able to stop Fulk."

"How?" Wren asked.

Sish shook his head tiredly. "The Gods only know. I'm making this up as I go. Got any better ideas?"

Wren looked grave. "Not any that don't result in Rena getting killed."

"What does he want her for anyway?" Sish asked.

Liv slipped the thimble on her forefinger and admired its dull red hue in the pale blue light, "She's a summoner, a natural-born catalyst. Like a wand or staff … even this thimble. She can be used to channel energy. My guess is he plans to use her to make this army come alive."

"That will kill her?" Wincott asked.

Liv pursed her lips.

"Well, it can't be good for her," Sish said.

Wincott looked at Ruddlefunt. "Is there any way to stop the army from reawakening?"

The dwarf was thoughtful for a moment, but it was the spider that spoke up. "There's a circlet the Lords would wear … it will be with the other devices that will awaken the sentinels. The one who wears it controls them."

"We have to steal the circlet before he gets to it," Sish said.

"How?" Terry asked.

Sish looked at Liv. "I don't suppose you know an illusion spell?"

"Ask me to grow a tree, get some roots to come alive, or bring on a heavy rain— I'm your lady. Illusions? Only a basic inanimate object and only for a few seconds," she said.

"That's all we'll need," Sish said.

"What are you thinking?" Wincott asked him.

"Marty," said Sish.

Wincott scoffed and rolled his eyes. "It'll never work. A Marty is a finesse job."

Sish leveled his eyes at Wincott. "I can do it."

"What is he talking about?" Liv asked, her eyes darting between the two thieves.

Wincott tugged on his beard thoughtfully. "A Marty is what we call a change-out or the old switcheroo—he wants you to use an illusion spell to make a copy of the circlet and switch them out at the last moment."

"It'll never work," Wren said. "We need to find another way.

"There's no other way," Sish told them.

"Lo!" the satyr called out.

The dungeoneers turned toward the goat man, who stood at the top of the stairs and pointed down the long, well-lit corridor they had entered from. Hundreds of soldiers wearing bright blue and yellow uniforms marched toward them.

"Guildsmen," Wren cursed.

"Well done, old man." Sish looked at his father accusingly.

"The Company is right behind them," Wincott said. "We ran into a contingent of those old fools tussling with some goblins near the base of the fortress."

Terry spun his sword around and said, "The corridor is narrow. I can try to buy us some time if I have a hand?"

The barbarian looked around. No one said anything. Wren sighed and drew his sword. As did Wincott.

"How about eight?" Petr the spider said, holding up half his arms. "We'll stay and help. It's what we were built for."

Dalla nodded, as did Seygan, though the satyr looked less than enthusiastic facing certain death.

"Good," Sish said. "Buy us a bit of time. Liv and I will deal with Fulk."

"Do you know what the circlet looks like?" Petr asked him.

"No idea," Sish replied.

The spider looked at Ruddlefunt. "Black. Simple. Made of the same composite as your skull. Help them?"

The dwarf nodded enthusiastically.

"Okay," Sish said, looking at the assembled group, "wish us luck."

The group split in two, with Liv and Ruddlefunt disappearing toward Fulk among the silent ranks of knights while Terry led

Wren, Petr, Dalla, and Seygan to the narrow end of the corridor to hold off the approaching Guildsmen. Sish and Wincott lingered a moment longer, the old man shaking his head quietly.

"Some luck, eh?" Wincott said to him.

Sish chuckled. "You think we're cursed?"

"Yeah," Wincott said after a moment, "but it's our own doing, not some purple gem we happened on once upon a time."

The words lingered between them, resuscitating a memory that should've hurt more than it did. Now it was just another story between them. He wasn't sure he hated the old man as much as he used to. Maybe hate wasn't the right word, really. It's difficult to hate someone you can't stop loving.

"Good luck, Dad," Sish said to him.

Wincott licked his lips, his eyes watering. He sniffed and said, "You, too, and remember—"

Sish rolled his eyes and nodded impatiently. "I know, I know— finesse, focus, and luck."

"No, son," Wincott said. "Trust your gut and follow your heart."

The old thief's eyes flicked down the column of soldiers to the green-robed wizard marching determinedly toward almost certain failure. Sish opened his mouth to offer a quick reply but thought better of it and just nodded quietly. He turned and ran after her.

Chapter Forty-One

IT'S THE MONSTER MASH ... A STOREROOM SMASH!

RASPBERRY WAS IN WINCOTT'S HAND before he knew he'd pulled it, his eyes fixed on the column of soldiers marching down the lit corridor toward them. *Raspberry. It's a stupid name. Why would a person name a sword after some fruit?*

He hefted the weapon and wondered about the swordsman with a sense of humor. Vik Tar Regare, whose heart gave out on him when the Pelican of Sitka of the Grand Valley startled him. *How strange life is,* Wincott thought, *for a man of such renown to come so far through the many trials of Roan only to have a jammer near the end. That's how life is though. No one's getting out of it alive, and most of the exits aren't pretty or even notable.*

Recalling that Mr. Regare had a sense of humor, Wincott decided his death might have been a perfect fit, almost poetic. But what death awaited the old thief? He was overdue, surely, having long since used up any natural luck the universe had afforded him at birth and done very little to generate the expectation that there might be some hidden reserve of it he was yet unaware of. He might be looking at it now—one of those soldiers, one of those swords or lances might be meant for him. He deserved it, probably, but he'd been alive long enough to know that deserve had got nothing to do with it.

The barbarian stepped in front of the old thief, sword drawn, feet set on the strange composite floor as if they anchored some unmovable object. Frankly, he looked ridiculous wearing only a sad loincloth and soft leather boots. What made it worse was that one side of the loincloth was caught between his ass cheeks, revealing entirely too much skin. When Wren came to stand next to Wincott, the thief rolled his eyes at the barbarian's back and grinned. Wren only shrugged and shook his head, his weapon held loosely in his hand, eyes fixed on the fight to come.

Behind Wincott were the three newcomers—monsters, all of them—but with seemingly decent dispositions. He eyed the spiderman curiously and then looked down the corridor past Terry.

"So, we just going to fight 'em?" Wincott asked no one in particular.

Wren half-turned toward him. "Got a better idea?"

Wincott looked at Petr. "You're a spider, right?"

The spider nodded.

"You can shoot web out of your butt?"

Petr looked heavenward impatiently but acknowledged he could. "But that's not where it comes from."

Wincott ignored him and pointed to the wall on either side of the corridor. "Could you create a barrier? Slow them down?"

Petr immediately saw what the thief intended and got to work, his large, hairy black body moving with lightning speed as its eight legs clicked across the composite floor and spun a thick wad of webbing that blocked the entrance to the storeroom. The Guildsmen immediately took notice of what the spider intended and broke ranks, sprinting toward the webbing with their weapons drawn. Several of them were immediately caught in the gooey mess, their bodies thrashing uselessly, while others backed off and attempted to cut their way through.

Terry wasted no time. The barbarian leaped forward with a great sweep of his sword. He cleaved through two of the Guildsmen, leaving their lifeless bodies hanging limply in the webbing. He thrust at another, and there was a terrifying scream of pain. Wincott held back, fingering Raspberry nervously. The Guildsmen changed their approach, sending a contingent of lancers forward to thrust their sharp weapons through the web at a safe distance, hoping to skewer someone on the other side. Wren deftly dodged out of the way as one of the weapons lanced toward his gut.

Wincott noticed that the webbing was already sagging beneath the weight of dead Guildsmen and the numerous blades that had swept through it. Terry's rhythmic hack-and-slash motion wasn't helping, and the thief guessed the enemy would burst through at any moment.

Wren batted away a lance that had gotten dangerously close to Wincott as the thief ruminated about their problem.

"We need to retreat," Wren told him, parrying another spear.

Wincott hesitated and found his eyes lingering on the gorgon. She stood next to the satyr, both looking at the melee with rapt yet innocent fascination that reminded him of spectators watching an arena fight. An idea popped into his brain.

"Gorgon," he called to the woman, "can you turn these men to stone?"

Her face shifted toward him, the thin black gauze covering her eyes billowing in the tumult of air swirling amid the battle. She nodded and turned toward the slackening wall of webbing.

"Spider, reinforce it, and then let her do the rest," Wincott directed him.

Petr's legs clicked across the floor again, and more webbing shot out across the corridor. This time, the Guild wasn't slowed, the men behind it pressing their attack with sword and lance that sliced through the gray strands with relative ease. Terry and Wren kept up the defensive but were only able to bat weapons aside and slide the advance.

Dalla stepped in front of Wren a moment later. Wincott pulled him back and gestured to the woman as she removed the gauze from her face. The snakes on her head writhed with renewed vigor, their heads snapping toward the advancing Guildsman.

The gorgon's natural abilities soon had the desired effect, with half a dozen Guildsmen slowing their attacks to a languid pace before hardening into stone against the webbing. The stone soldiers created a natural barrier that rose to half the height of the corridor and the webbing held, making it far easier for Terry and the others to mount a defense.

Dalla pulled the gauze back over her eyes and turned toward the thief, her lips curled in a small but satisfied smile. Wincott nodded thanks. Wren took a breath from the fight while Terry kept the Guildsmen at a safe distance with his sword point.

"It'll hold, for a bit anyway," said Wren, "but we better hope the others manage to stop Fulk before it's too late."

Wincott nodded and glanced over his shoulder at the columns of sentinels that filled the storeroom. A shudder ran up his spine thinking about being caught between a legion of Guildsmen and an army of sentinels, but all he could do was hope.

It was then that he heard the slap of naked feet against the composite floor and a gibbering language he'd thought he'd left behind in the valley. The hair on his neck stood on end, and he felt his face go flush. To his left, he spotted a band of goblins sprinting out of a hidden corridor toward him, weapons drawn. In the lead was Meat Cleaver.

"No shit," Wincott marveled.

Chapter Forty-Two

PLAN? WHAT PLAN?

LIV WAS A STRIDE AHEAD of Sish and ready to leap from the last row of sentinels onto the open floor below Fulk's platform when Sish seized the hood of her robe and pulled her back. She landed on the ground with a soft thud and struggled to get back on her feet.

Sish held her firm, whispering harshly, "What are you doing? You can't just charge out there. You'll get us all killed."

She stopped moving and turned toward him. "We don't have any time. We have to stop him before he hurts Rena, or worse."

They crouched between several sentinels but had a clear view of the platform at the back of the storeroom that Fulk was above, Rena in tow. Atop it was a series of white desks and several instruments that surrounded a fully reclined chair with a strange type of halo suspended above it. Fulk lifted Rena onto the chair and pushed her shoulders down roughly so she would lay back. The old trader's head darted back and forth as he searched for something, anything, Sish thought, that would help him turn on the apparatus, and likely the army of sentinels with it.

Sish hazarded a glance at the sentinels above him and Liv and was happy to note they remained still, and apparently, asleep.

"Do you have the illusion spell ready?" he asked her.

Liv wrested her robes from the thief's grip and knelt next to him, her eyes fixed on Rena.

"There is no illusion spell," she said.

"What do you mean?"

"I lied."

Sish sighed heavily, "But I thought you said—"

Liv slapped her hand angrily against her thigh to cut him off. "I know what I said. I. Was. Lying. There is no illusion spell. I'm a bloody farm wizard. You guys were taking so long getting a plan together, I needed something to get us moving."

Sish grabbed her shoulder, and she spun around to meet his eyes. "Then what the hell are we supposed to do?"

Her thin red lips tightened against her teeth. "We go after him."

Sish cursed and looked toward the platform, where Fulk had found what he was looking for, and lowered a small black circlet over his head. The trader fell to his knees and shook violently as the material touched his skin, but after a moment, his eyes opened and shone with the same cerulean haze that marked countless sentinels.

A thunderous chime rang through the storeroom as though the world were being called to attention around them. A series of translucent blue images leaped from the white desks on the platform and floated in the air around Fulk. Rena's chair began to lift toward the halo above her, which shone with a bright white light. The girl struggled against some unseen force that pinned her to the chair. Her head snapped from side to side, her hands and feet wriggling to no avail. Her eyes were round with fear, tears streaking silently from their corners.

"Screw it," Liv breathed.

The wizard twisted out of Sish's grasp and leaped through the column of sentinels, sprinting toward the platform. But Fulk was already on his feet, a strange, satisfied smile spread across his face. He raised his hands toward the ceiling, palms upward like some religious zealot. The translucent blue images solidified into a blue wall that surrounded the platform. Liv slammed into it, the wall repelling her backward with a crackle of electricity. She landed in a heap on the floor in front of Sish.

The thief ran to her side, Ruddlefunt next to him. Liv was conscious, but her eyes rolled around in her skull like two billiard balls.

Rena's chair halted once it was in line with the white halo. Fulk closed his hands into fists, his eyes closed. There was another eardrum-shattering chime, and the halo around Rena burst into a brilliant white light that enveloped her body. Her back arched in pain, and Sish could see her mouth open to scream, but nothing could be heard over the sound of the machine as it echoed like a cathedral bell through the vast chamber.

The white light enveloped everything around them until it was so bright that Sish had to close his eyes and shield Liv's for fear of going blind. Then, just as quickly, it winked out of existence, and the storeroom was bathed in pale blue light that seemed to sparkle upward from the mortar lines between the composite floor tiles.

A loud clicking noise sounded behind him, then the floor shook with the snap of a thousand or more mailed feet coming together in unison to stand at attention. Rena's chair lowered from the now quiet halo, and the girl tumbled to the floor, the blue shield around the platform vanishing. Fulk opened his eyes and smiled. He stepped forward and snapped his arm outward, his fingers flat like a knife, and pointed toward the corridor, where hundreds of Guildsmen battled to gain entry. Sish turned his head and watched Fulk's army charge toward the Guildsmen. Amid the ocean of movement, his eyes couldn't locate the spot where he knew Wincott and the others were trapped between the two forces.

Chapter Forty-Three

WE LIKE GOBLINS NOW

MEAT CLEAVER SAILED TOWARD WINCOTT brandishing a rusty butcher's knife. The thief was out of options. *This is it,* he thought. *I never should've robbed Shatterstill.*

He closed his eyes, waiting for the knife to bite into him, but he felt only the woosh of air as the goblin careened past him to knock a Guildsman's lance out of the way. He opened his eyes and turned to see the creature land expertly on its two feet, fold into a roll, and come up to throw the meat cleaver into the advancing soldier with expert precision, burying the blade in the man's chest, knocking him back and two others with him.

Wincott opened his mouth to ask what was happening, but a second goblin leaped past him, two short swords in its hands, and it quickly tossed one of them to Meat Cleaver. The lead goblin caught it without a pause in movement, spun around, and buried its point in a Guildsman who had gotten the drop on Terry, saving the barbarian from a grievous wound.

The barbarian nodded his thanks and went back to the fight. Meat Cleaver stopped and turned toward Wincott.

"Who are you?" Wincott asked the creature.

It stepped toward him, its sharp yellow eyes assessing the thief with something between pity and outright disdain. "Dirge Oyamason, Herald of the Shadowguard."

Wincott looked at him dumbly, unable or unsure what to say. He'd never heard a goblin speak the common tongue before, nor had one ever saved his life or demonstrated such skill with a weapon. The other goblins, a dozen or so in total, fought with similar skill, and he suddenly felt very outclassed.

Wren stepped forward. "Then the Shadowguard is real?"

Dirge nodded. "We are the descendants of the nine who fought to protect Roan from Myrrhmyth generations ago, and it's been our task ever since to protect this city from invaders."

"But … you're goblins?" Wincott said, realizing how stupid it sounded as soon as the words left his mouth.

There was a flash of annoyance in Dirge's eyes, but the goblin ignored him in favor of a conversation with Wren.

"You fools have led the enemy past our gates into the very heart of the city—if the army of the Lords awakens, there is little we can do to stop its advance. Here or anywhere," explained Dirge.

Wren nodded. "Then our purposes are aligned."

Just then, a gong rang out across the storeroom that reminded Wincott of a hammer striking a temple bell. The hair on his arms stood on end as an electric current spidered through the room. A white light blinded him, bringing the melee to a momentary halt.

His eyes cleared in time to see the army of Roan awaken, their heels moving in swift unison, armor clanking as they advanced toward the invaders. The pale blue glow of their eyes sent a shudder up Wincott's spine as he drew Wren and Dirge's attention to the newest threat.

"That's a problem," he said, pointing with Raspberry.

Behind them, Terry stood atop a pile of stone soldiers, swinging at unlucky Guildsmen as they came within reach of the barbarian's great sweeping blade. Past them, Wincott could see a fight breaking out in the rear of the Guildsman's column. More fighting, this time with a new enemy. E&E men.

The thief could only shake his head at the utter bloodbath unfolding before his eyes. Wren had seen it, too, and the men exchanged glances, unsure what to do. Behind them, a few of Dirge's goblins had engaged the army of sentinels. The blue-eyed warriors moved with rapid efficiency, not a single wasted motion or muscle, and were more than a match for the goblin's elite company. Atop the heap of petrified soldiers, Terry was being beaten back, the Guildsman having figured out how to press their lances forward in a way he was unable to defend against. Petr joined in the defense of the small square of space the companions held between the three advancing forces, and even Dalla lifted her gauze to target the blue-eyed soldiers, though it didn't seem to have an effect. They were outnumbered on all sides and would be cut into ribbons if they didn't move.

The satyr made the next move. Wincott wasn't sure if someone shouted to him to do something or if he'd been trying to get their attention and no one noticed amid the commotion, but the goat man put his pipe to lips and began to play a deep, mournful lament. The notes cut through the noise like a string of daggers slung from the satyr's hands, capturing the attention of the sentinel army. The blue-eyed warriors turned their attention to the satyr and marched toward him.

Seygan stopped and looked at Dalla and Petr in surprise. "Now what?"

"Keep playing," Dalla urged. "Buy us some time!"

The satyr fixed the pipe to his lips again and played while backstepping from the battle, the front portion of the sentinel army following him mindlessly. As that happened, Terry leaped down from the pile of stone Guildsmen, his eyes fierce and strained, his skin nicked with several dozen superficial wounds. Wincott could smell the heavy musk of the barbarian's sweat.

"We need to fall back," Terry said.

Guildsmen spilled over the barrier of petrified comrades.

Wren looked at Dirge.

"Where can we go?"

"There's an escape, a narrow tunnel in the east wall, hidden from passing eyes. It will take us up to the base of Shatterstill," Dirge said.

"We're under the old fort?" Wincott asked.

The rumor had been true, then. There was an entrance to Roan, and he'd been close. If only he hadn't gone for that stupid coin purse and woken the goblins up, he might've found it and avoided this entire catastrophe. He felt his face suddenly flush with guilt as he realized Dirge stood next to him, the goblin's yellow eyes narrow and fixed on him as realization crept over the thief's face.

Wincott opened his mouth to say something but thought better of it. The goblin's eyes lingered on him a moment longer, the short sword held comfortably in its hand. He had no doubt that Dirge would've gutted him then and there if circumstances were different, but the goblin stayed his hand.

"We can settle accounts later, if we survive this," Dirge told him.

Wincott swallowed heavily and looked away, his eyes falling on the platform at the rear of the room where he could see Liv and Sish ambling up to where Fulk stood and commanded his drone army. The trader was completely unaware, and for a second, the old thief thought his son and the wizard might get the drop on Fulk, but they ignored him altogether, moving instead to gather around a crumpled form on the floor behind him.

A heaviness tightened his chest then, followed by an overwhelming urge to sprint through the column of sentinels toward his son. Terry seized his shoulder and urged him onward, away from the encroaching armies on either side of them, to where the goblin said there might be an escape.

Seygan was only able to draw away several dozen sentinels from the fighting, buying a small but necessary amount of time for the others to slip away before the blue-eyed warriors and Guildsmen came crashing together in a rain of steel and armor.

As Wincott sprinted away, he heard the tooth-chattering scream of the monstrous reptilian beasts that formed the rear guard of the sentinel army. The creatures sprinted through the ranks of their mailed brethren toward the Guildsmen who flooded from the corridor into the storeroom in a flurry of barbed lances and flashing swords.

The storeroom was a cacophony of fighting, and no matter how many paces he ran, Wincott didn't feel like he could put enough space between him and the advancing army of sentinels. Even Terry and the goblins were forced to stop and fight as they made their way toward the east wall. Wincott tried to get a view of the platform at the back of the room and some idea of what had happened to Sish, but he was too short to see beyond the press of bodies.

Seygan successfully lured away several dozen enemies but ended up backing himself into a corner. When he ran out of breath, the music stopped, and the scream that accompanied the satyr's death cut through the fighting like a single piercing note that rang in Wincott's ears.

Despite the overwhelming fear that bubbled up inside him, the sound of Seygan's death struck a chord of guilt within him. He stopped then to help Terry fend off several sentinels, plunging Raspberry into a tall chain-mailed soldier wielding a hammer. Terry took care of the other two, but as soon as they were gone, four more stepped in to take their place. Wincott found himself in a sword match with yet another soldier.

He feinted to his right, and when the sentinel fell for it, he pulled back and waited for the soldier to go all in with its weight. He used the opportunity to trip it up and plunge the sword through its back. The brief gap in fighting provided him with an opportunity to see where everyone was.

Terry was busy beside him, fending off several other soldiers and a pair of blue-eyed raveners that had gotten into their mix. A little further away toward the east wall, Wren and Dirge were in a similar battle, while even further, Petr, Dalla, and the rest of the goblin band were in yet another fight. All three groups were surrounded. The entire storeroom was a roiling ocean of combat, and there seemed no order to any of it.

In the distance, atop the platform, even Fulk looked overwhelmed. The old trader's eyes darted over the vibrating mass of bodies seemingly without control. The Guildsmen were entirely inside the storeroom now and seemed to have struck momentary peace with the E&E men, both forces fighting alongside one another to cut a path to the trader.

Wincott couldn't see a way out for Sish and Liv. Acting on pure instinct, he threw himself back into the fight, swatting away his attackers, trying to drive a line through them to the platform. Terry saw what he was doing and followed suit, but still, the thief and the barbarian made little headway. The sentinels were simply too many and too strong.

As Wincott's muscles weakened, his chest heaving for air, he became slower to react to the lean, efficient counterattacks and parries from his opponents. He took a hammer blow to one shoulder, the edge of a blade to his sword arm, another to his leg. Each one breaking him down more and more. From the corner of his eye, he could see even the barbarian was slowing, his body peppered with cuts and tattooed in blood.

So, this was it, he realized. It ended here in a battle he never wanted or sought.

Another hammer blow forced him to his knees. A blade glanced off his eyebrow, blood pouring into his eye, clouding his vision. Terry screamed, his throat hoarse, next to him. The sentinels pushed them back efficiently with no voice of their own—like muted statues bred only for war.

And then Wincott heard a scream. An image flashed through his mind: a mother crying at the edge of the water in a seemingly unwinnable battle many years ago. A child drowning. Everything went black. He felt cold rush all over his body, his skin prickle with gooseflesh, and wondered if that was what it felt like when a sword was thrust through your body.

Chapter Forty-Four

DEUS EX RENA

SISH PULLED HIMSELF ONTO THE iridescent blue platform amid the clamor of battle. His mouth was dry with fear, the air filled with the stench of burned dust. Fulk didn't notice him. The trader's eyes were glued to the army he commanded into chaos as if he no longer had control of his own body or even his thoughts. The thief slid onto the floor and scooped Rena's crumpled form into his arms. He was certain she was dead. But as he descended the platform and walked her toward the rear wall of the storeroom where there was the least commotion, he felt the faint pulse of hot breath on his neck. He laid her on the cool tiles. Liv was there a moment later, coaxing her back to life.

The girl opened her eyes, dazed for only a few seconds before anger marred her youthful face. Her brow knitted together, lips pursed, a dark look emanated from her like nothing he'd ever seen before. He remembered then the great scream she had let out atop the promontory at the far end of the valley.

Summoner.

His stomach churned, and he wiped cold sweat from his brow, the smell of scorched air after lightning filling the air around them.

The girl sat up silently. The tremor of battle ahead of them filled the storeroom with the clang of weapons and screams that followed. Fulk's army had overwhelming control of the room, despite the press of Guild and Company men who cut their way toward the platform. Somewhere amid the swell of bodies, Wincott and the others were fighting for survival, but Sish couldn't spare a glance to locate them. The energy billowing around Rena captured him completely.

The summoner fixed him and Liv with a glare but said nothing. She didn't need to. The wizard's shoulders sunk in acknowledgment, as if conceding to a rage and power that was many times more than what Liv could ever hope to wield if she spent her entire life studying magic. It was respect, Sish thought, a recognition that despite individual abilities, there were things in this world—seasons, storms, rivers, volcanoes, earthquakes—that harnessed incomprehensible power, and when they were unleashed, all a person could do was take cover.

Rena was one of those things.

Liv held the ruby thimble in her hand and gestured, almost uneasily, for Rena to take it. The Catalyst of Nerjammer. A brash apprentice's attempt to duplicate his master's power to create life. A useless trinket to most. In the hands of a skilled wizard, it would provide the ability to channel greater power. In Rena's hands …

Sish got to his feet and stepped back. He realized he'd been holding his breath ever since the girl opened her eyes. He exhaled and sucked in breath as if he'd just come up from a long swim. He moved backward as the girl took the thimble from Liv's hand, her big, round blue eyes studying it wondrously.

Sish placed a hand on Liv's shoulder and drew her back as he created distance between them and the summoner.

The burning smell strengthened as the girl slid the thimble over her thumb, until all Sish could smell was the acrid odor of sulfur. Liv's eyes widened in sudden realization of what was happening. She turned and pushed Sish to the ground, taking cover at the rear of the platform.

Rena erupted in bright red flames. Her back arched, a horrendous scream of pain erupting from her lungs that shook the floor and cracked the tiles beneath them. The engulfing fire burned red, then blue, and finally white before her body was consumed and snuffed out. The scream stopped. Sish opened his eyes. He and Liv were crouched, shaking, against the platform some fifty feet away, their eyes fixed on a small pile of white ash where the girl had been. Sish's heart leaped into his throat, his eyes watering.

The battle raged behind them as the small pile of white ash began to vibrate. Then shake. And then, a six-inch-long black talon reached out of the ash and pulled itself up. Behind it were several more talons, each glinting blackly in the dim blue light of the storeroom. They were attached to a paw covered in dark brown fur, which quickly became an enormous, muscled arm. A second arm emerged next to it, and working together, they pulled upward, and from that pile of ash, a massive lion's head emerged. Atop it were two ram horns, black, with full curls drawing back against a shaggy mane of fur.

Beneath its horns were red eyes that burned like coals from an ancient fire mounted atop a mouth filled with teeth like white daggers. The creature pulled itself from the fire as though it were climbing out of some great stygian pit, its body all rippling muscles and clawed hind feet. At its shoulders was a set of black, leathery wings drawn back alongside its flanks, and its tail was that of a scorpion's—long, armored, and ending in a poison-tipped thorn the length of a footman's spear.

"Manticore," Sish breathed.

Liv said nothing, her face frozen with awe as the creature rose from the shattered floor tiles. It tossed its head back, its wings fanned like a dragon's, and roared with a guttural ferocity that shook the teeth in Sish's gums. It struck such a primeval chord of fear through his body that all he could do was hold Liv and pinch his eyes shut.

Everything in the storeroom froze. Silence filled their ears as every fighting man and creature stopped and turned toward the manticore. Even Fulk turned around then, his eyes glassy, and in them, for the first time, there was fear.

The manticore's tail snapped like a whip, sounding an eardrum-thumping crack through the chamber as the creature pounced toward its first victims. It leaped over the platform in a single bound, one of its rear paws glancing off Fulk, sending him to the floor in a splash of blood, the circlet atop his head skittering away from him.

Rena landed on one of the guardian sentinels, the gargantuan lizard creature Ruddlefunt had called Yig. An ancient one, he'd said, thought to be near indestructible. The manticore drove the first one into the ground with its front paws, its jaw closing over Yig's head and ripping it from its shoulders in one bite. In a single movement, Rena snapped her poisoned tail into the second one with several quick pokes that drove gaping holes through its chest before it, too, died.

There was another pause then as the soldiers realized the newest threat they faced. The Guild and Company men fled into the corridor. The army of sentinels turned on the manticore. Everywhere Sish looked, there was only fighting and running.

The manticore leaped into a phalanx of lancers and batted half their number away like they were pieces on a gameboard. Its tail whipped through the other half, and a second later, the creature leaped up and away with its wings sailing down upon another group of soldiers in another part of the room to wreak similar destruction.

Sish watched in stunned silence, his arms wrapped around Liv, as the slaughter careened through the room, decimating the glossy army of reawakened sentinels. Each time she landed, there was a great thump, and the storeroom shook, rock dust cascading upon them.

Eventually, the fear abated enough to allow Sish to gather his breath and shift his feet beneath him to stand. Liv pointed up to the cracks forming in the cavern roof as fist-sized rocks tumbled down around them.

"She's going to bring the mountain down on us," he said.

Liv was next to him, breathing heavily, her eyes darting between Rena's onslaught and Fulk collapsed on the floor. She spotted the circlet a few feet away and picked it up.

The trader groaned and got to his feet. The manticore's claw had opened a gash on his face that stretched from one side of his forehead to the bottom of the opposite cheek. He wiped blood from his eyes and saw the circlet in Liv's hand. He lunged at her, knocking the circlet from her hand. It careened off the platform into the melee around them.

Sish kicked him back.

"No!" Fulk screamed. "Give it to me. Only I can stop her— she'll kill us all."

"*No one* can stop her," Liv said, her lips drawn back against her teeth. "We can only hope to escape, which, if I have anything to say about it, you won't."

"Going to kill me, girl?" Fulk sneered. He turned to Sish, and his eyes flashed, "Or maybe you? Both of you are pathetic. Weak. Unable to command true power. Now get out of my way."

He strode between them when Sish swung at him. Even bloodied, the trader dodged the blow with ease and countered by sinking a fist into Sish's gut and pushing him backward.

The wind exploded from Sish's lungs. He stumbled backward. Liv swung at Fulk, but he dodged her, too, and pushed her to the ground and planted a foot in her gut. Sish felt his world go red. Without breath, he charged the trader and flung himself forward. They tumbled over the side of the platform to the floor below in a tangle of arms and legs, dust and rock raining down around them.

Fulk had the upper hand almost immediately, one hand gripping Sish's neck, the other pummeling his face. The thief began to see stars as he struggled against the weight of the trader. He drove his knee upward, hitting only air, then shifted and tried again. On his third attempt, he connected solidly with Fulk's groin, and the older man froze and tumbled over to the side.

Sish sat up, running a hand across his bruised neck involuntarily, a rush of air filling his lungs. It tasted like fresh mountain air, but he knew that couldn't be true with all the rock and dust cascading down around him. A chunk of cavern ceiling the size of his head landed next to him. Fulk coughed and struggled on the ground.

Sish got to his feet and hefted the rock, intending to slam it down on the trader's head and be done with him once and for all. Fulk's back was to him. Sish lifted the rock above his head and judged he had the perfect shot. Fulk wouldn't even see it coming. An image flashed through his mind of a knife in his hand, the feeling of it plunging into Davin Faithguard's back. The look of disgust on his face. The look of contempt on Liv's.

It halted him just long enough for a body to drive into him, knocking him back onto the floor. He hit the ground with another explosion of breath and felt the immediate annoyance and frustration of something continually happening without any way to see it coming. The rock rolled out of his hands, away into the crowd of struggling soldiers who fought, bled, and screamed in terror around them as the manticore shredded through their ranks.

When Sish's eyes cleared, he looked up to find Wincott on top of him, his face bloody, bruised, and cut in half a dozen places. The old man looked like he'd gotten into a fight with a bramble patch and been thoroughly trounced.

"What … what are you doing?" Sish asked, catching his breath, the anger rising in his throat at the thought that his chance to end all this had just been stolen away.

Wincott coughed and said, "Sish, you can't. You can't kill him."

The old thief closed his eyes, nearly out of breath, and was shaking his head.

"Don't tell me what I can't do; he's mine! Mine to kill! I have to end this," he screamed.

"Sish, he's your father."

He heard Wincott's words, but he didn't feel anything. It wasn't as though they went in one ear and out the other or that they didn't mean anything to him. It was just that he was numb to it. He was numb to it, to new information, to his own ability to see, think, or feel about things differently than he already did.

Fulk is my father.

His vision drifted toward the old trader on the ground nearby, blood welling from his hawkish features. He felt … *nothing*. He turned to Wincott, searching his fa—no, his dad's eyes. He knew the older man spoke the truth. But it didn't matter to him. Maybe it should have; maybe there was something wrong with him in that it didn't. But at that moment, the question of who his father was had long ago been settled. It didn't matter to him who had planted the seed that had created him or whose blood coursed through his veins. It was, in the end, only a curious little thing, like the name of a mountain you remember for a moment before you see the next one or the shape a cloud takes on a summer afternoon before a swift breeze blows it away.

Fulk was his father.

That might be true, he decided, but his dad was lying on top of him. His *dad* stayed his hand.

"Dad—" he began but was cut off as Wincott suddenly grimaced and the color drained from his face.

Behind him stood Fulk, a knife sticking out of Wincott's back. The trader wore a passive look, as if it was just a matter of business, something that got in his way, and now it wasn't.

Sish, pinned beneath Wincott, struggled helplessly as he watched the life bleed away from his dad's body. He cursed Fulk, but his words were dreamlike, a whisper amid the cacophony of war as the cavern raged with blood lust and crumbled over them.

This is it, he thought, *the Treasure of Roan.*

Fulk's eyes drifted greedily toward the abandoned circlet a few feet away. He stepped toward it, reaching out, his bloodied face determined to finish what he had started. But just as quickly, the shadow of the manticore descended on him, the creature's gaping maw sinking into the narrow space between his shoulder and neck, devouring his torso in a single bite. It shook the trader in its mouth like a rag doll before spitting his legs into the crowd of fleeing soldiers.

The manticore stopped and looked down at the two thieves, its eyes no longer burning red coals but blue eyes with black pupils. Rena's eyes.

It exhaled hard from exertion, its lion's body riddled with wounds, fur matted with blood. It seemed to breathe for Wincott as the old thief struggled for air atop Sish, the knife still protruding from his back.

Wren was there a moment later, laying Wincott next to Sish. Terry knelt next to the old thief, his eyes grave as he looked at the knife jutting from his back.

Sish stood as large boulders began to break away from the ceiling, crashing into the platform. There was a goblin next to Wren, urging him and the others to run while they still had a chance. He looked vaguely familiar, but the thief couldn't place him. Without thinking, he turned to Wincott and pulled the knife from his back. It was deep, but not to the hilt. There was a spurt of red blood. The wound was low in his back. His dad screamed in agony. Wren and Terry exchanged looks of alarm.

"Can you walk?" Sish asked.

Wincott paused a moment, his breath coming in rasps. "My legs. Can't … can't move them. Go. Go without me."

"Sish, we have to go, or none of us will make it," said Wren.

Liv's hand was on his shoulder then. She didn't say anything. He turned to look at her, half expecting to see the same disgust he'd seen there the night of Davin's death. But there was only sadness and love, a movement of the muscles in her face that suggested he should do what he felt was right, and that whether he lived or died—if any of them lived or died—she would still love him for it.

Sish squatted, slid his arms under his father's body, and stood up. The old man was heavier than Sish would've wished, reminding the young thief that he was weak and Wincott was carrying too many pounds. If they got out of this alive, which he doubted, he would have to start lecturing his dad about diet. And maybe learn a thing or two about fitness from Terry. He chuckled awkwardly at the thought, and everyone gave him a strange look, not sure what it meant.

"We're not leaving without him," Sish told them, "He's one of us."

It was Terry who nodded first and clapped Sish on the shoulder.

"Follow me," the barbarian said, his face split in a wild grin as he charged toward the east wall, weapon at the ready.

Wren was right behind him, Petr and Dalla at his side. It was then Sish noticed the manticore was gone and Rena was back. The girl offered him an exhausted smile, and he nodded a thanks to her. She ran alongside Liv. Sish followed, Wincott in his arms. The strange band of goblins that had stalked them since their first night in Roan protected their heels.

Between breaths, he tried to think of funny things to say and tease his dad about as they made their way toward the east wall. Later, he wouldn't remember any of what he said, only the look of contentment on Wincott's face as they ran, sprinted, stumbled, walked, and ran again toward the path that would lead them up to Fort Shatterstill as the fabled Treasure of Roan lay buried behind them.

Chapter Forty-Five

IN THE ARMS OF A GOBLIN

WINCOTT SAW A LOT OF strange things as his son carried him out of that dungeon. He watched a girl who had become a manticore become a girl again. He saw an army, not destroyed, flee to save what lives they had left and perhaps fight another enemy, another day, somewhere else. He saw a dwarf, scarred from centuries protecting a secret beneath the ground, pick up a small black circlet, appraise it curiously, and slip it into his red moth-eaten robes before disappearing amid the crowd.

He saw a sky of rock cascade around them in a way that made him think of a game of ball tag. There was a goblin with a noble face not running at them with a weapon but behind them protectively. There was a narrow corridor with many stairs and hidden rooms jutting off in various directions, and he could've sworn at least three of them were filled with glittering gold coins, tall treasure chests, jewels, and rare art. There was an endless spiral of stairs that climbed up to the heavens, a light so bright at its apex, he was forced to close his eyes against it.

Looking up at that light, he saw the face of his son, a man, exhausted, bleeding, dirty, and tear-streaked, ready to give up at every step, but somehow, with the urging of his friends, carrying on. There wasn't any finesse in it, and probably only a little focus. Certainly, a bit of luck. There was always that. But more than anything, there was determination. Grit, Wincott decided. True grit.

Eventually, he passed out. When he woke up, he wondered how he could be floating alongside Sish as they climbed out of the city. His eyes cleared, and he realized he was cradled in Wren's arms. Later, it was Terry's arms. And after that, Dirge's—the creature offering a strange grin that was halfway between triumph and murder. Wincott could only chuckle. But it hurt to laugh. And he passed out again, fading into a deep sleep.

He awoke in a canoe that drifted silently down a misty river. Was he awake? No. It was a dream. Maybe.

The soft white light gave him the sense of early morning, but he couldn't place the sun in the sky. He heard the soft trickle of water as a paddle dipped into the water and guided them forward.

Wincott sat in the bow. Ahead and above him were two cliffs that almost came together to form a bridge over the river. Atop them was a massive stone statue of a manticore, its front legs on one cliff, its hind legs on another. The creature's regal lion head turned toward their canoe, its forehead dipping in welcome ever so slightly.

But where was the dragon? It was Myrrhmyth's likeness that decorated those cliffs not a manticore, yet it felt strangely … familiar.

Wincott breathed in the fresh air. It filled his lungs without pain. He wiggled his toes. They were warm and dry. A nice spring morning, he decided.

He turned to find Sish paddling at the stern, slowing guiding them forward to pass beneath the stone manticore. Between them was Meridan. She was dressed in a white gown, stretched out along the bottom of the canoe, her hands held to her chest, a bouquet of brilliant purple fireweed clasped in her hands. Her cheeks were rosy, alive, lips upturned in a playful grin.

Sish smiled at him and pointed at the statue. "Dad, look! She's welcoming us home. We're going home."

Wincott turned to find the statue was gone, the sky cleared. Above him, the pale blue of dawn shone vividly. To the east, the horizon was aflame in beautiful puffy streaks of violet and pink as the morning sun crested the mountains.

The old thief awoke with a start. He was in a room with stone walls, but it wasn't Roan. Everything was silent, save the steady crackle of the small campfire. He was warm, not freezing.

The firelight cast shadows that danced along the masonry around him. Shatterstill.

Sish stood a dozen feet away, leaning against a doorway and looking into the morning light.

"You're alive," he said, turning around, "Everyone is camped outside."

Wincott sat up. A rough woolen blanket was laid over his legs. It wasn't his. He looked at his son. "I must've dozed off."

"You've been asleep for two days," Sish said with a wry smile.

Wincott stumbled as he got up, discovering he could only move his right leg. His left wouldn't budge. In fact, he couldn't feel it at all. Sish's face darkened with a frown.

"I was afraid that might be the case," he said. "For a while there, it looked like you wouldn't be able to use either of them. Consider yourself lucky."

Wincott chewed his lip for a moment and then looked up at Sish and smiled. "I always have."

Sish laughed soundlessly and put his arm around Wincott to guide him out the door. They stood on one of the higher battlements at Fort Shatterstill. It was midmorning, the sky gray with clouds, light snow cascading over the sharp peaks of the mountain range to the east. Below them stretched a white valley and an ice-covered river that snaked through the trees. Wincott wondered how long it had been since he escaped from this very fort across the valley to ...

The great black maw of Roan was directly across from them, a hole in the far mountainside. The entrance to the city gave him gooseflesh as he recalled what they'd discovered in its depths. He noticed movement at the entrance to the city, but he couldn't make out what it was.

"Sentinels," Sish answered for him. "Guildsmen, too, and E&E men. They've been streaming out of the city in small groups since we got here. Found their way out."

"And will go to the gods only know where," Wren chimed in, announcing his presence.

The hunter clapped Wincott on the shoulder and offered him a smile. "Glad to see you're up and moving. Thought we lost you."

"Would've been a shame," added Terry, coming around the corner of the battlement to join them. "You're pretty good with a sword when you want to be."

"And fairly sharp in your old age," Liv said, coming out of the tower door.

"And you have slippery fingers," a voice croaked.

It was Dirge. The goblin came to stand next to Wincott. They were practically the same height. Dirge had his arms crossed, Raspberry buckled at his side.

"Hey, that's—"

Sish stayed his hand. "Call it an apology. You did rob them, after all. Dirge and the Shadowguard have allowed us to rest up a few days before we decide where to go next."

"Go next?" Wincott asked.

Sish pointed across the valley to a dark shape that perched atop a jagged, ice-laden cliff overlooking the entrance to Roan. Wincott hadn't noticed it, but once his eyes picked it out from the mountainscape around it, he could hardly see anything else.

There sat Myrrhmyth, the great black dragon that had once claimed this entire mountain range and its valleys for territory. He had never seen the dragon, only heard stories about it, half of which he'd long ago decided weren't true. But maybe …

The great wyrm spread its wings as if announcing its presence. It dropped down in front of the city gate, landing with a thud that could be felt across the valley. A great jet of flame burst from its mouth into the throat of Roan. When the fire abated and the smoke cleared, the dragon slithered through the entrance he and Sish had camped in only days before, vanishing into the mountainside and the depths of Roan.

"Survivors means the secrets of Roan won't stay secret for long," Wren observed.

"More will come," added Terry.

"And the dragon … the dragon's return changes things," Dirge finished.

Wincott held up his hands. "Woah, woah, woah. If you morons intend to go back in there, you can count me out. I'll just camp out here, thanks."

Terry crossed his arms and gave the old thief a stern look. "There are still monsters to slay."

"And we never really did get to explore that library," Liv added reflectively.

"There's treasure, too. Lots of it. Spotted some on my way out," Wren commented.

An image of rooms filled with coins and jewels flashed through Wincott's mind Maybe, he thought. Just maybe.

He shook the thought out of his head like he would try to shake a hangover.

"No," he protested, "there's a bloody dragon in there—we barely survived the first trek. Sish, you're not going back there. You know what I had to do to keep you alive? No way. My pockets are empty after that venture. I wound up with 40 percent of nothing. I'd just as soon go back to the market in Fort Rivers and lift a few wallets, thank you very much."

Sish laughed and rolled his eyes.

Rena emerged from the tower then. She smiled when she saw Wincott. The girl approached the old thief and took his hand in hers, leaning her head against his shoulder to join them as they looked across at Roan.

Sish put an arm around Liv and stared across the valley at the endless rows of unexplored mountain peaks behind the city. He laughed then.

"Hey, if you want to just be a thief, I'm okay with that." Sish put his other arm around his dad, a playful look in his eye as he looked down at Wincott, his voice dripping with sarcasm. "But me? I'm more adept at pursuing worthwhile causes. I'm a Dungeoneer."

Wincott could feel the heat rise in his face. He breathed, pushing it away. "Fine," he said, "but I want 20 percent."

Sish scoffed and turned toward him. "Twenty? You'll be lucky to get ten."

"Fifteen, and I won't tell these guys about that job in Fort Bowron."

Sish turned on him. "The hell you won't."

Wincott winked.

Liv, hands on her hips, turned to Sish. "What happened in Bowron? Did you cause that explosion?

The group began to pepper Sish with questions he couldn't find answers for. Wincott only laughed and wandered back into the tower, where a warm fire, bed, and hopefully, a long, restful sleep awaited him. He felt a tingling in his left foot and managed to wiggle one of his toes. Things were looking up already, he decided, chuckling.

He crawled into bed and listened to his son do a poor job of dodging questions and avoiding answers. Sish really was the worst thief he'd ever met. Wincott thumbed a little trinket he'd nabbed during the argument—the ruby thimble, still hot to the touch. Might fetch a decent price in Chicken Town, he figured, or it might come in handy later. It tended to turn up when needed. He slipped the device into his pocket and rolled over, wiggling his toasty toes and thinking that things weren't all bad. His feet were warm and working. His son was alive. And there were probably a few treasures laying about Fort Shatterstill he'd overlooked before. He intended to find out as soon as he woke up, Dungeoneers be damned.

THE END

ABOUT THE AUTHOR

Joel McKay is an award-winning author, public administrator and former journalist. When not writing, you can find him enjoying the great outdoors of Northern British Columbia. He lives in Prince George, B.C., with his wife and two daughters.

www.joelmckay.ca